A STORY OF LOVE, HARDSHIP, AND THE
POWER OF FRIENDSHIP AND FAMILY.

KEN JAMES

BALBOA.PRESS
A DIVISION OF HAY HOUSE

Copyright © 2024 Ken James.

All rights reserved. No part of this book may be used or reproduced by any means, graphic, electronic, or mechanical, including photocopying, recording, taping or by any information storage retrieval system without the written permission of the author except in the case of brief quotations embodied in critical articles and reviews.

Balboa Press books may be ordered through booksellers or by contacting:

Balboa Press
A Division of Hay House
1663 Liberty Drive
Bloomington, IN 47403
www.balboapress.co.uk
UK TFN: 0800 0148647 (Toll Free inside the UK)
UK Local: (02) 0369 56325 (+44 20 3695 6325 from outside the UK)

Because of the dynamic nature of the Internet, any web addresses or links contained in this book may have changed since publication and may no longer be valid. The views expressed in this work are solely those of the author and do not necessarily reflect the views of the publisher, and the publisher hereby disclaims any responsibility for them.

The author of this book does not dispense medical advice or prescribe the use of any technique as a form of treatment for physical, emotional, or medical problems without the advice of a physician, either directly or indirectly. The intent of the author is only to offer information of a general nature to help you in your quest for emotional and spiritual well-being. In the event you use any of the information in this book for yourself, which is your constitutional right, the author and the publisher assume no responsibility for your actions.

Any people depicted in stock imagery provided by Getty Images are models, and such images are being used for illustrative purposes only. Certain stock imagery © Getty Images.

Print information available on the last page.

ISBN: 978-1-9822-8852-5 (sc)
ISBN: 978-1-9822-8851-8 (e)

Library of Congress Control Number: 2024906182

Balboa Press rev. date: 03/27/2024

CHAPTER 1

THE SLEEPY STARS WERE STILL HIGH IN THE SKY AND THE slumbering moon a silvery orb low on the horizon, as Thomas and Victor, quietly closed the rickety door behind them. "Use the latch lad, if you wake your sisters by slamming that bloody door, I'll take the skin off your arse with me belt buckle. Your mother won't want them up on this of all days!" Victor looked up at the scarred, smiling, face of this uncle. "You touch me with any belt Uncle Tom, and I'll tell my mam! You know she'll have your guts for garters if you don't look after me proper. "The older man winked his bright, left eye at the youth and chided, "Your mam is a sight to behold when she's angry. She's got a mouth that can blister the varnish off the chapel pews at a hundred yards and a temper to match it. "Specially where her darlin' little Victor is concerned. They both stepped quietly away from the door, their hob nailed boots ringing disobediently on the flagstones of the pavement. In the fast-fading gloom they could see other shapes appearing from Doors all along the terraced street. "Come on lad, step lively, we can't be late today, not on your first day down the pit. "Victor, shuddered, a feeling of hopelessness and resignation filled him, and his step seemed to falter. If Thomas had noticed the lad's discomfort and reluctance, he made no comment about it. "Don't worry lad, everyone 'ates it at first, it's the first twenty years that are the worst."

"If I live that long Uncle Tom."

"Let's get one thing sorted out right now young Victor, when we leave the house to go to the pit, we're butties, not relatives, everybody's butties down that bloody 'ole, even yore worst enemy. Just remember that and you will be fine, we all look out for one another down there see." Victor pulled his coat collar tightly around his neck and followed the dim shape in front that he thankfully knew was his uncle, only now, he was even more special, he was his butty.

"Don't walk so fast Unc, I mean Tom, let my eyes get used to the dark or I'll break my neck, before I get to the pit."

"Sorry lad, but we can't stop to enjoy the view or that bastard Gregory, will stop us a day's pay." Victor looked up startled, it was the first time his uncle had ever used, 'language', in front of him. Victor had only heard a few hushed whispers about Mr. Gregory, the mine owner's manager, they said he was a harsh man, chiselled out of coal, as cold as the frost on the windowpane on a crisp winter's morning and as kind hearted as a terrier down a rabbit hole.

"What's he really like Tom? Is he as bad as they say he is?"

"Don't expect any favours off him even on your first day, lad". Tom answered seriously. "He's as bad as about half of what you have heard, and that makes him a pretty mean sod. "He turned and hurried on. They were joined by several other miners, all trudging their way towards the eerie silhouette in the dim distance that Victor knew was the beginning of the end of his dreams!

"Why have you got a face like a smacked arse then Victor? Said a voice from behind him, that belonged to Stuart Thomas, a man Victor, vaguely knew as someone who had been kind to his mam, the day they brought home the broken body that had once been his father. They had carried him up to the bedroom and the family had waited four days for him to die! His mother had not shed a tear, but they all knew she was still an ocean of bitterness and grief inside.

"Good morning, Mr. Thomas, I didn't think anyone could see how happy I was to be going down the pit for the first time, in this gloom. "Victor said sullenly.

"Don't Mister me, boy! You are a man today, and you will call me Stew, unless you don't like me that is?"

Victor looked hard at the thick set miner but could not make out any expression on the fellow's face.

"I'm sorry Stew, our Tom, told me to use first names but I forgot, I'll get used to it eventually. There seems to be more to going to work than just leaving the front door and setting off!"

"You've got a good teacher in your Uncle Tom; lad just do as he tells you and you won't go far wrong."

Tom, tugged hard at Victor's elbow. "Come on you two, I can't afford to lose half a shift whilst you two silly buggers talk about names. "He looked at his nephew's elbow and arm and spoke thoughtfully, "You'll need to get some muscle in those arms of yours, if you are going to be worth more than, 'Tuppence' a day. You've got muscles like knots in bloody cotton you have, I knew our Kate, was bloody spoiling you but bugger me 'ow are you going to do a hard day's work with arms like a bloody pretty girl!" Victor pulled his arm sharply away from his uncle before retorting.

"Don't you worry about me; I'll do my share even if it kills me!"

"I'm thinking it'll kill me, more like. I've seen more meat on a jockey's whip!"

"Stupid sod! You have never seen a jockey's whip." Stew, guffawed, "You wouldn't know one if it bit you on the arse!"

"Leave me alone the pair of you," said Victor beginning to feel flushed." I was one of the biggest boys in my class, at Sunday school."

"Don't take any notice Victor, you'll have a lot more leg pulling to put up with before today is out. "Stuart laughed happily as they strode on.

They were now part of a swelling throng of men nearing the mine. As he Listened, he could hear them talking, moaning, swearing and even laughing together in hushed voices. The noise and comradeship seemed to lift his sagging spirit and his hob nailed boots appeared to be sliding over the cobbled ground. Victor looked ahead, standing tall in front of him, was the monstrous winding tower, stretching up to touch the floor of the heavens, although he knew that it led to hell, not the place they taught of in chapel. Victor could see that the men were doffing their caps to a man who stood outside a small slate grey building. He neither spoke, nor acknowledged the men's greetings.

"Is that Mr. Gregory?" asked Victor quietly.

"Aye butty, that's the swine, once seen never forgotten!" Answered a voice that Victor recognised as belonging to a man called Herbert Humphries. He's the one man in this pit that I look forward to attending 'his funeral. Herbert Humphries was a man, a little over five feet four inches tall, his dark hair almost hidden by his firmly pulled down flat cap. Victor could imagine his brown eyes flashing madly in his swarthy face as he spoke of the infamous Mr. Gregory. Though small of stature, Herbert Humphries, was, without doubt, the most well-respected miner in the locality. He was the agent, of the South Wales Miner's Federation, or the FED, as the men all called it.

"I expect the old bastard will have a few words of welcome for you on your first day, Victor". Just doff your cap and say nothing other than, good morning, and thank you for allowing me to start. "Reassured Herbert, with a pat on Victor's shoulder. "We are all right behind you so don't worry and don't let him upset you."

They reached the building where Thomas removed his cap and spoke to the mine manager.

"Good morning, sir. This is my nephew Victor, who you said could start work with me this morning. He's thirteen years old sir and as you can see, he's well built for his age and a God-fearing hard worker." Thomas stepped back, as Victor stepped forward, his cap also in his hand.

"Y_Yes Sir thank you Sir." Victor mumbled.

"Don't thank me yet boy, we'll find out if you are up to the work before you need to thank me. Work hard and I'll not bother you ..... much! But let me hear of you shirking and you will learn to hate me as much as these already do." He waved his hand at all the passing miners. "You'll earn your pay boy, let's hope you're worth it! One more piece of advice, don't let Humphries fill your head with a load of subversive nonsense."

"Owen's." The manager barked gruffly. Thomas stepped swiftly forward.

"Yes Sir."

"Take the boy to the west district with you. He can start filling the drams let's see how his lily-white hands manage a few shifts on a shovel."

Victor managed a last, "Thank you." Before Tom dragged him off. Victor strained to hear what was said between the manager and Herbert, but their voices were swallowed in the noise of the great steam winding engine that had coughed into life, hissing and groaning, as it began lowering men down into the inky depths. Victor's nostrils were filled with the sharp biting dampness, of the billowing clouds of steam, that began to drift around the tower and the mine shaft.

Thomas looked down at Victor. "Well lad, here we are. First day down! Yore mam didn't want this day to ever come."

"I know Uncle Tom, but I've got to earn some money to help Mam, pay the bills or we'll all be in the workhouse." Victor hugged his lunch box tightly to his chest and felt the cool smoothness of his drinking jack, filled with cold tea, against his hip. It was suspended from a stout leather belt. It had been his fathers before him and he rubbed it reassuringly, its roughness reminded him of his father, as did its strength and security. As Thomas watched the boy, a knowing smile touched the corners of his mouth.

"It was a strong belt for a strong man, young Vic, just remember that. I'm only sorry that he isn't here to take you down 'himself."

Victor looked at his uncle for several moments holding his eyes with his own. "I miss him of course, but I know that he wouldn't want anyone else to take me down, except you, if he couldn't.

"Victor Leslie!" A voice boomed out in the half light. "I've got something for you, here." The voice belonged to a man called Evan Dance. He was the mine's Banksman; he was in charge of all the loading and unloading of the pit cages at the top of the mine shaft.

"Morning Mr. Dance." Victor replied.

Evan came towards them with a lamp glowing brightly in his outstretched right hand. "This belonged to your father, they brought it to the surface a few hours after the accident. I kept on meaning to bring it to your house, but I kept putting it off, you know how it is." He shuffled about on his feet to hide his embarrassment. "Well anyway here it is, better late than never. I've given it a good clean, it's filled with oil and is all ready to go."

Victor looked at the glowing reminder of his father's last working day, one of his last days on earth. He put out a trembling hand to take the offered lamp.

Tom looked down at the swaying lamp, "Thank you Evan, we were always wondering what happened to his lamp but just thought it must have been smashed in the fall."

Victor, unable to look away from the lamp could only mutter, "We thought it was lost. I don't know if I should use it."

"Don't be bloody daft Victor!" Snapped Thomas angrily," It was your Dad's lamp who the hell do you think he would want to have it. He didn't do you any harm when he was alive, so don't think that his lamp will harm you now or bring you bad luck. If anything, it will mean he's watching over you!"

Victor was brought back to reality as he was pushed, along with a group of about twenty other miners, into the cage. In the depths below he heard the ringing signal of the bells and was staggered as the cage began its headlong descent down the shaft. He looked up quickly to see the surface glow disappear.

CHAPTER 2

KATE LESLIE HAD BEEN UNABLE TO SLEEP AND HAD STAYED IN BED weeping until her frame ached with emptiness and she had used every tear in her frail body. It seemed like an eternity since she had heard Thomas, take Victor to that God forsaken mine! It had already claimed the life of her husband, was it now to take the life of her youngest son! She had stayed in bed and not gone down to see the two men off, as a good wife and mother ought to do, but she knew she wouldn't have been able to let him go. He was still only a child, her little baby. Just thirteen years old! Once again, long despairing sobs consumed her as she gave herself up to the feelings of helplessness and bitter gloom that consumed her every waking thought. She prayed for the release of sleep, but it would not come.

She heard a tap at her door. "Mam, are you alright?" It was her eldest daughter, Christine. "Don't cry mam, Victor will be fine. Uncle Thomas, will look after him, you'll see."

Kate wiped away the tears with her bed sheet. It was still too dark for Christine, to see her red, tear-stained eyes. She must make sure that the girls did not realise how worried she was and know of the dark ache that would not leave her breast.

"Now don't fuss Christine!" She blurted out, without thinking. She only ever called her Christine, if she were worried or annoyed.

"I am perfectly alright; I don't know what's gotten into you this morning." She was shocked at how easily the lie slipped through her lips. She would have to see the Minister and seek forgiveness. Was a white lie allowed for the sake of the children?

"Go and put the kettle on the fire, dear. I'll be downstairs in a minute, let me get dressed." Kate uttered a long sigh, climbed out of bed and reached for her clean clothes.

Downstairs, Christine took the blackened kettle from the hearth to the tap in the bosh, where she filled it with cold water. She took it back to the fireplace and put it down. She picked up the poker and stirred the glowing timbers, raking the ashes and cinders into the grate bottom. Chris grimaced as she took several lumps of coal from the bucket that stood in the hearth. She hated the way it made her hands so dirty and collected under her nails she felt unclean, like one of the old hags in the mine washery. She placed the fresh coal over the reddening cinders and watched as the shining surface charred and blistered before bursting into golden flame that danced in her sparkling eyes. Picking up the kettle she lowered it gently onto the already growing flame.

Kate walked into the kitchen, she was wearing a plain, grey dress, with a black shawl draped around her shoulders.

"Good girl. I could do with a cup of tea, I see you've got the fire going nicely so the kettle won't be long. "Chris looked at her Mam, there wasn't a sign of a tear on her serene face. She smiled to herself.

Mam, was very good at trying to hide her feelings from the whole world, always wanting to protect her children from all harm and upset.

"Sit down Mam, I'll make us both a nice cup of tea and a piece of toast. The fire's going well now." She took a brass toasting fork from a nail at the side of the fireplace and stuck a thick slice of bread onto its prongs. "I'll make it just the way you like it, just lightly brown no black bits, I promise." She held the bread in front of some of the red-hot coals. "Tea and toast, the best way to start a new day."

"I'll have a cup of tea, but I don't think I can manage any toast thank you Chris." Kate stated wearily.

Chris looked over her shoulder and said. "You must have some food inside you Mam. Stop worrying about Victor, Uncle Tom will look after him, he won't let anything happen to him."

Kate raised her eyebrows and replied, "And who, young lady, is going to look after Tom? My Victor is only thirteen years old, he should still be going to school, not down that God forsaken hole. I was listening to him sing in chapel yesterday, his voice hasn't even broken yet! It was a beautiful soprano, he's not even old enough to be a tenor!"

Chris carefully took the toasted bread off the fork and turned it over so that the fresh side now faced the ever-increasing glow of the fire. "You know, as well as I do, that you couldn't afford to let him stay in school. He had to go out and earn some money to help pay the bills. He wouldn't have stayed in school anyway, not if it meant you going short to keep him there, you know how pig headed he can be, even for a thirteen-year-old."

"I know, I just wish there had been some other way, that's all. Kate watched as the kettle signalled its readiness by billowing steam from its charred spout. She rose wearily from her chair and used a clean flannel rag to lift the kettle off the roaring fire. She placed it on the black leaded plate of the oven, at the side of the fireplace. "Still, as my old gran used to say, everything seems better with a cup of warm tea inside you." Kate smiled bravely at her daughter, as she poured the boiling water into the gleaming, brown earthenware teapot.

Chris brought the toast back to the table and reached for the butter. "Why don't you go to the Manse this afternoon and see the Minister, I'm sure Mr. Morgan can find a reading and a few words of prayer, that will give you some comfort Mam. You mustn't let the others know how worried you are, especially our Ivy, you know how close she and Victor are."

"I didn't mean for you to find out Chris. Don't you let on a word of this to the others. I don't want Victor to be worried about me, he must only worry about himself." Kate added quietly.

You can't keep everything to yourself Mam, but don't worry, this will be our secret."

"I don't know what you are talking about Christine!"

She picked up the piece of warm buttered toast and ate it hungrily. It was nice to be spoiled occasionally.

"They will both be home starving hungry before you know it, Mam." Laughed Chris, "you know the way our Vic eats, you'd think he's got hollow legs."

"Kate smiled at her eldest daughter," It will be good to cook for two healthy men once again. We will need twice as much hot water this evening for them both to bath."

CHAPTER 3

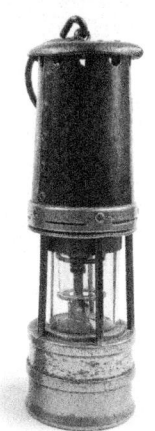

THE CAGE LURCHED TO A STOP AT THE PIT BOTTOM. THOMAS PUSHED Victor forward and said, "Come on lad we can't hang around here, there are another eighty men to be brought down in the next few minutes. We've got a long walk to reach the face." Victor looked around surprised at the room there appeared to be at the pit bottom. Tom, noticing the look on his nephew's face added, "Aye it's bigger than most people think, isn't it? There's got to be plenty of room for full coal drams to be brought in ready to be taken to the surface. Tom and Victor followed a group of men as they walked along the heading making for a well-lit building cut into the side of the roadway. "It's the underground lamp room Vic", Tom Nodded. "If your lamp goes out when we're working this is the only place to have it relit and it's a bloody long dark walk to get it done! If the overman catches you doing so, he'll clip your ears good and proper." Tom walked forward as Vic marvelled at the ghostly shadows that danced on the mine wall. It looked as though an army of silent colliers marched with them to the coal face.

"How many men are working down here today, Tom?" Victor asked, his voice echoing along the dark tunnels.

"This month we're working in the West District. I don't know for certain, but I think there's about sixty of us. There are about the same in the East and twice as many, in the North District." Victor looked but was unable to see his uncle's face as he have the reply. "Your Mam was relieved when she knew we were in the West. It's the least gassy district in the whole mine."

Victor, tried to stand as tall as he could as he said. "I realise Mam didn't want me to come here to work, she wanted me to stay in school, but I couldn't, it would have meant the girls going without too many things. They will soon be on the lookout for husbands and what chance would they have without pretty dresses? Anyway, I'm too old to be living on charity." His nose wrinkled and his lips puckered up, as they walked past another underground building, "PPhhh! What's that? It smells worse than a farmyard and a pig stye put together."

His uncle laughed, "That's the pit pony station, stinks a bit doesn't it! You'll get used to it."

Victor shook his head," I don't think I'll ever get used to a smell like that!"

"You will." Said Stewart Thomas. From behind. "You'll get used to all sorts of things down here. Wait till your Uncle Tom farts, then you will be glad to come back to these sweet-smelling ponies!"

"Give over," Tom laughed. "You'll be making him believe all the things they say about us rough colliers, is true!"

"They are, because I've heard you called, 'Bugle bum', more than once! I used to wonder why. Now I know!" Chided Victor.

They walked on, for what to Victor, seemed an age. The roof had been getting closer to his head, he found himself stooping over like an old washer woman. Glancing up, he could see that the timbers supporting the roof were getting further and further apart. Above them, he could see the glint of shiny black coal or the dull nothingness of shale and rock—the kind that fell without warning and crushed the precious life out of an unsuspecting miner!

"If you don't keep your head down, you daft bugger, you are going to spread what bit of brains you've got, all over the roof beams!" Declared Stuart.

"Aye," continued Tom," If brains were gunpowder, you wouldn't have enough to raise your bloody hat to the minister's wife on a Sunday morning! Keep your bloody head down, or do you fancy spreading your brains about?"

Victor grinned to himself. "Sorry, Tom, I was only looking for the roofing timbers, they seem to be a long way apart!"

"That bastard Gregory, says it costs too much to put them any closer," Stuart swore vehemently. "It's cheaper to buy off a dependant's family than pay for a safe roof!"

As they walked on, Victor could see the dim outline of a door, blocking the heading, a few yards ahead. The door stretched across the whole width of the tunnel. Tom, who was at the front, rapped his knuckles hard on it. The sound echoed through the narrow confines of the district.

"Who's there?" Quizzed a frightened, shaky voice.

"Open up Dai, some of us have got to get to work." Tom declared quietly. "It's only us!"

The door was dragged open, to reveal a boy of no more than twelve. His teeth gleamed in comparison with his dirty face when seen by the light of the miners' lamps. The small boy stared wide eyed at the group of men.

"I wasn't sure it was you; I heard your footsteps but I didn't know for certain."

Tom looked affectionately at the poor waif, he was too young to be working in a place like this, but his father has been gassed by the 'after damp', that followed the explosion in the west district last year and he was the oldest of six orphaned children! Boys became men early in the pit!

"Why are you sitting in the dark David?" Asked Tom, giving the boy a friendly Pat on the head.

"Hello Tom." The boy replied more cheerfully," I was just putting my lamp down, when a great, big rat, the biggest I've seen, ran over my foot. It made me jump so much, that I knocked my lamp over, and it went out. I've been sitting in the dark for about half an hour now!"

"When all the men have come through you go back to the lamp room and get it relit. Get a ride on one of the dram runs, tell the pony driver I said it was OK." Tom said reassuringly.

David Looked doubtful and added, "The last time I wasn't back, Mr. Morgan, the overman told me off and have me a belting! He said I wasn't to go skiving off again!"

"Tell Mr. Morgan, I, said you Had to do it!" Insisted Tom, making a mental note to have a few words, with William Morgan, about beating frightened children the next time they met, at the Miners' Hall. "Yes Sir." The boy replied gratefully, as the group walked through the open ventilation door.

"Make sure you close it tight behind us mind David." Whispered Stuart, giving the lad's hair a friendly ruffle.

The miners trudged through the ventilation door, the men all stooping low to avoid the low roofing timbers. Victor was able to walk along with only a slight bend in his neck.

"How much further is it, Stuart? We must have walked for more than half a mile. "Victor mouthed testily. "I didn't realise we had to walk so far to get to the face!"

"You'll try the patience of a saint, your miserable young sod." Snapped Stuart," As soon as we reach the bloody face, we've got to start work, real work! Then you'll wish you was still walking along this heading."

Victor became aware of the metallic ringing of metal striking metal and the dull thud of sledgehammer blows, together with distant voices, and curses intermingled with the odd burst of laughter all accompanied by the continuous, monotonous reverberation, as dozens of mandrils bit deep into the seam of coal. They were almost at the face. A few yards ahead Victor caught sight of a man standing to one side of the roadway, just ahead of them. Tom stopped to talk to the man.

"Morning Huw, how's the face seem today? Tom enquired politely.

The man he addressed was a short man, no more than five feet six inches tall he was the district fireman, the man was responsible for underground safety in the west district of the mine. It was his duty to test the mine workings for gas and if he detected any 'firedamp, to arrange for sufficient ventilation to blow the explosive gas away before the miners began work, if, the manager agreed to a delay in coal cutting, with the consequential loss of profits.

"Hello Tom, I tested the whole district about two hours ago everything seemed clear," He answered, taking another look at the safety lamp he held up to the roof, looking for the tell-tale blue flame that would indicate the presence of the murderous, 'firedamp', "Of course you never know what you might uncover, once you all start cutting. There are too many 'blowers', in this mine for my liking." He added meaning the hidden pockets of gas that were exposed without warning and could be ignited without mercy!

Huw looked at Victor, "Hello, young man. The first day is always the worst, you'll get used to everything before you know it and feel like one of the boys."

"That's what his mam and sisters are afraid of!" Added Tom. "They don't want little Victor, getting his hands dirty, worst still breaking a finger! You can't play the piano properly with a collier's hands."

Huw glanced quickly at Victor's hands before continuing, "Someone with talent like you didn't ought to be down the pit young Victor." He gazed up at Tom, who hadn't replied. "You know as well as I do, his mother can't afford for him to stay at school any longer, talented or not. The money isn't there! She's probably at home now breaking her heart! We are all going to try to make sure the boy keeps the music up, but the education will have to stop unfortunately."

"That's a pity, I've heard he's a bright boy." Confirmed Huw. He reached behind him and picked something up off the floor. "I've saved this for you, young Victor, it ought to have gone to one of your older brothers, but as they are all away working elsewhere you must have it. "He handed a metallic object to Victor. It was a mandril, the small pickaxe, that the colliers used to undercut the coal in the mine. "It was your father's, he used it well. When you become older, and are a collier yourself, perhaps you will be able to use it, as well as he did. He was a butty of mine. I'm sorry there's no handle in it, but it was destroyed in the accident, maybe you can put one in when the time comes." He handed the pickaxe to Victor. "Keep it safe."

Victor muttered his thanks and tucked it under his arm, as if he were cuddling a long-lost friend.

Tom spoke to Huw, for a few minutes and mentioned the problem with the young boy David, on the trap door. "That sod, Morgan has been giving him a real hard time lately. He'll be singing top tenor in the choir, not bottom base, if he doesn't leave the boy alone!"

"He can be a proper bully, can William," said Huw as the group walked on down the tunnel heading. "I'll have a word with him myself and I'll tell little David Davies not to worry, I'll see to his lamp."

The group walked to the coal face where a pair of miners entered their own stall. Tom led Victor to theirs.

"This is where we work Victor, this is our stall. We call it our 'stint', I will cut the coal out, you will shovel it into the tub. When it's full push it out to the roadway and transfer it to a dram, then come back for more."

Victor watched as Tom, stripped to the waste, lay on his side facing the seam of coal and began work, Victor watched as the sweat, began to run down his uncle's forehead streaking vividly through the coal grime that caked his brow. He sensed, more than saw, the effort and concentration on Tom's face. He marvelled at the muscle that had become apparent on his uncle's chest and arms, even in the pale lamp light. No longer would he think of Uncle Tom, as a thin weakling. With short yet powerful strikes of the mandril Tom slowly cut away at the coal, until he had undercut a considerable gash into the face. He squirmed further and further into the ever-enlarging gash to cut away even more coal. It was at this time that he was in the greatest danger, if the overhanging coal should fall, he would be crushed, like a mouse beneath the feet of an elephant! Satisfied with his efforts and the depth of the undercut, he pulled himself out of the hole he had made.

"Now it's your turn while I catch my breath," Tom panted, "Don't worry I'll tell you what to do and I'll watch you all the time. You are going to help me knock the coal down." Tom pointed to the sledgehammer and wedges that lay at the back of their stall. Victor turned and picked up the hammer and wedges before returning to the face. He was surprised with the hammer, it was quite heavy, but not nearly as heavy as he expected it to be.

"Put a wedge in the coal and tap it in, until it holds." Ordered Tom. Victor found it quite difficult to both hold the large metallic wedge and tap it into place with the unwieldy sledgehammer. Eventually he succeeded in burying the wedge to a depth of about 3 inches into the coal face. "Now's the time to put your back into it. Hammer the wedge in and split the coal. "Victor did as he was told. He had to spread his legs awkwardly in order to maintain his balance, and swing the hammer in sideways strokes so that he did not bring it into contact with the roof, which would have had a catastrophic result!

"Not too fast Victor, keep it steady, patience is what counts if you are going to do the job properly!" He patted the boy reassuringly on the shoulder. "Keep your eye on the end of the wedge."

Victor drove the wedge deep into the yielding coal and was soon covered in a cloud of clogging dust, that invaded every part of his body. As the wedge bit deeper and deeper he began to feel a dull ache begin to spread slowly between his straining legs. It spread slowly up to the small of his back and the sweat began breaking out on his forehead. Tom, noticing the strain and change of expression on his nephew's face smiled and said, "Spread your legs more Vic, brace yourself or your balls isn't going to be good for nothing by the time you are fifteen!" Victor grateful for any advice spread his legs in an attempt to lessen his agony and then became aware of the messages of agony that was being broadcast by his tortured shoulders. "Grin and bear it lad, it will get easier with time and practice."

Victor watched as the whole length of the wedge disappeared into the gleaming coal face. He was told to stop and noticed that a large crack had appeared in the gleaming surface, it was running in both directions up and down from the wedge."

"Put another wedge into the crack about a foot up from your first wedge and hammer it home." Tom answered, following a careful inspection of the sunken wedge and the cracked coal. Victor gazed at the split with uncertain pride, it seemed such a small investment for so much work and excruciating torture! He was dismayed when his uncle remarked, "Not bad for a first attempt, but we need another wedge up here!" Tom pointed to a place a foot along the crack. Victor, summoning all his resolve and determination, forced another wedge into the new position indicated by Tom. Before he could begin to hammer, he was interrupted by Owen's voice, coming from behind the pillar of coal. Get those legs spread young Victor or your knackers will be knackered!" This was followed by raucous laughter from all sides of the coal face, as Owen continued, "We only let you young ones do the 'ammerin', it's no good for married or courting men! Find your self a girlfriend if you want to be excused 'ammerin'. Then you can take up another kind of 'ammerin' between the bed sheets!"

"But that one will bugger you up even more than this one!" Shouted Evan Wilkinson from the other side of the face.

"Take no notice of them Victor they're only trying to put you off!" Shouted Tom. They are doing a damn good job of that thought Victor to himself.

"Just put your 'and in your pocket at the end of every shift and if you can count up to three everything is fine!" bellowed Owen.

Gritting his teeth, Victor hoisted the sledge and began to pound at the new wedge. Spreading his legs as widely as the space allowed, he began his laborious job. With tear-streaked eyes he completed the task. Never had he known such pain, as the one that he felt between his trembling legs, perhaps this was how they found the men to work in those eastern harems he had read about! At any rate he felt capable of singing soprano for the rest of his life!

He had to hammer in another three wedges before the crack was wide enough to enable the large lumps of coal to come tumbling down from the face, accompanied once more by huge clouds of the ever-present dust!

"All joking aside Victor, it does get easier I promise. "He looked behind him to see the beaming face of his proud uncle. "You've done a man's work today, Vic, you can feel proud of yourself, a man's work!"

Victor became aware that the other miners, on all sides were busy hammering the face. Victor noticed how Huw Steven's entered each stall with his lamp held high, searching for any blue flame indication that the dreaded firedamp gas was present. Satisfied, he told the miners to begin loading the coal onto their corves, the small wooden tub used to transport the coal from the face to the horse drawn drams. Victor began lifting and loading the largest lumps of coal, his fingers clawing and scratching against the smooth sides of coal pieces. He used a shovel to fill the corve's edges with smaller lumps and coal dust, which his uncle called 'small coal' before he began the laborious task of pushing and heaving the heavy tub to the loading point. Every movement caused clouds of coal dust to fill, the already coal infested air. "Make sure you take the lump coal," Reminded Tom, "The weighman will try to cut our wages if you take too much small! The swine still sell it, but they don't pay us for it! It's our donation to the owner's profit and retirement fund! The greedy bastards!"

It took Victor, seven exhausting journeys, before he cleared the hewn coal. He found his uncle busily undercutting the face in their stall on his return. He watched mesmerised as Tom hacked away with the vicious implement, sinking its sharp blade deep into the yielding coal, cutting a slit, like an enormous open wound in the soft underbelly of an immobile huge, black, bat. His uncle paused to support the roof cut with a short timber prop which he hammered into position with the flat edge of his mandril. Wiping the perspiration dripping from his forehead with the back of his coal-stained arm he said, "Go along the heading to Huw Stevens, he is going to blow the heading further into the coal face. I asked if you could watch and begin to learn how it's done. Go on be careful, he's expecting you." Victor picked up his lamp and walked along the heading where he could see lamp lights glowing, wondering how Huw could possibly, 'blow' the heading!

"Come on Victor," said Huw pleasantly, as Victor approached. "Watch how we open up the coal face so that we can cut more coal." He watched in fascination as a group of men timbered the roof and propped up its supports. A short way ahead he saw a few miners drilling into the shale and rock lathered between the coal seams. Each man supported a hand cranked twist drill on his shoulder; and was busily boring two-inch holes into the rock face in front of them. Although he couldn't see them, Victor could imagine the anguish and exertion that must be showing on the face of every one of the drillers, as the strenuous task was completed. It took the drillers about twenty minutes to complete their task; and all the time Huw explained to Victor the way the work was done; and the reason for the siting of each drill hole. The final hole completed the miners withdrew the drills and carried them back down the heading to where the colliers were cutting and hewing coal.

"Come on Victor," said Huw, "This is where I take over!" He walked to the rock face and held his lamp high, he searched for any tell-tale blue colouration of the pale flame that would indicate the presence of the explosive fire damp. Finding none, he called Victor to him. "I am going to place dynamite in the holes and blow it up, so that we can extend the heading." Victor understood at last what his uncle meant, when he said Huw was going to blow up the heading! Huw took sticks of explosive out of a small wooden box and capped each one with a detonator cap, to which was added a short length of fuse. He carefully inserted a stick into each hole and pushed it to the end of the bore hole with a round wooden stake, using a smooth, jerk free push. He joined the short fuses to a longer one, which he lay along the floor of the tunnel heading. The task complete he looked at Victor and said, "Mr. Gregory has said that we will soon be using electrical detonators in the pit! Just think electrically fired explosives in Cwmcarn mine! Back down the heading Victor, Back to Tom, then, you must find somewhere safe when the explosion goes off." Victor turned and walked back to his uncle's stint. As he arrived, he heard Huw's voice booming through the district. "Firing! Take cover! Firing!" Tom left the stall and indicated for Victor to follow him. All the colliers working in the district we're leaving their stalls and moving swiftly down the tunnel, as far away from the explosion as they possibly could. Every man and boy found whatever shelter they could, Tom pulled Victor into a small niche at the side of the tunnel. He covered his ears with his hands and told Victor to do likewise. The tunnel took on an eerie silence as hardened colliers cowered behind drams and corners dreading the dangerous explosions and the choking dust that would soon fill the entire district. A dust ten time more concentrated than that made as they hewed coal! The silence was broken by footsteps that announced the arrival of Huw, he came searching for his own haven. There was no sanctuary in a coal mine!

Victor held his breath and squashed his hands tightly over his ears. A rumbling blast filled the tunnel with its muffled roar, filling Victor's head with a ringing such as he had never experienced before. Then came the dust, it filled every living space completely! There was no escape if you wanted to breathe you took it in, in gasping mouthfuls of the choking, evil, filth. Victor could hear the sound of coughing miners wheezing and spluttering around him spitting huge black phlegm balls onto the floor. Distastefully Victor found himself doing the same! The dust seemed to envelope him completely, filling his mouth, eyes, ears and clothes. Gradually he could make out the vague silhouettes of coughing miners who were appearing around him, each with a face streaked with dust irritated tears. The colliers remained where they were as Huw Stevens went forward to inspect the roof. Satisfied he called the men forward whilst he issued orders about timbering the roof and where the pit props were to be placed. The men returned to their stints and began hewing and cutting the coal.

"Right, Victor, it's time for the sledge and wedge again, let's get this coal down and into your tub and away." Tom was breathing heavily and taking in lungs full of the dust laden air. Victor took a wedge and placed it onto the coalface and tapped it wearily in. His tortured muscles began screaming as he braced his legs and began to swing the hammer. He couldn't ever recall the coal tumbling from the face. He could only remember loading the large lumps of coal out of the stall, into the small wooden corve that he used to transport the coal to the larger drams that the ponies hauled to pit bottom. He wondered if he had a muscle in his body that wasn't tormenting him with agony that was almost more than he could bear! But there were another five back breaking hours of work left in the shift, and there was always tomorrow to look forward too, another full shift!

"Why doesn't Hue put explosives in the face and blow down the coal?" Questioned an exhausted Victor. "It would get coal down a lot quicker and, I bet it would be a lot easier!"

Tom, looked kindly at his nephew, before giving his answer. "As far as being quicker is concerned, it would be the quickest way into a pine box for all of us down here. Explosives have been tried on the face before, but it's too dangerous, there's too much gas. Hundreds of us have been killed when the owners wanted to get out more coal very quickly, to sell to a customer, but it's always ended in disaster! I have heard that in some areas they can use dynamite to blow down the coal, but that isn't around here. Most of us are shit scared when they blow the heading! There have been some nasty incidents then!" Victor put all thought of dynamite out of his head as he concentrated on swinging the sledge against the wedge. "We get enough accidents from sparks between the sledge and wedges!" Added Tom, "Without us wanting to commit suicide!"

CHAPTER 4

Victor had worked at the mine for more than six uneventful months. He had become stronger and could now lift quite large lumps of coal with ease. He was able to haul the tub of coal when it was full to the brim. Glancing down at his hands, he noticed how they were calloused and rough, not the hands you associated with a musician. Ha! How many musicians humped coal, three hundred yards underground, for a few shillings a week! He looked at his uncle Tom, straining to undercut yet another section of coal lying on his stomach, with sweat pouring down his back in torrent's. He was a common hewer of coal by day, yet, at night when the grime and filth had been bathed away, he was a gentleman! A rough diamond, a paragon. Who would think this rough collier was the conductor of the village male voice choir and the leader of the chapel's choral society. He was self-taught there had been no one to teach him, he was a self-made, musical perfectionist. Victor, thought of the advice his uncle always gave, "Just because we work on our hands and knees like animals, is no reason for us to behave like them. Too many people in this world think that is all a Welsh collier is capable of. Live your life with dignity, respect all men, and in time, you will earn their respect. "Tom laughed to himself and thought, back to the previous night's choir practice. Tom had been a harsh martinet. Victor chuckled as he thought of the way Tom had criticised the second tenors over a late entry. "Daniel Evans, you might want to be late for your own funeral, but don't you dare be late responding to the instruction of my baton. It is never wrong! You have put the whole tenor section out. We will have to do the piece again from the beginning!" Yet, he could change in the twinkling of an eye, consumed with delight. He could purr like the cat that had escaped with Skimmy Jones, the milkman's cream. "Beautiful lads! Absolutely bloody beautiful. That was the best rendition of 'Ilef', I have ever heard sung outside the Nationals!" Victor thought of his life underground, how was he going to develop his music. "You have more musical talent in you than the rest of the family put together." Uncle Tom had remarked on more than one occasion. "Including your mother, who has difficulty playing the triangle! Don't give up lad, talented such as yours must win in the end. I don't know how, but one day, some way, this family will listen to your applause in one of those fancy London theatre's. We will watch you conduct a symphony orchestra."

Victor stared away into the blackness. How do pit boys manage music lessons? It's nothing but a pipe dream, perhaps he could take over the choir when his uncle retired. If he lived that long!

Tom, his undercutting finished crawled out of the trench. He looked at his nephew and smiled, "Let's join the boys in the heading and have our grub, we'll knock this coal down afterwards." He picked up his food box and set off down the tunnel.

"Wait for me Tom! Don't run off, I want to see the other men as well!"

Victor caught up with his uncle and together they walked along the heading until they came to a section that was slightly larger than the rest, here they found a group of about fifteen colliers, sitting down, talking busily as they consumed their food. Victor noticed that one of the group was Huw Thomas, the fireman. He, like all the miners, was eating with blackened hands! Victor took a look at his own fingers they were as black as the night or should he say, coal!

Huw laughed aloud and said, "A bit of dirt makes bread and cheese taste like caviar at that posh bloody restaurant, 'The Ritz'."

Stuart Thomas added, "You silly little turd! You have been eating down here for nearly six months now, perhaps today is the only day you have got your hands dirty, is it?" Everyone laughed at the absurdity of the situation.

A miner named Owen Rees, the owner of a wicked sense of humour was the next to pipe up. "It isn't only your hands that get dirty down here you know, it's everywhere. Why if we didn't all bath when we got home, we would all be fathers' of bouncing black babies!"

"Give over!" Said Evan Wilkinson, an enormous mountain of a miner with the temper of a large lamb. "Yours' is black all the time in spite of all the washing you give it!"

"He's not washing it, you daft bugger!" Quipped Tom.

"It's mine and I'll wash is as often and as fast as I like!" Evan piped up.

This comment almost caused Tom to choke, and he turned to Owen.

"Don't forget there are some young boys down here, a joke's a joke, but don't get carried away!"

"Don't you, use that chapel voice with me Tom Owens," snapped Owen, "We are all men down here, and if he doesn't know by now that it's used for more than pissing through, it's bloody well time he learned!"

Victor loved the way the men joked and ridiculed one another; he knew that no offence was meant and non-ever taken. If an accident happened it would be their friendship, togetherness and cooperation that would keep them alive and be their only salvation, until help arrived. "Take care of your butties, then yourself," was the message that had been drummed into his skull from the moment he had been underground. "Outside help is a long time coming down here, you depend on your butty, and he depends on you!"

"Any way, with a randy old sod like you Tom Evans, he would have to be 'tupp' if he didn't know about the finer points of life. There isn't a widow woman safe from you and your charms. Smarmy old bastard isn't you Tom? And to look at him on Sunday, singing in chapel, butter wouldn't melt in 'is mouth!" Laughed Huw, his eyes sparking, even in the dim light of the safety lamps.

"All I do," responded Tom. "Is bring a little comfort to those who need it!"

"We all know what they need, and you are supplying plenty of it! "Chided Evan and as an afterthought, "you lucky old bastard!"

"Not so much of the 'old' if you don't mind." Added Tom cheerfully. "Theres plenty of life in this, 'old' dog yet! As my old dad used to say, 'You are only as old as the woman you feel!'

Evan paused, before taking a bite from a large chunk of cheese, "In your case that's a fair bit of feeling! I only hope you wash your hands first!"

Huw stood and looked back along the heading, "Hurry up with the food lads, that bastard Morgan, hasn't been to this district yet, I expect he'll be along soon to see that we are all hard at it." Victor noticed that Huw was carrying a canary in a cage. The poor thing looked petrified as it clung precariously to its perch.

"Why have you brought your pet bird to work Huw? Victor inquired.

"This is Billy, named after our wonderful foreman. I use him to test for gas. John Collins, the other fireman said there had been a lot of gas blowers and trouble with the ventilation doors, if there's any problems with bad air, he'll let me know." He said looking at the bird.

"How will he do that?" Quizzed Victor.

"He'll fall off his perch, stone cold dead!" Evan interrupted, "And we, all run like buggery, back to the shaft!"

Victor looked at Huw, "I didn't realise you was so cruel Huw!"

"I've a dozen birds just like him in a cage near the blacksmith's, up on the surface, but he's, my favourite. I cried like a baby when one of them died last year, but better one canary than a district full of friends. He's our only warning about bad air and gas." Huw put his face by the cage and clucked at the canary. He received an answering trill in return. "Yes, it will break my heart if I have to bury Billy, but I would rather that, than bury you." Victor was continually amazed by the warmth and gentleness of these rough and supposed coarse miners.

The Lamp

"Finish your food Vic, it's time we got back to the stall. There's work to be done and money to be earned for that kind Mr. Gregory, to give to the mine owners." Uttered Tom his voice heavy with sarcasm.

Tom led Victor back to their stall as the miners drifted back to their own stints. They had been working for only a short time, Victor had given the wedge no more than a dozen taps, when, they were both petrified by a hideous, terror crazed scream, that spread panic throughout the district! Tom, ashen faced, turned to Victor and they both stared ominously at one another for several seconds. "Come on!" Yelled Tom, the spell broken, "A blood curdling yell like that means some poor bastards in a bad way! "Grabbing at his lamp he ran off down the heading with Vic in hot pursuit. They were soon joined by other agitated miners running towards the source of the hideous scream somewhere in the formless obscurity ahead. Victor's heart was pounding within his breast and his breath was coming in huge heaving gulps of emotion. He was aware of the hair on the back of his neck standing immobile and erect, telling him to hide in a dark, dark corner until it was safe, but he was even more afraid of the weird, ghoulish blackness that was back at their stall, and where he would be all alone.

"Who screamed? It came from down this way" Agonised Owen Rees. Victor's back was a raging torrent of sweat despite the intense feeling of bitter cold that was consuming him. Every fibre of his being was telling him to hide, cringe away in the darkest recess he could find.

"Bloody hell! Oh shit!" Victor heard Evan Wilkinson exclaim. "The poor little mite. he's a goner for sure! It's little Dai, what's left of him! The poor little bastard's a mass of blood!"

"Let me through to have a look!" Demanded Huw. "He might be alright. You can never tell with this kind of light."

"The poor little orphan's, with his Da now, different light isn't going to change that!" Sighed Tom. "You know as well as I do, he's in a better place than we are. God protect you sunshine." He looked at Huw, how do you tell a widowed mother that she's lost her first-born son?"

Victor strained to see what they were talking about, peering into the darkness he was appalled to see, faintly illuminated by the glow of their safety lamps, the dreadfully mangled remains of what, a few moments ago, had been David Davies, the ventilation door trapper. His blood was seeping into the coal dust, covering the floor and his twisted broken limbs were spread eagled across the rail tracks that ran the length of the mine. A little further ahead Victor noticed a jittery pony, panting and squirming against its harness. It had been pulling a run of four full drams of lump coal. To the left-hand side of the tunnel Victor recognised the huddled shape of a sobbing man!

"I I I didn't see him until he screamed! The pony and all the drams went over the lad before I could stop Bella and bring her under control!" His whole body shuddered as he gave himself up to the tears that consumed him. "Why was he across the bloody tunnel?"

"He must have just fallen asleep Bryn, "said Huw, addressing the suffering haulier in charge of the pony and drams." You couldn't have known he was there. The poor little fellow was just plain exhausted, he's been working fourteen hour shifts this past fortnight because his sister needed new shoes!"

Victor stared fascinated; it was the first time he had ever seen death! It wasn't clean and peaceful, it was sordid, messy and dreadful. He turned away feeling the bile rising from the pit of his stomach. He wasn't much older than that, that carcass, which had once been, David Davies!

"Find a blanket to wrap him in somebody." Snapped Huw.

"Don't be bloody daft, Huw! Where are you going to find a blanket down here?" Answered Owen, "he can have my coat it will go around the poor little sod about five times anyway!" He handed his grey flannel jacket to Huw, who, gritting his teeth, wrapped it around the body and picked it up and placed it on the last coal dram.

His grisly task completed, he turned to the throng of horrified miners. "Back to work lads, there's nothing any of you can do. I'll take him up the shaft, then take him home. Do you think Kate, will come with me to see his mother, Tom?" Everyone could see the look of pleading that filled his eyes.

"Of course she will Huw, she'll probably take the girls with her, there's five more young ones in that house and I don't expect Mary Davies will be in any fit state to look after them for a while! Back to work lads, Huw's right there's nothing we can do and that callous bastard Gregory, will only dock our wages if our tonnage is down! After all it's only a child's life! Mustn't let it stop us making him money!!"

Huw put a comforting arm on Bryn's shoulder, "Come on Bryn let's get back to pit bottom, then it's home for you and straight to bed."

"You don't think I will be able to sleep do you? Every time I close my eyes I am going to see little Dai Bach, and his brothers and sisters. What am I going to say to his Mam?" He shuddered and fell to his knees. "Dear God, what am I going to do?"

"You are going to mourn little David like the rest of us, then get on with living, you've a family depending on you as well, remember!" He helped the distraught miner to his feet and led him off down the heading, leading the pony pulling its grisly cargo.

CHAPTER 5

KATE RUBBED HER FLOUR COVERED HANDS AGAINST HER WHITE starched pinny. She smiled contentedly, as she looked at the saucepan of rabbit stew bubbling on the fire and she placed the tin of dough into the hot oven. "That's the thing for hungry miners, rabbit stew and bread to mop the juice!" She hadn't asked the minister where the rabbit came from! If she didn't ask, then he wouldn't have to lie!! Lying is a sin so no questions asked, better for everyone. Anyway, there were plenty more rabbits where that one came from, and their need was greater than the landlord's or his gamekeeper's.

"The stew smells wonderful, Mam. I expect the men will be starving when they come in from work." Christine remarked as she walked into the aroma filled kitchen. Kate looked up, how easily Chris had used the word, 'men', the girls were already forgetting Victor was still only a boy! She had stayed awake for night after fretful night but she could see no way of removing Victor, from the mine and sending him back to school, where a boy of his intelligence and talented belonged.

Kate smiled at her eldest daughter. "Isn't it lovely, the way the smell of slow boiling rabbit stew fills the whole house when it's cooking over an open fire?" She turned to the pot and stirred the slowly simmering content's gently with a wooden ladle, "Rabbit has always been your Uncle Tom's favourite." She smiled at herself and thought, "And when he knows it was poached, he'll probably enjoy it even more!"

Two of her other daughters came hurrying into the kitchen. Both were quite short. Ivy the younger of the three daughters, was a pretty dark haired sixteen-year-old. Glenys, the other sister was almost two years older than Ivy and had raven coloured hair that hung to her shoulders. She had eyes that sparkled like the stars in a frosty sky, crowning a face that radiated peace and contentment.

Ivy flounced to the table sat down and said, "All the boys have been sparkling Glenys, Mam. She flutters her eye lashes and they all come drooling like little sheep off the mountainside, just like lambs to the slaughter!"

"You're only jealous, because none of them fancy you yet!" Snapped Glenys. "That's all it is jealousy!"

"Stop it you two! I am not going to stand here and listen to you squabble like common street girls. I may not be able to control what you get up to outside this house, but you will behave, like the ladies you were brought up to be, inside it!"

"Sorry Mam," echoed both girls.

"We went for a walk along the canal bank. We walked all the way to Risca and back. It was wonderful, there are a family of swans at Crosskeys and they have six cygnets." Said Glenys turning to face her mother. "We met a few boys from the village and a few young men who work at the brickworks." She smiled wistfully, a faraway look in her coal dark eyes.

"You should have seen the way she was ogling the boys, Mam!" Teased Ivy, winking at her two other sisters. "I thought we were supposed to wait for the boys to spark us, not go chasing after them!"

Kate raised her eyebrows in the reproachful way that they all recognised as a sign of an impending detonation of her temper. Ivy recognising the sign, hastily interrupted, "Don't burst a blood vessel Mam, I exaggerated a little!" She looked at the thunderous look she was being given by Glenys, "Well perhaps a lot. We saw them on the other side of the canal bank throwing stones at the cygnets you should have heard the way our Glenys told them all off! I bet most of them feel about two inches tall right now. You would have been proud of her Mam."

Glenys allowed her expression to soften, she even managed a small thank you sort of smile to cross her face and head in Ivy's general direction.

"Why were you down the canal bank anyway girls?" Kate demanded the stern look returning to her face. "You know I don't like you going there, you could meet goodness knows who and be sold to the gypsies for no more than a basket full of pegs!"

Christine not wishing to be outdone could contain herself no longer and quickly added, "They could be captured and sold to white slavers! They would end up in some Eastern harem. Just like you read about in books."

"Don't be so silly Chris," rebuked Kate, "What would white slavers be doing on a canal bank at Crosskeys?" She looked intently at her two daughters again, "I'm still waiting for an explanation, as to why you were on the canal in the first place."

"We simply went for a walk Mam, nothing else. It was such a nice day we just started walking and before we knew it, we were in Risca."

"It's been very warm these past few days, you didn't go swimming in the canal, did you?" Kate asked her eyes wide and insistant as she studied the faces of her daughters. "You know what I've said about that, young ladies don't do such things! You'll catch the plague! There are dozens of dead dogs in it and thousands of drounded kittens!"

"I Wouldn't be seen dead in the canal!" Snapped Glenys rattly.

"That's just what you'll be if you ever swim in it!" Stated Kate.

Ivy, not pleased with the direction the conversation was taking tried to interrupt, "The boys all go swimming in the canal, it's where they all learn to swim."

"And how do you know that, madam?" Ranted Kate her temper beginning to rise, as she stared at her youngest daughter.

"She always goes to spy on the boys when they go swimming, Mam." Replied Christine.

"Ivy! I'm ashamed of you!" Continued her mother. "You know they don't wear anything when they swim in that canal! It's not a sight for a 'Lady' to be looking at!"

"They do so mam," blushed a reddening Ivy. "I've seen them, they all wear white, swimming knickers!"

Before Kate could think of a proper retort to Ivy's naïve remark she was interrupted by a loud rapping at the front door.

"Good lord, it must be the policeman! No one else knocks at doors like that!" Blurted Katie, thankful for the chance to break the conversation, before things got any more difficult!

"Quick girls! Tidy up the kitchen before I answer the door."

The girls looked at one another, then the kitchen, it was the usual immaculately tidy place it always was! Not a thing was out of place. The China gleamed in the cabinet, the grate and oven were freshly black leaded and the floor had been swept and the flagstones scrubbed until they were as sleek as velvet! Kate's kitchen was renown in the village, no germ, speck of dust, or dirt was to be tolerated.

"Mam! The king could eat his dinner off the floor if he wanted too!" Declared Chris, laughing merrily at her house-proud mother. "You know you never have a thing out of place!"

"You never know who's going to call. It's like I always tell you all, make sure you always wear clean underwear, just in case you have an accident, and they have to undress you at the doctors. Just think of the shame if you've got dirty knickers on!" Scolded Kate.

As Chris walked towards the kitchen door, Glenys pulled Ivy, to one side and whispered. "The next time you know the boys are swimming down the canal tell me. We'll go down there together to watch them and see what's on offer!"

Tired of waiting for her daughter to open the door Kate overtook her and wrenched the latch open. She stood riveted to the spot, her eyes wide staring blankly at a coal blackened vision that stood before her. Her eyes began to fill with tears and small silvery steaks could be seen running from the corner of each dissolving ord. Her soft lips began to twitch uncontrollably, her dry tongue unable to move within her mouth. Kate, managed to take a step back into the room, straight into the arms of Christine, who realising something was wrong quickly looked over her mother's shoulder. She too, saw the spectre of Huw Stevens, still in his working clothes, covered in the grime of the coal face. Chris, clutched tightly at her mother she closed her eyes dreading the words she was expecting Huw to say.

Huw beginning to comprehend the anguish his appearance was causing quickly blurted out. "It's alright Kate. Victor and Tom are both fine! I've come on another matter, honestly, they haven't had an accident or anything!"

"Are you sure?" Sobbed Kate, wincing from the grip of Chris's fingers on her shoulders." What do you think we are supposed to think with you turning up here, in that state, halfway through the shift. I've been imagining my son and brother lying dead and mutilated at the bottom of that bloody pit shaft! "Huw looked incredulously at Kate, in all the time he'd known her, he'd never herd her, use strong language. "I know you must be thinking all sorts of things must have happened, but don't worry, nothing has happened to them."

"Don't stand out there dirtying the doorstep Huw Stevens, come on in." She said, moving back into the kitchen, offering him the room to isn't. "I can see from the look on your face that something is bothering you!"

"I can't come into, 'your' kitchen in this state, Kate, I've come straight from the pit!" He said doubtfully.

Kate smiled to herself being aware of what people said about the cleanliness of her house and kitchen. "Don't be daft Huw, come in and sit down. Where do you think Tom and Victor, bath after their shift? This is a home, not a house! We live here it's not treated like a residence, when it's dirty we clean it that's all!" Kate turned away from Huw and wiped away her tears. She looked at Christine and said, "Put the kettle on to boil, then make us a nice cup of tea, I think we could all use one, and, like my old granny always used to say, everything seems better after a nice cuppa!" Huw sat on a polished wooden chair next to the table, covering his face with his hands. The woman became aware that something was troubling their old friend, something that was eating him away from the inside. Chris, tried to ease his tension and said, "I hope you realise you made my mother swear! We didn't think she even knew such words, but perhaps it just slipped out! She'll have to clean the chapel from top to bottom for a month at least, if she is to be forgiven!" Huw smiled gratefully at the young woman before continuing, "Your family are fine but there has been an accident." Kate sat next to him and gently put her warm hands carefully around his massive, gnarled fingers and squeezed them soothingly.

"I think you had best tell me what's happened, there's only one way to do it and that's to blurt it straight out." She said gazing confidently into his eyes. "I admit I was worried, but I'm over that now, it will help if you tell me, I've got all day." Kate turned back to Christine and said, "How much longer is that tea going to be?"

Huw took a deep breath and began to tell Kate about the pit accident and the death of the boy. David Davies. He felt her grip tighten as he told the tale and saw the glistening tears return at its conclusion. "It might not be my Victor, but it is someone else's son! I will come with you to tell poor Mrs. Davies. Lord above what a thing to have to tell a mother!" She thought for a moment then added, "Heavens above! It's Mary Davies, of Feeder Row, she buried her husband less than six months ago!" Once again, her eyes were moist with tears as she began to move around the kitchen gathering her coat, hat and bag. "Chris, Glenys, Ivy get your coats you will have to come with me. There are five more children in that house, and I don't think Mrs. Davies, is going to be in any state to look after them! Ivy, you stay here and make sure the water is boiled for when our Victor and Uncle Tom get in from work. The dinners on cooking, don't let it burn or I'll skin you alive." Huw, much relieved now that Kate was taking charge of the hundred and one things, that needed doing, if the Davies' family were to be supported and taken care of, sat up and began to relax. "We'll see to Mrs. Davies and the children, Huw. You will have to get a message to Herbert Humphries, as soon as possible. The miners' federation will have to provide help for this family. I expect the owners will be whitewashed as usual and deny any responsibility. They left us all but destitute when my Edward was killed, if it hadn't been for Tom… …!" She left the sentence unfinished as she headed for the door with her girls following like chicks chasing after a mother hen, off to do battle with a sly old fox!

"What have you done with poor little David?" Kate asked Huw looking nervously up and down the street. "You haven't left the poor little mite out in the street, have you?"

"I can't take him home Kate!" He answered, shuddering. "Not even his mother, would recognise what's left of him! When I got him to the surface, we saw how badly he was hurt. It made grown men ill. I've never seen anything like it Kate! It's the first time I've ever seen Evan Dance cry! He was blubbering like a baby. Dear God! I've had to do some things, I've taken the broken bodies of too many friends, back to their homes'!" He stopped horrified; how could he have been so idiotic! Kates's, husband had been one of those friends.

"Don't worry Huw, you were wonderful when it was my Edward." She added quickly, seeing the haunted look that crossed his face. "You look as though the Grim Reaper, has just tapped you on your shoulder and Old Nick, is doing a tap dance on your grave!"

"You know my mouth is bigger than the Severn Estuary and I can't seem to keep it closed once I get excited or agitated! And my Lord Kate! The poor little lad!" Kate Squeezed his hand affectionately and whispered, "Don't say any more Huw, please. You must be brave for the next hour at least. If you can't be strong, how are we going to be? It seems to be a wife's lot around here to weep for her husband and sons! We can't do it for ever, when are they going to do something about these greedy coal owners and their unsafe pits! It's a dangerous enough job without all this insane, insatiable exploitation. They have the audacity to go to their churches on Sunday's, listen to our lord's teachings and milk us dry of all our dignity and humanity on a Monday! May the good Lord grant us retribution in the next life!"

"We could all do with a small amount of recompense, in this life, too, Kate!" Huw countered testily. "We have been bled dry for generations. But let's not talk of that now." He shivered convulsively once more. "This is a time for grief, sadness and comforting, God I need the comfort myself!"

They set off wearily, to walk the short distance to Feeder Row, the home of the unsuspecting Davies family.

"Run ahead to the minister's, Glenys, tell Mr. Morgan what's happened and ask him to meet us at number ten." Ordered Kate. "We will need him at a time like this!"

Glenys, glad of the opportunity to leave the wretched group hurried on in search of the clergyman, her feet echoing hollowly on the irregular, stoney road," If he's not at home, find him!" Kate shouted as an afterthought.

They walked along the narrow well-worn path leading towards Feeder Row, the grass had been worn away, by the hundreds of feet that trudged along its length during the past 30 years. The edges were strewn with wild mint that filled the air with its heavy diuretic, dulcet aroma. Here and there, large clumps of heavy stinging nettle stood waiting for any unwary hand or arm that dared to kiss its excruciating stems, a plant too quick with its umbrage! They walked by the house of Doctor Devlin, surrounded by its tall, ivy strewn wall. The girls always walked on tip toes, hoping to see over it into the grounds beyond. Its finely manicured lawns and orchard with trees laden with luscious ripe fruit, that meant a paddling on the backside for any scrumper unlucky enough to be caught inside by the doctor or Mrs. Ferguson, his housekeeper. Tanned because you were too slow, was the chant that surrounded any child captured and walloped! "Grab some apples and run like hell! Glenys, grimaced at the memory of the sour, crabbed, tartness of the unripe fruit, stolen during fits of youthful madness! They all marched on in silence, each conscious of the grisly task to be performed, at the end of their short walk. They look down at the silvery River Carn, as it splashed its way towards the murky depths of the river Ebbw. Each prepared what they were going to say or do. Feeder Row was in sight, its grey, stone walled houses standing resolutely together against the ravages, of both men and the element's. Several dirt streaked children were playing on the flagstones outside each door. Few were wearing shoes, none any clothes that had not been passed to at least three or four older brothers or sisters before them. Huw led the way to the Davies' front door where he stopped and took a deep breath! He knocked loudly, two or three times with his knuckles.

"We are right behind you Huw; this isn't going to be easy so perhaps it would be better if you let me tell her. It might be better, coming from one mother to another!" Kate could hardly believe that she had heard herself propose anything so preposterous! How would she be able to walk into someone's house and calmly announce such news.

"Thank you, Kate, I was hoping you would be able to help me out, but this is something I must do, it's a responsibility I can't shirk! It's my duty, I owe it to young David, and I owe it to myself. You see I took him to the pit to work." Huw admitted gravely." I arranged for him to start work, knowing how desperate the family were! They couldn't manage on the bit of parish relief they were receiving, together with a few coppers from the federation. They have had nothing but the promise of compensation from the owners!"

The door was opened by a small girl. She wore a tattered linen frock that had obviously belonged to at least two older sisters before her. Its hem was ragged and showed signs of having been altered in length twice previously, but it was spotlessly clean! The same could not be said about her hands and face, both looked as if they had not been washed for several days! She looked up and presented a mouth full of black teeth as she smiled," Ello, what d'you want? If you're after money, my mum said we isn't got any!" Once the sentence was finished, she turned away and began to close the door.

"Wait Sally! It's me, Mr. Stevens. I've come to see your Mam. It's very important, go and fetch her please." Huw smiled at the little girl, as he put his hand firmly against the door, to prevent it being closed.

A dishevelled woman, little more than skin and bone, came to the door "ooh the hell is it just bugger o—! She stopped short when she saw Huw and the party of women at the threshold. "Sorry Mr. Stevens, I didn't know it was you, I thought it was that pig who calls for the rent, an' I ain't got it!" She spoke honestly without a trace of shame," If he thinks he can get blood out of a stone, He's got another thing coming'!" She continued hardly pausing for breath," I wasn't expecting visitors you'll have to take us as you find us. Come on in, all of you. I want to get the door shut quickly so that, that bloody rent collector can't get in!" Mrs. Davis went quickly inside, urging the others to follow her, when they were all indoors, she quickly slammed and bolted the door. I thought you was working' this shift Mr. Stevens, still never mind I can make you a nice cup of tea." She stopped, as she became aware of the others who were looking at her, all her visitors seemed to be avoiding her eyes! "Oi! Why be you all looking' at me so funny? There be something' wrong isn't there?" She moved her glance from face to face, hoping for an explanation. Finally deciding to concentrate her attention on Huw. "Come on Mr. Steven's what is it." She stopped speaking as a dreadful understanding began to consume her thoughts. "Some thing's happened to my David hasn't it?" She took a step back into the room and bumped into the table, she put her hand down and clutched at its rough scarred surface.

Huw stepped forward a grim look in his eyes, "sit down Mary. I've got some bad news to tell you." He took a deep breath, gazing upward as he searched to find the words. What were the appropriate words for a time such as this?" You must try to be brave Mary, but David has had a very bad accident down the pit today." Before he could finish, she gabbled. "Is hurt bad? I'll do what I can, but I haven't got much money to pay for the doctor, perhaps I can clean the s surgery?" She stammered.

"Sit down and let us make the tea for you." Ordered Kate, "Christine put the kettle on and then find the tea caddy and make us all some tea. Come on Mary, sit down let Huw finish, it's time for all of your courage!" How easily the words slipped off her tongue, she had almost, lost her mind when her Edward died! Bravery was for soldiers and people without feelings! She had wept for months and even now a day did not go by when her eyes did not mist over, and sobs consume her every thought! She squeezed Mary's hand tightly and added, "Let Huw finish then we'll all see what we can do."

Mary, looked longingly at Huw, her eyes pleading with him not to say the words that she knew were coming.

"I'm sorry but little David won't be coming home, Mary. He's gone to a better home, one where all his cares and woes have vanished! He isn't in pain he's with his dad!"

"Oh my God! My baby, where is he? He might be alive bring him home to me! I'll look after him!" She began to cry, great husky sobs, filled the room. Huge, crystal-clear tears gathered in her eyes and began to roll uneasily down her contorted cheeks. "Y-Y-You said, you was going' to look after him! You promised he would be alright. My Dai, hated going' but he knew we needed the money! You should have seen ow proud he was when we bought the new shoes for our Molly to wear to school!" The tears were falling like rain and her body was shaking hysterically. "What a bloody price to pay for a pair of shoes! What a bloody price!"

Kate looked at Glenys, then at the young children. "Glen, take the young ones out to play, don't bring them back until I tell you too." She turned her attention to Christine, "For the lord's sake Christine! Hurry up with that tea! We are all dreadfully sorry about what has happened. If there's anything you can think of that needs doing, please ask." Kate felt an idiot as soon as the words were out of her mouth! Poor Mary wasn't capable of thinking of anything right now! They must let her weep for her son, tears were the only answer, along with time! But now was the time for tears. Kate put her arms around Mary's shoulders pulled her head forward and they both cried, the tears, that only mothers' can shed!

CHAPTER 6

PHILLIP GREGORY SAT ERECT IN HIS COW HIDE CHAIR BEHIND HIS leather-bound desk, several document's lay before him beneath a large sheet of pink blotting paper. He glanced up at the grandfather clock that ticked majestically in the corner of his spacious office, ten to two! They would be here in a few minutes, that subversive bastard Humphries, who didn't know his place and had little respect for his betters', and the members of his moronic committee! He confirmed that the chairs, he had ordered, were all in position in front of his desk. They were the smallest chairs in the entire building. "If you want to put someone at a disadvantage," his father had always told him, "Fix it so that you can look down on the buggers, show them you are superior, put them in their place, beneath you!" How he loved lording it over these semi-literate morons! The feeling of absolute power he possessed gave him an almost permanent erection, something that he would have attended to, before the day was out! He breathed deeply, sat up to his full height, closed his eyes and thought. He had to be at his best today, not give the ignoramuses an inch, they had to go away with nothing more than sympathy! Perhaps a few half promises, nothing concrete, after all, he was the master, they did as they were told and liked it, or else! He reached forward to a large inlaid rosewood box, he rubbed his hand erotically, wantonly along its surface, smoother than a tart's thighs! He lifted the lid lasciviously, inhaling deeply as the aroma of the Havana, coronas filled his more than ample nostrils!

He breathed addictively once more, before selecting a long cigar, the fattest he could find in the box. He lifted it appreciatively, rolling it between his thumb and forefinger. Opening his desk drawer, he took out, a small, ivory handled, knife which he used to make a small hole in the end of the chosen cigar. He lit it carefully using a gold lighter which he carefully placed on display at the edge of his desk. Closing his eyes he puffed a long blue stream of smoke, into the room. There was nothing like a large cigar for putting these miners down, giving him a wonderful feeling of superiority, when all they had was a handful of chewing Tabacco, or some indescribable, foul smelling, pipe weed! He sat back, he was ready!

There was a knock at the door and Mrs. Thompson, his secretary entered, "Mr. Humphries and the delegation from the miners' federation are here Mr. Gregory." She smiled seductively as she spoke. He Leered lustily at her ripe breasts, thin waist and wonderful hips, his perfect saddle!

He felt that age old stirring deep within his pocket. "Down boy!" He thought you'll have to wait a while! "But I promise soon, we'll spread eagle her on the desktop!" He spoke quietly. "I'm busy for the next few minutes!" He smiled at the thoughts and expectations that were going through his mind. Let them wait for a while, do them good to stew in their own juice! "I'll see them in five minutes." She closed the door and went outside.

"Mr. Gregory won't be long gentlemen, he has a bit of business to finish first, then he will see you." She smiled at Herbert Humphries, he was a real gentleman, treated everyone with respect, not like her employer! His respect was delivered according to the size of their bank account!

"Thank you Silvie, I would have been more surprised if he had been ready to see us at the appointed time!" Herbert Humphries answered, in his usual matter of fact way. He turned to the two men accompanying him, and whispered, "Don't forget, let me do all the talking! Don't say a word unless I ask you to, you know what a sanctimonious bastard he is! He'll be trying to rile us before having us thrown out. Try to keep calm, we are in the right!"

Silve, pointed towards some chairs and asked, "Would you like to make yourselves comfortable and sit down. He said five minutes, but I don't know how long he's going to be!"

"Thank you Silvie, we may as well, I expect he intends to make us wait a while!" They all sat down holding their caps in their hands'. "Have you heard from you husband George lately?"

"Yes, I had a letter off him last week. He's been promoted to Petty Officer and he's going to be transferred to a cruiser based in Plymouth. He said he might be able to come home in a month or two for a fortnight's leave." Silvie, replied wistfully. "The money will come in useful, but I wish he was at home more, it's hard with him away for more than eleven months of the year!"

"That's what you get if you pick up with a sailor when you go on an outing to Barry Island!" Herbert laughed, humouring her. "You must miss him; it can't be easy bringing up those boys with their father so far away!"

write at least once a week, and George, does the same, but you are right I wish he was home more often but if he was, where would he work? There's only the pit! He's always been a sailor; he doesn't know anything else."

Herbert smiled knowingly. Aye he thought, only men work down the pit and only a fool would leave you here for a bastard like Gregory! But all he said was. "It would be hard for him to settle down here, we don't have many openings for naval gunners!"

Silvie, looked hard at Herbert searching for any sign that he was trying to belittle her, but she could detect nothing. "I'll see if Mr. Gregory has finished and he's ready to see you." She knocked on the door once again and disappeared inside. She returned after a few minutes to announce, Mr. Gregory, will see you now, do come in."

The Three men went into the office, Herbert Humphries led the way.

"Come in and sit down!" Phillip Gregory snapped brusquely. "You can have five minutes only. I've a pit to run. It involves a lot more than going down a bloody great hole and swinging a mandril!"

Herbert, quite unperturbed countered, "Good afternoon, Mr. Gregory, it's nice of you to see us. We all know you are a very busy man." He paused to introduce the two men with him, "Let me introduce Bill Morris, another Union official from the pit and this is Jack Miles, from the Bedwellty area."

"Three to one, is it Humphries, I didn't think you were a coward! I thought you'd face me alone." Gregory puffed a long stream of smoke straight into the face of Jack Miles. We do things our way down here, we don't need advice from any outsiders on how to run our affairs!" The two miners although inwardly seething, remembered Herbert's advice and refused to rise to the bait, they sat quietly, facing Phillip Gregory.

"You've got them well trained if nothing else." Gregory admitted! "There's nothing like a nice cigar to help me collect my thoughts and sharpen my wits." He declared, pointedly refraining from inviting the miners to take one. "Come on then, let's get down to business, what do you want this time?"

Herbert looked him straight in the eyes without blinking. "We have come about poor little David Davies, the pit boy who was killed three days ago!" Before he could continue Gregory interrupted him. "It was the stupid little sod's own fault! He fell asleep!"

"Nobody knows for sure what happened Sir," Herbert continued, "But what everyone does know is a family, with five children, who have already buried their father because of an accident in this pit, now have another member ready to be laid to rest in 'Nazareth'! The Federation are hoping that, you, on behalf of the owners, will see fit to provide some compensation for the grieving family."

"Where do you think the money's going to come from? This is a pit not a benevolent society, I Can't give money away. Just because some poor devil falls asleep in front of one of the horses." He was beginning to warm to the task. "As far as compensation is concerned, The Davies' ought to pay me! That pony was worth more than thirty-five pounds, and it's been lame ever since the incident! This pit can't afford to feed and care for an idle pony any more than an idle bloody miner!" Take the buggers on, headfirst, don't be Subtle, it was the principle he'd started with and it was the one with which he would die! "While we're on the subject of money! West district stopped for nearly half an hour when the accident happened, I ought to dock them all an hours pay!"

Mr. Gregory, a little boy is dead, his family are grieving. They have lost not only their brother, but their bread winner, have you no compassion, no Christian kindness?" Herbert looked at the stoney faced man before him, looking for any sign of humanity, but there was none! "Can the company offer anything to lessen this deserving family's hardship? If not for the mother, then what about the children?" He paused briefly to collect his thoughts, "The men are angry and feelings are running quite high, there's even some talk of a strike, unless something is done for the Davies'."

Gregory took a deep contented draw of his cigar, exhaled slowly and added, "I don't think the men will strike over an issue such as this, but, I know the owners are anxious to avoid trouble before the investigation by the Inspector of mines. I will wait to see if the inquiry makes any recommendation about compensation. You never know the magistrate may be feeling generous! In the meantime, I am willing to allow the family to stay in Feeder Row, in the company's house for the next month, free of charge. Of course, if they are unable to pay after that, they will have to move out. I'll need the house for a working miner and family."

"I'm sure the company will not enjoy the bad publicity; it will receive over its treatment of the family after such a horrific accident!" Herbert was clutching at straws, without a reliable witness to the accident and its cause the federation had little with which to fight." A young boy has been mutilated! Killed stone dead because he was working too hard in your mine and all you can offer his bereft family is a month's free isn't?"

"As I told you earlier, this mine is here to make money, not give money away to every Tom, Dick or Harry. As far as the harmful publicity is concerned, do you think the press are going to be concerned with an unfortunate accident to a young pit boy. Good grief man! This is Nineteen Hundred and Nine! There are far more important things going on in the world! I have made my, first last and final offer. Perhaps the inquest will feel more sympathetic to your entreaties! However, I have business to conclude, you will have to leave!" Gregory ground out his cigar in the ash tray on his desk. He picked up his pen and began to read and sign the document's on his desk. One of his companions made as if to speak, but, with a wave of his hand, Herbert silenced him.

"I hope the owners' decide otherwise, there has been a very unfortunate accident. The Fed is not trying to apportion blame, we just want to see a poor, wretched family, that fate has decided to deal with so callously, taken care of! We feel that the owners would appear, to the public, to be more benevolent if they were a little more charitable towards this family." Said Herbert, looking for any trace of humanity in the representative's face.

"Don't try and soft soap me, Humphries! I don't give a bugger! There will be no adverse publicity about this incident because, there will be no publicity! The owner, the Duke of Bedwellty, is on the board of several newspapers, need I say more." Without looking up, Gregory resumed reading. The three men turned and marched from the room. It was raining quite heavily when they reached the outside.

Phillip Gregory allowed himself a contented smile! He had done well, single handed he had routed those moaners, he slumped contently in his chair, thinking. He needed a reward and at a time like this, there was only one thing that fitted the bill! He glanced at the still open door of his office and said, "Silvie, come into my office please, you won't be needing your notebook!" He stood to meet her as she walked seductively into the office, silently closing the door behind her. Forcing his bitter tongue between her half open lips he tugged her skirt high over her hips, before thrusting her back onto his desk and clawing hungrily at her panties!

"Even this is warmer than it was inside," grumbled Bill Morris, "He seems to be typical of the breed. As long as we make the money for him, he doesn't care what happens to us!"

Jack Miles pounded one fist into his other hand. "Let's call the boys' out we'll see if it's cheaper to pay the Davies' compensation or lose money in a shut down!"

"No way!" Snapped Herbert quickly," I am appalled at the stance the management is taking, but it was an accident, a tragic accident. I will not ask the men to strike over this. I don't think they will agree to it anyway!"

"I agree, with you." Said Bill, looking at Herbert. "It isn't right to ask the men to strike, it will only mean every family suffering not just the Davies'. We will have to ask the federation if they can help this stricken family."

"You make representations, to the' Federation' on their behalf. Bill, I am going to see if we can hold a pit head collection for the family it may not be much, but like the old lady said when she pissed in the sea, every little bit helps!" Herbert, smiled ruefully at his two companions. "It might not be a lot, but we try to take care of our own!"

"That unfeeling bastard Gregory, what an example of Christian brotherhood and com_____" Herbert, interrupted him before he could finish. "We all know what he is like and to be honest, we got as much as I expected, bugger all! So, I can't say I am disappointed. We tried but you can't get blood out of a stone, there's more heart in a stone. Let's go and do what we can."

"It's no use Huw, the man is made of stone! He won't do anything to help the family." Herbert was sat at a highly polished table, in a sparsely furnished room, at the local chapel hall. He was chairing a branch meeting of the Federation. "He was adamant that it was the boy's own fault because he fell asleep, so the mine is blameless." He looked appealingly at the sombre faces gathered around him. "If anyone's got any suggestions, I am willing to try anything, because you can bet that at the end of the month, that bastard will have the bailiffs in and the Davies' will be out!" This statement was met with murmurs of agreement, whilst several men merely nodded. "I am not prepared." Herbert continued, "To ask the men to strike over this matter because where does the blame lie? Does it lie with an affluent coal owner who's willing to let young children work, God knows how long, underground, just to sate his greed for profit and money! Does it lie with little David Davies, because he worked so hard, he just fell asleep! Or does it lie with a society that just doesn't give a bugger, as long as it happens to somebody else!" He thumped the table in exasperation.

"We have got to do something," Bill Morris interrupted. "The lad's got to be buried if nothing else!"

"Parish relief fund will take care of the funeral," stated Herbert. "The dead aren't the problem! There's a widow and five little mouths to feed and clothe!" He looked around the room, hoping for a glimmer of an idea that might prove the salvation of this destitute family.

"Aren't there any relations to take them in? Surely they must have somebody!" Inquired Huw.

"Nobody knows." Answered Herbert, "They moved here about seven or eight years ago, but no one knows from where. Dot Williams, from next door said they heard her talk of Rochdale, Manchester, there's no way we will be able to contact them up there, but the 'Fed' will try. If we can trace any relatives willing to take them, we will have to try to find the money to send them there. If not, it's the workhouse!"

Huw looked at the men gathered around the table. "What a bloody fine mess once again! How many more of us are going to end up in that damn workhouse before something is done to improve our conditions. After all, we are supposed to be living in a civilised country!" Thank the lord for Parish Relief! At least the poor mite will be buried properly. Mr Berwyn Morgan has agreed to hold the service. Kate would have skinned him alive if he hadn't! Tom has said the choir will sing in the chapel and at the graveside."

CHAPTER 7

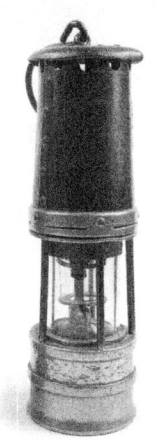

Kate wiped her eyes and removed the tear streaks from her cheeks as she stepped out of the door onto the Feeder Row pavement. Turning left, she began walking home to George Street. Seeing a group of neighbours talking outside number 14, she stopped and began chatting. "Good morning, Kate, what a terrible thing to happen!" Said Pam Smith, the lady from number 13. "It isn't right for the young ones to be took from us so soon. It isn't right!"

"Good morning, ladies. "Kate replied smiling pleasantly at all those present." It was a dreadful accident! It could have been any of our husbands or sons."

"Dirty ole pits! I wish my son Basil didn't aye to go down there," said Elsie Cousins, who lived in number 14." But where else can he work. There's nowhere else!"

Pam Smith, the other neighbour present, looked over her shoulder to make sure no one was eavesdropping, "It isn't safe down that pit! I don't want to cast nasturtiums at anybody, but, my son Fred, said that they don't have no proper roof timber and when they do, it isn't enough, they have to spread it too far apart to do any good! He said there's so much water down there that they'll all catch the' lumpago'! It's alright for that Mister Gregory he don't have to worry if he as to go to the doctor he can pay but my Willie, gets hurt we haven't got the money to visit any fancy physician!"

"Don't be daft Pam, your' husband Willie won't get hurt, he's never in work to get hurt!" Sneered Elsie Cousin of number 13. "He gets tired after opening is eye lids! Why my Joseph, reckons he's too tired to have got you pregnant and when it happened arf the night shift left the county!" All the women roared with laughter as Elsie continued, "Well at least your Willie didn't go anywhere! If what I've herd is right he shouldn't have been called Willie!

"You got up grumpy this morning didn't you." Snapped Pam.

"No, I didn't!" Replied Elsie. "I left the miserable old bugger in bed!"

This caused even more raucous laughter!

Kate although amused, whispered, "Ladies we ought to keep the noise down, we must show more respect for the grieving family!"

"You are right Kate. It's just that when she starts on about er Willie it makes me mad, the idle toss pot! Big Dick he should have been called!" Continued Elsie.

"Kate desperate to change the subject and stop the squabbling neighbours, turned to Mrs. Morgan and said "How is your Daniel doing at sea Doris? Is he still a stoker on that ocean steamer?

"Yes." Answered Doris Morgan. "Funny isn't it! Here's my Moses and the boys digging and shovelling the coal for all they are worth, to get it up the pit an there's our Daniel shovelling it for all he's worth into the boiler of his ship!" Her eyes crinkled with laughter, "Still, at least he's got away from the pits!"

"How is your Paul doing?" Enquired Kate." The last time you spoke to me he was doing well in New Zealand. Is he still there?"

"I think so, but I don't know if he's doing as well as he was. Cos last night I heard our Don and David talking about him. I fink he', must be down on his luck. I got the idea that he is having to go to the soup kitchen to eat cos they were saying as he was outside a brothel and was going to go in for a basinful! He's a big lad and he'll never survive on just soup and broth!"

Kate unable to control herself, hid her embarrassment by pretending to be overcoming a coughing fit.

"You 'ad better be careful of that cough." Warned a most concerned Pam, "If you are coughing like that in the Summer what are you going' to do when the weather gets really cold in the winter!" Kate grateful for the temporary relief, these naïve, uncomplicated, women provided from the overwhelming grief of the Davies' household, chatted constantly, away for several minutes.

"I hope you will all be in chapel on Sunday?" Kate enquired more through hope than expectation.

"I can't come on a Sunday, that's the only day my Joe isn't working'. We like to go for a walk then call in for a little drink together down the pub." Answered Elsie.

"Don't make me laugh, Elsie Cousins!" Added Pam, "You an your husband don't have a little drink any time. I've seen you coming home! I don't know who was carrying who! Neither of you was capable!"

"Well I've got news for you Pam Smith." She smirked and winked at Kate. "We was both more than capable when we got in! An' I was too tipsy to stop 'I'm ! I only 'hope the dull sod pulled it out in time! We can't afford anymore brats!" Kate could feel her cheeks reddening despite the fact that she had been a married woman herself for more than 20 years.

"And I spend all my time on my knees scrubbing' the floor. I don't fancy getting' back on them to pray on a Sunday!" Laughed Doris. Kate smiled at the three women, and added tolerantly, "If you change your minds, you will be very welcome at, 'Nazareth', most welcome. With our men working the way they do, a word in the Lord's ear, asking him to watch over them and keep them safe can't do any harm and it makes me, feel a lot better!"

Kate wished them a good day and set off to walk home. It was a pleasant day so she decided to walk along the bank of the brook. It was little more than a trickle, glistening and babbling its lazy way down towards the hebbw', half a mile away. She strained to see the gleaming stones nestling on its bottom, glaring like pieces of ivory from far off Africa. Since she had been a girl, she had marvelled at the way the crystal water had swirled and bubbled, boiled and foamed to overcome each stony barrier in its path before it joined its parental river, eventually racing off to that far distant maelstrom, the sea! Her thoughts ran to the times when, after a week's winter rain, the brook was a raging torrent defying all to stand in its way. It could be an ebullient, surging, vortex. Without thinking she slipped off her shoes and dangled her toes in the icy cold water. Closing her eyes, she was able to picture her beloved Edward, lying immobile, face down, arms outstretched waiting to tickle any unsuspecting trout that might swim by. Her mind wandered to the day when he crushed her in his strong arms, and his lips brushed gently against hers, softly at first and then more urgently. She tasted his hot breath hasty and demanding! They had toppled back into the lush fern, hidden. He had been so powerful, so forceful, so masculine that he had been completely irresistible, Kate surrendered completely and knew that this was the man for her, the man to whom she would remain faithful for ever! They had married two months later, and William had arrived seven months afterwards. She still told everyone that he was two months early! She was snatched back to reality as her foot slipped on the sharp edge of a piece of sandstone that took the skin of her big toe. The visions disappeared from her memory as she was drawn back to reality. Her eyes blurred as the tears gathered as they had a thousand times before. "Damn you Edward Leslie, how dare you leave me here alone! My darling, darling man. Wait for me, I will be with you, once again when my sun sets, for its final time! Pushing all sadness to the deepest recesses of her mind, she marvelled at the beauty that surrounded her. The plush green mountainsides, heavy with fern; the bushy stands of birch and his wonderful silver cousin; resplendent oak trees, gnarled but strong; and everywhere the melodic symphony of the birds mixed with the repetitive dirge of the crow. This was a day for love, for laughter and for joy. A day for thanking God for all that she had, not what she didn't or would never have again, not in this life, anyway! But, she decided, no one can take away your dreams!

    She sat down on the fragrant grass and put her shoes on her still wet feet. Lord! How she missed Edward! How do you bring up seven children without their father? Others had done it and with Tom's help she was as well. Rising wearily to her feet, she set off once more to complete the short walk to her home. No sooner had she reached the start of George Street, than she heard a voice calling her.

"Kate, Kate!" It was the village minister, Berwyn Morgan. He was hurrying after her puffing and panting as his portly frame struggled to catch her up. "Wait for me please Kate, I'm not as young as I used to be." Red faced; the religious conscience of the community caught her up. "I was hoping to have a few words with you concerning the Davies boy's funeral."

Kate, smiled at Mr. Morgan with genuine affection, he was a man with real regard for every human being, regardless of wealth social position or standing. "Come on home with me, we can have a talk over a cup of tea and one of Christine's bakestones."

"That will be fabulous Kate, just what the doctor ordered!" He answered eagerly. As a cake connoisseur, he regarded Christine Leslie's bakestones as the finest in the locality, and if he were not the local minister, something, for which, he would be willing to sell his soul! They walked slowly to Kate's front door when they entered Christine was busy cooking in the kitchen. She stopped as they entered and said pleasantly, "Sit down both of you I'll pop the kettle on and make you a cup of tea. And I know Mr. Morgan will want a bakestone."

"No, I don't!" He added, his face alight with humour, "I'll have three or four of, your, bakestones, Chris!"

Once the tea had been drunk and the bakestones hungrily consumed, he raised the matter of the forthcoming funeral.

"I don't like funerals' at the best of times and a child's, even less. The grave has hardly been closed for his father and here we are, opening it up once again! I understand that we are to start at Feeder Row. Tom and the choir will sing outside in the street and then the procession will walk to the chapel for a brief service before the burial."

"That's right Berwyn, Tom has made all the arrangement's. Please keep the service as short as you possibly can, I don't think the family can stand much more! Poor Mrs. Davies is at her wits end." Pleaded Kate.

"You know me Kate, I'll start off with the best of intentions but, once I start in the pulpit I get carried away! It's my one sin. I'm worse than a tory politician on voting day!" He said sincerely.

"You are not that bad. Its just that, you, do care about people, not just say that you do." Said Kate. "But it isn't the time for Bible thumping Berwyn, it's a time for some of your wonderful sincerity and compassion!"

"Kate, you could flannel the devil himself! After five minutes with you, I feel I could go out and convert a dozen Catholics for breakfast and have them baptised by tea!"

Kate, both amused and flattered by the minister's remarks went on, "What's to happen to the family after the funeral? That's what I'm dreading. Will there be much parish relief to look after them?"

"Precious little, I'm afraid. And there's no family to help. I have been trying to trace a long-lost brother that she hasn't seen for twenty years, but I don't hold out much hope!" The minister shook his head sadly and clasped his hands in exasperation. "I went to see Mr. Gregory and asked if he could help. I won't tell you what he said!"

"It looks like the workhouse then, or just another homeless family to wander the streets begging for a crust of bread," Kate was close to tears as she continued, "The Federation are trying to help, but they can't do much. They have already got as many destitute families as they can cope with. The Davies' will be the straw that breaks the camel's back!"

"I haven't given up hope of finding the relatives yet! The family are in my prayers. Every night I pray that something will turn up!" He said fervently, "God willing!"

"Everything is organised, and Lord knows we've been through this so many times before that we ought to be able to do it in our sleep!" Added Kate hopelessly, not knowing what else to say.

"What about you Kate, are you reconciled to Victor working down the mine?" The minister enquired.

"Not while there's breath left in my body, Berwyn, I'll never accept it or become used to it." Kate spoke earnestly, her voice alive with passion. It's had my Edward, I'll not let it have Victor. A boy with his ability and intelligence should be in school, he ought to be preparing for university. Every morning when I have seen him safely off to that, pit, I sit and cry and pray for the miracle that will save him. It isn't only his mind, but since he's been little more than six he's had this wonderful talent of hearing any piece of music and being able to play it on the piano. A talent such as that, must be allowed to develop! Our Tom's musical but Victor is gifted!"

"He's in my prayers every morning Kate." The minister admitted honestly, "I'm sure that everything will be fine in the end!"

The morning dawned, with its usual valley's whimper. The sun afraid to show itself through an unwashed blanket of unbroken cloud. Victor gazed through the half-opened curtains. Hardly daring to move he sat up. He glanced over to his uncle still asleep in his bed, on the other side of the room. He watched the steady rise and fall of the eiderdown, as it matched Tom's steady breathing, as yet he had not been affected to a great degree by the 'dust'. Victor rose quietly from the bed and went'to the window, gritting his teeth against the icy cold of his feet on the polished oil cloth, he looked out. A haze hung over the village like a pall! It was as if Nature realised the village was in mourning! The mountains had their usual covering of damp, dark mist, their tops could only be imagined, as the fierce, wind drove the pliant clouds billowing down, closer, to the sodden, unfriendly ground. He listened to the rain as it battered on to the roof before running into the pipe and splashing itself onto the bailey far below.

"What a perfect day for a funeral!" he said to himself. "A fitting end to a far from perfect life. Not even the weather will take any pity on the poor little bastard!" He shrugged his shoulders, he was starting to think like a collier, better not let mother hear him speaking like one! He would feel more than just the rough edge of her tongue! His mind moved forward to the service, he loved playing the chapel organ, he thought of Owen and Evan talking as they often did during their food break in the pit. They were always laughing about the 'swelling organ' sound! He meant to ask Uncle Tom why they found it amusing, after all the organ didn't swell! He glanced again at Tom, but he was still lost conducting a choir of champions at the National's. He decided to go in search of a cup of tea and a warm in the kitchen if the fire was still alight, scarcely breathing he tip toed to the door and went downstairs.

The four part harmony blended with the strains of "O Iesie Mawr," soared heaven ward. The choir sang as the small, austere coffin was easily carried out of the silent house by the four bearers; accompanied only by the mournful dirge of the choir, together with an undercurrent of weeping and wailing from the women inside. The rain fell in torrents, drenching all those standing outside the sombre house. The choir always claimed that it was the rain that ran down their eyes and faces, but it wasn't often, even in a mining village, that you buried your children!

The coffin was lifted onto four pairs of burly shoulders' and the cortege trudged gloomily off.

"I hope I never get used to that!" Admitted Berwyn Morgan, "Even I, was lost for words, when it came to comforting poor Mary Davies." The minister was addressing a group of about six men outside the wrought iron gates of 'Nazareth Chapel'. "We had all better hurry on to our own homes and change out of these wet clothes or we will all catch consumption!"

"Did anyone see any of the mine management at the funeral?" Demanded Tom. "I didn't expect Gregory to come, but I thought he would have sent one of his lackeys!" The men all agreed with the sentiment expressed but realised that the likelihood of the management turning up to pay their last respects to a pit boy were extremely remote and after all, it was raining!

Herbert Humphries joined the group. It was plain for all to see that he had been weeping unashamedly. "Lord I'm glad that's over! The inquest is next Tuesday, but I don't hold out much hope for a fair hearing, the Inspector of Mines holding it will be Rogers! We all know how he has whitewashed the owners in the past."

"I have listened to all the evidence that has been presented." The words were spoken by Stanley Rogers, His Majesty's Inspector of Mines. He was a pompous overbearing man, with a ruddy complexion, the result of too much whisky. He was speaking in the tap room of the Butcher's Arms, which had been cleared of all furniture, expect for a single table and several dozen chairs. The chairs were all occupied, and forty or fifty men were squashed in behind them. "I am ready to pronounce my findings," he continued, "On the poor unfortunate death of David Davies a youth of twelve years of age. In the absence of any corroborating evidence or witnesses I must bring in a verdict of accidental death. It appears to me that the youth was to blame for his own death, he ought to have been more vigilant. The mine's master cannot be held responsible for sloth and laziness! I have heard evidence that the pony involved in the occurrence has had to be destroyed a fact that has cost the mine owners more than thirty-five pounds! I am led to believe that, through their benevolence and thoughtfulness, they do not intend to sue for recompense!" This statement resulted in angry murmurs running through the spectators. Roger banged the table thunderously with his gravel, "If we can't have quiet, I will order that this room be cleared! He glared sternly at a police sergeant and constable who stood silently at the front of the room. "As I was saying, the owners intend to forego their right to just compensation as a mark of respect to the grieving family, something which I, find highly commendable. It is the finding of this inquest that David Davies, pit boy of Cwmcarn Colliery, died of accidental causes." So saying, he brought down his gavel with a resounding crash onto the table, to bring the proceedings to an end!

Herbert Humphries turned to Huw Stevens and remarked bitterly, "What did I say? Roger's gives the Davies' nothing! The bastard is more concerned with a dead bloody horse than a poor child! Mind you, the horse was worth thirty-five pounds, David was only earning six shillings and four pence a week!"

CHAPTER 8

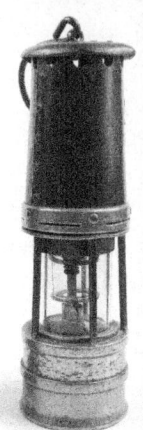

THE CHAPEL SCHOOL ROOM ALWAYS SMELLED OF POLISH TO Victor, a sweet and sickly aroma, mingled with the rough nasal assault of the bottles and bottles of caustic that his mother poured down the drains. "If the devil's down there." Evan Wilkinson declared once again, for the ten thousandth time." He must have the cleanest arse in the 'ole of South Wales! Bloody hell why does Kate put all that smelly, bloody stuff down there?"

The smell often made Victor's head swim. He frequently wondered if it was the same as being drunk! "You know how much my mam fusses about things being' clean. Well, she says, they have got to smell clean, not just look it!"

"If Kate, or the minister heard you swearing in this chapel she'd use your head for a mop on the floor!" Warned Tom. "Come on let's go inside its almost time to start practice. How is it going to look if the conductor and accompanist are both late!

They looked around the room which was lit by several oil lamps hanging from the ceiling, supported by heavy, rusty chains. Their smoky glow filled the room. Forty men sat in an orderly semi-circle facing a small upright piano and an upturned wooden box. Tom marched to the front and stood on the box, facing the smiling throng.

"Right lads! Let's get straight to business. We'll warm up with a chorus of, 'LLef'. On your feet boys you can't sing sitting down, you need to get some air into your lungs." Tom ordered the choir as he opened his arms wide as if he was embracing the whole world.

"And remember, I don't want any sluggish entries! Follow me, not the person by you!" He turned his head and smiled at Victor, who was seated at the piano, his fingers poised over the keys, ready to play the introduction. His whole concentration fixed on Tom's right hand which began to move rhythmically as he called out, "One two three four!" On the count of four, his arms swept down by his side and Victor began. On Tom's command the choir began to sing.

"Stop! Stop! Stop!" Bellowed Tom. The choir stopped singing and waited with bated breath, for the guilty parties to be given a large slice of the rough end of Tom's tongue, "What's the matter with you' bottom basses' tonight! You sound worse than a herd of pregnant water buffaloes, if you can't sort out one note between you, we've got a problem, because I heard about forty-two different ones! And that's pretty good as there are only sixteen of you! When Our Lord invented the piano, He had the good sense to put black and white notes on it. Trust you basses to be singing the notes in the cracks between them." Tom looked at the mortified bass section and noticed some of the second tenors smirking. "Don't you tenors' smile! The noise coming' from you was just like the one that came from the convent, when they found out that the toilet seat was up! Let's try it from the beginning, and everyone, had better watch me!"

Victor's fingers ran lightly over the keys as he became lyrically lost to the melodic blend of the choir and piano. The hymn's arrangement sounded as if all the angels from heaven had been collected for one harmonious extravaganza of singing perfection. At its conclusion a deathly hush overwhelmed the electric atmosphere The silent choristers, gazed eagerly at Tom, waiting for some sign of reaction or emotion.

"Wonderful lads, wonderful!" Tom breathed, rather than spoke. He was still savouring the thrill that was running between his shoulder blades, filling his entire being with wonder and exhilaration. "I don't think you've ever sung it better, if we do it like that at the competition there won't be a dry eye in the hall!" It was impossible to put into words the release that singing have to these men, who spent every working, backbreaking, day grovelling like trapped rats, almost half a mile underground. Singing was second nature to each and every one of them, as was the drinking! Victor had seen most of them drink until they fell down. He didn't know what attracted them to the drink, he just realised it had some sort of addiction and release just like music. He decided it was something that would need a far greater intellect than his to explain.

He was brought back to reality by the urgent tapping of Tom's ivory baton on the top of the piano. The baton had been presented by the choir, 'In grateful appreciation', to Tom, last Christmas. It was his most prized possession.

"Now then, let's go through, 'Laudamus', I wasn't satisfied with the top tenors after last practice." He thumbed through a copy of the hymn until he came to the correct page. "Here it is! Page 2 third line, some of you are under the D sharp. Top tenors up, the rest of you sit down and shut up! We'll go through line three, but!" He stared at them to emphasise his point. "When we reach D sharp, hold the note." Victor began to play and Tom brought in the tenors. When they reached the note, they held its pitch. Some of the tenors were seen and heard to struggle! "Stop! Shut up!" Moaned Tom "Nearly isn't good enough. We'll try it row by row. Starting with the back!" Each row of singers went through the required exercise until Tom, satisfied that the offending mistake had been remedied, announced, "Right we seem to have it now, let's try it once more, all the tenors together this time and for God's sake watch me and think!"

This time the music was sung to Tom's satisfaction. "Good. The rest of you have had enough rest let's sing it through, but I will be watching you tenors!"

Once more the hall was filled with the harmonic chorus as the musical performance echoed with ear shattering crescendos and barely audible pianissimos so intense that Victor was conscious of his heart pounding in his chest. He was always amazed at the way his uncle exhibited total control over this body of men. The universal concentration of each chorister on each and every gesture of the conductor's baton and facial expression. It was the opinion of more than one chorister that Tom, did more conducting with his eyebrows, than with his hands or baton. "He's like bloody Mephistopheles, trying to mesmerise some poor unsuspecting virgin before getting his evil way with her! We must be a stupid load of buggers' cos we all do exactly as he tells us to!" Tom slowly brought his arms to his side and the choir stilled. Victor could see that his uncle was well satisfied with the performance but knew, that praise was something that came hard to Tom's lips.

"Not bad boys, but there's still room for improvement, it's getting better but we are not quite there just yet." Tom stepped off his podium and announced, "We'll have a ten-minute break now, give you all a chance to get your second wind ready for some serious practice in a little while."

"Just like that miserable old sod," said Jack Taylor, one of the first tenors. "We sing our balls off, and ole misery guts can't say well done!"

"I heard that, Jack! When you sing to my satisfaction, I'll tell you. You are in the Chapel school room, watch your bloody language or I'll use your balls for a bracelet countered Tom!" Without a trace of emotion in his voice. Both men were smiling at one another." Sorry Tom, you know 'ow I do get carried away some times, clean forgot I was in the chapel!" Jack replied.

"Forgot my arse!" Countered Owen Rees, from the first bass section. "We all know what a complaining old sod Tom, can be, that piece was perfect, but, getting musical praise out of Tom is harder than getting a full day's pay out of Gregory!"

"I'll give praise where it's due, so when I say you have sung well, you'll know damn well you have sung really well!" Tom answered.'

"I don't know about anything else," said Bryn Smith, a bass with a voice deeper than the mine's upcast shaft, "But my throat is about as rough as a badger's arse! I am going to need quite a few pints tonight or we will all be out looking for my lost voice!"

"That's rich Bryn." Laughed Owen, "You have never needed any excuse to get several pints down your throat before. We might all be out looking for your lost body once your Sally 'as finished with you, if you go home in the same state as you did last night! Like something' demented she was. Bloody hell she scared me witless, and I didn't have to go into your street never mind your house!"

"Don't take any nonsense in your own home Bryn! Use your belt, show her who's boss!" This advice came from a young man called Maldwyn Evans, who was sat beside Bryn. "I wouldn't put up with it."

"Spoken like a single man!" Replied Evan scornfully," have you seen how big her brothers are? And there's three of them'!"

The choir practice continued for another hour's hard singing. Tom was a hard task master. A feeling of deep satisfaction filled all the members as Tom finally announced, "Well done lads!" He looked gratefully at Victor before continuing, "I Think we've all worked hard tonight, and most of us deserve a couple of pints."

Bryn looked up at the pleased conductor, "Good God! Did I see Tom smile then? It must be some kind of record!"

"Don't be such a daft bugger! Tom doesn't smile he' just suffers a lot from wind! It makes him pull a lot of funny faces that's all." The single men all made their way out of the practice room and headed toward the Cwmcarn Hotel. The married men, all with wives and children to support began to drift homeward, most too short of money to be able to afford a few halfpennies for a couple of glasses of beer. Tom caught hold of Victor's shoulder affectionately and hauled him to his feet. "It's home for us Vic, you are not old enough yet and if your mam found out I 'ad taken you she'd skin me alive and probably have you praying for forgiveness for at least a week. Anyway I 'haven't got a penny until pay day!" The two 'men' were the last to leave the hall. Tom unhooked each lamp in turn, and using the chain carefully lowered it to shoulder level where Victor gingerly raised the glass and blew out the flame. Once each lamp had been extinguished, they left the darkened room. They walked slowly once they had left the unlit chapel school room. Victor glanced up at the gloomy starless canopy that enveloped them with its tranquillity, muffling even their hob nailed steps, as they gingerly made their hushed way through the swarthy evening along the well-known street, Dark, shave for the occasional gas lamp standing like a beacon against the enclosing inkiness of the night. He was always disturbed by the neutrality that the night imparted to everything touched by its deathless fingers, Stealing colour like a merciless thief.

"Mam still wants me out of the pits, doesn't she, Uncle Tom?" He enquired, his voice low, less he disturbed the totality of the night.

"That's a daft bloody question, as if you don't know already." Tom replied, without even Faltering his step, "She'll never be used to it as long as there's breath in her body! You can't tell me you are used to it and enjoy it?" His voice adopted a harsh tone mirroring the inevitability that was consuming his body, "Damn it all, we have only got used to it because it's the only way to feed our families, we go down there because it's work! Not because we love it!" Anger was beginning to assume control of his senses. "How many of the choir do you think will be here or capable of singing in ten years time?" Victor sensed that his uncle was staring earnestly at him with tear frilled eyes. "There won't be many!" He continued, "The lucky ones will be the dead ones, not those still alive and too choked up with the dust to hardly move, never mind sing! No if there was any other choice there isn't one of us who could honestly say we wouldn't do something else, if we had the chance."

"What if they made the pit safer uncle, wouldn't that make a difference?" Whispered Victor, somewhat perplexed by Tom's outburst.

"It would help a lot. But do you think Gregory or the coal owners, give a toss about us, or our safety? I don't! Compassion doesn't come into sight when it comes to making profits for the owners and bosses! People, especially miners, are cheaper than timbers, air pumps and gas safety. It might mean a cigar less or a satin, instead of a silk ball dress! Perhaps it might mean a penny fall in the owner's shares, no, our lives are cheaper, we are only ignorant miners."

"Things must get better one day Tom, they must! It's not fair!" Blurted out Victor.

"What would have happened to us all if you hadn't been there to look after us Uncle Tom?" He continued. "I often stay awake at night wondering where dad is and what it must have been like after the accident. I still dream about him and wake up expecting to see him at the end of my bed. God, I miss him! And I know Mam does too." He peered ahead trying to catch a glimpse of his uncle, through the shadowy depths. It seemed as if he was always looking for his uncle through the half-light!

"More people than you think miss your dad, Victor. He was well liked and respected by many people, and he was loved by a lot more! If we can influence the lives, of as many people as he, did in such a short time we can regard ourselves as honoured. "Fair is the last thing to be considered in our work Vic. If it suits them by releasing a little of the control to make things a little easier for us, they may, but once we look like asking for anything like a fair share, they'll crack us like a nut even if it takes them twenty or thirty years to do it. They've got long memories even if we haven't!"

They walked on in silence. Tom stamping his feet angrily along the damp invisible pathway as they continued their way homeward.

"It's no good kicking the world Uncle Tom, it can't help it." Said Victor wincing as each tread fell upon the unyielding ground.

"Come on Victor, let's not get downhearted. I've had my moan and I feel a lot better so I mustn't burden you with the problems of the world must I. If you manage to better yourself don't ever forget where you came from and the way we are made to work like dogs for less than a decent wage!" Tom threw his head back and strode off into the deepening gloom with Victor tailing after him.

As Tom and Victor reached their kitchen door, a secret conversation was taking place in one of the large, comfortable, private rooms of the local Cwmcarn hotel. The room was brightly lit by three large oil lamps. One stood solidly in the centre of an oval oak table placed beneath a heavily curtained window, the other two were placed one at each end of a large mantlepiece above the fireplace in which a glowing coal fire was burning merrily, sending its warming glow into every corner of the room. Three sumptuous armchairs were drawn cosily around the fire and separated only by a small, lacquered table. Three, large, half-filled whisky tumblers stood on the table, together with an almost empty bottle of malt whisky. The chairs were occupied by three men engaged in hushed conversation. They were, Phillip Gregory, the mine owners' representative. Thomas Owen Price. The Bedwellty Steam and Coking Coal Company's General Manger and Sir Michael Fairfax a company Director.

"Capital show Phillip, capital!" Enthused Fairfax, "Keep the ignorant sods in their place, you handled that inquest really well. We haven't been doing too well at the exchange lately and bad publicity could have dropped us down a few more points!"

"Yes, old boy", added Owen Price, "We've come out of the whole affair smelling of roses. Any concession, could have been looked upon as a sign of weakness on the company's behalf and who knows what the bastards would have expected next!" He leaned forward snatched up his glass and gulped down the whisky hungrily. "Damn me, Phillip, that's a bloody good drop of whisky. I see you've plenty of the little luxury's necessary to make living here in this common little cow patch, almost bearable!" Gregory smiled, picked up his glass, acknowledged the compliment and with a smack of his lips drained it gleefully.

"Talking of luxury, are you still, 'Rogering', that secretary of yours? What's her name now?" Questioned Fairfax.

"Sylvie," Phillip replied as he reached to refill the glasses with a generous helping. "She is an excellent secretary too!"

"You dirty old dog, once your hand is up her skirt you don't worry if she can even write. "Leered Owen Price. "I'll pity you, if your Sadie finds out!"

"Sadie doesn't suspect a thing, and any way she likes the money I bring in too much, to cause any trouble."

"Doesn't her husband suspect?" Queried Owen Price as he reached for a large cigar that was smouldering in an ashtray on the table, the smoke from its glowing tip drifting lazily toward the celling. He rolled it carefully between his yellow stained fingers before drawing insatiably on it, reminding Gregory of a piglet sucking on a sow.

"He's a petty officer in the navy, only gets a few weeks leave a year," answered Gregory absent mindedly, his attention still on the vision of a large piglet slobbering busily away in the stye!

"That's different, all beneficent employers look after all the needs of their staff." Leered Fairfax, "Just so long as you don't get caught, the baby might look like you!"

"All babies look the same when they are born." Laughed Gregory. "Just make sure its surrogate father wasn't at sea when he should have been rising to the occasion!" Replied Fairfax.

Owen-Price looked at the two men through a haze of acrid cigar smoke and whisky. He was beginning to feel far too comfortable, and his head was starting to swim, "Let's get the business concluded before we become completely incapable." He fumbled in his inside pocket and pulled out two thick envelopes. He handed them both to Phillip Gregory, who gratefully accepted them and swiftly tucked them out of sight. "The thicker one's for you old boy," Stated, Owen Price, "A little thank you from those of us on the board who think you handled the situation well. The other one is for that coroner Rogers, just so long as he keeps his mouth shut!"

"Yes Phil, keep the bastards in their place, making sure the profits keep rolling in and we'll look after you and keep you in the place to which you've become accustomed!" Stated a smug looking Fairfax.

"One more thing, Phillip, the chairman is going to pay the mine a visit in a few weeks' time. His lordship is becoming concerned about the safety of his employees. I'll stall him for as long as possible, long enough to let the furore die down a bit. Make sure there's nothing amiss when he comes, there's a good chap." announced Owen-Price. "Now let's get drunk, we've to catch the ten o'clock train in the morning and the only way I can survive in a shitty place like this, is with a quart of best malt inside me."

It was a fine morning, as beautiful as an early November morning could be, when Kate pulled back the curtains to let the sunshine in. She looked at the huge trunks of beeches and silver birch standing their sentry on, the damp hillside. Many people loved Autumn, with its change of colour and the crisp biting feel of the frost laden air. She hated it! Everything dies during Autumn, it's the time of death!' She had said this to herself ever since she had been a child. "Nothing but withered leaves, rotting stems, and stark bare hillsides, a time when even Nature wants to withdraw from this world." Her thoughts drifted to poor Mary Davies in Feeder Row, her month, so graciously granted by Phillip Gregory, ended today. The minister Berwyn Morgan was still trying to trace her long lost family, he had even asked Captain Stroud, if the Salvation Army could help trace her Manchester relatives. Time ran out today, the bailiffs would be hammering on the Davies' door at seven o'clock this morning. Kate had done all that she could she had nothing else to offer, she slumped into a fireside chair and buried her face into her hands.

The crash of hard knuckles against the wooden door resounded along the length and breadth of the deserted street.

"Open up Mrs. Davies!" The voice came from the portly frame of Charles Griffiths, head bailiff of the steam and coke company. He, like his three companions was dressed in a dark suit, white starched shirt with a back ribbon bow tie and black bowler hat. They all carried a heavy wooden cudgel, "It isn't no use hiding' we've got the coppers with us an' a legal warrant to take over the house!" He turned to the policemen stood behind him, Sargent Parsons and Constable Haywood. He spoke to the Sergeant, "Come on Will, if you don't get her out I'll have to break the door in, and Mr. Gregory will have my guts for garters for the damage!" Sergeant Parsons pushed his way distastefully passed the gloating bully, "Please Mrs. Davies, come out. Don't make this any harder than it is already!" The sergeant's voice firmly coaxing and pleading with the distraught woman to give up her home. There were times when he loathed his job but, the law was the law! "Open up now, it will be better for everyone if you open the door and ..... He was distracted, as were the entire party in front of the house by a rumbling, clanking sound that came around the corner. The noise was made by a two wheeled cart that was being pulled around the corner of the street by Herbert Humphries and Berwyn Morgan. The wheels of the cart wobbled precariously on the dirt floor squeaking unmercifully crying out for grease. The two men brought the cart to a halt outside number 12, beside the bailiffs, Berwyn Morgan pushed his way through the bailiffs, "Excuse me sergeant, may I try!" He tapped gently on the door, "Mary, it's me, the minister, Mr. Morgan I've come to help. I've brought Herbert Humphries with me we brought a cart for your belongings."

"I can't come out and take to the road with my little ones," Sobbed a distraught voice from behind the door. "I'll burn the house down with us inside it first!"

"Don't be silly, Mary. Listen to me. Herbert and I have arranged for you to use Farmer Meredith's barn for a while, until we can sort things out. It's dry and you will be able to keep warm there."

"Come out Mary," Shouted Herbert, "We'll see you don't come to any harm."

"Do your duty sergeant!" Snarled Charles Griffiths, lifting his club as if to bater the door.

"I maybe a little bit too old to make you put down that stick," growled Herbert resolutely, his eyes a-flame, "but I know at least two hundred men who would deem it an honour and a privilege to take that stick of yours and cheerfully use it to break your back!" He looked along the still deserted street. "I've only got to whistle!" The bailiffs became decidedly nervous at this and began looking nervously up and down the street.

"Come on Herbert." Sergeant Parsons spoke authoritatively, "You will be frightening me next. I don't like it myself but it's my duty to enforce this warrant and help these," his voice took on a sarcastic sneer, "Gentlemen evict the inhabitants of this house."

"Open up Mary, there's a good girl." Berwyn, whispered soothingly through the door, "It will be fine, you'll see. Mr. Humphries is with me, we will take care of you and the children." After a short pause the door was opened, just sufficiently for Mary Davies to look out. "You are sure that we will have somewhere to go aren't you reverend?" Pleaded her weak voice. Her eyes searching the minister's face for reassurance. "We will take you somewhere where you can stay until we can sort out something permanent for you and the children, Mary, come on don't worry." The door was pulled back to expose Mary Davies, with her five children huddled securely behind her. Berwyn, looked into the room to see six sets of despairing eyes looking hopefully toward him. Herbert Humphries, on seeing the door open, pushed his way through the crowd of bailiffs gathered in front of the door, even though they were all much bigger and stronger than he was, stepped into the room and in a voice that boomed along the entire length of the street, confidently declared, "Chin up Mary, don't let these," he paused to turn and look at Charles Griffiths and his group, "Persons, worry you. Let me know what you want to take, and I'll make sure it's loaded safely onto my cart outside. These gentlemen," his voice was now heavy with sarcasm, "Have offered to help you move house. Get all your belongings ready." He turned and spoke to the group that were gathered before the door. "If one thing is broken or you are heavy handed with any of the children, if the minister will excuse me, vengeance will be mine, not the Lord's! Do I make myself clear?" Charles Griffiths grunted his comprehension.

It took precious few minutes to load the Davies' meagre belongings onto the hand cart. Herbert pulled it easily and the pathetic entourage followed. As they began moving, neighbours, as if by magic, began to appear outside their own front doors. The spectacle was watched in total silence, more complete than an undertaker's funeral. As the party turned the corner a lone voice rang out. "Good luck Mary! Rot in hell Griffiths you bastard!"

CHAPTER 9

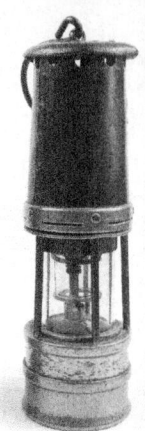

"Why hasn't Owen come into work this morning, Tom?" Asked Victor. He looked around at all the blackened miners sitting around taking their food break. Many were eating hungrily at their meagre meals, but the vast majority were slumped exhausted, occasionally sipping cold tea from their water jacks. Victor turned his gaze toward Stuart Thomas, he appeared to be totally drained of all energy and was leaning limply against a thick pillar of coal. Victor, looked down at his calloused hands, the year he had been working had transformed them into rough vice-like grippers, in fact the year had altered his whole body. The puppy fat had disappeared, to be replaced by hard muscle and sinew and with the strength had come a hardness, a hardness not of the spirit but of the body. He still had his hopes and dreams, but they seemed further away than ever, he was trying to keep his schooling up and the minister was tutoring him in mathematics. Mam and Tom provided him with plenty of books to read, he didn't ask how they obtained them, books just appeared at his bedside from time to time. Mam made him use sixpence from his wages every week so that he could continue with his piano lessons.

"Bryn Edwards told me that Owen, bumped into Beryl Cookson on the way to the pit this morning!" Declared Tom his voice serious and hushed." What's that got to do with it Tom? We meet all sorts of people on our way to the pit every morning." Replied Victor.

"Beryl Cookson's got crossed eyes!" Interrupted Evan Wilkinson who had been sat quietly, listening to the conversation, "He couldn't come to work after that! It's dead unlucky to come down to the pit after meeting a cross eyed woman!" Victor looked at his uncle and Evan trying to detect some sign of a joke or leg pull, but he could find none. "He's right Victor!" Continued his uncle. "There are lots of superstitions about working down here and that's one of the worst! I don't know if it's true, but I wouldn't want to take a chance on it. It's dangerous enough down here without tempting fate!"

"I didn't think you believed in old wives tales Tom," Declared a slightly amused Victor, astonished that his uncle could believe anything so ludicrous.

"Don't you go mocking' the old beliefs!" Snapped Evan who, was beginning to become quite irritated if not angry. "You haven't been down here long enough to tell us what we can and can't believe in!"

"I Wasn't trying to do any such thing Evan, I only wondered why Owen wasn't here!" Replied a subdued Victor.

"Perhaps it's my fault." Tom said butting into the conversation, trying to calm the situation. "I haven't told Victor about any of the old beliefs, but there isn't a miner working down here that won't go home if he meets a squinting woman on his way to the pit!"

Victor squirmed uncomfortably, there was still a lot he had to learn about working underground.

Evan looked at Victor and continued in his bass voice, which was almost as deep as the pit in which they were working, "'have you never noticed how the firemen never mark any of the timbers or drams with a cross when they be chalking! It's dead unlucky that's why! If any of the evil spirits that live, skulking' about down here, in the dark corners an' holes saw the sign of the cross, they would be so angry they would cause an accident!"

Tom noticing the wide-eyed look on Victor's face decided it was time to change the subject, miners' superstitions were best given and received in small doses. He didn't want his young nephew too petrified to come to work. He glanced up at Stuart Thomas who was leaning awkwardly against a pillar in obvious discomfort. "Stew, you look terrible do you feel...." Before he could finish his reply, the miner slumped unconscious to the ground! The colliers alerted by Tom's remark, threw off their own tiredness and fatigue and jumped to, the aid of their fallen butty. "Stand back give him some room ordered Tom, he's still breathing', let's try an' sit him up." Several pairs of helping hands reached forward and gently raised him from the floor.

"Wha Wha Whaasss going' on?" mumbled Stuart as he opened his eyes. "What happened I I I don't remember."

"I think you just fainted Stew that's all." Reassured Tom looking carefully into his friends face for any signs of illness or injury. "Somebody brings me his water jack so that he can have a drink of tea and some food inside him."

"Here they are Tom," said Victor bringing the water bottle and food tin to his uncle. "But they are both empty, 'he must have eaten already!"

"No, he 'hasn't" said Evan, "I see him come through he just sat down over by there, he looked bloody terrible now I come to think about it!"

Tom looked at the two empty containers then he spoke gently to Stuart, "What's going on Stew, why 'haven't you got anything to eat? You know how hard it is down here, you can't manage without something' to keep you going!"

Stuart, leaning on his elbow replied, his voice a croaky whisper, "Ceinwen and Rachel, both needed new shoes to go to school, my daughters won't go around with holes in their shoes, not while there's life left in my body!" He paused to gather his thoughts and catch his breath, "The only way me an' Morag could afford it was to cut down on food for a while. I haven't brought any food to the pit for nearly a fortnight. Me an' the missus just been having soup at night I thought I could manage but I bin so tired this last couple of days!"

"You stupid proud bastard!" Harangued Tom, "We would have helped!" he waved his hands to indicate the group of concerned miners, "Every man here is a butty do you think we would have let you or the kids starve."

Stuart looked sheepishly at all the faces that were watching his every movement hanging onto his every word. He took a deep breath and said, "I take care of my family I don't beg any man for charity they are my responsibility. The girls didn't ask to be born so it's my job to see that they don't go without."

"You stupid bloody swine, you don't beg off your mates." Tom was beginning to lose his temper, he struggled to control himself and make this silly, proud man see sense. "We all stick together and look after one another in this bloody pit, God knows nobody else will!" Tom looked through the crowd until he was staring at Victor. "Vic, go and get my water jack and food box." Stuart began to squirm and protest. Tom held him firmly and declared through tightly clenched teeth. "If you won't eat my food and drink my tea, I'll stuff it so far down your throat it'll come out of your arse and save you the trouble of going for a shit!" No one present had ever seen such a determined look on Tom's face and no one doubted the threat in his words!

Victor returned with the food and drink which he handed to Tom. Tom turned and spoke to the colliers, "Let's have a little bit of privacy lads." Everyone left the two miners alone.

"Come on Stew," said Tom gently, "Share my bread with me." Stewart smiled at his butty and took a greedy bite out of the offered bread!

A short distance along the heading Victor was watching Evan Wilkinson squirming tenderly against a rock wall. He appeared to be in a great deal of discomfort! He twitched and writhed from position to position as he tried to sit comfortably.

"Have you hurt yourself, Evan?" Enquired Victor. Afraid that his companion had sustained an injury whilst helping Stuart.

"Don't you worry Vic, Boy I'm fine. It's just a few, 'love bites', I picked up on Saturday, in the match against Blackwood!" Evan smirked as he replied. He was one of the most gentle men that Victor knew but put him on a rugby pitch in an Abercarn jersey and he became transformed into a rampaging fiend. "You can't beat a local, friendly match. We kicked the shit out of one another for hours on Saturday!"

"I thought a match was over in an hour and a half!" Quizzed Victor. "It is usually, but nobody had much money, so we just played on. The ref was about to blow the whistle when the two captains called everybody together and said as we were all broke, how about just playing on? So, we did! The second half lasted nearly two hours. If we 'hadn't kicked the ball in the river twenty or thirty times we would all have bin bloody knackered!" Victor looked at Evan with total disbelief.

"Just give yourself another year or two down here and you will be hard enough to play for us!" Evan continued with a big boyish grin on his face, "There's nothing' like a game of rugby for getting' rid of all your tension and frustration. Kick somebody's head in during' the game, clean your self-up an' then have a nice friendly drink with them afterwards!"

Victor looked along the tunnel to see the stooped figure of Tom making his way towards him. His uncle squatted down beside Evan.

"You haven't been trying to get Victor to play Rugby, have you?" Tom reproached Evan. "Kate will give you rugby if she finds out!"

"A young boy like Victor ought to be playing. Good mates' rugby players, you play as a member of the team." Defended Evan.

"I'll make my own mind up Tom!" Said Victor, quite taken with the idea. "Well, before you run out to play for Wales, we've got three or four wedges to hammer in!" Stated Tom, as he got to his feet and headed off towards his stint.

The hammer swinging no longer had the excruciating effect on Victor, that it had originally. It was now a chore to be endured. One that had firmed his arms and wrists with strength that was almost out of proportion, to his size. It was, however, damn hard work. By the time the last swing was completed, and the coal down, both men were drenched with sweat, it ran down their backs in torrent's and burned their eyes making it appear that Victor was crying like a newborn baby. Tom dragged his arm wearily across his sweat stained forehead before reproaching Victor," Now ask me if we work down here from choice, go on!" Victor, could only manage a feeble smile in answer to his uncle's sarcasm, before gasping, "At least we can sit down before we start to haul it away!" Both men selected a sturdy wooden prop to lean against. Victor looked at it, trying to imagine the tree, as it had been high above, growing in the gentle warmth of the sun. Now it was lifeless, condemned to everlasting darkness deep within the bowels of this hell hole. He closed his eyes feeling the lush, green, damp grass between his outstretched toes. He was forced back to reality when Tom used the toe of his boot to push him in the side. "Come on Vic, here's Huw, stop the daydreaming."

Huw Stevens, came to them, as he had done a hundred times before with his lamp held high, as he searched for gas. He stopped when he reached Tom. He put down his lamp, squatted on his hunches and said, "The earl is visiting the mine today. The word is that he is on an inspection tour, because of all the accidents that have happened during the last eighteen months. They are saying that David Davies' death was the last straw, as far as the Earl is concerned." Evan Dance said that he may even come underground, to see the conditions for himself."

"I'll believe that when I see it!" Said Tom, His voice an ejaculation of cynicism. "Coal owners don't come down these dangerous holes, not when they can find bloody idiots like us, to do it for them. After all, he might get his boots dirty and that will mean more work for his poor old butler!"

"I'm only saying what is being said on top." Huw answered. He rose to his feet and tested the stall before moving on. Tom and Victor began loading the lump coal into a corve ready for Victor to haul away. They had been toiling for little more than an hour in the foul, squalor when they heard a voice calling them from along the heading. It was the voice of James Fraser, the underground manager.

"Take care men, I'm coming along the heading with the mine owner. His Lordship the Earl, Fraser announced in a well-spoken bass voice.

What the hell is that silly old fart doing' down here?" Victor heard a voice remark.

A cultured voice boomed in reply, "The silly old 'fart' has come to see if your conditions are as bad as I suspect they are! And, if I catch the man who said it, I'll give the swine a good horse whipping. Who was it?"

"Who said what, your lordship? I never heard nothing!" The same voice replied. "Fings echo down here!"

Victor watched the two men approach through the gloom, picking their way through the partly loaded coal. They paused occasionally as the earl stopped to examine the roof supports and timbers, which he rapped hard, with his silver topped walking stick. Victor could hear the mumble of voices as the two men talked but was unable to hear what was being said. Eventually the men were close enough for Victor to see the Earl of Gwent for the first time. He was a well-built man, a little under six feet tall. He was wearing a tweed suit, with short trousers! Victor had never before seen plus fours. He smiled to himself, at the sight of this balding old man with his trousers tucked neatly into his socks. Old fart. Summed him up perfectly he thought! He remembered his manners.

"Good day Mr. Fraser, your Lordship." He spoke respectfully, not wishing to be mistaken for the voice."

"Hello laddie," replied the Earl. He smiled broadly at Victor. "How old are you my boy, you don't look old enough to be down here?"

Victor was startled by the easy manner with which the mine owner spoke to him.

"F f f fifteen, Sir." He stammered I've been working here for about eighteen months now Sir!"

"We have fifty or sixty boys working in the mine your lordship." Interrupted Fraser, before continuing quickly," But we don't use any young children!"

"Can you read and write boy?" The earl continued.

"He was the best scholar in the school before he had to come down the pit Sir." Interjected Tom. "He is the finest young musician in the entire Western valley." The mine owner looked keenly at Victor before asking," Why are you working here instead of being in school?"

"His Dad was crushed under a roof fall almost three years ago your lordship." Answered Tom, "Victor's my nephew, so I help the family all I can, but there isn't enough money for him to go to school, so he has to earn his keep!"

"This is Thomas Owens your lordship," interrupted the under manager, pointing to Tom. "He is the miner who conducts the choir that sang at the eisteddfod you attended a short while ago in Newport." The earl looked at Tom with renewed interest, it was difficult to imagine that the conductor, who stood on the podium at St Woolos Cathedral, was this same dirty miner! Yet, if one looked hard beneath the dirt and grime it was possible to see the gentleman hidden away!

"Step forward man!" Ordered the earl, "Let me get a better look at you." He thrust his hand out. "I want to shake the hand of the man who could inspire a male choir to produce such a wonderful sound. Lady Charlotte still talks about it even now. In fact, it's been her favourite conversation piece during the last two or three dinner parties!" Tom hesitated and looked down at his grubby hands, they weren't exactly in a fit condition to shake the hand of an earl! The mine owner, noticing Tom's doubt said, "It's honest dirt, I'll not take offence if none is intended. Damn it all this is a coal mine, mine in fact!" Tom grinned broadly, wiped his hand along the side of his trousers and grasped the outstretched hand firmly. The two men stood talking together for several minutes. Victor was amazed to hear his uncle talking so freely with the earl even though the conversation consisted entirely about music and male voice choirs in particular. He heard his name mentioned several times as both men glanced in his direction. He watched as they walked along the heading, almost out of sight. "Your Lordship," continued Fraser, "We have a lot more to visit and inspect. If we don't hurry, we won't have time to do it. These men still have a lot of loose coal to load, if they don't do it, they won't be paid for a full shift's work today." He moved closer to the earl's ear in order to whisper, "It isn't safe for you here, the roof hasn't been properly timbered yet!"

"We'll move when I'm good and damn ready, Fraiser!" Snapped the mine owner, beginning to feel somewhat irritated by the bombastic manner of the under manager. "But I won't stop these chaps from earning their pay, let's move on ———," Before the earl could finish his sentence everyone in the district, was silenced by a fulminating detonation, that came reverberating along the tunnel. It was a double boom, that pierced the very soul of each person at the west district of the mine.

"For God's sake get down!" Screamed Huw Stevens. Tom hurled himself at Victor and knocked him to the floor as the others tried to find what cover they could. Victor could hear a thunderous roar tearing its headlong way through the tunnel, as if the top had blasted off the lid of hell itself and was racing to engulf them. A raging whirlwind ripped through the district knocking down anyone either too crass or tardy, to take heed of the urgent warning. Victor saw several friends and neighbours swept away as if they were no more than paper puppets. Several props buckled under the colossal force, bringing down large rocks, timbers and roof beams. Then the impenetrable clouds of dust and smoke saturated the district. He strained to see through the impervious billows, but his eyes burned with an intensity that made him scream until his lungs were ready to burst. Then everything was silent.

Victor forced his eyes open, they felt as though they were on fire, as if red hot coals had been dropped into them, but he kept them open. His lamp was still alight, as were three or four others. He tried to get to his feet but was held firmly down by his uncle.

"Stay where you are you daft bugger!" His uncle shouted harshly into his ear. "Let some of this filthy muck and dust settle before you get up. There may be gas!"

"When did the earl go down underground, Dance?" Phillip Gregory, interrogated Evan Dance, the banksman. "Who's gone with him?" If the owner wanted to go underground, he wanted to be the one to show the old codger around, thought Phillip Gregory. After all, it wouldn't do for the silly old fool to go anywhere too dangerous!

"'He was with Mr. Fraser, sir," replied the banksman. "They descended the pit about forty-five minutes ago."

Phillip took his watch from his waistcoat pocket, glanced at it quickly, swung it on its chain and replaced it, 1.25pm. He had ordered them to shot fire the coal in the east pit today, in order to meet the French contract! The silly old bugger would turn up unannounced, today of all days. He hoped Fraser, had the sense to keep the old man well clear of the explosions. They had to double production, if they were to keep the Frenchmen happy. The gas hadn't been too bad there, these last few weeks. He wouldn't have ordered John Collins, to use dynamite today, if he had known! The Blackvein seam in the east pit was nearly eight feet thick. Just a few days of taking a chance with the dynamite, would be worth the risk, just as long as that nosey old fool wasn't snooping around!

"Heard his Lordship ask Mr. Fraser to take him into the North District, but they were talking for a long time, and I didn't eavesdrop sir!" Continued Evan," I was very busy supervising the unloading of a pair of drams, empties had been loaded onto the cage and I rang down to pit bottom to let them know the cage was ready, the answering bells rang so we lowered the cage. Mr. Fraser and his Lordship then came over and said they were going down next trip. When Mr. Fraser gives an order, I jump Sir!"

Gregory, a thunderous look on his face replied, "Carry on with your work Dance, I'll see the two of them when they come up. Let me know the minute they do." Phillip Gregory left the pit head and was walking towards the blacksmith's when he felt a rumbling vibration run through his feet, he staggered and had to quickly spread his legs and grab hold of a large stack of rough-hewn, pit props, that had been delivered the previous day, they were ready to be taken underground. The sudden tremor ceased almost immediately to be followed by a muffled, double report as if a naval destroyer had fired its front guns.

He turned to stare at the pit head, frozen to the spot. He watched in fascination as an enormous pall of black smoke erupted from the pit shaft itself. Rooted to the spot by some spellbinding enchantment, he believed he was watching the smoky fume spewing prelude, to a volcanic eruption. The sombre, sooty haze ascended lazily into the heavens before being dispersed by the affronted breeze! He was snatched back to reality by the raucous, strident blaring of the mine's hooter. Its cacophony swelling to ear shattering proportions before dying into silence only to begin all over again. Emitting the most feared sound within the entire mining community —— Disaster, calamity, God help us all! He rushed to the pit head trying to collect his scattered thoughts. Other workers had also responded to the catastrophe and were shouting and yelling uncontrollably at the pit shaft's mouth. Several men were helping Evan Dance to stand, he had a gaping wound on his forehead, that was oozing blood down his cheeks and slowly soaking into his collar. Pushing his helpers away, Evan struggled groggily to his feet and yelled, "Shut up all of you! We want calm heads, not bloody idiots here. Somebody brings me something to put on this cut." He put his hand to his head in an attempt to staunch the flow of blood. Someone said, "You need that seeing to Evan!"

He turned angrily and snarled, "Don't be bloody daft, there's work to be done! There will be plenty of time to see to this scratch when we find out how things are down below!" He pointed a sharky finger towards the now silent shaft. Everyone had their own ominous thoughts of what had happened in the hellish depths below! Phillip Gregory arrived and began to bark out orders. "Check the shaft for any signs of damage. Let's see if we can get the cage up!" He looked around and spotted one of the office clerks, "Terry Priddle, get a message to the Crumlin pit straight away. See if they have any colliers who can help us, I think we are going to need them!"

Kate had put the men's washed shirts on the line to dry. She wiped her hands on her pinny, it would soon be time to start dinner. It had to be cheese and potatoes again today, they had finished the last of the bacon yesterday and there would be no more for a few days until next pay day. Well, at least they wouldn't starve. There was plenty of bread in the house. She turned to Ivy, who was wringing the water out of a freshly laundered bed sheet, "Wait a minute Ivy, it will take the two of us to wring that dry, if we don't get most of the water out it will never dry, not in a month of Sundays!" She went to her daughter, and they squeezed out as much water as they could, by twisting the sheet between them.

Ivy wiped her brow and remarked, "I hate washing! In fact, there's only one thing I hate more and that's ironing the dry clothes!" Her mother looked sympathetically at her headstrong daughter, wondering if she would think the same once she had a home and family of her own to care for and protect. They began walking towards the back door when they heard it! It was the pit hooter, and it wasn't blowing for the end of the shift! Kate fell to her knees and Ivy stood petrified. Christine came running through the door, "It's the Hooter! Theres been an accident!" Kate got to her feet and silently went into the house. Wrapping a shawl tightly around her head and shoulders she went out of the front door. The street was full of weeping, distraught women. The entire village seemed to be on the move with everyone heading towards the pit. By the time Kate reached the closed mine gates she was part of a huge crowd of wondering frightened onlookers. "The angel of death has come to visit us!" Someone shouted from the back of the throng, whilst other women could be herd chanting the Lord's Prayer. It was the lack of knowledge about what had happened, together with the certainty that there was no way in which they could help, that made their suffering almost more than they could bear! Fathers, sons, husbands, brothers, uncles and friends were somewhere far below out of sight but not out of mind!

CHAPTER 10

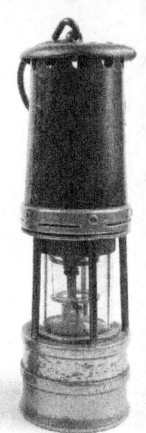

VICTOR LAY STILL, BENEATH THE RHYTHMICALLY BREATHING body of his uncle. He took several deep sniffs of air trying to detect gas, but what did gas smell like! The only gas he had come across was the kind that emptied the room when his uncle farted! He sniffed again, there was a slight charred odour, nothing else.

"What's wrong with your nose boy? His uncle whispered, "Are you hurt?"

"I'm fine Tom, I was trying to smell for gas." Victor replied, glad to hear the comforting voice of his uncle. The quiet was total, he let his mind wander trying to sense those who must still be around him. He wouldn't believe it, but he found himself listening to the silence! He was completely surrounded by its quiescence. Tom, somehow realising the turmoil that had invaded his nephew's mind put a comforting arm onto Victor's shoulder and squeezed it affectionately, "Lie still; there's a good boy. Wait until you are told to move. We are alright for now, 'where there's life there's hope. And I've got plenty of both!"

Huw Steven's got warily to his feet, and raised his lamp high, he turned the flame down in an attempt to see a tell-tale blue flame that would indicate the presence of more explosive gas. Finding none he turned the lamp up again and began to search for survivors and injured comrades. "All those who can, make your way to me, I'm holding my lamp up for you. If you can't, shout, but don't all shout out at once, we'll help you as soon as possible. I've tested for fire damp and haven't found any, but I haven't got the canary with me today so don't move around too much." Said Huw, quietly yet firmly. Tom hauled Victor to his feet and joined Huw, who was busy making a head count.

"Thirty-six, thirty-seven, five missing from this section!" Huw stated. "Victor stays with me, Tom and Evan see if you can find anyone injured. If you do, bring them here. Bryn Lewis and Daniel Morgan, take a lamp and see if the way back to pit bottom is clear." Victor sat gratefully at Huw's feet, marvelling at the calm, concise way he assumed control and began to plan for their well-being and survival.

Evan returned with a look of desperation on his face, "The stall where the Corbett brothers, Jack Cooper and Bill Higgs was working' is gone! The roof's down, there's no sign of them nor any sound!" Huw wasn't with him to see if there was anything that could be done. They returned to the party after a few moments. "It looks hopeless, we'll need help if we are to get them out, but I don't think they could have survived a fall like that! Whispered Huw, his voice barely audible.

"We must try to do something!" Insisted Ted Maggs a miner with badly scarred arms and face.

"We are not going to move anything until we know how safe it is." Huw stressed, let's look after the living first. We'll do what we can for the others in a while." Tom returned with the body of another miner named Peter Archer draped over his shoulder.

Huw looked at Tom, "Is he……?"

"He's still breathing but I don't know what's wrong with him." Answered Tom. "I didn't find anybody else. Bloody Hell! Tom exploded," Mr. Fraser and the Earl were here, talking to me an' Victor a couple of minutes ago!" Huw thought for a while. He came to a decision and said, "Tom you and Evan try to find them. I'm taking everyone else back to pit bottom!" He looked around him at the relieved miners staring at him in appreciation. "Help anyone who can't walk and keep an eye out for survivors on the way back. Tom, don't be too long, they wouldn't look for you!" He led his group of thirty-six miners along the heading toward pit bottom, hoping it was the haven, he was willing it to be. Victor detached himself from the rear of the party and quietly slipped back to his uncle.

"What the hell are you doing back here, it isn't safe! Go with Huw, as you were ordered to do!" Tom raged.

"It's no good throwing a tantrum Uncle Tom, I'm staying with you so bugger the orders!" Victor answered. "I'll go when you do. The sooner we get this search over and done with the sooner we can get out." Seeing that argument would be futile Tom surrendered but made a mental note to exact future retribution. The three miners began the grisly duty of searching the district for the missing under manager and the mine owner. Victor began to search carefully and methodically along the stalls praying that he would find them all empty. He crawled alongside a half filled corve when he heard a slight groan, a weak sob. He inched his way behind the wagon to find the mine owner, his face a mask of blood, slumped over the mine cart. Victor lifted his lamp to inspect the man's injuries but quickly lowered it as he illuminated the body of James Fraser impaled through the chest with a four-inch pit prop! His scream brought both Tom and Evan. A Quick examination of the gruesome injury showed no spark of life in the under managers mutilated corpse. Victor looked at the poor man's face. He had died with the most ghoulish expression, that Victor had ever seen. It was an expression that exuded both terror and agony and was to remain with Victor, for the rest of his life!

"The poor bastard's a goner!" Declared Evan, after giving the under-manager's body the briefest, of stomach-churning examinations. "I didn't like the bugger when he was alive, but I've never wished any man dead! Gord! Look at his face 'he must have suffered!"

"His Lordship is still alive," Confirmed Tom tearing his gaze away from the horrific mutilation that had once been a man! "The old sod's going to take some liftin'. He must weigh twenty stone!"

"Probably full of brandy and pudding and such like, I expect." Stressed Evan. "Well done, Victor! We would never have found 'him in here!" Evan thought for a while then continued, "Mind you, now that we've got to carry him, I wish you had gone straight by him!"

"I heard him moan Tom. There's a nasty cut on his head and I think his arm is broke, it's a real funny shape!" The three men pulled the mine owner's unconscious body into the tunnel, where there was a little more room. They wasted no time in examining the injured man but began carrying him the long way back to the pit bottom. It took all the three men's strength and determination to accomplish the task. A few hundred yards from the lamp room they met the anguished figure of Huw Stevens hurrying down the roadway.

"You stupid young bastard, I've been at my wit's end wondering what's happened to you! How do you think I felt when I found out you weren't with us?" The anger in Huw's voice eventually giving way to relief. "What's it like down there Huw?" Quizzed Tom, putting the earl's body down upon the floor, glad of a chance to give his aching muscles a short breather.

"It's a hell of a mess. As near as I can tell there's been an explosion in the East district. It's like the doorway to hell in there! Fires raging all along the heading. We are all in the underground lamp room and the stables. There's thirty-six of us from the West, fifty-eight from the North, but no one from the East!" He looked down at the still unconscious earl breathing erratically on the floor, "Let's get him to the others. The cage has been damaged. We can hear them banging about on the surface trying to fix it. We haven't been able to signal them because the bells aren't working." Hoisting the owner's body between them they trudged sombrely to the stables. Victor gazed around him, wherever he looked he saw soot blackened, frightened faces, staring blankly at floors or ceilings! They put the unconscious earl down on a pile of horse soiled hay in an attempt to make the old gentleman as comfortable as possible. Few had escaped the explosion unscathed, burns seemed to abound, Victor glanced at his arms for the first time since Tom had yelled the warning and became aware of the sting that was spreading along them. He examined them and the discomfort became an agony.

"We have been bloody lucky up to now!" Said Huw, to a small group of colliers that stood with him." We have plenty of injuries, but nothing too serious. The trouble is, I don't know how long the good air is going to last! There's bound to be plenty of after damp following an explosion like that, so it's going to reach us sooner or later!" The assembly nodded their agreement. Many of them had experienced fires and explosions in the past, but nothing on the scale of the one that had just occurred! "There's at least twenty men missing from the North! A few of the boys have stayed there to search and some have gone back to help! There's a hundred and twenty-three of us here, some have got pretty bad injuries!" Spoke a wizened old miner called Will Thomas, "We haven't heard a thing from the East! A couple of boys went along the heading to see if they could find out what's happened down there 'cos that's' where they copped it worst! But they 'haven't come back yet!" They all thought of what must have happened to the friends and neighbours who had been working there.

"If those searchers are not back soon, we'll have to look for them. I don't want anybody else wandering off and getting lost." Huw ordered. "We are not safe here, if that 'afterdamp' gets here before they send the cage down, they'll find us all asleep down here, for Good!" Huw paced around nervously, a thousand and one questions were flooding through his mind. Would they repair the cage in time? How long would it be before the after and blackdamp reached them and would they keep the fan running to supply them with good air, or would the manager decide to turn it off so as not to fan any fires that might have been caused by the explosion! As the senior man left unharmed below ground, he had to try to resolve these problems. He had to know what had happened in the East, and if it were still a place of danger and what risk it presented to their safety and well-being! He had to have first rate information. He came to a decision. He would have to try to enter the East district to see the situation for himself.

"Will, you look after things here. When that cage comes down try and stop everybody making a dash to get on it or nobody will get out. Tom, you help him." Huw felt his courage building as he issued orders to the miners gathered around him, and he would need plenty of courage where he was going! "We must know if there's any hope for those in the East and if conditions there are a threat to those of us here. But most important of all, we must find out what needs to be done to help the poor sods down there!" Huw picked up his lamp and began to leave the stables. Before he had reached the doorway, Tom pulled him roughly around looked him hard in the face and said," "Don't argue with me but I am going with you, it isn't safe alone". I could always thrash you when we were boys an' I can still do it now so don't try to stop me I am going with you! Somebody has got to look after you. "Huw, seeing the determined look in Tom's eyes and the fierce set of his chin nodded. He said. "I don't suppose I could stop you even if I wanted to! Ted Maggs, Daniel Morgan, help Will get everything organised here. Evan, you are the biggest chap down here, get as many of the rugby boys as you can and make sure everyone does as Will says!"

Tom turned to Victor, who was trying to wrap an old rag around his scorched arms in an effort to lesson the agony they were causing. "I am going with Huw. This time, stay here! No stupid bloody nonsense about following me or do I 'have to bash you unconscious!"

Huw returned when he heard Tom warning his nephew. He looked down fondly at the injured young man. He would be a boy no more, if, he survived this day. His gaze shifted to the senseless form of the old earl, his body inert save, for the spasmodic rise and fall of his chest. When fate struck half a mile underground it was no respector of title or position, he was an injured man, no more no less.

Huw turned back to Victor and said, "I want you to look after the old man. See he comes to no more harm. Ask Evan to help you get him onto the cage when it arrives. I promise to look after Tom. I'll bring him back don't worry." The two men left the comparative safety of the stables and pit bottom and wentt along the heading towards the East district of the mine! Resolutely they entered the heading that would lead them to the source of the disaster which they knew was approximately two hundred yards ahead. They reached the first ventilation door where they stopped to listen, hearing nothing they opened it carefully and carried on. The light from their lamps bounced malevolently from wall to wall, as each man strained to see a safe way ahead. Tom stopped to listen, straining his ears, he caught a faint crackle and hiss that proclaimed the roaring inferno that was waiting in front of them. The air was becoming thick with smoke so both men covered their faces with their dirty caps, trying to keep the choking filth out of their lungs. Tom's body was awash with sweat as he inched his way forward. They came upon the body of a dead horse, still shackled to a run of coal drams, it was spreadeagled from one side of the heading to the other making forward movement very difficult. It took several nerve-racking minutes before they were able to move on. The heat was growing more intense with every step. Movement was becoming more and more difficult as the fetid air made each step harder. Huw have a shout as he saw the silhouette of four or five men outlined by some burning roof timbers. Forgetting his own safety, he rushed onward. Each 'man' was little more than a charred hulk covered in a blackened carbonized crust. They had been incinerated instantaneously, by the engulfing conflagration that consumed every spark of life out of them, totally, without warning.

Both men felt the bitter taste as bile began to rise in their throats. "Who the bloody hell did those poor bastards used to be?" Huw croaked, his voice straining to overcome the nausea that was leaping within him!"

Tom, his eyes full of tears and his heart appalled at the repulsive mutilations before him, could only sob, "God knows! We never will! Theres nothing left to recognise!" The heat was becoming almost unbearable, and the fire ahead was an impenetrable inferno. We'll not get any further until that fire is put out. Have you seen any sign of the two men Will Thomas sent down here?" Demanded Huw urgently, as he gasped for breath in the foul air.

"Bugger those two!" Snarled Tom, his knuckles white as he clenched his fists helplessly. "There's at least sixty poor sods on the other side of those flames!" He stared viciously at the wall of fire that was slowly eating its way, hungrily towards the pit bottom. He screwed up his eyes trying to see into the pyre, for pyre is what it most certainly was, especially for the poor bastards trapped behind it! He gave up, his eyes were streaming from the heat and the strain. It was like trying to stare into the heart of a furnace, hotter than the deepest recesses of hell! He felt an urgent tug on his arm, he turned to find an equally anguished Huw pulling him back down the heading towards safety. "Come on Tom!" Yelled Huw, his voice raised to overcome the noise of the blaze which had become an ear-splitting roar. "We can't do any good here, let's get back to pit bottom and see what we can do from there. As the two men departed, they were accompanied by the crack and frizzle as more and more roof timbers ignited, adding their dry kindling to the burning frenzy!

Phillip Gregory and the men at the top of the pit were feverishly trying to free the cage from the girders that had been dislodged by the underground explosion. Evan Dance, with little thought to his own safety, or advancing years, had climbed the winding gear with a block and tackle and was busily tying a rope to one of the wheel supports. He lowered the secured rope to the crowd of workers gathered below, then shouted. "Get someone to get an end attached to that steel girder Mr. Gregory, if we can move that, it ought to be plain sailing then!" Phillip Gregory moved quickly and organised a pulling crew. The rope was securely fixed to the offending girder. With a shout of 'Heave! Heave! The piece of metal was inched slowly but surely up the shaft. "Quickly!" Gregory bellowed, his voice raised above the grunts and groans of the heaving men, "Somebody get another rope around that bar so that we can pull it sideways, safely onto the bank." His words must have been anticipated because someone was already hitching a hawser to it before he had finished speaking! With the large girder out of the way, it took only a few resounding blows with a sledgehammer to remove the last of the debris. Evan Dance, who had climbed safely down onto the pit head, pushed his way to the front. "Let me through, damn it!" He snapped angrily, "Let me check that cage! I must see if the 'winding' rope is damaged, we don't want the cage smashed at the bottom of the shaft!" He looked at the bond cage very briefly, jumped up and down inside it two or three times, to test the rope! Then declared confidently. "It'll do for now!" Phillip Gregory, along with a party of a dozen volunteers was the first into the cage.

"I can't ring you down Mr. Gregory, the signal bell isn't working." Said Evan as he closed the cage securing the volunteers safely inside, "If there's anybody left down there, they'll be waiting for you, without any announcement's! Five minutes after you reach pit bottom, I'm pulling the cage back up." Phillip Gregory looked up at the winding Hawser and the tower wheels. He spoke quickly to Evan Dance, not wishing to delay the rescue attempt any more than was necessary, "The cage seems alright, but don't lower us too quickly, easy does it, we don't want to crash into any obstructions on the way down. Make sure the winder knows my orders!"

"Don't you worry, Sir." Answered Evan earnestly, "You know Paul Morris, he's been the winder here for nearly twenty years. he knows his stuff. It'll be as gentle as a tart getting on a vicar!" Evan turned away and signalled the winder in the engine house to begin the descent. With a creak and a groan, the cage began to inch its way down the shaft.

Victor clenched his teeth against the signals of undiluted agony that were being sent by his inflamed forearms to his brain. At least his hands didn't feel too bad, but he felt certain that his fore arms would be permanently scarred! He turned to look at the frail body, of the old coal owner, lying in the dirty straw. It was the first time Victor had ever seen an earl. He looked like any other man, yet Victor had been expecting some kind of monster, considering all the tales the miners had told him about 'coal owners! The old man began to squirm and writhe as he began to regain consciousness, his eyes flickered and Victor knelt painfully beside him.

"W W W here aaaam I? Croaked the old man his voice barely a whisper, "What in damnation happened and where's Fraser?" Victor put his hand gently on the earl's shoulder to prevent him from rising. "There' has been some kind of explosion Sir. Just stay still, I expect they will come to get us out soon. I hope so!" Victor looked anxiously at the stable doorway hoping to see the reassuring figure of his uncle coming to them.

"Where's Fraser?" The earl repeated, "We were walking along the tunnel and that's all I can remember!" He closed his eyes trying to will the throbbing, that was turning his head inside out, out of his agonised mind! He looked up at the young man kneeling at his side, noticing his singed hair and eyebrows and the dirty sacking wrapped untidily around his badly burned arms. "We look a right pair between us, don't we boy?" He glanced around the room at the dozens of injured miners who were sitting or lying in the straw. He began to realise that a major catastrophe had happened. "Is Mr. Fraser out inspecting the damage, er, um, what did you say your name was?"

"I didn't your Lordship, but it's Victor, Victor Leslie. Mr. Fraser had an accident sir, 'He's dead. Me,' Uncle Tom an' Evan found you so we carried you here, but Mr. Fraser was dead!" The old man closed his eyes and turned his head away for an instant before he turned to look at Victor.

"Well Victor, let me thank you and your uncle Tom for carrying me to safety. It can't have been easy!" He said looking at Victor's burnt arms, before adding. The doctor's been telling me for years that I ought to eat less!"

"Yes sir," Replied Victor without thinking, "Tom did say that we ought to leave an old greedy guts like you where you were!" He stopped abruptly as he realised what he had just said to the injured Earl! "I I I!" He stammered but the old man roared with laughter that echoed around the sombre stables, "Wait till I get back to my club, I shall dine out on the stories I've to tell! Firstly I'm an old fart, now a greedy guts!" he laughed once more, his voice rolling off the low ceilings and resounding through the tunnels. "Wait a minute, you're the young musician I was talking to a few minutes ago, aren't you?"

"Yes your lordship, only it was a couple of hours ago!"

"What's that! Hours, you say! Why in damnation haven't we been rescued yet?" The Earl's voice was raised to a shout and all the miners present were looking at him, wishing he would perform some sort a miracle that would see them all rescued and safely on the surface. The air was becoming more and more foul, breathing was becoming almost unbearable. Each breath left an acrid oppressive taste in the back of the throat. Miners were coughing and trying to clear their lungs of the cloying smoke that was drifting through the mine workings. In the shadows a miner began reciting the Lord's Prayer in a haunting tone that filled the stable with an eyrie atmosphere.

"Don't worry your Lordship, I'll look after you until we get out. Uncle Tom and Huw, will take care of everything!" Said Victor trying to reassure the old man. "I promised them, I would look after you until they returned and when I make a promise to my uncle, I have to have a very good reason for not keeping it. You have had a nasty bang on the head, please lie still until we get you out and then the doctor will be able to check you over!" The old patriarch lay back and closed his eyes. He felt weary, wearier than he had ever done before, in all his sixty-eight years. He felt weaker than a kitten, the thump on his head was throbbing unmercifully and he felt sure that he had broken an arm. In fact, every last square inch of his body was announcing itself to be in need of some attention and soothing medical care!

A Crowd of several hundred worried wives, mothers and children had gathered outside the mine gates. Many wrapped in shawls were weeping quite openly, others unsure of what to expect were staring blankly at the locked gates and the frantic efforts being made to free the jammed cage. Most, were just standing mute, lost in their own feelings of dread and foreboding as they hoped for the best, yet secretly expecting the worst! Kate looked around at the crowd standing with her. The absolute silence was the most eerie experience she had ever experienced, the feeling of helplessness was totally all consuming!

Everyone seemed unwilling to cry out and ask for information, fearing that they be the one responsible for the bringing of horrific news. The crowd watched in amazement as Evan Dance climbed up the winding gear and lowered the rope. She remembered to her dying day the cheer that broke the silence as the cage was freed! Someone in front of her, a woman leaning against the Collery gate, screamed." Bring our men up Gregory, or you an' that harlot Thompson, won't be cheating' on your partners in the office any more cos we'll cut it off" An angry murmur of agreement and threat ran around the crowd. Kate clasped her hands together and began to pray silently to herself, as the tears began to roll down her cheeks, harder than she had ever prayed in her whole life before.

She heard the shout as the cage began its descent into the bowels of the earth. Damn coal! Damn the people who used coal, damn the coal owners who expected the men to win it for them and damn the miners for being stupid enough to go underground to get it! She opened her eyes. Lord, forgive her! She had never damned anyone, it was fright, a fear that was consuming her every thought! Please God, let them all come up safely.

"They'll all be safe Mam; I know they will! Won't they?" Said Ivy. She was trembling uncontrollably at her mother' side.

Kate hugged her daughter tightly, more for her need, than Ivy's! "Tom will take care of Victor. He'll look after him, don't worry!"

"But who is looking after Uncle Tom?" Croaked Ivy, fighting hard to hold back the tears that were threatening to engulf her.

"You know who!" Soothed her mother, "That's why we say our prayers!"

CHAPTER 11

THE CAGE INCHED ITS WAY SLOWLY DOWN THE SHAFT, REACHING the pit bottom without incident. Phillip Gregory wrinkled up his nose as the acrid, smoke filled, atmosphere, hit the back of his throat. A feeble cheer was raised as the rescue party stepped from the cage. Gregory looked around noticing that there appeared to be only superficial damage to the pit bottom. Several injured miners were to be seen standing or leaning against the tunnel walls. The vast majority seemed to be suffering from burns of one type or another. A few had wounds judging from the blood-spattered appearance of their clothing, but the men were orderly. There was no sign of panic as the colliers waited for the rescue which they knew would come.

"What kept you so long Sam?" Called out Will Thomas as the men stepped off the cage. "We've all shaved twice, we was waiting' so long!"

"Shut up Thomas," Snarled Gregory, as he surveyed the scene at the pit bottom. "Who's in charge down here? I want a full report!"

Will looked around, trying to find Huw. He eventually replied, "Mr. Stevens, the west District Fireman, is the senior man left Sir. He's gone over to the East district cos that's where the explosion 'happened! he 'hasn't come back yet!"

"Let's get these injured men up the shaft as soon as we can load them." Ordered Gregory, his voice thick with the effort of talking in the heavy fouled air. "Do you know how many are safe?"

Will looked around, trying to think before he replied, "As near as I can tell there's about a hundred and twenty, but I'm not sure. It's been a bit chaotic down here as you can see. Most got out of the West an' North, but we 'haven't heard a word from the East since the bang! I don't hold out much 'hope for them poor bastards!"

The rescue party, under the orders of Phillip Gregory began to quickly load the injured miners onto the cage. He have orders for its return as soon as possible. It began to ascend to the surface five minutes after its arrival, just as Evan Dance had said it would.

"The men who are worst are in the stable Mr. Gregory, there's some bad burns an' broken bones in there. We are going' to need some boards an' stretchers to carry them out!" Stated Will Thomas as soon as he had seen the cage safely on its way to the surface. Just as they were about to enter the underground stables they were halted by a shout from Huw Stevens. "Sir, He called out." Thank you, Lord, help has come. My advice would be to get the injured men up as soon as possible. The East pit's a shambles, it's burning hotter than hell! I don't think anyone down there stood a chance! Every roof timber we saw was a blaze, so the chances are, the roof's caved in all along the heading."

Phillip Gregory thought for a moment then replied, "Right, you stay here and organise the evacuation, I'll take some of these fresh men with me to see if we can start to get the fire under control." He turned to his party, selected half a dozen of the fittest and strongest and said, "Come on you men let's go and see if we can sort out that fire. There may still be a chance of saving someone in the East if we are quick! Let's get those fire hoses unrolled and ready to use." His party left the pit bottom and began walking slowly towards the East district, dragging the heavy hose with them.

A Buzz wentt round the waiting crowd at the surface as the first cage full of miners appeared at the pit head. Most staggered out to the gates where they were gratefully received by weeping relatives, and eagerly questioned by even more still worried wives and mothers. A cry wentt up and quickly spread around the gathering, "It's pretty bad, lots of injured but it's the East District that's really copped it!"

Kate caught hold of Ivy's hand, crushing her fingers so tightly that her daughter cried out with pain, "Did you hear that! They should be alright; they've been working in the West for nearly eighteen months now." She caught her breath as she realised that there were at least sixty men and boys working in the East District of the mine! She looked around her as the message began to spread. She saw the look of dread, as its meaning began to sink into those who had loved ones working that fateful district! She noticed the looks of horror that were replacing those of bewildermisn't as understanding of those few simple sentences began to sink in! The appearance of hope that had been on some waiting faces was being replaced with dread! She found herself muttering, "Damn All Coal!" Silently to herself once again!

Kate's attention was taken by a loud cheer that came from the rear of the crowd. It was followed with shouts of, "Clear a path! Get out of the way and let them through! It's the rescue miners from the Crumlin pit!" The crowd parted willingly, allowing the lorry load of rescuers through. "Come on lads save our men for us!" A woman shouted as the team prepared to enter the pit head, "You 'have to save them cos they are all family men, they're all we've got, and we need them!"

Victor, gently shook the Earl and announced, the shaft is working again, they'll soon 'have us out, you'll see." The coal owner opened his eyes and looked at the young man. He managed to give the youngster a smile before saying, I'll be glad to get out of this bloody place, it's been a pain everywhere, not just in the arse! Tell whoever is in charge to get the most seriously injured out first, I'll wait. Bad form to leave your men and run! Didn't do it with the Boers, can't do it now." He closed his eyes a lay back into the straw.

Tom, walked into the stable to find his nephew still sitting at the Earl's side. "How are those arms boy?" He asked as he squatted stiffly down beside him.

"The pain has eased a little now thanks, but they are pretty badly burned Tom." Replied Victor through clenched teeth, "They hurt more when I think about them, so I've been trying to think about other things!"

"You won't be using them under the bedclothes for a while anyway!" Added a concerned Huw, as he came into the stable. We'll 'have to find you a nice woman to take care of all your needs! Better than using your hand anyway!" He turned and winked at Tom, as Victor began to protest and blush all at the same time.

"Don't take any notice of 'him Vic, a woman will nag you more than your right 'and!" countered his uncle, trying to take his nephew's mind off their predicament.

Huw looked at Victor and said, "Seriously Victor, Tom will be staying underground with me for a while to help organise the rescue attempt. You must tell your Mam, that he is alright. Ask her to tell Mrs Stevens that I am too. Say we won't be long, but they are going to need all the help they can get to put out the fires." Victor jumped to his feet and shouted, "If you 'an Uncle Tom, are staying then so am! I told you before I am not going without him!"

"Sit down Victor!" Ordered Tom, "We are not going to volunteer to do anything brave or stupid, not for the benefit of these pissing coal owners anyway!" He noticed the Earl's left eye half open as he continued. "You look after his Lordship, You helped carry 'him, this far, so you see he gets out safely, then get those arms seen to. Don't argue just do as you are told! We won't be long, somebody's got to make sure that bastard Gregory doesn't leave the men and run, and Huw's just the boy to do it! And I've got to help him!"

The two men turned and left the stable. Victor slumped down disconsolately beside the Earl. The old man opened his eyes and seeing the distraught youth said, "They were right! You can't help much with burned arms. Take the messages they asked you to, that's your job now." He lay back waiting for the pain to ease before continuing. "How old are you lad?"

"Nearly fifteen, Sir," Victor replied." Why aren't you still at school, a bright lad like you should still be learning?!" Continued the Earl.

"I had to leave school, Sir, there wasn't enough money for me to stay on. My dad's been killed so I had to help support the family." Added Victor. Four strong miners came into the stable, they were carrying a wooden door that they had taken from its hinges, putting it beside the Earl they lifted him gently onto it. As they were carrying him to the cage he bellowed, Come on Victor, you are coming too! Help the lad someone."

Victor, try as he could, was unable to remember any of that ascent to the surface. In later years, all he could recall was becoming completely smothered by Mam and his sisters!

Victor woke with a start; he sat bolt upright! Looking around, he realised he was in his own bed. The back of his throat felt like a piece of raw meat. "Mam" He croaked; he had difficulty in speaking. "Mam!" He managed a little louder the second time. "How's Uncle Tom, is he alright?" His mother came rushing up the stairs beaming at him as she entered his bedroom. "Hush now Victor, the doctor said you mustn't talk after the scorching your throat has had. Tom's fine. Both he and Huw came up the pit a few hours after you did, they are both unhurt!" She sat comfortably on the edge of her son's bed and her daughters came in to join her. "We were ever so worried." Whispered Christine planting a huge smacker on her brother's forehead, despite his protests. "It was the worst three hours of our lives!" She concluded.

Ivy looked down at Victor and asked, "Are your arms hurting much now? The doctor plastered them in cream, he said they should be fine in a week or two."

"Never mind my arms!" Croaked Victor, "Tell me about Uncle Tom. Is he safe?"

"He's fine." Reassured Kate, he's gone to the Fed meeting to decide what's to be done for all the widows' and orphans. There's so many of them!" She looked out of the window, how peaceful it seemed out there, masking the turmoil that must be happening in so many fatherless houses!

"You must try to sleep Victor; the doctor said you were to have plenty of rest." Said his mother getting up to fluff up his pillows.

"I won't be able to rest until I know what happened!" Demanded Victor defiantly. "If you tell me I promise I'll go to sleep."

"It was terrible!" His mother said, "One of the worst disasters of our time! They have found sixteen bodies in the North, eight in the West as well as Mr. Fraser's but they haven't been able to get into the East because the fire is still raging!" She stopped as a shiver ran along her spine, it was as if an army of snowmen were inside her body trying to kick themselves out!

Ivy continued, "They think there are still about sixty men in there! But they don't think any of them are alive. There's no way to put out the fire, the rescue team said it will have to burn itself out!"

"If they use any more water on the fire," Continued Glenys. "They will flood the workings completely. We are all so thankful that both you and Uncle Tom are safe!" Unthinkingly she gave his hand an affectionate squeeze, Victor yelped with pain.

"Be careful Glenys!" Chided Kate, "You know how painful his arms are!" All four women gazed down at Victor's arms; they were more than twice their usual bulk with all the packing that had been put around them. He tried to flex the fingers of his right hand but found it extremely painful. Kate noticed the look of doubt that ran behind her son's eyes, a question of ominous uncertainty, he tried flexing his fingers again trying to make a fist but the pain stopped him bending his digits more than a fraction of an inch.

Kate looked lovingly at her youngest child, ran her hands delicately through his lank dark hair and cooed, "Everything is fine, Doctor Devlin's said you are bound to feel some stiffness in your hands and arms because you have been badly burned. But once everything has healed properly you will feel no pain in your arms or hands." Victor slumped back onto the bed with a huge sigh.

"Tell me more about the pit please." He croaked, his voice little more than a rasping whisper, "And can I please have a drink of ice-cold water? My mouth feels as dry as a China man's chin strap!"

Ivy rushed off to the kitchen whilst Christine continued with the story, "It was awful! Uncle Tom told us that once all the injured men were brought to the surface, the remainder began to search for those who were missing. There were fires everywhere, and the air was foul, more than a dozen canaries died within a hundred yards of the pit bottom! The trouble was so many of the ventilation doors had either been broken or burned, that they couldn't get the air circulating properly. In the end, they were using tarred sheets to help the ventilation blow out the bad air."

The women were watching Victor's face as the story was retold, looking for the first sign to escape from his eyes, but Victor, listened resolutely to every word spoken, his attention engrossed in the description. Christine continued. "They found the missing men in the North and dug out those buried in the West but none of them were alive. They said the screams when they brought the bodies up were horrendous. We were all here with you, waiting for the doctor to come. Uncle Tom's said that the whole time he was underground Mr. Gregory was cursing the fact that they wouldn't be able to fulfil the contract for the French navy and it would mean thousands of pounds lost! Not once did he say he was sorry for those who had died. Whilst the rescue teams were trying to put out the fires and save lives, he was busy planning how to reopen the mine and start work as soon as possible! They say he's been a swine!"

"Christine!" Rebuked her mother. "We don't have sayings like that in this house whether they are deserved or not!"

"Uncle Tom said worse than that Mam!" Countered Christine, defiantly. "I herd him talking to Huw Stevens in the kitchen this morning!"

"That's quite enough, thank you young lady." Snapped Kate her eyes flashing with anger, "You have been brought up not to eavesdrop on other people's conversations."

Victor at last gave in to the tiredness that was overwhelming him and silently closed his eyes and surrendered to dream filled oblivion. Kate, noticing the sleep overtaking her suffering son, noiselessly beckoned the girls out of the bedroom.

"I hate this filthy bloody mine!" Snarled Phillip Gregory as he tore of his shirt and tossed it in a crumpled heap onto the brown leather

Chesterfield chair in the corner of his office. "If you can't get out of that dress any quicker, I'll rip it from your bloody back! After what I've been through there's only one thing I need and it's right between your legs. Hurry up, damn you!" He hauled Sylvie harshly onto the floor beside him, forcing her legs apart with his coal blackened hands, he mounted her.

"You could have washed first!" Countered Sylvie. She winced as she felt his erect manliness forcing its urgent way into her inner sanctum. "I'll be filthy by the time you've finished!"

"Don't worry Sylvie! The way I feel at the moment this isn't going to take long! I feel like the beast those bastard miners reckon I am. Get on your hands and knees!"

His lust sated, he collapsed exhausted onto the floor. He looked at Sylvie still kneeling beside him and said, "look at us! What a fine pair we make. You with your husband blissfully at sea and me, with the blood of at least sixty miners on my hands!" He looked at his dirt encrusted fingers, "Even Pilate washed his hands clean of the blood. Me, I just couldn't wait to lift your skirt!" He pushed her roughly to the floor and yelled, "Leave me, I need to think." As he stood, his legs were still shaking from the exertion and ecstasy. He thrust his legs savagely into his trousers before walking to a wash basin where he bathed the coal dust and Sylvie's snatched from his hands. He returned to his desk as Sylvie, her clothes draped loosely around her slim frame, closed the office door.

He had to have a cast iron excuse, that pathetic bloody patrician had been in the mine at the time and sod it, the pathetic, indulgent, bastard had survived! Mercifully the soft-hearted noble couldn't remember or didn't know the reason for the explosion. He decided to brazen it out. There were no survivors from the East District, who really knew or could prove that he had ordered them to blast there! That French contract was worth too much to worry about a little bit of gas! He'd deny under oath, if necessary, giving permission to use dynamite. Let them prove it. All the witnesses were carbonized by now. He had friends who had too much to lose if they didn't stand by him. They would have to see that the right palms were well greased if they wanted to keep out of the shit! He wasn't going to take the blame alone; he'd take a lot of them down with him! He yanked open the door and went out to Sylvie. "Sorry about that dear!" He breathed his words urgently against her neck. He squeezed her breasts hard in the palm of his hands feeling her, nipples harden to his touch. "I've got a lot on my mind. I've thought things through, and everything is going to be fine. Come on back into the office. I need a second helping!"

Doctor Devlin sat comfortably at Kate's kitchen table as he spoke to Tom and Kate, in his broad Irish accent. "It's a wonder that more of you weren't killed, a heaven-sent miracle sure enough! But I've seen some terrible injuries this last week, enough to make even the holy Mary weep." He looked kindly at Kate, "At least you have been spared the ultimate sacrifice this time."

"Yes Doctor, we have been thanking the Lord for both Victor's and Tom's deliverance, together with all those other fine men he saw fit to save." Kate closed her eyes and added another silent prayer. "How long will it be before Victor is fit and well Doctor?"

The Doctor looked solemnly at Kate before he answered. "He'll be fit for work in three to four weeks. He's a healthy young man and once his arms have healed, he'll have no problem in holding a shovel. Victor will be back to full strength in a couple of months. His arms will be scarred but none the worse for that." He looked disconsolately into the blazing fire hesitating over his next sentence, searching for the right words. "We were all so worried!" Added Kate not noticing the Doctor's hesitation because of her relief. "He's been so brave; he hasn't once complained about the pain. You have been marvellous Doctor, but if it hadn't been for the miner's federation medical fund, I don't know what we would have done!"

"Don't worry about it now," He answered slowly, choosing his words very carefully, "I've been well paid and was glad to do all that I could. I only wish I was able to do more, but I've done all that I, or anyone else can!"

Tom, who had been watching the Doctor carefully noticed his apprehension and tentativeness of speech. He interrupted the conversation with an abrupt question. "There's something you are not telling' us isn't there doctor! What's wrong with Victor?" Kate slumped back into her chair her eyes wide unwilling to comprehend the meaning of Tom's question. "What d-d-d-do you mean Tom? The doctor's told us Victor will be back at work as good as new in a month or two!" She looked appealingly at the doctor waiting for confirmation.

"There's nothing wrong with Victor." Doctor Devlin continued. It was at times such as these that he wished he'd stayed at home on his father's farm in County Meath. "But his arms have been badly burned. His hands are untouched, unfortunately, the tendons that control his fingers have been damaged! His fingers will still function properly, and he will still be able to play the piano, but he will not have the dexterity and control to further his musical ambitions!"

Kate, Tom Ivy and Glenys were sat cosily around a blazing coal fire some hours later. It's warming glow flooded the room with contentment and a welcoming fellowship. The senior family members were trying to resolve the problem that had troubled them all ever since the doctor's deliberation. "How do you tell someone that their dreams are over?" Sighed Ivy, as she stared into the glowing mass of coal that spread its licking tongues of heat eagerly around the room, busily hunting out for any cold dark corners with which to battle.

"What you really mean is, how do you tell someone you love?" Continued Kate, her eyes still scarlet from the tears that had flowed freely all afternoon. "That their hopes and means of getting out of this dead-end existence have been destroyed! Snuffed out by those ravaging flames half a mile underground."

"At least he's upstairs in bed!" Snorted Ivy indignantly. "Don't feel sorry for Victor, not yet anyway! Just feel happy that he's alive! There are more than a hundred families, who would settle for badly scarred arms instead of a cold, wooden box on the mountainside!" She looked defiantly around the room daring anyone to disagree with her logic. "He's not a cripple nor is he hideously scarred."

Tom looked proudly at his niece always ready to jump to the defence of her 'baby' brother. "We all thank the Lord for his mercy in sparing so many lives, but music was Victor's life his greatest joy and passion."

"He'll still be able to enjoy it!" Exclaimed Ivy.

"I know," Continued Tom gently, "But it was more than joy, it was Victor's passion. When he played the piano his soul was bared for all who cared to look. I could never caress a lover with the tenderness with which his fingers fondled the piano keys. You have never seen him like I have, lost to the world, totally absorbed in the dream world that only music can induce. To Victor, it's a drug far more potent than any the chemist can give or the doctor prescribe!"

"Well, I'm just glad he's alive!" Snapped Ivy tartly.

"I know, darlin'," Soothed Tom, "We all are. But when Victor realises the extent of his injuries, he'll be devastated, it was his way out!"

Kate took a deep breath and sighed deeply. Her troubled family all looked at her. She had decided, and woe betide anyone, who disagreed; he was her youngest son, she would protect him for as long as she possibly could. She spoke quietly but firmly, leaving no doubt in the minds of those listening that she demanded compliance and obedience. "We are not going to tell Victor anything yet! If he asks or mentions the stiffness, we will tell him that the doctor said that it is perfectly normal for his injuries to take a while to heal. He must just be patient."

"That's no-good Kate," Chided Tom, "He will realise there's something wrong before too long."

"Maybe so, but I want him fit and strong before he learns the full extent of his burns. Nothing must hinder his recovery!" Said Kate. He was her youngest son after all! She had done all she could to protect him and would continue to do so, for as long as there was breath left in her body. She folded her arms defiantly in the posture that everyone knew as discussion ended, I've made up my mind!

CHAPTER 12

Phillip Gregory pushed open the window to its fullest extent and filled his lungs appreciatively. He repeated the process, enjoying every distasteful aroma. Opening his eyes, he took in the hustle and bustle of the hundreds of people marching about their daily business, God, he loved London, every last sight and smell! This was where he belonged, not that isolated Welsh bloody valley. He had ideas, drive and ambition and none of it involved those ignorant, sheep loving, sanctimonious have nots. The intrigue and opportunities were all here, this was where he needed to be if he was to realise his every hope and aspiration. He had shouldered all the accusations and persecution alone, but it would soon be payback time! The company was quick enough to take the profits, it was time for confederates on the board to make sure his arse was well and truly covered during the official investigation or he would take several accomplices down with him! Fairfax had seen him alright thus far, but he was not someone to rely on. when the chips were down, Fairfax always looked after number one, he had said it often enough 'Bugger everyone else!' …. His thoughts were interrupted by a sharp rap on his hotel room door.

"Come." He bellowed. The door opened to reveal, A hotel porter escorting three men dressed to the height of London fashion. Pushing the employee roughly aside, Sir Michael Fairfax entered the sumptuous room. "Glad to see you Phillip, I hope the journey up wasn't too bad. I've brought a few friends to see you and discuss what's to be done, then we can all go out and paint the town red!" The porter closed the door leaving the three visitors in the colliery agent's room. Phillip Gregory recognised Owen-Price the mining company's general manager but had never seen the other gentleman before. He stood a little over six feet tall, had a ruddy complexion, white hair and the largest moustache and mutton chop sideburns that Phillip Gregory had ever seen. He shook hands with his two associates and waited to be introduced to the third. It was Michael Fairfax who made the introductions. "Phillip, may I introduce Sir Oliver Fairfax-Stowe, my second cousin through marriage." Turning to Phillip he repeated, "Oliver meet Phillip Gregory." The two men shook hands. Phillip ushered his guests into his room to some comfortable armchairs well away from the door and any prying ears. "Oliver, has been appointed to handle the investigation into your mining disaster!" The words oozed from the lips of Sir Michael. Phillip noticed the emphasis placed on the 'your mining disaster' and waited for further disassociation. Sir Michael continued, "He is most sympathetic and understands the importance of improving coal production to meet the French contract. He has agreed to deal carefully with our problem and placate the miners and the dependant families, with an agreement that will be mutually beneficial!" He stopped and smiled at everyone seated in the room. Tell us what happened Phillip.

Phillip Gregory looked thoughtfully at the three gentlemen sitting before him, wondering if they meant to trap him into some admission of guilt or individual responsibility. Owen Price, noticed the hesitation cross Phillip's face and was unable to contain himself. "Damn it all Phillip!" He Bellowed, "We are all in this together, we've made quite a tidy sum so far, and if we all keep our heads and trust one another, we ought to make even more in the future!"

Phillip, realising that the details would have to be correctly arranged told of the event's leading up to the mine explosion.

"So you are sure that no one heard you order the fireman to shot fire in the East district?" Asked Oliver Fairfax purposefully. "You must be sure on this point, it could prove to be awkward, and we will need to discredit anyone who might come forward!"

Phillip, smiled triumphantly before answering, "The only people who heard those instructions are squashed flat at the bottom of the mine. I may be many things, but a bloody fool isn't one of them!"

The three visitors nodded pitilessly before The Mining Inspector added. "In that case, I don't think there's anything to worry about, there won't be any hard evidence just hear say and the company's lawyers should be able to quash that. There has been a great deal of publicity concerning the accident, even His Majesty has sent messages of sympathy to the bereaved families and dsentonation of three hundred pounds to the disaster fund being organised by the Mayor of Newport." He stopped for a short while to gather his thoughts before continuing. "Despite all this I can safely say that the company will be exonerated of any blame as long as Phillip sticks to his story." All three men stared at Phillip looking for agreement.

He was quick to reply, "You look after me and I'll do the same for you. We've all too much to lose, unless we can whitewash the whole issue!"

Sir Michael Fairfax smiled gleefully to himself making a mistral note that the time was fast approaching when it would be necessary to jettison Gregory and replace him with someone possessing a less compromising influence over their affairs. Not just yet, he'd wait until the furore, over the disaster and the inquest, had died down. Then an anonymous letter to a betrayed sailor about his wife's indiscretions with her employer, might have some interesting results! His face remained an impassive mask as he said. "We can work out the details later. I think it would be an excellent idea if the miners East District were to remain unworked for a year or two as a mark of respect, just as long as we can meet the French contract ....."

Phillip feeling more at ease with every passing second. "No problem! I'll double the output in the other districts, unemployed miners are two a penny down there, I'll just take on an extra sixty or seventy men. If we take on unskilled workers, we won't have to pay them as much, just leave it to me."

"The Earl's gone to the South of France to recuperate, he's expected to be away for several months, with any luck we should be able to get the inquest and investigation over and done with before the silly old bastard sets foot back in the country." Said Michael Fairfax. "Hopefully the old codger could be out of the way for at least six months." His cousin continued, "It will be much easier if his Lordship's kept out of the way. I don't want the proceedings to trigger his memory so that he asks any awkward questions."

Sir Michael stood up and beckoned for the others to follow him. "I promised Phillip some fun and games, so let's not waste time here. The cab's waiting to take us to my club for a meal. We'll catch the train to Epsom in time to have a wager on my filly in the three thirty then it's back to town for a spot of riding ourselves. I've arranged a couple of tasty fillies for us to enjoy! I think we can leave it safely with Oliver to see to everything and trust him to ensure that the company is vindicated of any blame." He smiled happily at his cousin, before concluding, "And it won't cost us too much!"

"This inquiry has considered more than six hundred questions, and I am now ready to deliver my verdict." Announced Sir Oliver Fairfax Stowe the Inspector of Mines. The enquiry had taken almost three weeks, numerous questions had been posed regarding the safety measures taken in the mine but no first-hand cause for the disaster could be proved. Throughout the entire inquiry, Phillip Gregory had resolutely denied issuing any order allowing the use of any type of blasting in the East district of the mine. Whenever he was challenged, he vigorously refuted any implication that either he, or the mining company, could have said or done anything that caused or produced the unfortunate accident. Witness after witness was called regarding the appalling working conditions endured by the miners, prior to the explosion, but no one under oath, was able to give the exact reason for the explosion on that fateful morning.

"Before I deliver my findings, on this most unfortunate occurrence. I have a few remarks to make. We have herd much evidence and even more speculation, much of it wild speculation. However, during the last nine days that this inquest has been held, one name has been cropping up continually, that of Mr. Huw Stevens, one of the colliery foreman. A most able mining deputy! This inquest would like to commend Mr. Stevens for his quick thinking and leadership, which undoubtedly, saved the lives of many of the miners trapped underground. I think I can safely say that they owe their survival to him. At the conclusion of this hearing, it will be recommended that Mr. Stevens be honoured by the Humane Society with a reward that befits his courage. Our thanks are also extended to a small, but brave band of miners who carried the Earl of Gwent, who happened to be visiting the mine, to safety. The whole sorry affair has been punctuated with deeds of heroism and bravery, a matter of which the community may take pride." He paused before continuing. "I have listened attentively to all questions, queries and challenges that have been presented to this inquiry." Fairfax Stowe rose to his feet to deliver his findings. "It has been a truly horrendous accident, and I am convinced that accident is what it was." He paused as angry murmurs ran through the hall only to be halted by the pounding of his polished wooden Havel on the desktop, "I have listened to others and consequently I demanded that I be afforded the same courtesy. I will have silence, or the room will be cleared of all spectators!" He looked pointedly at the police contingent of an inspector and half a dozen constables who had appeared, as if by magic, at the first sign of unrest. "I can only speculate on the exact cause of the explosion, unfortunately, this tragedy has robbed us of the only persons who might have been able to shed some light on this calamitous affair. As to what caused the explosion no concrete evidence exits. I can only speculate that a spark from a metal object, or a flame from a faulty safety lamp may have caused the ignition of a gas blow out or accumulation. An occurrence that could not have been foreseen and only prevented by the miners themselves being more thoughtful and less ignorant of safety measures. No evidence as to the guilt of the company, exits. I do find fault with the late under manager, Mr. James Fraser, also tragically lost in the disaster Mr. Fraser did not keep adequate records of the atmospheric pressure measurement's within the mine which could have accounted for the gas build up in the East district.

I also found fault with the ventilation system within the mine, something I am pleased to say, that has already been addressed by the company. Nevertheless, it was a fault that added to the explosion. I therefore rule that the Bedwellty Steam and Coke Coal Company be fined for each offence together with costs of two pounds and ten shillings. "At the conclusion of his verdict Fairfax Stowe brought his gravel down heavily onto the table to mark an end to the proceedings.

An angry crowd of miners were gathered outside the Newport Magistrates Court House. Humphries was deep in conversation with Huw Stevens and several interested listeners.

"It's no more than I expected," Snarled an irate Herbert. "Another bloody whitewash. Eight pounds ten fine! A bloody disgrace, an insult to the eighty-one dead miners. A bloody disgrace! Everybody heard the blasting all shift right up to the explosion and that bastard Gregory swearing he had not ordered John Collins to shot fire, the lying bastard!"

"I've just worked it out in my head," Snapped an equally angry Huw Stevens, "Eight pounds ten fine works out and about two shillings a dead miner. According to that inspector, we are all worth about two bob each!" Several members began yelling and shouting that Gregory be brought out and they would make him tell the truth.

"Not now lads." Urged Herbert, noticing the approach of a large detachment of police, "Save your anger for another time and place!" He indicated the policeman at the head of the rapidly nearing detachment, "That inspector Love, would enjoy running us all in for illegal assembly and causing a riot!"

"Let them try," bellowed Evan Wilkinson, "There's enough of us here to give them buggers a good hiding'!"

"Shut up Evan!" Shouted Herbert impatiently, "That would be playing right into their hands. All of you, back to the station it's time to catch the train home. We'll decide our next move when we've had a federation meeting, not a brawl in the street." As the assembled miners began to move off along Dock Street, Herbert turned to the Police Inspector and said loudly. "Very nice of you to offer to escort us to the railway station officer, but we know the way, we won't get lost!" He turned and hurried after the rapidly disappearing miners.

Kate looked out through her gleaming kitchen window. The sun had turned the mountainside to an explosion of colour. Looking at the bronze bracken as it whirled in the breeze, she found it difficult to imagine the carnage that had happened underground just six weeks previously. Tom and Victor were both back in that dark death trap, where the fifty-six men and boys were still entombed. It would be too difficult and dangerous to retrieve their bodies the inspectors had said. She shuddered uncontrollably as she thought of all those empty coffins being lowered into their still resting places. She thought too of the weeping families, women and children, crying themselves to sleep each and every night. There had been reporters from the national and London newspapers, but they had disappeared once the ordeal was over, leaving the widows and orphans to cope alone, as they searched for more sensation and disaster. The appeal fund would help. The word was every dependant family would receive seven pounds six shillings and a pension of eight shillings and sixpence a week from the public subscription fund. It seemed like a fortune but many of the families were six or seven strong, it wouldn't feed, house or clothe children for very long! How do you set a price on a man's life? Who knows his true worth? She thanked the Lord that, this time, her loved ones were safe. Looking along the street she noticed Berwyn Morgan, hurrying busily towards her door, puffing and panting as his short legs found great difficulty in negotiating the gully steps. He was smiling brightly; it was the first time Kate had seen him smile since the disaster. She opened the door in response to his sharp rat a tat tat!

"May I come in Kate?" He puffed, clearly out of breath. "I am getting too old for all this running about at my age but, I couldn't contain myself any longer. If I don't share this with someone I'll burst!"

"Come in Berwyn, before you do yourself a mischief." Laughed Kate, a smile dancing across her face at the sight of the beaming minister. It was wonderful to see a happy face even in these troubled times. "Sit down and stop fidgeting or you are going to pop all the buttons off your coat. Then, what will the neighbours think!" She teased.

He laughed heartily, as easily as the pressure valve popping on the shunting engine. "I realise I must look foolish but I've some wonderful news to tell you." He sat down comfortably by the welcoming fireside and watched Kate busy herself making the compulsory cup of tea.

A Steaming cup was placed before him together with a doorstep slice of rich Sunday best cake. Berwyn bit hungrily into the ambrosia!

"I've had some excellent news to tell you. My mind is in such a dither I don't know where to begin, "He spluttered his mouth crammed full of cake.

"Eat your cake Berwyn, there's plenty more where that came from, but no prizes for being the first to finish! The way you gobble it down anyone would swear that your wife never makes any!" She looked mischievously at his ever-expanding girth, "but those of us who know, you, know full well that Megan says you have hollow legs as far as cake is concerned!" They both laughed heartfully as he added. "It's not my fault that everybody feeds me cake. I can't imagine how the rumour, that it is my one weakness, got around!" He said.

"Perhaps it's something to do with the fact that you have told just about everyone in the village." Kate added. She waited for him to remove the last crumb from his plate before she continued. "What is this news? You've been here for a least five minutes and you haven't told me. It must be a record!"

The minister drained his cup appreciatively put it down carefully then began. "I've had a message from a captain in the Salvation Army. He read about the village and the pit disaster in his local paper. Well, it seems that he has been in touch with a man called William Davies, he's a blacksmith at Rochdale colliery near Manchester.

"I don't think I've herd of the gentleman before; I don't know anyone living that far away, my family come from the Cotswolds." Interrupted Kate.

"It turns out that he's a long-lost cousin of Mary Davies from Feeder Row, and he's willing to look after her and the children. Isn't it wonderful?" The minister was on his feet banging his first on the polished top.

"That's the best bit of news I've had in a month of Sundays." Agreed Kate her mind drifting to the destitute family living like paupers in Farmer Meredith's old barn. "However, did it happen?"

"It appears that news of our tiny village and accident has travelled the length and breadth of the country. As you know I have been writing to people everywhere asking for information concerning relatives of the Davies' family. This William Davies was at his union Lodge meeting when they were discussing our plight and he mentioned that he had a cousin working here. He didn't know that he had been killed nearly two years before the explosion. Well to cut a long story short, his mining lodge contacted the salvation army to see if they could help their member's relative, and that was it. When he herd about the family he agreed to look after them. He's a single man living with his mother."

"At least some good has come from this tragedy." Agreed Kate. "I only wish there had been some other way to have spread the word, about the plight of the Davies family!"

CHAPTER 13

Victor had been working underground for more than a month following his accident. The strength had gradually returned to his arms after their burning and were quite badly scarred. He wasn't too worried about scars on his arms, after all his face was totally untouched. What was causing him sleepless nights, was the stiffness that wouldn't go away from his fingers, and they ached and he couldn't control their movements as well as he used to do, they seemed to belong to someone else. He had enjoyed playing the chapel piano on Sunday, his first session since the disaster, but he had found great difficulty in using the fourth and middle finger on his right hand. He had put it down to rustiness, after all he hadn't played for almost seven weeks. He had counted his blessings after looking at the congregation and noticing the large number of empty spaces, that had until recently, been filled with loved ones and friends. A few stiff fingers, seemed of no consequence when compared with the real suffering that had been, and was still being endured, by so many families in the village.

"Are you going' to 'hammer that wedge or what?" Shouted Stuart Thomas, from the next stall. "Only some of us would like to go home sometime today. If it's alright with you!" The jibe snapped Victor away from his daydream. He gritted his teeth braced his legs and began to swing the hammer as he had done so often in the past. Just thinking Stuart, that's all. I was miles away!"

"Daft bugger, it's time you stopped thinking about women, and started chasing' them!" Retorted Stuart.

I wasn't thinking about women ..." He began to deny it fervently, before Stuart interrupted him once again, "Wasn't thinking' about women! When I was your age I couldn't 'help myself I used to wake up every morning in bloody agony it was that stiff! Every time I saw an attractive woman it stood to attention."

"I can put up with that stiffness easily enough." Victor retorted quickly, "I know what to do with that. It's my hands that are stiff all the time. I was hoping that they would be better by now, but they ache continually."

Tom, looked pointedly at Victor, wondering how long they would be able to withhold the information regarding the real extent of his injuries. His mother had ordered that he be told nothing at present, he doubted the wisdom of this course of action, but Kate was the boy's mother. "Leave the boy alone," laughed Tom, "Hes got plenty of time for the sins of the flesh.

"Why is everything' I enjoy a sin?" Shouted Evan from out of the darkness. "When God invented g pleasurable, they, said it was a sin. But if he invented anything' better than a man an' woman enjoying' a jump, he kept it to 'himself! It's the only pleasure that we can 'have free of charge!"

"Unless you are really desperate and 'have to catch the train to Newport and go down the docks!" Shouted Stuart Thomas, "But in your case Evan, even those Jezebel's down there, take one look at your pick handle 'an offer to do it for free!"

"No they don't!" He snapped, "They offer me money!"

"You are both wrong," said Tom enjoying the banter between the two workmen, "They'd take one look at that thing of yours and ask for double the money! A boy's wages and a donkey's dick!" Laughter soon filled the heading, proving that the conversation had been enjoyed by all those within hearing distance. Victor, oblivious to the joke being enjoyed primarily at his expense, finished driving home the wedge and began tapping in another one. He had soon learned where his uncle wanted the wedges placed, and hardly ever needed telling to move theme to a more advantageous position. The split was beginning to widen when he heard the voices of Huw Stevens and his uncle talking quietly behind him. Huw had arrived to test for gas and check the roof supports.

"Good news about the Davies' isn't it Tom." Said Huw, as he squatted onto his hunches. "And let's be honest, we need all that we can get at the moment."

"They've had it hard these last twelve months." Tom answered. "It was a cold winter and a barn on the mountain isn't the best place to keep five young kids! It's a wonder none of the kids wasn't down with consumption although the two youngest look as though they are full of rickets!"

Victor hammered the wedge and the coal began to tumble dustily down. Huw said, "I have to go and blow another twenty yards of heading in a short while. I just want to check everything is safe, first!" He shuddered every time he said it these days, wondering how long it would be before they suffered the same fate as those in the East district. Victor had also come to dread every shot firing. It was one of the only times he enjoyed the darkness, no one could see the way he hid away like a frightened rabbit. He put down the sledge, and using the dim glow from his lamp he made his way to his uncle and Huw. He too, squatted beside them.

"It was good to hear the lads laughing again." Said Huw, "I know it's hard, but life must go on. We must put the past behind us, pick up the pieces and carry on with our lives. A good laugh down here will do us all a world of good!"

Several other miners began to join them as they too, awaited the shot firing. Huw Stevens made his way to the face, ready to begin testing for gas. He wondered if the others dreaded the firing, as much as he had come to do.

"Stand by!" Shouted Huw, his voice masking the turmoil that was churning its way inside his heaving chest. "Firing!" He returned to the miners hiding anxiously against the tunnel walls. Every face he saw in the dim illumination afforded by the safety lamps, exhibited a countenance of resigned terror! He realised, every man present shared his abject horror of the explosion that might condemn them, to the same fate as their comrades, still unburied, half a mile away. You were never alone when you were underground, they all shared his fear! The explosive roared into life, causing the heading wall to tumble heavily down. Huw waited, listening to the coughing and wheezing all around him. Safe again! The men were soon shrouded in the envelope of dust that invaded every corner of their bodies, slowly but surely filling and clogging their lungs, and eating away at their very souls and existence.

"Bloody dust!" Exclaimed Stuart, "It gets everywhere."

Huw gave the signal for the miners to return to their stalls and restart work. The choking and spluttering men began to move the fallen coal into the empty corves, using hands and shovels, whilst others began the far more important task of strengthening and reinforcing the roof with timbers. Victor, his back on fire with the effort and continual bending, heaved and strained to manoeuvre the largest lumps of coal into his tub. It was always at this time that his hands were at their worst, he gritted his teeth, believing that strenuous exercise was the only way to strengthen his weak fingers. Victor pushed the full corve along the heading to Bryn Edwards, the haulier, who was waiting with his pony hitched to a run of drams. The coal was quickly transferred into the nearest empty dram before Victor returned with the empty tub. He repeated the journey seven or eight times until all the loose coal had been removed. He collapsed exhausted watching his uncle undercut the seam once more, his rippling muscles shiny with sweat as he swung the mandrill powerfully, the sharp steel cutting an arrow straight groove at the base of the coal seam.

"Every time I see you, you are sat on your bleeding' arse." Laughed Owen Rees. "I come over to have a quick word with your uncle and find 'him doing' all the work, and' you doing' bugger all."

Tom climbed out of the stall to meet the packer, one of a team of miners responsible for packing as much of the coal spoil as they could, safety behind the colliers, as they advanced through the coal seam."

'Hello, Owen, haven't seen you for a while." He said, "'How's it going'?" "Not bad butty,". Replied the black faced miner. He was stripped to the waist. His grimy chest streaked with rivulets of stale sweat that marked his exposed body, bearing silent witness to the physical strain and effort that he continually endured. His arms bulged with muscle that seemed to exceed his small stature. His fingers were calloused and gnarled from constantly lifting and stacking stone and slag into neat walls, behind which the coal waste and spoil was stored. "I just popped over while it was quiet, to ask when we are going to start choir practice again?"

Tom looked deeply into the packer's eyes, they still shone with an inner spark, the spark of hope and a yearning and zest for life. A Yearning that had not been dimmed by twenty years of flogging his guts away, day after weary day, for a starvation wage in the blackness, three quarters of a mile below ground. It was the hope and expectation that there had to be something better for everyone, it was just a matter of time, even if he had to wait from beyond the grave. "I don't know if we will be bothering again." was all that Tom managed by way of an answer.

"Don't be daft mun!" Snapped the usually placid worker. "We've been practising too 'hard an' too long, for the Nationals, to give in now!"

"It's not daft Owen! All but three of the top tenors are still buried in the East!" Tom looked down at his coal blackened hands and continued, "St Peter must 'have a wonderful choir up there, he's got some of the best tenors I ever heard! I don't know if we will ever be able to replace them, let alone in just a month's time!"

"Can't you push some of the second tenors up to first?" Owen suggested. "Not unless you are willing to use a razor on them!" Snapped Tom testily, he looked sadly along the dark tunnel that led to the funeral home district that now entombed so many fine men. Miner's, who were now adding their voices to the choir of heaven. "I can't work miracles! And that's what it will take, they were irreplaceable, but I think it's a damn bloody cheek of you, to come here, and suggest we try to replace them, when they 'haven't even been given a Christian burial."

"Don't you get stroppy with me Tom Owens!" Owen defended, his temper beginning to rise, "I've got some real good butties in the East as well!" Huw, realising that tempers were beginning to rise, jumped between the two squabbling miners. "Come on lads." His voice was quiet, yet firm, "This is no way for you to behave, not down here anyway. I remember the time when you were working side by side trying to put out the fires, when we all thought there was a chance. "His eyes were pleading with the two long-time friends to come to their senses, before something was done or said that might inflame the situation even further. "I'm sure the boys in the East don't want to be responsible for your quarrel. What a memorial that will be!"

The softly spoken words soothed Tom's temper and his anger subsided, as quickly as it had risen. His soot black face was split from ear to ear by a grin that almost cracked the lips off his mouth, his teeth glowing like South Sea pearls in contrast to his grimed cheeks.

"I'm sorry Owen. I'm as annoyed about it as you are, but it's hopeless! I've thought and thought, and there's just no way we can replace them. It will take years to train anybody else." He held out his hand to his long-time friend and butty, "It's the waste that annoys me, all those good men! It makes my blood boil every time I think of them. Shake 'hands butty it's this bastard job!" The two men grasped hands warmly the tension between them gone. Tom added, "you are right though, we must start singing again. We will never replace those who are gone, but we owe it to them to continue! I'll see about letting everybody know about starting back, as soon as I possibly can." The squabble between the two men had stilled the humour in the district. The laughter subsided and a resigned melancholic depression returned as the miners continued their repetitive existence of hewing, loading, carrying and hewing, as they had done for time beyond memory.

"I'm leaving you at home to make sure the men have their dinners and there's plenty of hot water for them to bath when they get in."

Shouted Kate as she turned her shoulders against the biting winter wind as she hurried off in pursuit of her two other daughters. They were a short distance in front of her, trudging wearily up the side of the frosty hillside heading towards farmer Meredith's barn. The barn of a place that had been the Davies' home since their eviction by the mining company. Berwyn Morgan had contacted her cousin and arranged for the family to move to Manchester, Today was moving day! Glancing behind them, her daughters slowed and allowed her to catch up, her feet scrunching through the crisp frost hardened bracken, as she lengthened her stride to join them.

"Be careful mam," Shouted Ivy as she took hold of her mother's bony elbow, "We don't want you to fall and break your neck!"

Kate smiled, ever grateful for the consideration shown by her daughters. "Thanks dear, but I'm not as ancient as that yet! I'm still pretty nimble on my feet, even on a slippery old hillside like this." Despite her remarks, she was pleased to allow the comforting hand to remain and support her. Farmer Meredith's barn lay below the crest of the mountain. It was surrounded by a large copse of beech trees that afforded some shelter from the icy blast that seemed to blow all year round. A stream of crystal-clear water ran to the stone trough that stood before the barn door. It had been the perfect winter haven for pregnant ewes and young lambs, now it had been the home of Mary Davies and her five young children. It was a miracle that they were not all dead from consumption. The clean water had kept the cholera away! She glanced at Ivy and Glenys as they struggled wearily upward, tugging two battered cases that had been kept in the chapel schoolroom to hold the crockery for the annual Whitsun tea party. Not one single objection had been raised when she suggested their donation to the Davies'. A visit to Jones and Porters the grocers, had provided two sturdy carboard boxes for the cups and saucers. "Be careful with those cases girls!" She shouted, raising her voice against the angry howl of the persistent blast. "They may not look like much but they are all we have!" The struggling girls looked back and managed only an agreeing nod as they strived to retain their footing on the slick path. It was hardly a path, merely a thin track along the mountainside, where the grass had been worn away by the thousands of walkers, men, women, children and courting couples who had wandered the mountain in search of peace and solitude. There had not been many courting couples seeking the seclusion of the barn since it had been occupied. Kate smiled to herself as she thought of how many sunburned or wet backsides the barn's occupation must have caused! All three women were panting hard by the time they stood before the barn. The battle against the ice and wind had taken full toll of the daughters' youthfulness and Kate's resolve. Mary Davies pulled the heavy door open for them to quickly enter. She slammed it closed behind them, before too much of the meagre heat escaped. Kate stared around in the gloom at the five small, frightened children who stared at her apprehensively. Mary Davies had done her best to turn it into a home, but a barn was still a barn! Bethan, the youngest child, recognising Kate, ran forward and hugged her knees. "Auntie Kate! Auntie Kate! You will never guess but we are going' for a ride on the train!" Kate bent down and picked the small child up. Opening her shawl she cuddled the tot against her warm body. "I know my darling, it is going to be lovely, better than going to the seaside!"

"Will it Auntie Kate?" Asked four-year-old William, "Only we isn't never seen the seaside so we don't know what it's like!"

"Don't you worry!" Kate looked at all the five children in turn. "Your Mam's going to be with you to look after you. She won't let anything nasty happen to you. All of you must listen to your mam and do exactly as she tells you." She looked at eleven-year-old Sandra, the eldest child. "You must be really brave and help your mam with the others and make sure they don't get frightened." Kate glanced around the barn as her eyes slowly became used to the dimness. She made out the shadowy figures of Herbert Humphries and Berwyn Morgan sitting at a roughly hewn wooden table, standing in front of the barn's only window, a small square of gleaming, frequently polished glass; set in a frame of unpainted oak. They both smiled when they saw her look in their direction. "What am I going to do Mrs. Leslie?" Pleaded

Mary Davies. "I don't know these people who have offered to take us in. What might I be takin' the children into?" Kate looked reassuringly at Mary Davies, hoping that she would find the right words to help this distraught lady. "You've answered part of your question yourself." She said. "They have offered to take in you and the children. No one has forced them!" She looked towards the minister hoping that he would come forward with some words of encouragement and help, but he was still engrossed in conversation with the union agent. Kate took a deep breath and continued. "Don't forget, they are family. They are miners so they know about the struggle to survive, they know how hard it's been for you these last three years trying to bring up the family without a man to help. But!" She paused to emphasise her words, "But, the most important thing, as far as you are concerned, is, things can't be any worse there, than they are here. That would be impossible! Heaven only knows how you have survived this long! It's a wonder you haven't all died of the plague or consumption or something worse!"

"It's been very hard Mrs. Leslie, I'll grant you that, but Rochdale is the other end of the country!" Said Mary Davies, her voice charged with emotion as she clasped and unclasped her fragile hands.

Herbert Humphries overhearing, Mary Davies' outburst moved from the table and approached the two ladies. He placed his arm tenderly around her shoulder and said, "I give you my solemn promise that everything is going to be fine. The Federation has been in touch with the Rochdale branch, and they have vouched for your relatives; they are hardworking Christian folk." The minister, also noticing the mother's anxiety, came forward to add his reassurance to Mary. "Don't you have any fear Mary, William Davies and his mother Annie, are looking forward to your arrival and have promised to give you a good Lancashire welcome and to take care of you and the children. Captain Thomas, of the Manchester Citadel for the Salvation Army, has said he will drop in on you to see that you are settling in. He will write to me to tell all of us, here at Cwmcarn, how you are getting on. "Kate smiled at Mary before saying quietly, "With all these people looking out for you and caring for you, what have you got to fear?" Let's get that train so you can start your new life!" Mary Davies looked gratefully at all those gathered in the barn. Her doubts settled; she began to prepare the children. Their few meagre belongings were gathered together. A few changes of threadbare clothing, some well washed sheets and half a dozen well-worn blankets were quickly layered into the two cases. "Not a lot for a lifetime's toil and back breaking work, is it?" Said Mary reflectively, as she observed her scant belongings half filling the two cases. "Don't worry Mary." Replied Kate. "It's the amount of love that's gone into the washing and mending of the clothes that's important. You've put in what you had, and that's a thousand times more important than money!"

"Talking of money!" Added Herbert. He pulled his wallet from his jacket pocket, "Here are the tickets for you and the children." He handed her the small cardboard tickets which she took and placed safely away. "You will catch the twenty past one train to Newport, then change to the three o'clock train to Manchester Piccadilly Station, then change for Rochdale. You might have to change trains at Crewe. Whatever happens, your relatives will be waiting for you at Rochdale station, ready to take you home." Herbert reached into his wallet once again." The lodge have decided to give you a small gift to help you on your way, it's not a lot but it may come in useful." He handed her five, ten-shilling notes. "One for each of the children." At the sight of the money, Mary's eyes became awash with tears. Her trembling hands were unable to grasp the notes as Herbert forced them on her.

"Come on Victor only one more wedge and then we'll be ready for loading. Victor, his eyes closed with determination pounded, the hammer, driving the wedge deeper and deeper into the glistening coal face. The task completed; he watched as the coal fell precariously to the ground. It was a thing of constant amusement to him now, of the way he had struggled, in the beginning, to control the sledgehammer and hit the wedge! It no longer caused him agony, it was now, just all in a day's work. He wiped the sweat from his brow with the back of his coal black hand. He winced as he felt a speck of grit break the skin, high near his hair line. A minute smudge of brick red blood covered the back on his knuckles. He dabbed the weeping graze with his finger tip in an effort to stop the modicum of blood that was trickling down his forehead. Tom, witnessing his nephew's efforts, bellowed with laughter. "Don't rub coal dust in the cut you silly young bugger! It will turn your scar blue!" Victor stopped. He remembered all the men he had seen with their blue scars. 'A permanent memento of coal mining!' His father had always called them! He remembered being told how coal dust permanently scarred a miner with livid blue scars.

"If that turns blue, your mother will kill the pair of us!" Joked Tom. I think you had better start combing your 'hair forward for a while! Just in case, you never know it might heal up proper!" Victor wiped his fingers as clean as possible on his breeches before touching the scrape once more. The graze felt no more than a quarter an inch long. "Mam won't even notice it!" He replied.

"Don't be bloody daft! you know as well as I do 'how she fusses over you, she'd wipe your arse if you let her! There's no way she'll not notice 'her little boy has been scarred!" Tom's voice was deadly serious as he made the remarks and Victor did not see the way his eyes sparkled or the knowing wink he have to Huw Stevens who had been an amused eavesdropper just outside the stall.

"You had better get that clean as soon as you get home." Said Huw after carefully examining Victors 'wound'! "You can never be too careful with cuts underground it could turn septic at the drop of a hat!" Stuart Thomas crawled out from his nearby stall to add his words of warning. "I don't think there's a girl in the village will let you touch 'her with a poxed up, scarred face like yours!" He cautioned. Victor, who had begun to show some concern, realised that his leg was being pulled, well and truly off by these 'serious miners'!

"Now I know you are takin' the piss out of me!" He retorted, looking at Stuart, "If a Bastard, as ugly as you, can find a wife and father three daughters, which thankfully don't look like their father!.....

"The milkman's a good looking fella down their street!" Interrupted Tom, glad to encourage any banter that lessened the tension that had existed in the mine ever since the disaster.

"One little scar!" Continued Victor, "Isn't going' to spoil my looks, just ask my mam!"

"Never mind your mam!" Laughed Stuart," I'm going' straight home after work and bury my working boot in the arse of the bloody milkman's 'orse!

CHAPTER 14

THE WALK FROM THE BLEAK, COLD, BARREN MOUNTAINSIDE TO the station passed in a flash. Kate remembered little of the journey, save for the continual grunting of the minister, as he struggled on the slippery paths and walkways with the half full suitcases. Her eyes twinkled, as she heard the occasional semi whispered oath leave Herbert Humphries lips, when his foot slipped on a white frosted leaf, or a withered brambled snagged at his woollen socks. How different, from the way her daughters had carried the suitcase up the icy mountainside! Herbert hadn't lifted anything heavier than a pen or his best Sunday hat for more than twenty years; and Tom, had maintained that the minister wasn't strong enough to carry even a message! He sweated if there were more than a double handful of ha' pennies on the collection plate. She pinched herself hard. How dare she think such shameful thoughts about these two wonderful men, who had inspired and led the community! Yet the twinkle remained in her eye.

They crossed the bridge over the River Ebbw. Kate glanced down at the black filth that roared beneath her, forcing its way down the valley, would it ever run crystal clear again? Its evil smelling muck, an imitation of the water that had once flowed by, it was now little more than an open sewer!

"We are here to help Mrs. Davies and her children onto the train." Answered Berwyn as he placed the suitcase down upon the cold grey stone of the platform. "She has her tickets. She's going to Rochdale, to live with some relatives." The minister rubbed his hand appreciatively now that it was no longer straining to hold onto the unwieldy handle "Evans!" Yelled the station master, to his station porter. "Help this lady with her luggage. These gentlemen look as if they need a rest!" Gordon Evans appeared from the station office wheeling a small wooden handcart, on which he placed the two cases. If ever a man was unfortunately named it was Gordon! Forever being called by his station master to 'help', the travellers, he had become known as Evan Elpus! A name that followed him around the village to his dying day. The railway bureaucrat examined the tickets meticulously, before allowing the party to follow Helpus' along the platform, to await the arrival of the Newport bound train.

"The next train's expected in ten minutes!" Said the porter pleasantly. He took the cases off the trolley and placed them on the platform. "This is a nice spot to wait, you can watch along the track and see the train as it approaches." He smiled at the children, who were all staying close to their mother's side, "I love a ride on the train, I guess you young ones do too?" The children made no attempt to answer but huddled even closer to the protective skirt of their mother.

"Don't mind them Mr. Elpus," Answered Mary Davies. "They are all feeling very nervous today, we are moving away, and it's all been too much for them!"

"I'm sure you're aware of the family's problems. 'Mr. Evans'!" Kate replied with a heavy accent on the name Evans.

The porter chuckled at the mistake over his name and the hasty correction. "Course I 'have, I have been helping people at this station for nearly fifteen years now, so there 'isn't a lot goes on in the village that I don't know about." He smiled reassuringly at Mrs. Davies. "I have been 'helping people with their luggage so much that I often forget what my real name is too!" Herbert took a penny from his pocket and handed it to the porter, "Here you are Gordon, I know the railway's pay, isn't much better than the miner's!"

The porter took the coin and tucked it away in his own pocket. "Thank you very much Mr. Humphries. All contributions gratefully received. Every little bit 'helps as the old lady said when she piddled in the sea!" The bitter cold was intense on the exposed platform and the group began to shuffle from foot to foot in an attempt to stay warm and keep the harsh cold at bay. The children, with only thin coats and dresses were shivering uncontrollably. Mary Davies pulled her smallest children to her, to warm them as best she could.

Kate, who was also beginning to feel the cold in the tips of her fingers and at the ends of her toes, remarked, "The train will soon be here and you will all be safe and warm, inside a nice comfortable carriage. When you get to Newport Mary, make sure you wait in a nice, warm waiting room. The matt black train puffed into the station with a woosh of steam and a screech of breaks. It slowly ground to a halt, stopping with a jerk that made all the children jump with alarm. Berwyn pulled open a compartment door and took the cases inside. The excited children gathered around the open door and had to be pulled back by their mother, until the minister had finished loading the bags.

"In you all get." Said Kate as she lifted the youngest girl in, "Find yourselves a seat and do as your mam tells you." She have Mary a peck on the cheek as she entered and added, "It'll all come out right in the end, you'll see. Be brave! You will be in all our prayers!"

Herbert took five shillings from his pocket and handed them to Mary I expect the children will be hungry before you get to Rochdale this will get you all a hot meal." He handed Mary a pile of coppers. "These are for the porters, you will need help with the cases." As they were saying their goodbyes, the 'up train' from Newport to Ebbw Vale screeched to a halt, opposite them on the other platform. The compartment became foggy, as steam from the arriving train flooded in through the open door. Berwyn quickly secured the door with the Davies family seated snuggly inside the carriage. Kate stood waving as the small train huffed out of sight, heading towards Crosskeys and eventually Newport. The party made their way back to the village, their way partly obscured by the white clouds billowing out of the tall funnel as the Ebbw Vale train set off on the next part of its valley journey. As they crossed the canal bridge from Chapel Farm. Kate thought she saw a sailor hurrying a few hundred yards ahead. She only knew one sailor. Sylvie Thompson's husband, George, but he was at least two hundred miles away at sea!

Victor closed his eyes and waited for the explosion and the clogging cloud of dust. He heard Huw shout the all clear and began to trudge back to the stint, his nose and mouth full of the bitter tase of coal dust. His life seemed to be filled with monotony, hammer, hide, lift and shove; repeated endlessly, day after weary day. Most nights he was glad to go home, bathe, eat and sleep! His head felt as if it had hardly touched the pillow when it was time to start again. The men might joke but when would he ever have time to meet a girl, never mind anything else! He reached the face and its pile of broken coal, which he began to gather.

"We seem to be working harder than ever. "Said Tom, as he wiped the back of his dirty hand across his sweating cheek, "Still, at least we are being paid for all this lovely steam coal we are sending up the shaft!"

Victor closed his mind to every thought except the one-of moving the coal in front of him. Lift the lumps, shove the corve! Lift and shove! Victor, on the verge of exhaustion pushed the empty corve back to the stall, where Tom was finishing the propping of the roof with a heavy wooden wedge which he was hammering into place, on top of a prop, with the side of his mandril. The job completed Tom looked around at his nephew, "You looked bloody knackered Victor. Take it easy for a while, you've got to give your self time to get over the accident."

"I'll be alright Tom." Victor replied, glad of a chance to sit down and talk for a few minutes. "It's just that we don't seem to be doing' anything with our lives, just work and sleep work 'and sleep!"

The older man looked fondly at his nephew, seeing himself twenty years ago. There had been a fire in his belly then, a burning ambition.

The pit had soon extinguished it. Talent didn't matter, potential was for those who could afford to develop it. Workers and miners had to know their place, and if they wanted anything better, there were those who made sure that they remained subservient! Dig the coal and if you are lucky I'll continue to let you work for me, be grateful. I'll throw you the occasional bone from time to time! If you don't do as I say I'll close the mine and starve you into submission. It had always been so and would always be so. The greedy would always bleat the word envy, when they saw the hungry asking for a fair share at their trough! "Victor, You have got brains, the only way the likes of us are going to achieve anythin' is through the Union! Help the 'Fed'. The bosses will just milk us for all they can get. The only way to help your self is to fight to improve the lot of everybody. But mark my words, never let your guard down. 'cos they'll get their own back, even if takes them twenty years ! If you ever think the struggle is won or over, that's when they are at their most dangerous, you can never trust them!" Victor had never heard his uncle speak so passionately or angrily about anything before, he was panting with emotion. "I didn't mean to upset you Tom. It's just that everything down here seems so pointless! We all seem resigned to our fate and accept it. If we are not killed in an accident, we'll end up as invalids or cripples!"

"Never accept it, Victor!" Tom Jabbed his nephew in the shoulder to reinforce the message, "but you can't change anything by yourself. Get involved with the 'Fed'!"

"Bloody hell! "Who's the morbid bastard on the bloody soapbox? Evan Wilkinson called out from the darkness. "If I 'had a 'hankie I'd 'have a bloody good cry! Sod them all is the only answer, if you get the chance kick them where it really 'hurts, they'll do the same to you if you let them."

"I'll tell Kate he was on about kicking somebody in the taters and she'll stop him in 'his tracks!" Shouted Stuart. "We try not to start your uncle off 'cos once started e goes on for ever and a day!"

"Alright I'll stop, but you all know how I feel about the only way to change things down here!" Concluded an exasperated, Tom.

The Lamp

Petty Officer George Thompson, marched briskly past the hotel and along the dusty main street. His brightly polished boots sparkled as their well nailed soles scuffed over the exposed stone of the roadway. He looked neither left nor right but strode purposefully towards the mine, dressed in his best 'parade uniform'. He patted the comforting heavy weight that bulged out of the knapsack that he carried effortlessly. Perhaps it wasn't true, and he wouldn't need them! He had walked through George Street and was approaching the narrow track along the mountainside that the miners used to walk to the mine, every morning. When his nerve began to fail him, he stopped and put the bag carefully at his feet, reaching into his tunic he pulled out a tattered letter, and, read it for the thousandth time! He stood and cried like a baby for several minutes, with tears streaming down his salt hardened cheeks. His nerve and anger restored, he snatched up the knapsack and marched on. Leaving the last terraced house behind him, he walked past the entrance to the Cwm Gofapi valley. The locals always called it the 'lappy'. In fact, when he asked for the Cwm Gofapi, no one knew where you meant! He slowed down to look at its entrance, guarded by almost half a dozen towering beech trees, their bare branches clawing defiantly up at the overcast sky. He had courted Sylvie in that secluded valley, when they had been much younger. She had run barefoot through the honey sweet grass and had splashed merrily in the pure, bright stream. He had thought the stream was the perfect reflection of her purity and devotion. He had marvelled in the slimness of her waste as he held her in his arms, almost afraid to hold her lest she shatter in the urgency of his grip! Closing his eyes, he remembered the clear brilliance of her eyes and the deep flush of her cheeks as their lips met. Her hair had radiated with a luminescent flame as she tossed it against the fading sunset. Sylvie! How could you? He dragged himself reluctantly away striding to the 'spout', another streamlet; this time, one of pristine quality. He cupped his hands under a diamond bright overflow, feeling its icy coldness cascade through his palm, numbing his clamped fingers. He raised his hand to his mouth tasting the ambrosial nectar as its frigid freshness dribbled over his tongue. There had been no frigidity when Sylvie had surrendered to him on their wedding night! Her warmth and sensuality had completely overwhelmed him. Her passion had overshadowed his ardour as she had enjoyed, not endured him! The chill of the water brought him back to his senses and be resumed his dreaded journey. He walked through the open colliery gate and headed purposefully for the manager's office. A Shunting engine was loading coal near the pit head and the mine blacksmith was toiling with a red-hot iron bar which he was bending across a massive anvil. The ringing of his hammer resounded around the colliery, as he pounded away with his heavy hammer. No one shouted a greeting or waved a welcoming hand as he reached the office door. He turned the handle silently and entered. Sylvie's office was empty, the seat she occupied with such pride and confidence was thrown back against the wall, her hat and coat hung neatly on the dark stand in the corner. Removing his cap, he placed it quietly on the desktop, before tip toeing to the manager's office door. Placing his ear against its varnished smoothness he listened intently. He heard Sylvie moaning breathlessly, with an urgency that he knew only too well!

Soundlessly he turned the handle and opened the door. Clothes were strewn around the room and the two naked lovers were intwined on the large desk, which creaked unmercifully in response to the powerful thrusts of its occupants. Sylvie her eyes tightly shut, had her legs wide open as she knelt below Phillip Gregory urging on his thrusts to increase her delight and abandonment as she submitted to him totally. George, his face an impassive mask, his eyes ablaze with anger yet filled with the tears that ran from his very soul, quietly opened his knapsack. His hand closed easily around the plain wooden grips of the seventeen-inch Lee Enfield sword bayonet, its razor point gleamed wickedly as he withdrew it from its scabbard and brought its cold steel out into the cold light of day. With the stealth and cunning of a Bengal tiger stalking its unsuspecting prey he crept behind the oblivious, squirming couple. "Deeper! Deeper!" Moaned Sylvie. "Oh that's it! Oh Phillip! Faster faster!"

Standing behind Gregory's heaving naked back, he raised the bayonet in both hands with the hilt cupped firmly in his right palm, with a muffled oath, he closed his eyes and plunged the weapon down with every ounce of his strength. The bayonet entered between the fifth and sixth ribs, passing through a lung and bursting the heart, before appearing through the unsuspecting mining official's chest in a torrent of blood and gore. Gregory's dying body shuddered, his eyes opened wide in terror and the scream of agony died in his mouth as his teeth clamped together severing his tongue! Sylvie annoyed at his interruption of her sexual enjoyment opened her eyes and began to complain when she noticed the horrendous gash that had appeared in her paramour's chest, soaking her with his precious life blood. He collapsed onto her, a lifeless bloodied corpse, driving the breath from her body and stifling her screams deep within her throat. George lifted the bayonet and impaled the body three more times before dropping the gore drenched shaft. Sylvie tried to push the corpse away, but the lifeless body pinned her to the desk top. Unable to move, she became aware of the grisly form of her husband looming intimidatingly over her. She had never seen such a look of loathing on his face, a dreadful, grim, detestation of her! She began to plead but one flash from his malevolent eyes silenced her; and chilled her body to the bone! Leaving his wife trapped beneath her employer he reached onto the floor to pick up Gregory's tie and belt; using both he tied the living woman to her dead philandering lover.

"Don't you say a single word," He snarled, through tightly clenched teeth. "Not a single word or you will join your lover now! Your actions have spoken for you today, more loudly than any words that might come from your betraying lips!" He took the creased letter from his pocket. "I received this!" He waved the letter in her frightened face. Reading from the letter he snapped out. "Your wife has betrayed both you and her marriage vows with her boss. Come home quickly and unannounced to find out for yourself the truth of her deceit!" He picked up the sanguine blade, pushed the note onto the shaft and impaled it once more into the corpse, where it protruded grotesquely into the air. "Is it too much for a man to expect his wife to be faithful?" The tears had returned to his eyes and were unashamedly running down his cheeks in torrent's. "Have I treated you badly? Have I not provided for you?" He looked at his blood encrusted hands and arms. "You'll not win, the whole world will know what you are! You'll die with this on your conscience, although I doubt if you have a conscience; you always placed yourself first, second, third and every place in between it and last! At least your own kind will know what you are and the evil spell you have cast." He put his hand into his large tunic pocket and pulled out a Webley 455 mark IV service revolver. He waved it in his wife's petrified face, "The hangman won't have me, but the gutter shall have you!" He gathered all the discarded clothes off the floor and took them to the office window, where he drew back the curtains, pushed up the sash and thew out the clothes, before reclosing the window.

"I loved you with a longing that filled my soul! I wasn't to sleep every night, when I was at sea, with your name on my lips. But you have been betraying me, and my love and devotion. What a fool I have been!" He placed the revolver's barrel against his wife's temple and pulled the trigger. "Wait for me in hell!"

The pistol's report echoed throughout the office and pit head. George Thompson, bent over, pecked his wife once on the cheek, sat on the floor and put the pistol into his mouth!

The scandal spread through the village faster than a message carried around the chapel's pews. Accidental death occurred with a heart wrenching regularity, but murder and violence; it was almost unknown in a small village like Cwmcarn! Two bloody murders and a suicide, it was more gossip than a miner's wife could bear; and the wagging tongues were out in force! This was too much for spreading over the garden fence, this called for communal gatherings. The small River Carn rushed by the solid houses of Feeder Row, as it ran alongside the feeder stream for the clogged waters of the Newport to Crumlin canal. The feeder was little more than a trickle, ever since the Nantcarn reservoir had burst, almost thirty years previously, and drowned the workers at the ill-fated flannel factory. The dam had been drained and several houses had been built on its dry bank, modern brick buildings, each with its own outside lav. The ladies of Feeder Row had stopped their washing and cooking and were outside in the street, their woollen shawls pulled snugly around their shoulders.

"They were stark naked! Not a stitch between them, when her 'husband caught them at it! Cackled Doris Morgan, to the eager crowd that had gathered around her. "I heard the police had to get her off him with a crowbar!" They all giggled.

"My husband needs a crowbar to get on me, not off!" Giggled Elsie Cousins. She looked around before continuing in a whisper. "They reckon it was still stiff when they pulled 'them apart! And it wasn't that rigor whatever that is!"

"It couldn't have happened to a more deserving' sod!" Added Pam smith. "I'm wondering how they are going' to get the coffin lid shut?" Screeched Elsie. "Perhaps they'll have to snap it off!"

"That isn't a problem they'll have with your husband's coffin lid is it Pam?" Laughed Doris.

"Just leave my William out of this if you don't mind!" Shouted Pam, her eyes blazing. She was always ready to leap to the defence of her husband. "Your, 'little Willie', you mean!" Joked Elsie as all the other wives screeched with laughter.

"Stabbed him right through the heart he did. And I didn't think the swine had one!" Elsie continued, her captive audience lapping up every word. "Then 'he must 'have blown her brains out before 'he did himself in! My Moses was one of the first to go in the office. 'He was helping Mr. Stevens take more explosive down the pit. Two bangs it was, so they all ran to the office." She paused to look at the listeners and ensure she had their complete attention. "Blood and brains all over the place he said there was! With Phillip Gregory and that slut tied together. her poor 'husband must have caught them at it!"

"I wonder if he let them finish?" Sniggered Elsie.

"Would you?" Snapped Doris annoyed at the interruption! "Anyway, as I was saying', they didn't 'have a stitch between them.

There was a note on the knife in Gregory's back. My Moses don't read to good but 'he reckons as how Mr. Stevens said it was one telling' George Thompson about 'is wife's carrying's on!"

"I wonder who sent it?" Said Pam Smith. "It is responsible for three deaths!"

"I don't know who the hell it was." Answered Doris. "But it wasn't their fault, it was them two adulterous buggers in the office! And anyway, Gregory got 'is just desserts. Good riddance I say!" An angry murmur of agreement ran around the crowd of women, fuelled by feelings of genuine hatred, for the man held responsible for the explosion that had devastated the village.

"I've been really depressed what with all that has been and happened to the village this last twelve month and' more, but," A huge grin split her face and beamed across her toothless mouth, "The thought of going' to that old buggers funeral has cheered me up no end!" Cackles and gurgles filled the air as the women gave full vent to their feelings.

"Yes!" Guffawed Elsie, almost doubled up with laughter. "After the old buggers buried, let's ask to have him dug up so, we can enjoy it all over again!"

"The more I think about it," laughed Pam Smith, "I'm only sorry I didn't owe the dirty old sod any money!"

Thomas Owen Price picked up the earpiece of his telephone. As with many of his social class, he had a great mistrust of all new-fangled contraptions. "Hello! Owen Price here."

"Just be quiet and listen Thomas!" Shouted a voice that he recognised as belonging to Sir Michael Fairfax. "Gregory's been topped, that letter to his floozie's husband, did the trick! He was starting to get too greedy for his own good. He knew too much, especially for one of his sort! If the papers' get on to you old boy, just say how shocked we all are etc. And our thoughts are with his family at this time. You know the usual stuff. Mention that the company intends to send the family five hundred smackers to help them cope."

"I heard that he'd bought it!" Responded Owen Price. "I haven't heard about the circumstances, but at least he's out of our hair now and we are in the clear."

"Just play it by ear old boy. Say, we don't know anything, but we are terribly shocked and are sorry that something like this should have happened." Fairfax hung the earpiece back on the telephone. He reached across his polished rosewood desk and opened his cigar box. He selected a thick Havana from inside and rolled it appreciatively under his nose. He closed his eyes and began to think. Now that Gregory was out of the way, the company would have to find another representative to manage the Cwmcarn Colliery. It would have to be someone less demanding than Gregory, he had become a grasping bastard! It would have to be a chap from the right background, a fellow who could do as he was told, keep his mouth shut, and make sure the coal came up the shaft, or he smiled to himself as he put a match to the end of the cigar; he would have to write another letter!

CHAPTER 15

The days had begun to lengthen, marking the beginning of the winter's end. The silver birch and majestic beech trees were starting to show all the welcoming signs of rebirth. Tiny green buds were appearing, that would soon explode with the joy that Spring had arrived. Life was still hard, but, at least when the sun shone, it made it easier to forget your troubles and heartaches. Kate gazed from her kitchen window. The blackbirds were busy in the bushes, squabbling with one another for the best nesting materials. Her attention shifted from the dough she was kneading, to the mountainside. It no longer seemed all grey, the colour was gradually reappearing. The bluebells would soon burst from their lazy slumber and carpet the hillsides with their wonderful mauve sheen. She thought then, of her youngest son. Victor had taken the news of the seriousness of his burns remarkably well. Too well! The whole family had gathered to break the news that he would have to forget his dreams of ever gracing the stage as a concert pianist. He had smiled in a way that she had never seen before, it was a way that even she did not understand. "Don't worry, I guessed something was wrong when the stiffness didn't go away. How can a pit boy expect to be trained for anything other than pit work anyway!" He had left the house and walked the mountain tops, alone with himself and his tears, for five or six hours. He returned to the house red eyed and exhausted, and no one had mentioned the subject for the last three weeks.

"Penny for your thoughts." Ivy said, she came quietly into the kitchen, whilst her mother gazed listlessly at the mountainside.

"What! Oh, it's you Ivy." Kate smiled at her daughter, as she came up to the table. She looked at her, she was growing into a beautiful woman. Spring was in the air; she began to wonder when the men would start to come calling. As her own grandmother had always said, 'It', will drag them ten times farther than gun powder will ever blow them!' Looking at the way Ivy was growing there was going to be some pretty big blowing in the months ahead!

She kept her thoughts to herself and replied, "I was just looking out and thinking Spring is on the way, I can't wait! This has been the worst Winter I can remember." She shuddered, as invisible icy fingers clawed their way along her spine. "We have had nothing but trouble, I can't remember a year as bad as this one! And there have been some bad ones."

Ivy put her arms around her mother's neck squeezed hard and said, "We'll be fine, you'll see. There's too much love in this family for this to get us down! We'll pull together, help each other and always look out for one another." She looked deeply into her mother's serene brown eyes. "It can't be any other way mam, after all, it's the way you brought us up!" Misty eyed, Kate placed her flour white hands around her daughter, and with tears splashing down her cheeks planted a kiss on Ivy's forehead. The two women remained wrapped together for several minutes before Kate pulled herself away and remarked, "Come on Ivy let me make this bread or there won't be any for supper!" She loved all her children with an intensity that often filled her with dread! The dread of being unable to cope with the thought that she wouldn't be able to survive, if anything happened to any of them. Yet, in a mining community, you often had to!

The afternoon sun had dipped behind the mountain's crest and was beginning to cast long shadows behind the trees. The house was filled with the taste tingling aroma of freshly baked bread. It was a smell that would have driven a hungry man totally and utterly insane. Ivy had hovered around the kitchen in the hope of cutting the freshly baked crust, off the cooled loaf, before it got too cold, smothering it with a pat of golden butter and sating her desire for the mouth-watering morsel! She had touched the loaf several times, only to discover it was still too hot to cut. She happened to glance out of the window. Bouncing and bumping its way along the dirt road was a large black car. It was the biggest car Ivy had ever seen. The black paintwork gleamed and shone in the afternoon sunlight, the chrome of the radiator and wheels sparkled intensely.

"Mam! There's a car coming along the street. It's even bigger than Doctor Devlin's!" Ivy watched as it weaved slowly in and around the holes of the rough stone filled track, that they used as a road. She laughed as she watched the posse of young boys running, screaming and laughing after the dark mechanical monster, that was chugging slowly onward.

"Perhaps the doctor has had a new car." Answered Kate rather disinterestedly, "If it's not his, it must be the undertaker's. Nobody else has a car! It might be the new manager's he's expected soon."

"If it is the new manager, he's well and truly lost!" Added Ivy. Her interest aroused by this unusual sight. Cars never came into the village; they always went along the main road! The rapidly approaching vehicle must have been doing almost ten miles an hour! It was being driven by a man in a dark suit wearing a black peaked cap. "There's a chauffeur, driving the car mam!" She shouted, "It must be someone really posh. I wonder what they want in our street!"

Kate, her interest aroused by the excited urging of her daughter looked out of the window. Ivy was right, there was a large motor car driving fairly quickly up the hill. She was able to see the outline of the passenger sitting in the roomy rear seat, although she couldn't make out who the passenger was, or what he wanted.

"No doubt the gossips, will be able to tell us all about it later on." Kate replied. "Come on, let's get on with the men's dinner or we'll never get it ready in time." Kate left the window and walked across the kitchen to the fireplace, its dull gleam a testament to the morning's black leading. A pot of stew was simmering gently over a small fire, it's lid rising from time to time to allow a spurt of heavenly scented steam to escape and disappear up the chimney with a sharp hiss. She lifted the lid and gave the stew content's a stir with a smooth polished ladle. She lifted the large wooden spoon to her lips and tasted the brew appreciatively. She smacked her lips in satisfaction. It was amazing what you could do with scrag end and a little patience!

"Mam! Come quick!" Exclaimed Ivy, so suddenly and urgently that Kate dropped the lid back onto the pot with a clatter. "The car's stopped outside our house!"

The chauffeur parked the car outside Kate's front door. Pushing his way through the crowd of excited children he knocked loudly. He turned to stare at the mob of ruffians mobbing his beloved Rolls Royce, smiled and said through clenched teeth, hoping that his passenger didn't hear, "Bugger off you little sods! Go on, bugger off before I fetch me 'and around some of your ear' oles!" He smiled once more, turned, and rapped his knuckles once more on the door.

Kate, busily brushing the flour from her hands and pinny rushed and opened the door.

"Are you Mrs. Kate Leslie?" Enquired the driver glancing over his shoulder to scowl at one bold youngster who touched the car's paintwork with a dirty, sticky finger. He turned back towards Kate, his face now wearing a wonderfully artificial smile. The kind that hired help always used when addressing those they considered to be their inferiors.

"The mother of Vitor Leslie and sister of Thomas?"

Kate, her mind racing and her heart bouncing could only manage to squeak out, "yes, there hasn't been any trouble, or another accident has there?"

Oliver Robson, the chauffeur, renewed his condescending smile before answering, "I don't believe there's a problem, but his Lordship." He indicated the passenger in the rear of the car, "Would like to speak with the two gentlemen in question."

"They are both down the mine and won't be home for at least another four hours." Answered a somewhat surprised Kate. She never felt inferior to anyone, believing that all respect, had to be earned, not simply inherited as the result of an accident between the bedsheets. The situation had caught her off guard, and this man's attitude was beginning to irk her. "They are both working! The men in this house, work hard for their living!" The chauffeur smiled again, touched his cap and returned to the car, where he spoke quietly to the passenger. Robson, returned to Kate, "His Lordship, the Earl of Gwent, asks that you allow him to wait with you while I go to the mine and fetch your son and brother."

Kate and her daughters watched thunderstruck as the old patriarch sat comfortably in an armchair as the car roared off to the mine, pursued by the boisterous group of children. Kate looked from the Earl to her children and back again. In a situation such as this, there was only one thing to do! Put the kettle on!

CHAPTER 16

THE DOOR BURST OPEN, AND VICTOR RUSHED BREATHLESSLY, INTO the kitchen, closely followed by Tom, who was also showing signs of exhaustion and anguish.

"What's the matter Mam?" Snapped Victor, his eyes exhibiting the worry that was eating away inside his aching head. "We had a message to leave the pit and come straight home! What's happened Mam?"

"Is it one of the girls?" Interrupted an equally distraught Tom. He thought back to when they had both been working at the face, a little over an hour previously and the paralysing effect that the message had, had on them." Huw Stevens just said we were to come home immediately!" Tom continued. He remembered the way they had stumbled and ran back to the pit bottom. No one had spoken a word to them on the journey, everyone must have known of the message and been afraid to speak about it, jumping to the same distressing conclusion as the fleeing pair. He had listened to every creak and groan as the empty cage ascended the shaft. At the pit top they had both run! Victor's, younger legs and lungs had ensured he arrived home a few seconds before Tom. Both men, covered from head to foot in coal dust, stood at the kitchen door; almost afraid to enter, in case their fears proved to be true. Looking in, they saw all the family members gathered around the table, which was covered with the Sunday best tablecloth and the 'special' China, that was only ever dusted, never used! Kate and the girls were drinking tea from the fragile, porcelain cups! Victor noticed a well-dressed man sitting comfortably, in Tom's armchair toasting his toes in front of a blazing fire. He leaned back smiling at the two filthy miners. Victor was sure he should recognise the man sitting in the chair, he was certain he had seen him before, but couldn't quite remember where!

Kate jumped to her feet at their arrival and clucked disapprovingly at their appearance. "We have a guest who's come a long way to meet you both, all the way from the South of France and London!" She nodded politely at the venerable old man sitting contentedly in the armchair. "It's his Lordship, the earl of Gwent our mine owner. He's come to say thank you for rescuing him from the mine!" Victor then realised that the man in front of him was the same man that he had carried, and sat with, on that fateful morning. No wonder he didn't recognise him, he had looked haggard, pale and extremely dirty; in fact, much of his face had been covered with dried blood; it was often impossible to recognise your own grandmother in the half light of the safety lamps! Before either man had a chance to speak Kate ushered them both out into the back yard where Ivy was already filling the tin bath with hot water. "I know its cold out here, but you can't wash in front of the fire today, not in front of the Earl anyway." Kate ordered. "Clean yourselves up, then upstairs the pair of you and change into clean clothes. Make sure you put on some decent clothes, no frayed cuffs or collars. We may be poor but, you are both gentlemen!" Ivy left towels and a large square of coarse flannel at the side of the bath. "I've dropped a bar of carbolic in the water for you both to use." Ivy said as she wasn't back inside the house.

"I wonder what the old bugger wants?" Said Tom, stripping to the waist and washing himself in the warm water. "There's only one way to find out I suppose...." He scooped a large double handful of water over his face and chest before fumbling in the bathtub for the evil smelling soap.

Tom and Victor stood at the table, they positively gleamed, following their open-air bath. Both were dressed in their Sunday chapel suits. Their only suits! When Kate ordered you to make yourself presentable, you did, or else!!

The earl stood up and faced the two men. His florid face adorned with a smile from ear to ear, a veritable throat slitter! A livid scar, visible just under his hair line, was to be a permanent reminder of his escape and rescue from the underground inferno. He held his hand out to both men and said, "I thought it was about time I came and thanked you both personally, for saving my life. There are those, however, who won't thank you for that! I would have come sooner only I've been out of the country. Doctor's orders. Said I had to have plenty of sun and relaxation!" Tom allowed himself a knowing smile, he had been back at work the morning after the explosion. It was alright for some! The earl noticing the quizzical look cross Tom face continued. "I don't remember much about the accident, or the next month following it, for that matter. Something to do with the blow on my head, according to the doctors. Although, they have said, my memory should get a little better. The only thing I can recall is being looked after by young Victor in the stables. I understand you both helped to carry me out."

"We did have help your Lordship." Tom answered, then he continued with a smile on his face and a twinkle in his eye. "There's no way just me an' Victor could have carried you out!" The earl guffawed heartily and patted his paunch happily, before responding, "That, I can believe, there's far too much roast pheasant gone into making me what I am, for me to take offence. But I believe I could forgive you almost anything. One of the few things I remember about that day in the mine was being carried to the pit bottom, and, if the ladies will excuse me," He looked at Kate, "Was the continual moaning about carrying, old lard arse!" He bellowed with laughter once more, whilst Tom and Victor looked sheepishly at one another. "I've been called many things in the past; some of them to my face, but mostly behind my back." Victor could feel the colour rising in his cheeks and his ears began to tingle as they became hotter and hotter. The earl noticing Victor's embarrassment laughed all the louder and said, "Don't worry lad, I think the name fits me to a 'T'. You will never know how much I admire you, and the others, for carrying me out of that hell hole, when you were also injured."

"I just hope your lordship's memory doesn't improve too much!" Joked Tom, "In case you start remembering' a few of the other phrases!"

"I was sorry to hear that young Victor won't be fit enough to realise his musical ambitions." The earl sympathised. "But perhaps I can make amends. I have many business interests as well as my mining ones. Steel, shipping and textiles to name but a few. I would like to reward both of you for saving my life."

Tom was the first to speak, his words firing out automatically, before the earl had time to finish his well-rehearsed speech. "There's no need for any reward your lordship, we done what we would 'have done for anybody who was hurt in the mine. Down there, when we 'have a disaster, we all 'help one another and anybody injured is a butty to take care of!" The earl looked at the determined expression and marvelled at the frankness of this 'uncouth' gentlemen! "I did not mean to offend, but I am the coal owner, I am forever in your debt, therefore, you will accept my reward."

Kate, annoyed at her brother's outburst and lack of manners, quickly interrupted. "Tom, where are your manners. His lordship has come a long way to speak to us, at least listen to what he has to say!"

"I meant no offence your lordship, it's just that we are so used to looking out for one another underground, that I couldn't help myself!"

"I intend giving both you, and Evan Wilkinson a reward of a hundred and fifty pounds each!" He paused, waiting for the excited gasps from the girls to subside, noticing that Tom remained unmoved. "What's the matter man! Anyone would think I've just ordered you to be flogged. Hell! Isn't it enough?"

Tom, visibly shaken at this last remark, answered, it's more money than I have ever seen in my whole life sir. In fact, I don't know what I would do with an amount like that! If word of it got out, we'd all be murdered in our beds." It was the earl's turn to be shaken at the realisation of the implications, to them all, of a few hundred pounds!

"I know what you can do with my reward your lordship. Some of the miners was badly injured, the federation is doing' it's best to help them, but doctors' bills are expensive. If you don't mind, I'll just keep twenty or thirty pounds, to help the girls get their bottom drawers together, and the rest I'll use to help pay the doctors! I know some families who don't know where to turn to for help. Well, they can turn to me. That money, will give many people a good night's sleep, without worrying' about treatment or pain!" Kate looked proudly at her brother with more admiration than she had ever done before; he had moved in and supported her and the children when her Edward had died; he had never complained once or moaned about himself; his only thought had been to take care of her and the children. Now, once more, his thoughts were of others! If only the world were full of men such as this, poverty, injustice, greed and self-interest would be diseases that would disappear off the face of this earth!

"Only! Don't say the money came from me!"

"You shame me sir!" The earl replied." I should have realised the kind of man you were, as you struggled to carry me to safety, with little regard for yourself! You will accept the money for yourself and family, he said forcefully, that will not be argued about. I will pay another two hundred pounds to the federation on the understanding that it all is to be spent on medical care for the injured miners. And don't worry, I won't mention your name!"

The earl turned his attention onto Victor, who's mouth had dropped open at the mention of such sums of money, and the way in which they had been dismissed by his uncle. "You impressed me greatly in the stables young man. Your hands were obviously causing you great discomfort and distress yet, you were attentive to my needs and well-being. A credit to your mother's, upbringing and regard for your fellow man!" Kate, was certain her heart would burst with pride, hearing this gentleman paying her Victor, such glowing praise.

"I have made some investigations about you, young man," He smiled warmly at the bemused Victor. "Everyone speaks well of you. Your teachers complain that you should have completed your education, you were far too bright to end up working down the pit!" He noticed the frown appear on Victor's face, "Don't worry I won't send you back to school!" Kate's joy subsided at these words; education was her son's only hope!" I will allow you a few options." He paused to collect his thoughts, before continuing with his offers. "You can remain at the pit where I will see you are trained as a fireman, and I will ensure that you eventually become a mine manager, managing one of my mines. Or, I will arrange for you to be employed in my Newport shipping office, where you will train as a shipping clerk and bookkeeper. I will arrange weekly lodgings for you and allow you to come home at the weekend and for choir practice." Before Victor could reply, Kate shouted out. "He'll be delighted to work for you at Newport, your lordship. Explosions don't happen in offices!" Her heart was leaping, and the tears began rolling unashamedly down her beaming cheeks. He had seen the last of that dirty old mine, and it had seen the last of him!

CHAPTER 17

THE FAMILY WAITED EXCITEDLY ON THE DESERTED PLATFORM for the arrival of the five thirty Newport train, only Tom was missing, he had been at work in the pit for more than an hour. Kate and the girls, were busy fussing around Victor, ensuring he had enough clean shirts and vests. If Ivy didn't brush at imaginary specks on his collar two or three times, Christine did, at least a dozen! Kate clucked like an old mother hen, unable to decide if she was pleased to see Victor safely away from that dangerous pit, or unhappy at saying goodbye to her baby! Sanity won; he wasn't going to descend that gloomy shaft ever again. She smiled happily and squeezed his hand tightly. "Take care of yourself and don't do anything that you shouldn't!" She blurted out. "Don't be silly mam!" Victor answered, as he placed an arm affectionately around his mother's shoulder. "I'm only going to Newport; I'll be back on Saturday night."

"You listen to our mam!" Snapped Ivy, "You've never been anywhere on your own before, so just listen and be careful!"

"Newport is full of Jezebell's," Added Christine, her eyes twinkling and her mouth aflame with laughter, "They'll take one look at a strapping valley boy like you, and you won't stand a chance!"

"They won't stand a chance you mean!" Interrupted Ivy. "If they dare try to get their hooks in our Victor, mam will be down there like a shot! Won't you mam!"

"Stop teasing, all of you!" Kate ordered, "Victor is probably worried enough as it is. If he doesn't know the difference between a decent girl and one who will be after him for his money, I'll give up now!"

"Perhaps he wants to have a wild time himself mam." Continued Christine. "I said stop it!" Warned Kate, who was beginning to have second thoughts herself about letting her little boy, go!

Victor, who had become used to all the fuss and 'smothering', waited passively for the train, almost oblivious to the scheming women surrounding him. His mind in turmoil! The girls were right, he had never been anywhere alone! But it was a chance to succeed, a way to better himself and, he didn't have to go down that bloody pit, ever again! He thought back to the previous evening, when he and Tom were alone in their bedroom. Tom had seemed somewhat subdued, as he began to advise him. "I'm going to miss you young Victor, more than you will ever know, but I want to give you a few words of advice. I hope you don't mind, but even if you do, I am going' to say them anyway. There's no shame in striving to get on to better yourself. But there is disgrace in turning your back on your roots and disowning your birthright. Always remember where you came from with pride. Always remember, the love and care that you received from this family that made you what you are now, and what you are capable of becoming. Help others, and, if God is willing, you will get on. Don't become a boss with your nose always stuck in the trough of plenty. Treat every man with dignity and respect, look deeper than the dirt on his hands! Just remember that there is a house full of people here, who will be following' your every movement, make us proud of you. Never forget, it's people who are important, always remember people before profit! Care about people!" He was snapped back to reality by the loud hooting of the rapidly approaching train.

"Don't worry mam, I'll be fine!" Victor announced with more fervour than conviction, "After all, I'm only going to Newport, and it isn't ten miles away!" The train arrived at the same time as the tears! The train with a bellow of steam; the tears came in floods. Victor found it impossible to console his mother and three sisters so decided not to try! Four spotless white handkerchiefs appeared under four sobbing noses, as Victor, suitcase in hand, entered the empty carriage, after hugging his sisters and pecking his mother lightly on the cheek. He was somewhat bemused by it all. How did a sixteen-year-old say goodbye, even for a week? "I'll be back on Saturday. Cheer up all of you!" He shouted as the train shuddered and left the station with its usual Jerk. He settled back in his seat and watched the grim brown water of the Ebbw River run alongside the carriage. He watched the bright, clear water, of the Carn brook, become swallowed and tainted, as it met the filthy river at the ruins of the flannel factory that had been washed away, by the flood, almost thirty years previously. As Crosskeys approached, he closed his eyes and began to worry about what lay ahead. He smiled; it could be no worse than his first day underground!

Newport station seemed enormous, Victor was amazed by the hustle, bustle and constant movement that occurred, even at five to six in the morning wherever he seemed to look. Lifting his battered suitcase, he strode along the immaculately clean platform. Looking above his head, he saw the signs indicating the exit, up and over the foot bridge. He followed the crowd, marvelling at the way, each person remained aloof, no one talked, or even passed the time of day with those around them. Back home, a crowd such as this would have been a raucous gathering. Here, people seemed too busy and in too much of a hurry to enjoy the company of others, especially strangers! Tom had always said, it was more interesting to meet a stranger than an old friend. In Newport, no one seemed to have the inclination or patience. The crowd, with Victor at its tail, reached the barrier and the ticket collector. The official stood stiffly at attention accepting the tickets as they were offered, giving each cardboard oblong a scant glance, before depositing it into a tin resting on a small table at his right hand side; occasionally he would cut a small piece from the edge of a ticket with a shiny chrome clippers, before returning it to the traveller. Victor handed over his ticket which was consigned to the tin. "Excuse me." Enquired Victor pleasantly, "Can you tell me how to get to number 54 Stow Hill, please? The ticket collector looked at Victor, recognised him as a lost stranger and smiled, "Certainly sir." He replied in a deep bass voice. Impressing Victor immediately with the address of 'sir'. "Go straight out of the station walk ahead until you come to the High Street. Turn right walk for about two hundred yards and you will come to the Westgate Hotel. Stow Hill is the second turning on your right, just go up the hill until you reach number 54. That hill, is Stow Hill." Thanking the official, Victor lifted his bag and set off. He had never seen such tall buildings, some of them, must have had four floors! Even at this early hour activity was occurring, doors were being opened, windows cleaned, and pavement's swept clean. Walking along the High Street, he had his first sight of Newport's electric tram system, as an open topped tram rattled by, with its long feeding arm gulping in the electricity from the overhead power cable. Victor saw several people sitting in the lower, covered compartment, whilst no one ventured to sit upstairs in the early morning chill!

He Paused gazing as it disappeared along the road. He decided to tell his sisters, when he next saw them, about seeing his first tram. Perhaps, before the day was out, he might even ride on one! Walking briskly, he soon came to the Westgate Hotel it was an enormous hotel, it was the most imposing building, Victor had ever seen. Without stopping, he began the steady ascent up Stow Hill and was soon stood outside number 54. The lodgings had been arranged by the earl's merchant, Mr. Lewis Hay-Jones. He rapped loudly on the highly polished mahogany door, with the heavy brass handled knocker. The door was answered by a petite girl, wearing a lacey mop cap and a heavily starched pinafore, over a plain cotton dress. "Good morning," Said Victor, "I'm Victor. I have come to lodge with Mr. and Mrs. Woodland." He tried hard to pronounce his words very carefully. 'None of that common pit talk mind you!' His mother had warned him, 'make sure you talk proper, I don't want folks thinking you were just dragged up!'

THE LAMP

"Come in please sir," Replied the young servant." You are expected. If you'll wait here I'll fetch Mrs. Woodland." She left and disappeared up a wide, gleaming staircase, that rose from the hallway. Victor looked around, he was quite impressed, the whole house smelled of polish, just like home! But there was even more furniture, than in the manse! Hearing a stair squeak he looked up. Descending was a lady who looked a match for any of the prize fighters Victor had ever seen at the Risca Whitsun fair! She had arms that could crack a walnut at twenty paces; and a bosom that bounced and strained with every downward step; but she had one of the kindest faces Victor had ever seen, complemented by the happiest of eyes! "Hello Mr. Leslie, or may I call you Victor!" Thus began a friendship that was to last to eternity! "Melanie and I, will show you to your room, we've been told you like comfort and that's something all our guests get." Continued Eva Woodland. She lifted Victor's case as if it were a feather duster and headed back up the stairs. "Follow us. I hope you had a pleasant Journey. We'll let you settle in for a few minutes then I've instructions to send you to your office. We may not be the biggest lodging house or the poshest!" She continued, proudly. "But we look after our guests better than anywhere else in Newport." They took Victor to a small room on the second floor. The room was dominated by the bed. It wasn't particularly a big bed, it just looked it in the room. There was a thin wardrobe and a matching chest of three drawers, both gleamed with polish. Victor swore that they were more reflective than a glass mirror! A bowl and jug of water stood on the drawers. There was a slate fireplace surrounding a cosy coal fire that was burning warmly in the grate. The thing that held Victor's attention was a gas mantle above the bed, the house was lit with gas! Eva, noticed Victor's awed gaze and remarked, "Like I said, we've got everything here, we've had gas lights for two years." She placed the suitcase on the bed and continued, "We will help you unpack this evening when you get back in, you will have to go out now if you don't want to be late on your first morning!" She ushered Victor towards the door, "There'll be a nice hot meal waiting for you when you get back. Chin up it's better than a poke in the eye with a sharp stick! Melanie will take you to the tram stop. Catch the number 14 to the Docks. It goes right through Commercial Street to Commercial Road; tell the conductor you want to get off as near to number 94 as you can. Ask for the Kings Arms Pub!" Eva closed the door behind them. She was well known for her long speeches and instructions! She smiled to herself and sighed, 'it paid to be nice to someone recommended and sponsored by an earl!' He seemed a nice young man. A little rough around the edges maybe, but he seemed bright enough, and would learn quickly how to stand up for himself.

The youngsters left the house and made their way down the hill towards the Hotel. It was a pleasant Spring morning, and the sun was beginning to peep over the rooftops and warm the streets, that had previously been covered in shade. Melanie walked briskly, somewhat taken aback, that Mrs. Woodland had asked her to take this 'boy', to the tram stop! She was a house maid not a wet nurse! Why, he was at least two years younger than her! Victor, still awe struck with the size and strangeness of his surroundings dawdled, a few steps behind this' cool' young woman. "Keep up Mr. Leslie!" She snapped over her shoulder, "The trams run every four or five minutes, but there may be a queue and then you'll have to wait. It will mean you might be late for work!" And if that happens, she thought, it will be me who gets blamed! "It's only a little further."

"I'm sorry." Answered Victor pleasantly, "It's just that everything is new to me, and I was looking around to get my bearings."

"There will be plenty of chance for you to do that when you have more time! If you are late for work, the mistress will blame me, and I'll probably have to blacklead all the grates as a punishment! I did them all yesterday, and it's the one job I hate!"

Victor ran the three or four paces necessary to catch up with Melanie, "Please call me Victor, no one ever says Mr. Leslie!"

Melanie smiled at the strange valley boy now walking beside her, "it's something you can get used to, everyone will call you it when you work in an office. Anyway, Mrs. Woodland would have my guts for garters, if she ever heard me call you Victor!"

Victor began to realise that it was going to take even more change than he had imagined, if he was going to adapt to this new lifestyle. "Please, when no one is around, please call me Victor. I don't know anybody here and I would like to think I have one friend at least!"

Melanie, beginning to warm to this, 'lost boy', repeated the smile and said, "Alright, when no one is around, but if I get into trouble, I'll say it's your fault!"

"Where I come from," answered Victor, "Everyone is nice to one another, we don't bow and scrape. I need a friend, that's all. If you don't want too that's ok, but I don't think anyone will get into trouble, for just being friends! Anyway, I've three older sisters at home, and we are all friends, as well as relatives!"

"Come on Victor, she announced as they reached the tram stop, "My first friendly piece of advice is, sit downstairs, you'll freeze upstairs! The tram causes quite a draught when it moves. Ask the conductor for the nearest stop to the Monmouthshire Steam Ship Company offices. Most tram stops are about two hundred yards apart. If you look at the side of the road you will see a sign it says, 'Car stops here by request', stick your hand out and a tram will stop." A tram was rattling into view and Melanie waved her hand to flag it down. It screeched to a halt and Victor got on. 'Bugger the weather and the advice!' He thought, so he climbed the stairs to the top, he wanted to see everything! He wished he had taken Melanie's advice, a minute after boarding, as the wind began to whistle around him. Pulling up his jacket collar he stared wide eyed as the tram trundled along Commercial Street.

"Here we are sonny!" The conductor's call echoed up the stairway, "Monmouth Steam Ship company offices." Victor began descending the stairs as the tram began to screech to a halt. He stepped to the pavement and walked in the direction indicated by the conductor. A swarm of butterflies were churning away deep in the pit of his stomach and his legs felt as though his boots were made of lead, as he opened the imposing door that announced, 'Monmouthshire Steam Ship Company'. He was confronted by a severe looking man, wearing a dark blue, three-piece suit. He was almost completely bald except for a grey border around the back of his head, just above his ears, which stuck out almost at right angles, and supported a pair of gold framed circular reading glasses. A heavy silver chain ran from one side of the man's waistcoat to the other which, Victor, supposed must hold a similarly styled time piece. William Hyde, the office manager was sat behind a high wooden desk, it reminded Victor, of being summoned to face the teacher in school. He wondered if there was a cane hidden in the desk drawer.

"Good morning," Mr. Hyde remarked as he took his watch from his pocket, opened the lid and glanced at the time. "You will be Mr. Leslie? I'm pleased to see that you are punctual, ten minutes early in fact! Much better to be early than late!" He put the watch back into his pocket with a flourish but made no effort to rise to meet Victor.

"Yes sir! Good morning, my ma… I mean mother brought me up to believe punctuality is a virtue. I have been told to report here, to start work as an office boy."

"Mr Hay-Jones will see you in a short while, to see if a coal boy is suitable to be trained to become an office boy. Personally, if I had known they were looking for someone I would have recommended my nephew, a young gentleman!" He emphasised the last word, before continuing." With a fine education behind him, and a pedigree of family service to this company, of more than thirty-five years!" The man's obvious animosity began to irk Victor, he had always judged people on the way they worked and behaved. This man was implying with every word he uttered, that respect was not to be earned but delivered to those chosen by birth or some pre-ordained decree. This attitude, Victor decided, many years afterwards, was the primary reason for his determination to succeed against all odds! "Please take a seat until Mr. Hay-Jones is ready to interview you!"

CHAPTER 18

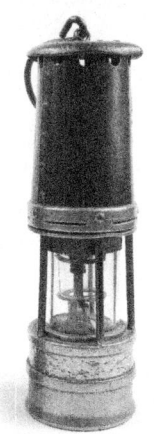

Lewis Hay-Jones welcomed Victor into his large, well-furnished office, but left him with the distinct impression that his apprenticeship and presence was to be endured more than appreciated. The man exhibited an aura of condescension, that Victor found extremely off putting, feeling acutely aware, that simply doing his best, was not going to be good enough. He would have to excel if he were to receive the most grudging of respect, he could expect little praise!

"The Earl told me that you are to start work in the office today and that you are to be trained in all aspects of ship management and coal and iron merchandising, I'll try …. as long as you are up to it!" Hay Jones paused waiting for Victor to make a comment, but none came. Victor sat silent and calm. 'Let the aggression come from others. Uncle Tom had advised, 'If they cannot provoke you, they will have to tolerate you. You must earn respect, no matter how hard it is. You will have to work twice as hard, for half the praise and recognition, because of where you come from!'

"The company runs Four Ships out of the Alexandra Dock." Hay-Jones stood and walked to the far side of his office, where a large map was displayed on the wall. "We export coal to Spain, France, and Italy. We do occasionally trade with North Africa." He pointed to the various countries and places as he mentioned them. "We import iron ore and pit wood from the Spanish port of Huelva. However, it is a great deal more complicated than it sounds!"

He returned to his desk where he sat down into his creaking leather backed, armchair. He picked up a gold nibbled pen, which he twirled between his fingers, before continuing. "You will start as an office boy, under Mr. Cuthbertson and his clerk Mr. Bailey. You will do as thy tell you and hopefully, learn."

He picked up a small brass bell that stood at the side of his blotting paper pad, rang it twice and waited for the door to open." His Lordship has arranged for you to be tutored on Monday, Wednesday and Friday evenings. A Mr. Mortimer Salvage will arrive at your lodgings for two hours at seven o'clock. He will teach you bookkeeping and endeavour to improve your grammar and mathematical skills. The earl has said you are to receive three pounds twelve shillings and six pence a week! A preposterous amount of money for a young man like you, if you ask me! Your lodgings will cost fifteen shillings and six pence per week. His lordship has paid the first week." The door opened and a young lady dressed in a full-length black skirt, and a white blouse topped with a high lace collar entered. Her dark hair was pulled high at the back of her head into a severe bun. "Naomi, take this young man to Mr. Cuthbertson, tell him it's the young man he's been expecting."

"Yes Papa." The girl answered. Victor guessed, that despite her harsh appearance, she was approximately his own age. They left the office and Naomi closed the door behind them.

Victor summoned up the courage to speak to this aloof young lady, "Hello my name is Victor, I am going to be working here. I hope we can be friends?"

Naomi turned to face this, 'common young man', of whom she had heard her father speak. The harsh look on her face disappeared, her appearance softened as she smiled, "I don't know, my father disapproves of me mixing with the office staff. "She took him through a door lined corridor, to an office labelled, 'Crewing and Dock Hire'. Mr. B. Cuthbertson. She knocked before taking him inside. There were two men in the office, which was lined from floor to ceiling with document's and journals. Both men sat at either end of a large letter strewn desk. Brian Cuthbertson looked up and smiled at the arrivals. "Don't tell me Naomi, this is my new office boy, Victor Leslie." He limped over to greet them at the door. As if guessing Victor's unasked question, he answered, "It's a wooden peg. Lost the real one to the Boers!" He said as he tapped his left 'leg'.

"Pleased to meet you Victor, I'm sure we will all get on just grand!" Naomi left the office closing the door securely behind her.

"Come and meet Trevor, Trevor Bailey the office under clerk. My right-hand man and," He said with a twinkle in his eye, "Very often my left leg man as well!" Victor shook hands enthusiastically with both men. It was a relief to find friendly faces, men willing to give him a chance before prejudging he was beneath contempt.

"Thank you." Victor replied, "I hope I can do a good job for you and be of help. I don't want to get in the way or cause any problems. Brian Cuthbertson allowed himself a satisfied smirk, as he thought of the interview that must have occurred, a few moments earlier, in the merchant's office. "Hay-Jones gave you a hard time no doubt. Always was and always will be an awful snob. He thinks he runs the company, but no one notices when he's away. In fact, more work gets done when he's not here to interfere!" He pointed to a chair mid-way along the document covered table and told Victor to sit down. Victor sat and looked around the office at the chaos that seemed to surround him. The room looked worse than the school room during a chapel jumble sale! It was amazing to think that either of these men would be able to find any relevant document without a major search!

Trevor Bailey laughed and said to Victor, "Looks a right mess, doesn't it? Well! We know where everything is, including contracts and document's we dealt with five years ago!"

"Yes," Continued Brian." There's method in our madness. Who are they going to replace us with? No one can come in here and take over from us without a great deal of problems!" Victor could see the merit in their argument, the office looked like the proverbial pig stye!

He felt at home immediately! He then glanced at their own work areas., both were scrupulously tidy.

"More to the point young Victor. "Added a smiling Brain. "We're both bloody good at our jobs." Victor sat straight in his chair and looked Brian straight in the eyes and asked the question that had been on his lips, ever since the earl had offered him this job in the shipping office.

"Please sir, what exactly am I expected to do?" He pleaded, "I expect you know about me and how I come to be offered this position." He shifted uncomfortably in his chair, before continuing, "I'm a miner who …. "Don't worry about who you were or where you came from." Interrupted Brian. "I started off as a puddler, at an iron works, then." He tapped his wooden leg. "I joined the army and fought in the Boer war. I was the earl's batman, he was a colonel then, I stopped a '303'! It shattered my knee; it was meant for his lordship. So, you see the place is full of those of us who have taken care of the old boy at one time or another, and he repays favours. But don't dare cross him!" Victor began to feel more at ease and warmed to these two jovial men. "Apart from Hay Jones," Brian continued, "We're all family men, from ordinary homes, who come to work to earn a decent wage to support our families."

"What about Naomi?" Victor enquired, "She seemed like a nice young girl."

"Just listen to the young bugger!" Laughed Trevor, "Hasn't been here five minutes and he's ready to take a shine to the bosses daughter!" Victor began to blush profusely and squirmed deeper into his seat, hoping that the floor would open up and swallow him whole, and hide his obvious embarrassment!

"Stop teasing the young fellow, Trevor!" Chided Brian, "It's Spring so obviously the sap's started to rise in the young lad's pencil! But you had better aim it a bit lower than the bosses daughter, cos if he catches you sniffing around there!" … He left the sentence unfinished, as he picked up a pencil from is desk and snapped it between his fingers, a warning of the retribution that would be exacted!

"What work am I going to do?" Asked Victor, making a hasty attempt to change the subject and move the conversation into an area that he wouldn't find so difficult. "I don't know anything about office work, but I'm a quick learner. I don't want to go back down the pit!"

Brian sat back in his chair and began to tell Victor something of the Monmouthshire Steam Ship company. "The company has four ships, they all sail from the Victoria dock, here in Newport. The earl owns coal mines and iron works. His coal comes down here, it's loaded onto a ship and is taken out to the customers. At the moment that happens to be in the south of France, the French navy uses our coal in their battle ships. We also send coal to Spain and Italy. Our empty ships sail to Spain, fill up with iron ore and take it to Liverpool, where the earl has it melted into iron. The ships then come here for another cargo of coal. It's simple!"

"It may sound simple to you," said Victor. "But what exactly, do I do?"

"The firm has four parts." Brian continued. "We take care of hiring dock workers and the crews' wages. Next door they handle all the storing and bunkering requirement's. Michael Porter and his office take care of the ship repairs and maintenance, and finally. Hugh Nelmes handles the ships' victualling, that means he makes sure the ships have enough food, and provisions for every voyage!" Victor was looking decidedly uneasy, as he struggled to take in all that has been said to him, it all seemed far too complicated for him to work out, let alone master!

"Don't worry Victor, you'll pick it up a little bit at a time, then before you know it you'll know more than all of us put together!"

"Don't worry!" Trevor added, "For a while, you'll just be our office boy. Making the tea, running errands, taking messages, fetching and carrying things. You know, just ordinary matters like that. Then when you become more proficient, we start you on some simple bookkeeping and who knows, you may even get to the docks side to see the ships loaded and unloaded."

The first day passed in a blur, before he knew it, it was six o'clock and Victor found himself on a tram, returning to Stow Hill. Despite the cold he sat upstairs once again, his youthful exuberance, totally overruling his common sense. He wanted to see more! He looked at his hands; then his clothes; it was the first time in his short life; that he had ever done a day's work and not gone home filthy dirty.

Victor pushed the empty plate away and sat back contentedly, with food like this and a lack of physical work it wouldn't take too long for him to become a 'lard arse'! He had just eaten a lamb chop all to himself, and it hadn't been a special treat!

"How about some of our special treacle tart to finish off the meal with Victor? Asked Mrs. Woodland approving as she surveyed his clean plate, "It's a pleasure to cook for someone like you. Why, if I didn't know better, I'd swear you have hollow legs! Where do you put it all?" Victor squirmed with embarrassment, "I'm sorry I didn't mean to eat too much, but I really did enjoy it. It was wonderful! Mam's a great cook, but we don't have much meat except for bacon, stewing beef or rabbit." "Don't apologise. Cook will be thrilled to know her food is appreciated. We won't tell her you are only used to bacon, rabbit and stew!" Laughed Mrs Woodland. "I have been told that a Mr. Salvage is coming here three times a week to tutor you. You may use my husband's study on the first floor. We have also been informed that you love to play piano, everyone is hoping that you will play ours for us. My James, bought it years ago, but it's never been played, we've kept it as an ornament in the parlour, if you promise to play for us from time to time, you may use it whenever you want too." Victor's eyed sparkled with delight, feeling he must be in heaven. All this food, a cushy job and a piano as well! "I love playing!" He could hardly contain himself as he replied, "I'll play for you, whenever you want me too, but I'm not as good as I used to be. I was burned down the pit and it affected my finger control. "He rolled his sleeves back to show her the scars on his arms. His left forearm was badly disfigured and extremely discoloured, whilst his right arm showed vivid scar tissue.

"You poor dear!" Sympathised Eva Woodland, "I had no idea. I wouldn't have dreamed of asking you if I had known."

"It looks worse than it really is." Victor answered, re buttoning his cuffs, "I can still play, it's just the doctor said I wouldn't be able to improve my playing as much as I had hoped to do. I would love to play for you."

"That would be wonderful. If you don't mind, the servants would love to sit in as well. Your tutor is due in five minutes. You could play for us after that, if you feel up to it?"

"It's the only way I know how to relax and unwind I can hardly wait!"

Thus began the first of many two-hour sessions with his new tutor. Mortimer Salvage. They always seemed to last forever. His head swam like a drunken priest, as he tried to memorise and cope with the mathematics of bookkeeping, with which he was bombarded and force fed. The long division and multiplication left him perplexed, but not once did he admit defeat and give in. It was a hard twelve-month study and at its conclusion, he could balance an account, keep a register or a journal that showed a profit or loss. He became more adept at bookkeeping than most other members of the company.

Victor always remembered that first evening when he finally closed the door on Mr. Salvage. He could hardly wait for Mrs. Woodland and the others to come to him and say all was ready for his. 'performance'. Eva led the way to the parlour. Victor hadn't known of its existence until she mentioned the piano. It was a large room at the rear of the house overlooking a large sloping garden. A fire was blazing merrily in the fire place, around which, were arranged several comfortable arm chairs. A six-place mahogany table was at the rooms centre, together with a set of highly polished chairs. A matching dark mahogany, cabinet stood against the rooms sidewall, it was resplendently Covered in the finest collection of Wedgewood pottery and crockery that Victor had ever seen; it was Eve's pride and joy! Victor notice none of these things as he entered this inner sanctum! His whole attention was drawn to the far end of the room!

It was dominated by the piano, the like of which Victor had never seen before, let alone played. It was an Ebony black, Steinway grand piano. He stood petrified with wonder, as he appreciated every curve and corner of its grace and beauty. Eve Woodland stopped, a worried expression on her face as she inquired, "What's the matter Victor, there's nothing wrong with it is there?"

"Definitely not!" Victor infused, as he rushed across the room to touch the wonderful instrument. He lifted the cover to look at the keys, each one spotless, reflecting the warm glow of the brightly burning gas mantels. He raised the piano's top and supported it with the metallic arm. Never had he seen it's like! He pinched himself hard, expecting to wake from a wonderful dream, but the piano and surroundings remained! "We haven't any music for you I'm afraid! "Eva apologised, "You are the first person to play it!"

It's not the kind of version I dreamed of, thought Victor, it's a bloody good second best! "Don't worry! I can remember plenty of pieces and I can play some songs that I know, perhaps we can have our own concert, if everyone joins in and sings." He sat comfortably on the piano stool and flexed his fingers appreciatively. Then he began. His mind was in a world of perfect contentment as the room filled with the haunting refrain of Beethoven's 'Fur Elise'. Everyone sat down and remained quiet as the refrain finally dimmed and ended in the now silent room.

"Victor! Cried Eva, "that was wonderful, why I am almost in tears, it was beautiful, you must play something else for us please." She was almost begging as he raised his hands over the keys once again. He had to admit, he loved being flattered and Mrs. Woodland was perfect at it, no one 'flannelled' better than she did! It was time for some Chopin, he began to play the Waltz in C sharp major. The entire gathering held their breath until the final strains ebbed slowly into silence, when Eva, unable to contain herself jumped to her feet and began clapping gleefully. "Let's sing something I think we should all know," said Victor. How about, 'Beautiful Dreamer'? He began to play as Eva and then her cook, Joan Davies, joined in to sing the Stephen

Foster favourite. Soon everyone present was joining in with the well-known chorus. Victor became aware of a dull ache, slowly spreading from his elbows, through his wrists to his fingers. He gritted his teeth and began to bite lightly into his bottom lip. He had been playing for little more than 10 minutes, yet his arms were telling him it was time to stop. At the song's conclusion he tried to rub some feeling into his complainant digits. He clenched and unclenched his tired fingers. Eva, noticing his obvious malaise remarked, "Are you alright Victor? You seem to be in a little discomfort. We aren't asking too much of you, are we?"

"Of course not!" He quickly replied, "I told you earlier, I love playing. It causes me a little pain, how are my hands and fingers going to improve, if I give in at the first twinge of stiffness or cramps. The more I play, the better my hands and arms will become." He had decided the only way they were going to get him off the piano, was with a Crowbar! He had never been near such an instrument before, not even in his wildest dreams. He was going to make his first session last as long as possible! He sat and played for well over an hour, his audience listened, sang and generally enjoyed themselves. It was Eva Woodland who finally called a halt to the evening, remarking that it was almost ten thirty and heaven only knew how they would manage to get up in the morning! "I'll have a good glass of 'Andrews' liver salts before I go to bed." She remarked, "That'll wake me up in the morning! I dare not stay in bed after a dose of that!"

Reluctantly Victor closed the piano. He had fallen in love, totally and utterly his dreams had been fulfilled, he had played a Steinway grand piano! He couldn't say if it was better than having a woman, but that would have to have been really special, if it was to better the sensation that he had just experienced. His thoughts strayed to Naomi Hay Jones as he went slowly to his room. Perhaps she wasn't as cold and unfeeling as she appeared. Without that strained hair style and some cheerful clothes she could be a beautiful woman!

CHAPTER 19

IT HAD BEEN AN EVENTFUL WEEK. HE WOULD ALWAYS REMEMBER the bitter scowl on Lewis Hay Jones' face, when he paid him his first week's salary. He had walked from the office with his feet barely touching the floor. Three pounds twelve and six pence! He had never before seen that much money in his life! He touched it, then put it in his pocket just to feel what that much money felt like. He took it out once again to make sure it was still there and was real. He rode home on the inside of the tram, afraid that, outside, the breeze might blow his wages away. At the Westgate Hotel, his usual stop, he decided to walk along the bustling High Street to the indoor market, where he bought two pounds of sausages and a whole leg of lamb. Mam and the family were going to have a tasty supper, and a wonderful Sunday dinner!

His first task had been to pay Mrs Woodland the fifteen and sixpence for his next week's rent, before heading to the railway station carrying his meaty parcel. He sat in the window seat for the whole journey home to Cwmcarn, thinking of some of the previous times that he had travelled by train. The annual Sunday school trip to the seaside at Barry Island was the one that came to mind, the compartment crowded with excited children, himself included, all fighting to sit by the window. Mum would always play the peacemaker, "for pity's sake, take it in turns!" Their favourite trick was to undo the strap, lower the window, and lean out to see where they were going. No one ever reached Barry Island dry eyed! Tears always fell like rain, as coal Smuts were wiped from streaming eyes with a spit wet handkerchief! He looked around the deserted carriage, it was strange, now that he could sit by the window, without the need to compete with his sisters for the privilege, he had no urge to open it and look out!

He stood alone on the spotless platform, being the only passenger to disembark at Cwmcarn. Looking across the gleaming track he could see the station master, William Jones, giving a perfect imitation of being busy, writing some pearl of information of paramount importance into his weekly journal. Hoisting his packages effortlessly onto his shoulder he strolled over the cast iron footbridge, each stride echoing loudly as the bridge bounced beneath his feet. He paused at its centre to gaze across the valley floor, at Cwmcarn, laid out like a photograph before him. The mine was tucked away in the valley, out of sight but definitely not out of mind! Looking left he could see the Abercarn, Prince of Wales colliery, idle these last twenty years since the accident that had killed two hundred souls. Just beyond it he could see the tall chimneys of the tin plate works and foundry, belching out the spiralling columns of blue, yellow smoking filth ready to attack the already congested lungs of the locality. He handed his ticket to the collector and set off along Chapel Farm Terrace, over the canal bridge by the blacksmith's, and headed ever closer to George Street and the family. How they had all screeched as he opened the front door! He had been smothered in hugs and sisterly kisses, even though he'd only been away for a few days.

The pride he felt as he put the meat and one pound and ten shillings on the table for the first time, he took with him to his grave! Looking after loved ones wasn't a duty, it was a pleasure! They sat around the fire until well into the small hours of the morning, demanding he told them every detail of his work and new companions. It was good to sleep in his own bed, but it felt strange sharing a room once again. Uncle Tom had made him promise to return on Wednesday evenings, the choir were resuming practise, and he was the only person good enough to be the accompanist. "We will only be singing for pleasure, it will be years before we are ready for competition again." Tom Mused.

He enjoyed playing the Chapel organ and thrilled to the congregations rendering of 'Yield not to Temptation, wondering if the Minister had chosen it especially for him! He thought wistfully of Naomi, as he ran his fingers lightly over the keys.

Victor had worked diligently at the steamship company for three months and towards the end of May, Bryan Cuthbertson announced, "C'mon victor, it's time I took you to the docks so that you can see what we do at first hand." He carefully placed several sheets of printed contracts in a small leather case, indicated for Victor to follow him, and left the office. "We'll take the tram to the dockside, I need to speak to Bernhard Owen he's the company's dockside foreman. He handles all our dock labour."

"Do we employ a lot of men at the docks?" Asked victor, "I've only seen document's and wage bills."

The two men continued the conversation as they boarded the tram for the dock gates.

"We export only coal. Although some companies handle other cargoes they do concentrate on coal. Our company is somewhat different in that we export coal from our owners' own mines. Much of the coal shipped through Newport, is bought at the coal exchange in Cardiff. We very rarely deal through the exchange, although Mr Hay Jones is a member." This is more like it he thought! At last, he was, was being given an insight into the actual working of the company. "We don't employ any workers at the docks, we only hire them when we have a ship to load or unload. The hiring is done by Bernhard Owen. He will hire the men required. He usually hires the men who buy him beer and cigarettes. The company doesn't ask too many questions, just as long as the work gets done." Victor began to wonder what kind of man this, Bernhard Owen must be, Some kind of dictator with the livelihood of hundreds of men and their families in his hands, and always in their pockets!

"Don't we pay the dockers a weekly wage like us?" Victor asked, as he thought of the uncertainty of the Stevedores Waiting at the quayside, hoping to be selected by the company's foreman or master stevedore as Brian called him.

"We don't employ many dockers," Brian continued, "We export coal, So we use the dock's tippers, they are men who tip the coal into the holds of our ships. They control the large cranes that lift our coal waggons and turn them out onto the shutes that pour the coal into our ships. The tippers are employed by the dock owners. Owen Just employs the coal "trimmers," for us."

"Who are they?" Asked victor eagerly. At last, he was being given an insight into the workings of the company.

"The 'trimmers' are the men who go into the holds of the ship and shovel the coal so that it is even. The weight in the ship's hold must be evenly distributed or."

"The ship may capsize!" Interrupted Victor, without giving Bryan the chance to finish.

"Exactly." Replied Brian, pleased that his young apprentice was catching on so easily. "It's a very dirty and dangerous job!"

"Not as bad as working down the mine in the first place!" Added Victor. "True," Brian continued, "but it is a very skilled job. If the coal isn't levelled and the weight evenly distributed, the ship may sink, and the crew lost!

"Last year, in 1910, there was a strike at the dock." Continued Brian, "A London company, Bouldon Brothers tried to cut the dockers wages by bringing in a scheme to pay the workers a daily rate, instead of a rate for each ton loaded or unloaded. A man called captain Edward Tupper organised the dockers and seamen. They went out on strike. It affected us because the tippers came out in support of the dockers and then the coal trimmers joined in as well." The tram pulled up at the dock gates and the two men, by then the only passengers, stepped down onto the cobbled road. It was a bright summer's day. Victor squinted against the glare of the sun reflecting off the rippling water in the dock. He looked behind himself at the Waterloo public house, dwarfed by the imposing transporter bridge in the background. He had walked over its huge lattice work towers and looked Along the River Usk and the town dock. "The Bouldon Company brought in labourers from London, Brian continued, it caused a riot on the dock side with the London workers besieged in their owners' ship. There were fights everywhere. In the end commonsense prevailed with the owners and the unions going to arbitration. The arbitrator ruled that the companies could hire men in whatever way they wished. Bouldon Brothers pay daily rates, We and nearly all the other Newport companies, pay piece rates. It's worked here for more than forty years! We don't need any outsiders coming in and changing things to suit themselves, making a fat profit then running off." Victor was led along the quay side until they stood beneath the S.S Tintern, One of the company's four steamships. The ship's stern seemed to tower up and up above Victor's head. The ship was a hive of activity. Seamen scurried busily around the deck side. Great clouds of dust could be seen rising from the ship's forward hold as the cranes poured ton after ton of the finest steam coal into it. They walked towards a man who seemed to be directing the loading procedure, Victor guessed he must be Bernard Owen. Brian limped up to the man and they shook hands. Owen was a tall, heavily built man with a Florid complexion, The result of frequent heavy drinking bouts. His face was almost hidden beneath a huge black beard.

"Bernard, let me introduce Victor," Said Brian, nodding to Victor, "He's working with us at the office, and who knows," he added with a wink, "One day he may be running it!" Victor took the offered hand and grasped it firmly. Bernard applied plenty of pressure, which Victor returned. "A good strong grip!" Bernard laughed, not the usual foppish office squeeze. "I think you've done some hard work at one time or another?" "I worked in the pit before I transferred to the office," Countered Victor. "Believe me, it's harder work there, than it is here!"

"You could be right!" He bellowed, "Most people complain like buggery when I shake their 'and, but you give as good as you got! We'll get on just fine." He concluded slapping Victor heartily on the back.

"When will the 'Tintern' be ready to sail?" Brian enquired." She'll be loaded in another fifteen hours, and ought to catch the tide four hours after that." Bernard answered.

"Only I've got to arrange the payroll for the crew who signed the articles for the voyage. I must talk to the master."

"He left the ship with Hugh Nelmes, about an hour ago. They were talking about the meat provision for the crew." Replied Bernard, "The mate is on deck supervising the tipping. D'you want to see 'him?"

"No, I'll leave a message for the master to call and see us before he sails, Come on Victor let's have a look while we are here." He led the way up the gangplank and Victor followed. It was the first time he had been on board a ship. They stood high on the quarter deck looking down at the trimmers scurrying about far below them in the dirt and grime of the hold, they were undertaking the backbreaking business of levelling the coal that had been tipped into the ship. Victor could see at first glance, the skill, as well as the brute strength, that was required to equalise the loads in the ship's hold.

"Watch what you are doing' down there you dozy bastard! Yelled Bernard at one of the trimmers who was sitting exhausted in the corner of the hold. "We're not paying you to sit on your arse. Get shovelling or get 'home!" The worker jumped to his feet and rejoined his workmates. Give the idle tosspots an inch and they'll take a mile! Owens concluded. Looking down at the dust and sweat streaked 'beavers', made Victor realise how grateful he was to be away from the filth and back breaking slavery of the pit. He could see trucks many of them bearing the name, 'Bedwellty Steam and Coke Coal Company', each patiently waiting its turn to be shunted to the dockside, where it's hard won content's would be taken from it, and loaded once again away from the sunlight, ready to be exported far, far away. He realised he was probably the first miner from Cwmcarn to see the coal once it had been loaded onto a Great Western truck and hauled away! He looked back to the grimy hold and its dirty toilers. He shrugged his shoulders and sighed loudly. It was still the same old story, the workers sweated in the grime and muck, faced all the dangers for a pittance, While the bosses sat back and raked in profits. He knew now, how much a ton of coal was worth and how much it actually cost to dig, transport and sell it! There was always plenty of profit! A crane coughed into life, Belching smoke and steam. It lifted a large truck, tipped its cargo onto a Shute and the coal poured into the hold. The ship rocked and complained against this intrusion and swayed disapprovingly in her moorings. Once the empty truck was lowered the trimmers set about equalising this latest load in the hold.

"Come on Victor, let's get back to the office." Said Brian, as he gave Victor a jab in the shoulder to bring him back to reality. "I know they look hard done by, but the company pays as good wages as anyone in the South Wales docks, in fact, we pay more than most!"

"It's not a quarter of what they ought to." Victor responded. "And I know, believe me, I know. It's backbreaking work shovelling coal!"

It was a subdued Victor who travelled back on the tram with Brian. He was deep in his own thoughts the whole journey and Brian decided it was best if Victor thought things through for himself.

"Mr Hay Jones wants to know how much longer the 'Tintern' is going to be in port?" William Hyde asked as soon as they walked through the office door. "He's quite concerned as time is money and the 'Chepstow' is due back within the next 36 hours."

Brian pointed at Victor and said, "Go on lad, you were there, I hope you were listening! Off you go and give Mr. Hay Jones a full report. Tell him what he wants to know."

William Hyde began to object, "Bu...!" A glance from Brian, that would have defrosted the South Pole shut him up. Victor a discomforting feeling in the seat of his trousers went to the merchant's office. He knocked the door.

"Come in!" Naomi called pleasantly. Victor opened the door and went nervously in. Her expression brightened immediately as he walked in. "Hello Victor, I haven't seen much of you since that first day." "Hello miss. I've come with a message for your father." Victor answered. Her mouth dropped but her eyes continued to sparkle as she continued, "Oh! You didn't come to see me!"

Victor could feel a colour burning its way up in his neck and inflaming his cheeks. "I I have a report for y yy-our father." He gabbled. Naomi, enjoying his shyness, baited him even further. I am disappointed! If I didn't know better, I would say you have been avoiding me on purpose. And don't call me miss! It makes me feel like an old maid. My father makes me wear these dowdy old clothes to work, but I am definitely not, either!"

Victor began to squirm with embarrassment, he had never been this flustered around his sisters, but this young girl was tying him in knots. "II haven't been avoiding anyone." He stammered. "It's just that I have been trying to learn my job. I have to succeed, I need to prove that I can do the job as well as, if not better than, most people!"

"I have been told that you are doing wonderfully." She answered. Looking deeply into his eyes, before he averted his troubled gaze. "Nearly everyone speaks well of you."

Lewis Hay Jones wrenched his door open and shouted, "Who are you talking to out there Naomi?" Looking around the outer office he saw Victor. "Oh it's you! What do you want?"

"I've come with a report from S.S Tintern Sir." Victor answered. He was still feeling flustered by the attentions and gaze of this strange young woman. "Mr. Cuthbertson sent me along."

"Don't stand out there then, come in," Hay Jones led the way into his office and closed the door.

"So you see Sir, she'll be ready to sail with a full cargo in nineteen hours. Victor answered, and the 'Chepstow', will be birthing in thirty-six hours. He concluded.

"A full report." Snapped a Curt Hay Jones, well delivered, give my compliment's to Mr Cuthbertson". He resumed his seat and with a nod dismissed Victor.

Victor found Naomi waiting for him outside her father's office door, "Don't judge all the family on the same level as my father! He can be nice at times. He can't help himself, that's all. He can't accept people for what they are. To him, background is the most important thing."

"I may not come from a 'named' background," Victor answered, "But, I am proud of my family. We have always worked hard for every little thing we have. I am not ashamed of my background, I was a miner grovelling underground to keep this company going, In fact I'm one of the lucky ones, I'm still alive!"

Her look softened and she placed her arm gently on his shoulder as she said, "Everyone should feel proud of who they are and where they come from. It makes you more of a man, more human not to deny your birthright! But it is also very important to be concerned about where you are going and, what you intend to do with your life. You are not denying your parish's background by trying to get on in the world."

He returned her gaze, peering deeply into her pale blue eyes, marvelling at the wisdom hidden deep within them, but more so at the concealed beauty mysteriously buried, fathomlessly at the edge of her soul. He saw, for the first time, the beauty of a woman standing before him. He felt the flame tinge his cheeks once more, he managed to smile and then made a dash for the door! Naomi watched, a knowing smile playing across her unblemished face, as he left. Victor ran back to the office; his cheeks were still scarlet as he sat down. Brian looked up from the sheet showing the 'Tintern's' articles and manifest. He noticed Victors ruddy colour and the agitated way in which he was rolling his pencil between his fingers. I didn't think Mr Hay Jones was in a bad mood or I wouldn't have isn't you in to see him! Or have you been taking a shine to Naomi again? Both he and Trevor, laughed heartily, as they both saw Victor's complexion deepen.

"A cold bath is what you need my young friend." Teased Trevor. "We told you before, you can't take a shine to the boss's daughter. We know what a flash of ankle does to you red blooded valley boys, but I guess it's not a stiff neck, you're suffering from. Right?"

A gleeful Trevor was unable to resist continuing the torment, "His mother told him he'd turn to stone if he ever saw or thought anything naughty! Judging by the bulge in his trousers when he walked in, he's started!" Both men doubled over as Victor squirmed even deeper into his seat. Victor picked up a list from the table in front of him. He stared at it, trying to ignore the taunting of his companions. Where is the 'Tintern' sailing to? He asked attempting to change the subject. "Somewhere exotic and romantic!" Trevor teased.

"If you must know," answered Brian, "She's sailing to Salerno in Italy with a full cargo of coal."

"I wonder what it's like there?" Victor Added.

"Docks are the same everywhere!" Replied Brian, "But the countryside is beautiful. It's nearly always warm and sunny."

"I've read about lots of foreign countries," said Victor, "Perhaps one day I'll be able to visit one."

"The only way you'll ever see a foreign shore is to join the army or navy." Countered Brian, "But then," he tapped his wooden leg, "You don't always come back with all that you started out with!"

"Don't forget the Monte Carlo run!" Interrupt interrupted Trevor.

"What's that?"

Trevor continued, "We have a contract to take Coal to Monaco in the South of France. It's for the Monte Carlo gas company. We take four cargoes a year, the ship and crew must be smart. The 'Raglan' always makes the voyage, she's the prettiest ship in our fleet. It takes six days to Unload the coal, and during that time the officers are allowed free admission to the gambling casino, while the crew gets shore leave. The company shares this trip among the employees and each year an office worker and companion are allowed to go!"

Brian, looked at Victor before saying, "You will have to wait for at least 20 years for your turn to come along!"

"I never thought I'd leave the pit, so who knows what will happen! My lucky number has already come up, perhaps it will again." Victor replied, his eyes full of hope and his mind on a certain young lady in the South of France. The trio spent the next four hours calculating Seamen's wages for the trip to Salerno and back. Several members of the crew had asked for wage advances, which had been agreed with the ship's master. These were reckoned and draughts were prepared for the merchant to take to the bank to withdraw the necessary sum of money.

I can't find any record of the master's salary. Queried Victor, as he searched through journal after journal.

"Shave your breath," warned Trevor, "The master always reports directly to the merchant. We have nothing to do with his salary. The mate gets nine pounds ten shillings a Fortnight, So the master is on a lot more. Victor returned to his calculations and concentrated on his own work. Once the work was completed, Brian allowed his two office workers to relax, He possessed a keen sense of humour, but work came first. He glanced through the documents his companions handed him, both waited silently as he checked quickly through the figures. Satisfied, he signed them and placed them in a wire tray on the tabletop, ready for collection and delivery to Mr Hay Jones, who was a perfectionist. Pity helps the clerk, who made a mistake or allowed an inkblot to sully his documentation. As he was signing the last one, there was a knock at the door. Naomi entered; she was carrying a contract. She was smiling brightly and spoke pleasantly to Brian. "My father wants you to check through this, it's new articles for the 'Chepstow', when she arrives. Daddy wants her back at sea within two days of arrival! He knows it's asking a lot, but the French contract must be completed." She handed the papers to him, before turning to smile at Victor.

"Thank you miss Naomi," replied Brian, "I'll check them through personally." Noticing the smile and Victor's embarrassment at the 'smile', He added, do you think our new worker will make the grade or will we have to send him back to where he came from?"

"Oh no! Definitely not!" She blurted out. Realising, she had answered much too quickly, in a most unladylike manner, she added more slowly and in a much more composed manner, "I mean, we have to give everyone a fair trial and make sure they have every opportunity to prove themselves worthy."

"He's working well." Brian added, enjoying the scene of a purple faced Victor, trying to disappear through the seat of his chair. "He's a clever young man. Did you know he is very talented musically?"

"I have heard nothing but good things about him, from all the office workers. I had heard a rumour that he played the piano, but I thought it was nothing more than that!" Naomi replied.

"More than a rumour miss." Continued Brian, "Why he's almost a virtuoso. He gives regular concerts at his lodgings, me and the wife have gone along and had a wonderful time. He also goes home to play his chapel organ every Sunday."

She looked at Victor her eyes bright and appealing, "I had no idea, Victor. I love music!" She left the sentence unfinished, hoping that this shy young man would realise its implication, but Victor sat tight lipped. Naomi, smiled at Brian and walked slowly from the room. "That's a lovely young lady, she's going to make someone a wonderful companion. Have you notice she's been wearing her hair much looser? She doesn't strain it back anymore. It makes it look much more attractive; don't you think? Brian remarked, as Naomi closed the door behind her. If I were twenty years younger and also liked music, I, would have accepted her invitation. The older men watched Victor closely, his ears seemed to prick up as Brian mentioned the word, invitation. Brian picked up his pen and quickly wrote a note on a piece of paper. He folded it and handed it to Victor. "I forgot when she was here, take this requisition to Miss Hay Jones asking for more ink." Victor took the letter and went to the door.

When it was closed firmly behind him, Trevor remarked, "Don't let Mr Hay Jones find out you've been matchmaking with his daughter, or you could end up being an ex-employee at this firm!"

Brian Cuthbertson laughed scornfully. "He tapped his wooden leg and replied, just like young Victor, I've got insurance! No one is going to dispense with my services while the Earl is in control, and anyway, I've saved a small nest egg for when that day does finally come. So, you see, I don't give a toss what Mr. Lewis Hay Jones, thinks!"

Victor was walking along the corridor with his note, trying to decide how to approach Naomi. He had played with many girls in Cwmcarn, but, they had always been school friends and neighbours. The fear was beginning to mount within his chest as he neared the door, Naomi wasn't just a girl she was Mr. Hay Jones' daughter, the company's merchant! He had noticed the change in her hairstyle, he loved the serene look in her clear blue eyes, and the sweet scent as she passed or stood near him. It filled his head with excitement and longing. He knocked at the office door. "Come in!" Replied the voice that was becoming to mean more to him than he was afraid to admit. He went in. As soon as he caught sight of her refreshing smile and welcoming eyes, his anxiety returned. I've a requisition order from Mr Cuthbertson for some I I ink." He stammered.

"I'll see to it immediately," she answered warmly, then continued. "I didn't know you were an accomplished musician. I had a few piano lessons myself before Mama died."

"I'm sorry, I didn't realise." Replied Victor "I would hate to be the one to remind you of unhappiness or bad memories."

Her smile was wide and luxurious, it made the hair on the back of Victor's neck tingle. "It was a long time ago. We missed her dreadfully when it happened. She caught the consumption, there was nothing anyone could do. You would have adored her, had you known her, she put everyone at their ease." Victor stood mesmerised as he stared into her radiant eyes, drinking in her delicate grace and elegance. He took a deep breath gathered his courage and blurted out.

"I was wondering if you would care to come to one of the musical evenings, if your father doesn't mind?"

A Coy grin replaced her warm smile, "I'll have to think about it and let you know. I adore music but my father may not like me travelling across the town late in the evening."

"I quite understand. Your father might think it totally improper for you to accept an invitation from his office junior." He said as he turned to leave.

"It isn't that at all!" She countered, "I would love to hear you, only it is such a long way from our house at Caerau Park."

"I am tutored before my little concert, but, if it is alright with your er um father …. I would see you safely home afterwards."

"I'll have a think and let you know." Was her parting remark.

As Victor was walking back to the office he bumped into Hugh Nelmes, the clerk in charge of the ships' victualling. He was a heavily built man possessing an imposing air of self-importance and a distrust of everyone and everything. In the three months Victor had been working for the company, he had hardly exchanged half a dozen words with the man.

Victor smiled and said, "Good afternoon, Sir, I hope you are keeping well?"

"Quite well thank you, Mr. Leslie." He replied, "I have been told by Mr. Hay Jones, that he has been instructed that you are to transfer into my office next month. I am supposed to train you in all the finer points of obtaining the provisions for a voyage. This is most irregular; you have only been with Cuthbertson for a short while and now it seems that I am to allow you to pick my brains as well! Most irregular indeed!"

Victor was taken aback by this outburst, and could only utter, "This is the first I have heard of this. I am perfectly happy with Mr. Cuthbertson and Bailey, I still have such a lot to learn, there's still so much I don't know!"

"My point exactly," Huw Nelmes continued, "Jack of all trades and master of none! That's how you will end up. Just because you happened to be in the right place at the right time you are receiving all these favours and privileges. It's not on! Some of us have worked here for twenty years and have had to work our way up from the bottom relying on sheer hard work, not favouritism!"

"I know nothing about any of this!" Victor replied honestly.

"Well, I was told earlier this morning. Three more weeks with 'dock hire' and 'crewing' then it's with me as my under clerk where I am to train you! A Most unsatisfactory state of affairs." His speech concluded Hugh Nelmes spun on his heels and disappeared back into his office.

A disgruntled and confused Victor went back into his own office. Trevor looked up and noticed that something was troubling his young trainee. "What's the matter with you Victor? You look as if you have lost a ten bob note and found a tanner!"

"Hugh Nelmes, has just told me I am transferring into his office in three weeks!" Replied Victor sullenly.

"I was going to tell you," Interrupted Brian, "But it seems that I have been beaten to it. You will find it a little strange in there, you will be about as popular as a boil on a nuns bum!"

CHAPTER 20

NAOMI HAD DECIDED TO MAKE VICTOR WAIT A LITTLE WHILE FOR her reply, and not appear too over eager to accept his invitation. She found him intriguing, he was a good-looking man. He was extremely strong, a legacy no doubt of his time spends working underground, he was also extremely intelligent and, despite the opposition towards him, from certain members of the company, he would succeed. He was quite coarse, compared with the young gentlemen with which she was acquainted, but he was much more interesting! In the right hands, if the rough edges were smoothed off, he could be the answer to a young woman's prayers. Father would disapprove of course, but she had always been an independent thinker, she had to be, ever since mother had died. It was time to let Victor know she would love to hear him play the piano. She'd heard Brian Cuthbertson and some of the under clerks say how much they had enjoyed the 'recitals'. If father didn't like it, he would have to learn to live with it, after all; he couldn't get rid of Victor, he was the earl's favourite. A fact that was making him unpopular with many of the senior members of the company. He also learned things too easily and much too quickly. She stood, smoothed a few creases from her skirt, went over to a large mirror hanging on her office wall and removed a few pins that were holding back her hair. She shook it seductively around her face down onto her shoulders and went through the doorway. She knocked at Brian Cuthbertson's office and entered.

"Excuse me Mr. Cuthbertson," She explained as she went in, "Could I borrow Mr. Leslie for two minutes please? I must study something in The Monte Carlo Gas Company's account for Papa, and I can't reach their portfolio, it's right on the top of the bureau." She smiled helplessly, hoping that it would add a little credibility to her plea.

Brian returned her smile before adding, "Certainly! Victor help Miss Naomi with that Gas Company account." Victor, pursued by Trevor's amused gaze, followed as if he had been shot from a cannon!

"It's true, you can't deny it!" Trevor laughed. "There's the proof. It will drag them father and faster than gun powder can blow them!" Both men guffawed loudly once the unsuspecting couple had disappeared. Naomi and Victor reached her office totally unaware of the speculation and amusement that they had caused.

Naomi pointed to a large buff, dust covered folder, at the top of the high office bureau. "There it is, Victor. That's the one I want." Victor carried a sturdy wooden chair to the bookcase, and with its help, had little difficultly in reaching the required document.

"Here you are miss." He replied as he placed the grimy record on her desk.

"Thank you ever so much." She cooed, and then said. "Oh! I've just remembered, it slipped my mind until a moment ago!" It had been constantly on her mind ever since Victor had invited her. "If the invitation is still open, I'd love to listen to you play."

Victor, his ears reddening looked deep into her wonderful eyes and became instantly mesmerised by their mystery. He was able to stammer. "Of course, it does, I would love you to come. When would be convenient?" His mind was racing. He had learned in the short time he had been working in Newport, if you wanted something, you had to go out to get it! And he wanted this astonishing young woman, more than he ever wanted anything before!

She beamed at him before replying, "when is your next concert?"

"Anytime you can come along!" He blurted out.

"You don't put a performance on just for me!" She warned, that won't be proper. "There will have to be others present!" The words came tumbling out from her mouth in a torrent of lies, as her heart yearned to be alone with this, 'rough diamond', who set her pulse racing.

"Mrs Woodland has asked if I will play for a group of her friends on Thursday night. If that is suitable?"

"What time shall I come?" She replied.

"We usually start at 6:30. I don't have my tutor on a Thursday. I'll be there, but I hope you will be able to arrange an escort home for me? She pouted.

"That can be arranged!" He answered, thinking if anyone else offers or interferes I'll break their neck! "I look forward to seeing you on Thursday." He returned to the office, his feet barely touching the floor, it seemed as if the top of his head was brushing the ceiling, he felt so tall. Brian and Trevor exchanged a knowing look, recognising the faraway look in his eyes as he sat at his desk and began to thumb through a cluster of contractual registers.

"Boom!" Shouted Trevor, "What did I tell you, farther than the gunpowder!" "Victor!" Shouted Brian," Wakey wakey! I don't know what's on your mind, but it certainly isn't the company's business!" Victor jumped from his seat as both men shouted at him and his mind was returned to thoughts of the present, not what he hoped might be! Three days practise, I must be at my very best on Thursday', he thought.

He completed the pay docket for George Olsen, an Able Bodied Seamen aboard the 'Tintern', four pounds eight shillings and four pence. Victor examined his figures again. Finding no mistakes he placed the document near Brian, ready for his authorising signature.

"Do we pay as well as the other shipping firms?" He asked, indicating the letter tray with the pay dockets in it. "Better than many." Brian replied. "There's been trouble in some ports, especially Cardiff. Some ship owners are trying to cut the wage bills by employing cheap Chinese seamen and workers. There's been a bloodbath down in Canton, in Cardiff. Chinamen beaten up, and their houses and shops ransacked and damaged. We've been quite lucky here! Victor, shook his head sadly, was there any where, that a working man could earn a decent wage without some greedy spectacular trying to worsen his working conditions, or make greater profits at his expense.

"There hasn't been any trouble at all since I've been here." Victor replied, keeping his thoughts to himself. Brian put his pen into the inkwell before replying, "There's nearly always trouble at the docks. We had that strike because of Bouldon Brothers, that I told you about. We've had other strikes with the dockers, and labourers. It's been quiet these last few months but believe me trouble will break out again before too long. We are affected by outside strikes as well, if the miners go on strike, we don't have any coal to ship, It's the same if the amalgamated Society of railway servants call a strike we get no coal, same again with the pits we're buggered again!"

It was a beautiful summers evening when victor walked out of the shipping office, so nice he decided to walk instead of catching the tram. He was beginning to learn some of the intricacies and problems that had to be solved, if the steamship line was to function. It would run much better, he thought, if respect and honesty were exercised by all parties. The ship owners would have more than a favourable return from their business and the workers made less demands, if equity was demonstrated by both sides. He had been taught by his uncle to deliver a fair day's work for a fair day's pay, but not to let anyone exploit him. "Fight for your own fair share," Tom had always told him. "Fight as dirty as the next man, if necessary!" He glanced over his right shoulder at the mighty Transporter Bridge standing its tall sentry over the Muddy Waters of the River Usk. He wondered what stories it could tell, if it only had a mouth that could speak. How many ships had passed beneath its metallic arms taking the 'black' cargoes to every corner of the world? Looking ahead once more, he strode off towards Westgate Square, and its imposing hotel, the site of the Titanic fight and struggle for freedom many years earlier. He could not carry the weight of the world on his shoulders, he could only take care of his own family and loved ones, but he swore to himself,

I will not do so at the expense of others, 'if I ever reach a position of wealth and power, I hope, I am strong enough to care for others not just myself and my own!'

The streets were almost deserted as he walked past the Isca Tavern, where he heard the raucous sound of laughter and raised voices. Hurrying on, he soon left the Westgate behind him as he turned up Stow Hill for the comfort and company of the Woodlands and their lodging house.

"I still marvel at the way you demolish a meal!" Laughed Eva Woodland, As she surveyed the empty plate in front of Victor, "you eat as if every meal is to be your last one.

"You leave the poor lad alone." Answered Joan Davis, the house cook. "It's men like Mr Leslie as makes my job all the more worthwhile. Why! I've never seen an appetite like his before, never mind cooked for one!"

"The trouble is," added James Woodland, "I don't think the way Victor gobbles up your offerings could be regarded as a compliment. You could feed him slops and he would wolf them down!"

"Slops they definitely are not sir!" Joan continued; "He's grown two inches since I've been feeding' 'him. Look at the spread on 'his shoulders. I know 'he was broad 'and strong before he came here but he's a strong bloody monster now! A good farmer would keep him for his manure!" Victor unaware of the comments his appetite always caused looked at Eva Woodland and asked, "I was wondering if you would mind if a friend came to our little concert on Thursday?"

"Of course not." Eva replied, "Who's coming?"

"Naomi Hay Jones." He answered and began to colour up at the look his statement generated. "A lady friend!" Said Eva, "I haven't seen Naomi for a few years, a scrawny, homely looking girl, as I remember!"

"She's beautiful, Victor snapped immediately, "She's warm, generous, has wonderful eyes and a gorgeous smile!" Eva, winked at James before continuing. "It sounds to me as if she has grown up since I last saw her. Pale as a ghost and hair twisted back out of her face, she was!"

"I dissolve, when I look deep into the bottomless pools that are her eyes!" Victor, added, barely breathing the words.

Eva looked at her husband as she said, "Did you ever get breathless at the thought of me?"

"Only the thought of having to carry you over the thresh hold my darlin'!" He joked, "You were always generous by nature and even more generous of proportions."

"Sarky devil!" She squealed happily. "You don't mind snuggling up to my broad beam on a cold night!"

"True, it's warmer and much more comfortable than a warming pan." He laughed.

"Does this mean you have no objection to me having Naomi here on Thursday?"

"Course we don't. Don't take any notice of us." Eva stated, then warned, "I hope her father doesn't mind!"

"What did your father say about you coming to my lodgings for the concert?" Victor asked Naomi, a worried frown wrinkling his youthful forehead. She smiled at the apprehensive youth before her, thinking 'faint heart never won fair maiden,' "Does it matter what he thinks?" She asked.

"Of course, it does!" He replied. "I want you to come, but your father's opinion must be taken into account." She looked hard at the young man before her, he was going to have to develop a much stronger backbone if he was going to survive in this prejudiced world, especially if he wanted anyone such as her. There were those whom background was all that mattered. He would have to prove himself, not fall at the first hurdle. "I want to come. Do you want me to?" She said tartly!

"I do, but I don't want to be responsible for you getting into trouble."

She smiled again, trying to reassure him, "I would love to come on Thursday."

"Right!" He replied, "That settles it, come to the lodgings at six thirty, we'll worry about the consequences later." He returned her smile and thought, 'If there is any trouble, I'll say it was my fault'. "I'll see you home safely afterwards."

Brian had followed the progress of his young worker with considerable pleasure and a great deal of trepidation. Victor's arrival and introduction into the company was an almost identical image of his own. Resentment from his co-workers, jealousy because of his sponsor, grudging praise from overseers, no matter how well deserved, added together with suspicious mistrust, meant constant vigilance, especially from behind! There was always those looking for an opportunity to put you back in your 'place'. Trevor left the office in search of the dock workers' payment slips. Brian looked up, made sure they were alone and said, "Victor. I have wanted to, have a word with you alone for some considerable time." Victor glanced up from his work, fearing a rebuke. "I want to warm you to watch out for yourself. There are plenty in this office who only want half an excuse to send a common pit boy back to the mine where he belongs! We are two of a kind, I came to these offices in almost an identical situation to yours, so let me try to warn you how difficult it is going to be for you to succeed. We both enjoy the favour of the earl, but he's not getting any younger. If anything happens to him, we'll both be out of here so fast it'll scorch our trousers." He paused, ensuring they could not be overheard and continued, "You have more potential than anyone else working here, and that is going to make you plenty of enemies. If you want to stay, keep working hard and while the earl is with us you will do well. Try to consolidate your position, make yourself indispensable, for the day when he no longer controls the company. Don't be afraid, if you want something, everything is going to be against you, but if you really do want it, you will have to try to overcome the bias and favouritism you will encounter." Before Victor could question, Brian further, the door opened, and Trevor returned with the wanted documents. A glare from Brian shut him up. It was a troubled Victor who returned to his ink blotter and leger. It did stiffen his resolve as far as Naomi was concerned however! He might be beneath her in social standing, but, as far as mam was concerned, there wasn't a girl good enough for him!

CHAPTER 21

Naomi knocked lightly on the door; it was a half-hearted knock if she was honest with herself. She had set off brimming full of confidence, but it had gradually evaporated with every step she had taken down Stow Hill. She had paused, opposite the imposing tower of St Woolos Cathedral, her nerve had almost deserted her there, but she wasn't on. The door tap had been her last chance of an excuse to run home and bury herself in her pillow at home. Melanie opened the door, have a short curtsey and said, "You must be Miss Hay Jones," She smiled politely then added, "Please come in, you are expected." Naomi followed the maid to the parlour where she found at least a dozen people sat in a loose circle around the piano. She saw Brian Cuthbertson and his wife Alice, accompanied by Eva Woodland coming to greet her.

"Good evening, Miss Hay Jones." Said Alice. "May I introduce Eva Woodland, the landlady of this house."

"There's no need for that." Eva interrupted. "I've known Naomi for many years, and her mother before her for even more!"

Naomi smiled, beginning to feel more and more at ease, with every passing second. "I had no idea you were Victor's landlady!" She said with genuine surprise.

Eva answered the question she could see forming on Alice's puzzled lips. "Many years ago, before I married James, I was a seamstress. I had many client's, one of them was Naomi's mother. We became friends and I used to see her often. I made most of Naomi's baby dresses. We lost touch, until her father asked us to take in a new lodger. It was Victor!"

"It's certainly a small world." Alice remarked.

"I didn't tell Victor, I thought I'd surprise you!" Said Eva.

"I didn't know you lived here. It must be more than ten years since I last saw you!" Naomi answered.

James left his chair and said, "Ladies! Let's sit down and get on with our sing song."

Naomi sat next to the Cuthbertson's with Eva in close attendance. Victor began to play one of his favourite pieces, Beethoven's moonlight Sonata, he had practised it for many years but had never played it with such feeling and intensity, he played it only for her. As he concluded, Naomi stared adoringly at him, her eyes moist with the emotion the music had aroused.

"That was a lovely old piece of music." Said Eva, "Let's have something a bit more cheerful. How about 'A Hunting we will go'!" The spell broken, Victor began the old folk tune, Eva joined in with her high-pitched soprano voice, encouraging everyone to join in with each chorus. They sang until they were hoarse, then begged Victor to play something soothing, he obliged with Mendelssohn's Spring Song and Tchaikovsky's October. Naomi looked at Victor with even more wonder, he really was a wonderful pianist his playing sent shivers up and down her back, charging her whole body with a spine-tingling electricity!

Eva supplied the gathering with glasses of dark ruby sherry and large glasses of white-headed stout, which ensured the evening was enjoyed by the entire throng. Naomi had never heard or been part of such merriment in her life before, she was totally unused to such abandoned high spirits and exhilaration. The people she knew, were composed at all times. According to her father it showed weakness if one allowed one's feelings to become known in public, but, she was enjoying this completely frivolous glee. These people knew how to enjoy themselves.

Victor looked deeply into her eyes and said, "Come on Naomi, it's your turn to sing a song for us now."

She returned his penetrating gaze for an instant, before she realised what Victor had suggested, then she began to panic. "I can't sing!" She stammered.

"Don't worry none of us can dear." Eva replied. "That's why it's so much fun, we all do our best."

"I only know hymns, from church, and I don't think they would be appropriate!" She was grasping at straws, looking for a way out an excuse, but Eva was insistent.

"You must know something from school perhaps?"

Naomi thought and thought.

"I can remember part of a song we sang at school; I'll try that one if Victor knows it!" Victor looked at her again, praying as hard as he could that he did. "It is called 'Cherry Ripe'," Victor breathed a sigh that started at the soles of his feet and burnt through his mouth like an express issuing from the Severn Tunnel! He played a few bars of the old folk song, waited, cued a note and accompanied Naomi as she began 'Cherry Ripe, Cherry Ripe, Ripe! I Cry; —Full and fair ones, come and buy!' She sang with a sweet contralto voice. Victor played as if possessed, hoping the song would never end.

"My dear! That was beautiful, I hope you can come again and sing something else for us." Eva remarked, speaking for the whole room. Naomi was looking at Victor hoping to catch some sign of agreement and approval in his eyes. Victor's eyes were riveted into hers, he realised that this one moment was the time when he completely lost his heart and soul to this mysterious, alluring young woman. There would never be another woman for him until eternity, not if all the numberless stars in the sky were to lose their sparkle and revert to infinity! She was the whole world to him!

The evening was over much too quickly, for Victor. Mrs. Woodland announced that it was time for Naomi to be going home. Victor had planned a fitting end to the evening and began to play,

'Brahms Cradle Song, it's quiescent melody filling the air and all the room's occupants with contentment.

At first, they climbed Stow Hill in silence, merely enjoying one another's company. Naomi, unable to keep silisn't any longer asked, "Are you always this quiet, or is it something I've done?"

"Of course not!" He answered hastily, "I was just enjoying the peace and quiet and sharing this still evening with you. It's wonderful, listen!"

She stopped and did so but could hear nothing, and said so, "I know!" He answered, "Perfect tranquillity, it's as if we are the only two people in the world, no one else is sharing this evening with us!" She looked longingly at this young man, ashamed that she had thought him a 'rough diamond'. He was deep, thoughtful, sometimes coarse in speech, but his manner was gentle and his feelings sincere. He was all that she could ever imagine wanting from a husband, and, she blushed at the thought, a lover! They strolled slowly in the starlight moving from one gaslit island to the next, until they stood outside her home, 202 Caerau Road. A large, detached house, with light appearing from many of its windows. They stopped at the gates.

"Thank you for a most enjoyable evening, Victor. I don't know when I enjoyed myself more." She said.

"I'm glad you enjoyed it I've enjoyed your company, more than anything else. But I'm glad you had fun, the Woodlands are nice people, they have really made me feel at home. I was worried to death about leaving my family behind and coming to work in Newport. But, if I hadn't, I wouldn't have met you! If I never meet another person, after sharing this evening with you, I will still be a very fortunate man!"

"Oh Victor!" She murmured, but he interrupted her. "It's alright I know a lady from your background must find someone like me very boring, that's fine. But I was hoping that you might like to come to the 'Lyceum' theatre with me next week? They're putting on a performance of Gilbert and Sullivan's, "Yeoman of the Guard". It's a wonderful operetta. I think you'll enjoy it."

I'd love to come with you Victor. She replied gazing wistfully into his eyes, longing, hoping that he would touch her, but he dared not. I'll see you at the office and you can tell me when it's on I must go now, it's very late for me to be out, and I do not find you boring! She turned very quickly, and before he knew it, she was inside. He was alone.

Brian had given him the task of taking a large sum of money to the master of the 'Tintern'. It proved that he was becoming recognised as one of the more trustworthy company members. Even Hay Jones had agreed his choice! He had been ordered to take a leather briefcase containing fifteen pounds and ten shillings to the ship's master Griffiths Prance. The case also had twenty gold sovereigns. "If you lose any of this, throw yourself off the Transporter Bridge!" Laughed Brian, but his eyes were deadly serious. He handed Victor a paper receipt, "Ask Mr Prance to sign this, then come back straight away."

Brian opened the top drawer at his table, took out a small cash box, which he opened with a key on his watch chain, took out tuppence handed it to Victor, locked the box and put it away. "This is your tram fare. Be sure to sign Mr Wilson's receipt book on your way out, or he will deduct it from your wages." Victor left the office, crossed the road and flagged down the first tram. He hurried from the dock gates, the Tintern was due to sail in three hours, any later and she would miss the tide. He walked along the dockside, watching as men unloaded deals of timber, the six feet lengths of rough sawn softwood, that were imported through Newport. The cranes spewing billowing white clouds of steam as they chugged into life hoisting the large wooden bundles on to the quayside, where the dockers swarming like ants, undertook the backbreaking slog of carrying the deals to their storage positions. He passed ships unloading pit props, which he recognised as similar to those his uncle had used to shore up the roof of their 'stint'. Everywhere his eyes looked, he saw men labouring strenuously to load and unload the ships waiting patiently at dockside. He arrived at the 'Tintern' and noticed, at once, that all dockside activity had ceased. The crew were all busy on deck completing their tasks, making ready to set sail. The column of black smoke was spewing from the single, tall funnel. She was still moored securely with two thick, salt bleached hawsers, fore and aft. He climbed the gangplank and halted at the top." I am Mr Leslie with a special package for the master." He called out to the nearest seaman. The man who had been greasing a length of cable indicated that he should stay on the gang plank and called for the second mate. The second mate arrived, he stood a shade under 6 feet tall, with muscular arms and a barrel for a chest. He sported the thickest beard of jet black hair that victor had ever seen.

"What can we do for you young Sir?" The mate asked gruffly.

"I have a very important package from the company. I must deliver it personally to the master." Victor replied, taking an instant dislike to this wild looking seaman.

"Give it to me. I'll see 'he gets it!" He snapped brusquely, as he held out his gnarled shovel like hands.

"I have it to give it to the master personally." Victor insisted.

I can't wait for long, and I don't think he will be pleased if you sail without it, especially when he learns you refused to let me on board with it!" Victor replied defiantly. The sailor was an inch or two taller than he was, but there was no way he was going to back down, if it came to blows, he was certain he would come second, but he was sure he would get in one or two good ones of his own!

"The company wants this package delivered immediately!" Victor stated. For a moment, Victor thought the second mate was about to explode, but reason took over and he snarled, come on board, I'll take you to his cabin." Victor stepped aboard the ship and followed the mate. As he walked past the seaman who was greasing the cables he heard him mutter," well done young 'un. 'He's a mean bastard and no mistake. Don't take any lip from him!"

The master was a gentleman, White haired and distinguished. He welcomed victor warmly with a firm handshake. Victor waited until the mate left the cabin before handing over the wages and sovereigns. The master counted it carefully, then he opened the ship safe with a large key and deposited the money safely inside.

"Thank you, Mr Leslie." He said, we are ready to sail, I hope to be out of the dock within the next two hours. The engineer will soon have a good head of steam up and then it should be plain sailing."

"Where are you going? "Asked Victor.

"We're bound for Marseilles in the South of France. We've a full cargo of best Welsh steam coal for the 'frog' Navy!"

"The South of France!" Repeated Victor. "The furthest I've ever been is Barry Island!"

"We will be off Barry in about three and a half hours, out in the Bristol Channel, then down South to the sunshine." The master replied, his mind mentally planning out the course and the passage ahead. He was a man of the sea, spending as little time as possible ashore.

"If you've a yen for travel and foreign parts sign on, it's a grand life!" Prance answered.

"No thanks." Replied Victor, "I like solid ground under my feet, if I change my mind, I'll let you know!"

"I'm afraid I'll have to ask you to leave now. The master said pleasantly, we sail in two hours, and I have lots to do before then. The next time we're in port come aboard, I'll be pleased to show you around a real working ship! He stated proudly. Perhaps I can persuade you to take up a nautical career!"

Victor walked quickly down the gang plank, pleased to be back on terra firm. He would leave ships to those who enjoyed them. He would take a coal mine before a ship!

As he was walking back along the dockside he saw the company's foreman, Bernard Owen, a short distance ahead, talking to a group of men, the conversation appeared to be quite agitated. Bernard noticing Victor, left the group and walked towards him.

"G day Mister Victor. Here's a surprise seeing' you. He said agreeably. "Good morning to you, Sir." Replied Victor.

The foreman looked back over his shoulder as the men resumed their unloading of a cargo of pit props. He shook his head and muttered as he turned back to Victor.

"Tell Brian, it looks as though the trouble is going to start again. They," he pointed to the dockers, just told me that some of the crew on that ship said that there's a seaman's strike in London. It seems that the seamen's union 'have asked for a uniform scale of wages but the owners 'have said no. The strike is bound to reach us sooner or later. Tell him, Captain Tupper, the seamen's union leader, is bound to be on the warpath again. 'He's certain to call all the Bristol channel ports out in support." Victor, looking at the worried expression on the foreman's face knew the hardship that strikes brought, but it was the only way most workers had to try to obtain fairness and a decent living wage. With most bosses and owners, fairness and honesty were the last things to be considered; he had suffered during the numerous shut outs and strikes, that had affected the family at Cwmcarn.

"Will it have much effect on us?" He asked the foreman.

"It's bound to! The tippers and trimmers will be persuaded to come out, and that will mean we won't be able to load any coal." Was the reply.

"The company will lose money if they can't export."

I only hope we don't try to bring in any 'black legs,' there will be riots if they do!"

Victor travelled back to the offices in a thoughtful mood. This information placed him in an awkward dilemma. He now worked for a company that was in the business of exporting coal, but, if a strike was called, there was no way his conscience would allow him to do anything to undermine its effectiveness or the solidarity of the seamen and docker's! He had experienced first-hand, the hardship that had to be endured during a strike. He closed his eyes and said a silent prayer that the information was false.

"Bernhard Owen, told you all this at the dockside?" Hay Jones questioned Victor. Brian had taken Victor to the merchant once he had told him about the news from the docks fore man. He had told the story again, to Hay Jones exactly as he had been ordered to do. Both men sighed and became agitated as his story unfolded.

"I had heard a rumour about it earlier in the week. The merchant said, I have telephoned a few friends in London asking for information, but they said they thought it would all blow over and it would be best to keep quiet about it."

"All we can do now is carry on working, it's a bridge we will cross if we have to." Brian answered.

Victor left the two men and returned to his office; on the way he met Naomi. She looked more beautiful than ever. She was wearing a spotlessly white, lace edged blouse, it was gathered tightly at her slender waist accentuating her swelling breasts and voluptuous hips. Victor gazed deep into her eyes, and she returned his look with a long lingering one that made the hair on his neck tingle with both longing and delight.

"You look wonderful this morning!" He said. Her lips parted, as a look of absolute pleasure took command of her face and revealed her flawless pearl white teeth.

"Thank you, Victor, it's nice to know that someone appreciates the way I dress."

"I hope you enjoyed last night and will come again very soon. The sooner the better as far as I'm concerned. He infused. I hope you haven't forgotten about going to the Lyceum to see the Operetta?"

I know very little about Gilbert and Sullivan you will have to explain most of it to me. She responded.

He looked into her luxurious orbs searching for the slightest sign of a tease but could detect only sincerity.

"We'll learn together!" He laughed, his eyes sparkling at the sight of this wonderful, warm woman in front of him, I've never seen a complete operetta before although, I do know several pieces that I play for the choir to sing."

"I've heard you play the piano, I would love to listen to you accompany the choir you play for." Naomi announced. She longed to share as many of his interests as possible, but had to beware of appearing too eager, after all a lady waited for the man to declare himself.

"My uncle conducts the choir. He's a miner!" He said it half apologetically, expecting it to show some sign of amazement or disbelief, but she did not.

"If you take after him, then he must be a wonderful man". She answered quickly.

"He has a talent for and a love of music but has had to teach himself! He said, he began in the pit at six years of age, there was no time or money for him to develop or learn. He lives and breathes music. I believe he would rather die than become deaf!"

I hope we can arrange to go to the Lyceum." She cooed as she disappeared into the maintenance office, her tone driving Victor into a frustrating frenzy.

The telephone in Hay Jones' office rang Shrilly, it made him jump, he had been slumped, half asleep in his chair, gazing out the window, enjoying the pleasant summer warmth. It rang again, urgently, he picked up the receiver.

"Gwent Steamship, Hay Jones, merchant speaking." He replied. He loathed the contraption; it always seemed such a cold dispassionate thing to him. If you wanted to judge a person, he always believed you had to look at the handwriting. You could put your heart and soul into a letter. You just barked words down a Bakelite trumpet when you used the telephone. "Hay Jones," a voice answered. "Michael Fairfax here."

"Damn!" Thought Hay Jones, what does the pompous ass want this time! He replied, "Sir Michael, how nice to hear from you what can I do for you?" The seamen have gone on strike up here. We're pulling all the strings we can to keep it out of the newspapers for as long as we can, but it's bound to spread. Owen Price is trying to organise a trainload of free labour to help load our coal, but the Earl is afraid it will cause trouble. He will stop us, he doesn't want any more bad publicity following that bloody mining disaster!"

"He's right Sir Michael!" Hey Jones, shouted into the mouthpiece, "The dockers won't stand for any imported labour, and what's more they'll 'Black' our ships, if we use it. My advice would be to try and hold out, we can do so for longer than seamen can!"

"You may be right, but we must try to keep the coal flowing!" Came the reply. "Talking of coal, how is that pit lackey his lordships saddled you with?"

"I am loathe to say it, but he is proving to be most able. I was expecting some coarse valley bumpkin, but he's quite refined, for his class that is!"

The voice cut him short, "His lordship can be an utter arse sometimes, he attracts waifs and strays like flies around fillies' backsides! Just keep an eye on him, we don't want any union types causing problems inside the office, there's going to be enough on the dockside. Do what you can and keep us informed if any trouble develops. We may have to call a board meeting to overrule his lordship and send you some labourers!"

"I'll keep you fully informed Sir Michael. Goodbye Sir." He replaced the earpiece onto the phone stand. It appeared that trouble was on the way!

CHAPTER 22

Victor stood beside the entrance to the Westgate Hotel, it was possible to peep into the reception area and still see the bullet holes in the walls that had been left as permeant reminders of the Newport Chartist riots seventy-two years previously. It was still discussed, with hushed voices, how soldiers had ambushed the protesters. Following the battle, at least ten valley men lay slain upon the ground. He hopped from foot to foot impatiently, Naomi had agreed to meet him here at seven, according to the clock above the corn exchange it was gone five past! If she didn't hurry up, they would miss the performance at 7:30! He tried leaning casually against the wall, but the stonework made his jacket dusty, he brushed up his sleeve and decided to stand as inconspicuously near the hotel entrance as he possibly could. He began to fume inwardly, like a long dormant volcano on the edge of eruption as the clock chimed the quarter. His imminent outburst, which saw him about to storm up the hill to The Woodlands, subsided as he caught sight of her rushing down the hill towards him. Naomi had decided to test Victors resolve and arrive a little late, consequently, she decided to walk instead of catching the tram. It was a warm clear evening, and she was enjoying the stroll. Her happiness turned to anguish as she heard the clock chime 15 minutes past! All her ladylike intentions vanished, as she caught hold of her skirt and ran 'pell mell' into the square. He laughed as she appeared breathless and dishevelled before him, he loved the 'lost' lock of hair that had escaped onto her forehead and the ruddy complexion of her flawless cheeks.

"I'm sorry!" She panted, trying to push her hair straight smoothie skate free of several wrinkles, "I must look an awful sight. I decided to walk and didn't realise it was so late!"

Victor looked long and hard at her before approving, "You look wonderful, you could never look anything else, to me". She smiled happily at the compliment, but promised herself, the next time they met, she would be composed, elegant and not have a single hair out of place. Damn that loose lock!

Victor grabbed her hand, and, without giving her any chance to protest, rushed her into Bridge Street, where they could see the magnificent theatre, one hundred yards in the distance.

"Come on!" He said, "We've plenty of time, as long as we walk quickly!" He made no effort to let go of her hand, and Naomi made no protest as she returned his warm touch. They walked under the six Corinthian columns, and beneath the magnificent statue of Queen Victoria, into the box office.

"Two circle tickets please." Asked Victor, letting Naomi's hand loose as he reached into his pocket for the ticket money. They walked up the plushily carpeted stairs to the circle, where he handed over the tickets to the young lady waiting to receive them.

"Third row from the front, seats eight an' nine "she stated." You'll 'have to hurry it's going to start in about free minutes!"

This time, Victor took deliberate hold of her hand and led the way to their seats, where they sat hand in hand throughout the entire performance.

Victor had only one word to describe the walk to Caerau Road, bliss! Naomi had leaned on his shoulder enthralled through most of the performance, and now as they walked home, she had hooked her arm through his and snuggled! He was becoming intoxicated with her perfume and her very nearness, he had only been closer to one woman before, and that had been his sister, Christine! They had 'top and tailed' a bed together one Christmas many years ago.

He nuzzled her hair, drinking in its aromatic scent and cleanliness, the last thing on his mind was 'topping and tailing' a bed. He pushed the urge to the back of his consciousness and concentrated on enjoying her company. He was falling for this beautiful woman, there would be thousands of obstacles in their way. If he were not to spoil any chance he might have with her, he would have to be respectful and patient. He laughed to himself; she was the first girl he had ever held hands with! Talk about the blind leading the blind!

They walked together, in an exclusive dreamworld, the world was excluded yet, not a single word was spoken! It was their arrival at the garden gate that broke the spell. She looked up at him and said, "I don't think I've ever had a more wonderful time."

"Neither have I." was his only reply. All the while, aching to reach down and kiss her, but fear held him back. Would she object? They might be seen. He didn't want to place any possibility of offence between them. He had never before felt this complete, or tranquil, as when he was with her.

"I'm glad you enjoyed yourself." He said eventually, "I love being with you, you are fun, caring, happy and above all the most beautiful woman I've ever known!"

"I bet you say that to all the girls!"

"I've never said it to anyone before. You are the first girl I've ever held hands with! I've never been to a theatre in my life before, there isn't much chance when you are down the pit for twelve hours a day!"

She caressed the back of his hand lightly with her slender fingers, before giving it a gentle squeeze. "That's all behind you now! You have impressed everyone with your sincerity, your honesty, your intelligence, your intention to do well and your warmth!"

He smiled happily, encouraged by her enthusiasm, but saddened by the thought that, despite her insistence he was not unique. He had been the one lucky enough to be in the right place at the right time, or ought that to be the wrong place at the right time!

"There are thousands of others, many of them much better than I am. They'll never be given the chance to improve their circumstances, not the way things stand now."

"Well, I think you are special!" She insisted, "And don't let me hear of anyone suggesting you're not!" Her eyes flashed and a thunderous look flashed fleetingly behind her eyes.

"I bet your father doesn't approve of us going to places together, does he?"

"I haven't told him, so there's nothing for him to disapprove of!" She answered defiantly. "I've always picked my friends without any interference, and I will continue to do so."

"You can't deceive him!" Victor snapped, "I can imagine how angry he'll be if someone tells him about us."

"Let me handle my father in my own way. I've been looking after him for more than ten years, ever since, mother died." Victor noticed the sadness that seemed to overcome her, replacing her usual vibrant guise with one of sadness and regret. He too, experienced a transitory sense of guilt for his part in reminding her or her loss.

"Don't be down hearted!" He whispered, feeling genuine sorrow. "We all have to look to the future, with hope, and remember the happier times from the past with fondness and gratitude." She gazed intently into his eyes, ave his hand one last affectionate tweak, and rushed inside. Closing the door softly, she tiptoed up the lavender scented, staircase. The tears came as she threw herself onto her bed." Oh Victor, you great hulking adorable ox!" She sobbed!

The 'Chepstow', berthed safely, her cargo of iron ore having been discharged at Garston in Liverpool. The race was on to load her with a full payload of steam coal, before the expected seaman's strike reached Newport. 'Tippers' and 'trimmers' swarmed around the steamship, under the vigilant eyes and abusive tongue of Bernhard Owen. Victor, together with all the other office members beavered through mountains of paperwork, at breakneck speed, to ensure the ship had a record breaking 'turn around. Victor had seen and was used to hard work, but, he had never seen anyone work as hard, or in such conditions, as the trimmers, deep in the bowels of the 'Chepstow'! The dust was blinding! They endured purgatory for the promise of an extra shilling on completion of the loading, providing it was executed quickly. The office staff and foremen were under strict orders to make no mention of the rumours regarding the impending strike. The ship sailed barely seventy-two hours after tying up. A relieved Hay Jones watched her depart.

"We don't have another of our ships expected for at least twelve days." He said to Bernhard, who stood beside him." The 'Monmouth' is expected back from the River Plate area then." He had advised against the company trading so far away. He had considered the length of such a journey would tie up the company's largest ship for much too long, she could make two, more profitable trips, in the time one was taking! The board had disagreed.

"Stockpile our coal ready for loading. I'll try to sell some of it at the exchange. We may be able to export it with another line.

"If they haven't heard about the seamen!" Bernard answered.

Victor sat still at his desk, his head swimming with all the calculations and reckoning he had been called upon to make. He was as exhausted as if he had just under cut and tumbled tons of coal at the face, yet the heaviest implement he had used was his blotter! Hay Jones entered and smiled warmly, "Well done one and all." He announced. "You all know how important the French contract is. There will be an extra half-crown for everyone this week!"

It gave Victor immense pleasure to hand the coin over to his mother, she had accepted it gratefully before tucking it safely away in the tobacco tin under her mattress. She had saved a Florin a week out of his money. She had three pounds eight and six in it now! It was her insurance money, just in case there was a shutdown or a strike. It would ensure they didn't starve, even if Victor wasn't able to help out. They all looked forward to his weekend visits, not because of the wonderful cuts of meat he brought from Newport market, but they were all proud of the man he had become. Confidant, self-assured and sure in his developing intellect and business acumen. He was no longer her little boy, his shyness had gone, but he still retained his humility and care for others. He was still her son. He showed no shame, only pride in his family and upbringing, together with gratitude for the sacrifices they had made for him. "The dock workers don't have it any better than the miner's, mam." He said to the family, as they gathered cosily around the fire for their usual late-night chat, "They work like dogs for a pittance, the only thing about their work is they don't have to face the dangers you find underground. The trimmers shovel coal for hours on end, in the ship's hold. It's as dusty as any roadway explosion, set off by Huw." They loved to hear him talk of the mighty ships and the wondrous places they visited. Marvelling at the tales of far-off countries, even though he had never visited any of them personally.

"I have some news for you." Announced Christine. She looked to her mother for encouragement, receiving a nod she continued, "I am getting married!" Victor looked dumfounded, "I didn't know you were seeing anyone special." She smiled and at him and added, "I met him at a chapel outing, you'll like him when you meet him."

"Who is he?"

"His name is Eric Birtles, he's just been made a fireman in Risca pit. 'Mam's agreed and we are getting married next month. Mr Morgan is doing the ceremony, and we will live with his mother in Tredegar Street, Crosskeys. Say you are pleased for me Victor.

He grabbed her in his arms and almost crushed her with a bear like hug. "If mam is satisfied with your choice, who am I to argue? I'm sure I'll like him."

The talk turned to weddings and lodgings, and he listened politely to her dreams and hopes, wishing that he could feel as confident about his future with Naomi, as Christine sounded about Eric.

Choir practice Saturday evenings had become a ritual, it was an addiction from which he would never be free. He had taken Naomi to concerts and operettas but male voice singing he decided was his musical passion. Tom complained about the 'top tenors', swore at the 'bottom basses' and moaned about everything in general, but the choir was improving with every practice.

"Come on you miserable old bugger!" Snorted Evan Wilknson. "That was perfect." A point that Victor had to concede. The pitch and timing had been first rate, then he looked at his uncle!

"How would you know?" Snapped Tom, "You just open your gob and out comes a note or two, you can't hear the whole sound like me out here!"

"I thought I saw you smile?" Said Hugh Stevens, "But it must have been all that rich food Victor, is bringing you from Newport. It was probably wind! The worst case of indigestion ever seen."

Tom would never change, he would go to his grave a musical perfectionist, where he would criticise the heavenly host!

"Victor has brought me the odd piece of 'shoe leather steak' I will admit, but it doesn't make you sound any better!" He snapped, as the choir smirked one with another, realising the pleasure that he had taken from their near perfect performance of Wagner's 'Pilgrim's Chorus'. Praise wasn't something that fell from his lips in copious amounts.

"He has brought something else." He waved a wad of sheet music in the air. "It's a bit modern for my liking, not a serious piece, but I thought the women and children might enjoy it when we give the concert at the chapel in a couple of months." He passed out the sheets, which the singers shared. "It's about pirates, a light piece written by a man called Candish – whoever he is? Victor said he thought we might sing it well." He pointed to the title, "As you can see it's called, 'The Song of The Jolly Roger'. Victor will play it through for us, so that we can get a general feel of it. You can follow it as he plays. Victor began to play and those who could read, followed the words. A murmur of approval ran through the choir as he ended the piece. Tom, as usual, unwilling to show any emotion or pleasure remarked, "Just as I expected, anything, as long as it is new, will appeal to you Philistines! Let's start with you tenors, first two bars, note at a time Victor." Victor played the notes deliberately and singly. The tenors sang the notes through two or three times until, parrot fashion they could sing the two bars almost note perfect. He repeated the process for the first bass and Tom had the two sections sing together. "Not bad for a first try!" He snapped, "It can only get better." The other two sections repeated the procedure until all four sections of the choir were singing the first few bars of the song. Intense practice took place for the next hour before Tom called a halt.

"That's enough for today lads, we don't want you to sing yourselves out!" He put his conducting baton into its case on top of the piano and stepped from his conducting stool. A miraculous change then occurred, as it did every week. Tom became human again, he was the tyrant conductor no more, but Tom, miner and friend. He moved among the men talking and joking, with his usual humour and friendliness.

"He's like a bloody fiend when 'He's got a baton in 'his hand!" Laughed Evan. "But talking' about a changed man, what's this I've heard about you and' a little darlin' from Newport?" He caught hold of Victor's ear and began to tweak in unmercifully, "Come on Vic, out with it, what have you been doing' eh? Norman Heywood, the policeman what plays hooker for the rugby club said, he's seen you in the 'Lyceum' with some little gal wot was all over you!"

"Piss off Evan!" Snapped Victor pulling away from the agonising pinch. "Heywood wouldn't know a lady if she bit him on the backside!"

"So you admit it! You was there with a woman!"

"I took a friend to a concert." Victor lied. "I don't have to account to you!" He concluded rattily.

"Keep your hair on. It must be serious if you can't take a joke!" Laughed Evan.

Tom, who had witnessed the scene, raised his eyebrows and smiled to himself, perhaps Christine wasn't the only one with some news for the family.

CHAPTER 23

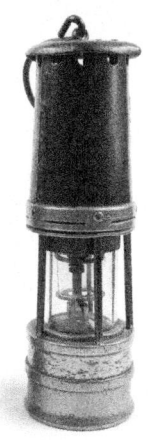

Victor and Naomi strolled hand in hand through the gnarled trunks of the huge beech trees in the park. Naomi had made up a basket of Victor's favourite cheese sandwiches and suggested that they take them into the park to enjoy the warm July sunshine. They enjoyed a secluded picnic. The food finished Naomi kicked off her shoes and strolled through the lush grass. Victor followed her as she smiled and leaned against a particularly large trunk. He walked purposefully towards her and pulled her to his chest. His arms slipped behind her back, his hands enjoying the slenderness of her waist. She showed no resistance as his mouth lowered and caressed her ruby red lips, tenderly at first, then urgently. Her lips parted and his tongue played gently over her teeth, before making exquisite contact with her willing eager tongue, sending electric vibrations through their entwined bodies. They gazed lovingly at one another and without saying another word they kissed again. "I've wanted to kiss you from the moment I first saw you!" Said Victor breathing the words passionately on her neck. "I've wanted you to, too!" She admitted, "But I didn't want to frighten you away"!" There's no way you could do that." He replied kissing her lightly on each eyelid before hungrily searching for her mouth once more.

She allowed him to kiss her with mounting passion but decided to cool his fervour on feeling the stiffness of his manly hardour pressing strongly against her thigh. Pushing him at arm's length she said,

"Calm down Victor! I love you but I'm not the kind of girl who is going to let you get carried away like this. We were both brought up to act differently, I hope you want more from me than just a moments wild abandonment here in this park."

"I've loved you from the moment I first met you. I have been going almost insane with love and longing. You have been my main reason for living he continued. "I look into your eyes, and I am hopelessly lost! Lost in wonder and love, wonder at my fortune that such a beautiful woman as you can be associated with someone like me!"

"I've already told you," She rebuked him "You are worth ten times more than the fops I've been seen with". She smiled wickedly and continued. "Now if you promise to not get carried away, will you kiss me again, then we must get back to the office. Their lips met and for a fleeting, bliss full, moment they were the only two people on earth.

The earl ordered Victor to accompany him to the docks telling him to get into the car before ordering his chauffeur to drive them there.

"At once your lordship!" The chauffeur replied, closing the door before walking round to the driver's seat and starting the engine.

The old man looked appreciatively at Victor, approving the changes that had obviously occurred. At the mature, confident man who had replaced the shy, retiring boy, that had left the colliery, and grown -into a dependable trustworthy individual with a spread to his shoulders that spoke of strength and stamina, a testimony to his improved circumstances.

"What do you make of this situation, Victor?" He asked. Victor thought for a moment before he gave his carefully considered answer.

"Do you want, what I really think, or do you want me to tell you what you want to hear?" He replied.

"Don't get smart with me young man. If I thought you were anything other than honest, I'd have left you in the bloody mine!"

"The dockers don't want this strike any more than you do, but they have had enough of being lied to and being treated as less than human, just because they haven't had the luxury of a fancy education and fine clothes. All they want is to be treated fairly. Be honest and faithful with them and they will be the same with you."

"You don't think they're being unreasonable?" The Earl inquired. "No Sir!" Victor responded, "This whole dispute has been engineered by the greed of Bouldon Brothers who want more for themselves and don't give a toss about the people they employ! I expect you know plenty of people who think that way, in the circles in which you move". The old man could only nod his head in agreement. He thought of the members of the board of his company. Many would sell their own granny for an extra Bob or two. Have you any suggestion as to how I can help solve the situation? Victor sat back in his seat; this was more than he had bargained for. It was a question that he thought was beyond his comprehension or reasoning.

"I don't think I'm qualified to answer that." He replied.

"Come off it lad!" The old earl barked, "You have been on both sides of the fence, and I hope I haven't wasted my money trying to have you educated, what do you think?"

Victor swallow hard, beads of sweat began to break out on his forehead as he began to answer.

"I think it might help if you spoke to all the local employers and try to persuade them to accept a compromise. A reasonable pay increase and a return to piece work, for all companies. I'm sure the dockers will return to work if they are offered a fair compromise. Strikes hit everyone, but it is the only weapon they have to fight injustice and believe me, I knew plenty of that before I knew you!

The old man gave Victor a warm glance. The car pulled up at the side of the waterfront. In the distance, a group of men watched the car stop and the two men get out. A few of the watchers from the crowd began to run towards the car and its unwelcome occupants. Victor scooped a yard long piece of three by two rough timber, off the floor. He hoped reason would prevail, but it was just as well to have a slight edge, if the rapidly approaching group needs some friendly persuasion! The earl was amused by Victor's actions, but he felt grateful for the concern shown. He had faced drunken mutineers in the past, the only difference then, was, he held a service revolver, primed and loaded and was perfectly prepared to put a bullet through the frontal lobes, of anyone foolish enough to show any aggressive intent! He stood facing these strikers, legs slightly apart, hands on hips. He laughed loudly as they neared.

"Who's in charge of you rabble?" His voice boomed, bringing the men to a sudden stop. "I want to speak to whoever is in charge of this strike. And I want to speak to him now!" The group came skidding to a halt about ten yards from the earl. They seemed slightly bewildered by this 'old man' who stood his ground and bellowed orders at them, like some determined old bull, following a visit to a vet who had used a rusty old razor! A voice rang out from the back. "What makes you think the strike committee will want to see a worn-out old relic act like you?" The earl laughed scornfully and then replied, "I may be old, but I don't hide at the back to name call! I want to try to solve the problem, you want to get back to work and I want you back. The only way that is going to happen is if we talk!"

Victor stepped forward, standing between the Earl and the strikers. "Let me speak to them your lordship, you will help much more if you talk with the local owners." He made a show of throwing away the timber club he had picked up for protection, a gesture that was noticed by most of the group. Victor shouted, "Let me meet the committee, I'll tell the owners your demands, then I'll help, not all owners are willing to take advantage of you. The earl will help!"

"Will you be alright Victor?" The earl asked.

"They are my own kind." Victor answered. He walked towards the strikers and held out his arm to shake the hand of the nearest man. "You go and talk to the owners; I'll see what I can do from this end". The earl returned to his car; he was the only person to notice his chauffeur reapplying the safety catch of the colt automatic pistol and put it under the driver's seat before closing the rear door securely. The earl wound down the window and called, "I'll see you back at the office in a couple of hours, God willing!"

Victor walked along the quayside chatting amicably with the men. It's never ceased to amaze him how nice people really were, if you only took the trouble to talk to them. They were almost all from the Pillgwenlly area of Newport, where they lived with their families. They took victor to a warehouse on the dockside. They walked beside huge stockpiles of pit props that had been discharged, by the delivering ships, but they would go no further until this dispute was settled. Lines of laden coal trucks remained as if welded to the tracks along with their attendant shunting locomotives, still and silent. The strike was total and complete. The only activity that Victor observed was aboard the ships unfortunate enough to be stranded in the port, although many of them carried seamen actively involved in, and supporting the strike. Victor was taken into the largest of the warehouses on the dock. It was piled high with deals of timber. And at it's centre a large space had been cleared, where tables together with several wooden chairs, had been arranged in a circle. Four men, dressed in dark suits, were involved in a heated discussion, which stopped when Victor arrived. One of the men George Jackson, the Seamen's leader came to meet them. He was a small man, who sported a well-trimmed moustache on his well-rounded face. He shook hands with Victor, they had met one another during Victors frequent visit to the docks.

"Hello Victor" Jackson called, "What are you doing here, there aren't any Gwent steamship's here today?"

"He was with that fancy panted earl, who was driving' into the docks!" The voice reported.

"I'm sure he can speak for himself." Jackson interrupted.

"I was with the Earl of Gwent," Victor said. He walked to the men seated around the table before he continued, "He wants to try to settle the dispute. He asked me to listen to your demands, then take them back to him." He looked around the small assembly, he knew most of the men by sight although he had never actually met them. He looked at George Jackson, who took the hint and began to introduce him. Henry Seer of the dockers, Albert Kinsey and John O'Leary of the labourer's union and Sam White of the Railway Servants." Jackson introduced them one by one.

"Why are you here?" Questioned Sam White, "We don't need a bosses spy!" "He's alright!" Snapped Gordon, "He used to work in Cwmcarn pit! He knows what it's like to be on strike!" Victor spent the next twenty minutes telling the strike community about himself and his connection with the earl. His story seemed to satisfy even the most doubtful of them. So, you see I am here to help you if I can. Tell me what you want, and I will do my damnedest to see your grievances are herd."

"The seamen want an end to the owners using cheap Chinese labour, we give a decent day's work, all we ask is that the owners treat us like men, not cattle and give us a fair day's pay!"

The strike committee all agreed with this statement.

"You see, Victor," Albert Seer continued, "We are all supporting one another. We all want a 'closed shop' with our members being guaranteed employment. We are fed up to the back teeth with 'free labourers' and 'black legs' being brought in so that the owners can shave a couple of pennies on our wages and swell their greedy pockets. We know how much they're making, and we're doing all the work. It's worse than the Hebrews in Egypt, we haven't got a Moses!"

"I know the Gwent, pays regulation wages, as do nearly all the local firms. It's the national company's and 'big boys' who are causing all the trouble!"

"We agree with some of that." Albert Kinsey continued, "But, even the local firms can afford to pay us a shilling or two more."

"I don't need convincing about the justice of your claims. Albert, I've seen how all your members work on the quayside and on board. Your conditions are only a little better than the miners. Let me tell the Earl what you have said, he's meeting the owners. I'm sure that between us we can sort out an agreement that's agreeable for you and acceptable to the owners." Said victor.

"Let us discuss this on our own for a while Victor." Please wait outside, if you don't mind?" George stated. Victor left the men as they discussed his proposal and went outside into the warm sunshine. Gulls were Whirling and cawing overhead and the sun was gleaming on the spume covered water. He wandered to the quay's edge, where he picked up several pieces of discarded coal and began tossing them into the water. He had scattered the floating gulls far and wide when he heard George Jackson calling his name. He returned to the warehouse where he found the committee seated awaiting him. "Take this message to his lordship and the owners." Stated Henry Seer. "We are willing to fight on single handed if we must, we are determined not to give in, but these are our terms, we want no more outside labour brought into the docks, we have worked here without fame or favour since many of our grandfathers" time. We want an end to the 'black legs', and the trouble they bring. We also want an extra shilling a week for all crane men and similar increases for all workers. The seamen want a guarantee that no Chinese seamen are to be used as cheap labour."

"I will tell him your message, or would you rather write out your proposals and I'll deliver your letter." Victor asked the seated assembly. He would take their message but felt that it would seem much more official if the message was written by the committee themselves. "No"! answered George Jackson, we thought about that and decided, these are only our first proposals. If the owners are willing to discuss them, ask his lordship to arrange a meeting and we will attend. We will present our formal written demands at that meeting. Good luck Victor and thank you for trying to help. There will be many Newport families who will thank you if you can help pull this off."

"Those are their demands sir." Victor spoke to the earl and Hay Jones who were both seated comfortably in the merchant's office. He had enjoyed the walk from the quayside to the dock gates. He had never seen the water look so calm and peaceful. The only sound that disturbed the evening was the occasional raucous call of a frightened gull. He walked beside several towering ships, wondering what tales they could tell of far-off places. He placed his hands against the side of a chunky tugboat, expecting to feel its heartbeat throbbing through its red leaded side, but it was still. No need for engines because there's no ship movement' he thought to himself.

He had been the only passenger on the tram as it rattled and sparked its way along Commercial Road. He had paid his penny and sat upstairs at the front, enjoying the cool breeze in the open topped vehicle.

"Thank you, Victor, you have done more than expected. Well done!" Commented the earl. "If you go back to your office and carry on with your normal tasks, I'll know where to find you if I need you."

CHAPTER 24

It had been almost a week since Victor had spoken to the strike committee, and he had heard nothing since. The earl had been busy meeting all the local employers and ship owners. He hadn't been able to spend much time with Naomi, there hadn't been another' home concert' and the weather had been particularly unpleasant, with almost continual downpours. He had managed to steal one long lingering kiss in her father's office, when the merchant had gone to the Cardiff coal exchange to try to sell some of the company's large stockpile of steam coal. It wasn't a problem at present, but it would be, if this strike lasted for much longer. He couldn't even remember the excuse he had used to go to the manager's office, but he could remember her soft inviting lips as they brushed tantalisingly against his. He had folded her in his arms, and there she had nestled running her hands gently through his thick black hair as he gently stroked the small of her back. They had clung together in a final passionate kiss before Naomi begged him to leave, in case they were discovered.

The earl, accompanied by the merchant, called Victor from his office, much to the surprise of his fellow workers, who, from the looks feared for his continuing employment with the firm." Do you think they've discovered the secret romance?" Asked Trevor.

"I don't know." Brian answered, "I don't think so, because Hay Jones didn't have a razor in his hand when they fetched him!"

"If he thinks our Victor has laid so much as a fingernail on his precious darling, it won't be anything as gentle as a razor. It'll be a rusty bread knife!" Both men laughed loudly before returning to their bookkeeping.

Once in the merchant's office, the earl spoke to Victor." I have seen all the local owners and they feel the same way that I do. We must settle. This London group, Bouldon brothers' maybe a larger and powerful combination but they are not going to dictate the terms for Newport. Victor, go back to the docks, see the strikers and arrange a meeting, wherever they would prefer. I will meet them there, with representatives of the employers, and we will try to reach an agreement."

Victor had been well received by the strike committee, all of whom, were willing to meet their employers in an effort to solve the dispute. George Jackson's suggestion that they hold the talks at the 'Salutation', a public house on Commercial Road at six o clock the following evening was accepted by all parties.

"We are resolute and determined to hold out for our just demands." Stated George Jackson. He was acting as spokesman for the strikers. They sat stiffly along the side of the large rectangular table that had been placed in the 'Salutations' saloon bar, the employers sat, rigidly along the opposite edge. The only person who seemed at ease, was the earl. He listened intently to the opening statements; he leaned forward over the table with his hands clasped loosely in front of him.

"The men have told us they will not return until their demands are met." George concluded.

The Earl waited until Jackson had finished, he placed his palms flat on the glass like surface of the massive table, looked around, eyeing each man on the other edge individually. Victor, sitting at a small bar table slightly behind the old patrician, thought he looked a formidable adversary.

"I am sure, you, as well as we employers, wish this strike to end as soon as possible. The earl rose to his feet as he began to speak, he always felt more comfortable that way. It has cost everyone far too much money, money that none of us," He pointed to the strike committee, "especially you, or your members can afford to lose!"

Victor sat silently, as the discussion moved from one side of the table to the other. He enjoyed the way the arguments changed and shifted, as proposal and counter proposal drifted in and out of the discussion. He gazed, with mounting respect, as the strikers stuck manfully to their demands, despite threats and even conditional promises from the owners and employers. Although, voices became raised and tempers rose, the earl sat serene and calm throughout the entire proceedings.

"We are prepared to hold out for our rightful demands." reaffirmed George Jackson, "You know as well as I do you won't be able to move any cargo out of the port, and our brothers at all the Bristol Channel ports are of a like mind, so you cannot transfer your business elsewhere. We will return to work as soon as you recognise the justice of our claim. We are asking for a small increase in the wages in the pockets of our workers. The other conditions demonstrate we require security and freedom from worry."

The Earl stood again and said, "I suggest we separate for," he took his pocket watch out of his silk waistcoat. Looked at it and spoke. "Twenty minutes. We can discuss all the offers and proposals made, as well as enjoying some of the hospitality of this fine establishment." The strike committee left the room and made their way into the public bar. The earl left the owners talking at the bar and walked over to Victor. He was carrying two large glasses of whisky.

"So far so good, young man." He gave one of the glasses to Victor, "Here is a large one for you." Noticing victors alarmed look as he added, "I know your mother wouldn't approve, but it's time to start enjoying some sins of the flesh! A twinkle appeared in the old man's eye as he continued, although, if what I've heard about you and Naomi is true, you've already started!"

The fiery taste of the whisky added to the earl's remark, caused Victor to splutter and gag, which only added to the old man's enjoyment, as he thumped unmercifully on Victor's back.

"What do you mean?" Gasped Victor, trying to get some feeling back into his throat. The sudorific liquid was blazing along the back of his mouth and turning his eyes into deep pools.

"Don't cry!" Whispered the earl, "I won't tell her father."

"I've been a perfect gentleman!" Coughed Victor, "My intentions have been nothing but honourable, she's wonderful, the most beautiful woman in the world as far as I'm concerned!

"Glad to hear it. If you had said anything differently, I would have horse whipped you myself. She deserves respect, but more importantly she needs a man who loves her, she has had precious little of that since her mother died!"

"She means the world to me, your lordship, and I think she feels the same about me, but we are both worried about what her father will do and say if he finds out about us!"

"The secret's safe with me, but if I know, you can bet others do as well. They may be looking for every opportunity to do you down. They may not be under the same obligation to you, as I am. They will take any chance, they can, to send you back to where you came from, the coal mines!"

"I hope I have done enough to justify your faith in me, but as far as any obligation is concerned you have paid that back more than one hundred-fold!" Victor replied. The two men stood talking a short distance away from the other group of ship owners and employers. The latter group involved in heated and animated discussion. The earl looked towards them and said, I had better join the others. I think they're beginning too loose their tempers; this is a time for cool heads and compromise, not anger infested principals!" He left Victor and joined the others. Victor noticed the mood of the group change, as the earls calming influence and persuasion took control of the situation. It was as if a bucket of ice water had been thrown over a pack of fighting dogs. He sipped at the whisky, it still burned as hot as the hobs of hell, but in small sips he quite enjoyed it. He just hoped no one told mam!

The meeting reconvened and the discussions continued. Victor saw how the earl's diplomatic persuasion was having a subtle effect on the two groups, gradually bringing them together, to a compromise which both parties were able to agree, with a feeling, that they had not been the ones to capitulate completely.

"That's agreed then." The Earl announced, his voice booming around the quiet room, "We will agree to the pay rise and the local owners will return to the piece work method of payment. None of the Bristol Channel ships will employ cheap foreign crews, all crew members to receive the agreed rate of pay. Unfortunately, we cannot speak for Bouldon Brothers, who refused to take part in these discussions. We for our part, will keep to our side of the bargain."

"Fair enough!" George Jackson replied, "The strike committee feel that you have made a fair offer. We are of the opinion, that without exception, the Newport employer is a man to be proud of, he doesn't take advantage of the workman's weakness in discussion and bargaining. You are fully aware of the sacrifice involved in the dispatch of all Newport cargoes, by the Newport work men and are willing to pay a more than favourable recompense." What a windbag thought Victor, why didn't you just say thank you!

"I'll see you get some credit for what's happened here today." The earl said to Victor, "But there will be those who will not thank you for it. We will sign the agreement tomorrow and then it's back to work as usual." Victor left the pub and walked along the road; he had decided to walk when he heard a tram rattling along behind him. He was almost at a stop so, he put out his hand to halt it, he was back in Stow Hill before the earl had drunk his fifth glass of whisky.

Victor had worked for the company for more than eighteen months; he had gained experience in every department of the business. It came as a shock to some members of the staff when he had been chosen to replace Hugh Nelmes, as company 'victualling' clerk, when the former retired. It had made him unpopular with several more senior members, especially the under-clerk Leslie Saunders. Despite their hate and jealousy, no one could deny Victor's ability. He had introduced a scale of provisions, that were distributed to the crews, that had pleased both ships masters and crews. It included, a generous daily meat and bread allowance, together with a liberal quantity of fresh vegetables, when available. The success of his stewardship was witnessed by the fact that the company's crews signed articles for voyage after voyage. As a company head clerk, he was earning the fabulous sum of seven pounds and ten shillings a week! He was able to take his mother more than two pounds ten shillings every week. He had begun to save money for himself and now had almost seventy pounds in the bank!

He enjoyed Christine's wedding, her husband was a wonderful man, they had looked the perfect couple as they walked from the Chapel. He had received his greatest pleasure when quietly handing them two five-pound notes. Eric, protested and tried to hand the money back, but Christine, the wiser one of the two, pecked Victor softly on his cheek before tucking the notes into the bodice of her dress. She whispered softly to Eric, if you are a good boy, I'll let you look for them in a little while! And if you are a really, really, good boy, who knows what else you might find!

Victor winked at Eric and added quietly, "it's a special wife that keeps a little bit tucked away for a rainy day." He laughed, "Isn't it a pity there isn't a cloud in the sky!" He concluded looking skyward. "Don't you worry about me!" Eric replied. "I've got a bloody good imagination."

Christine pecked her husband gently on the lips and murmured softly to him, just wait a while and your days of imagination will be over, I've been saving myself for you, for a long time!

The wedding had also been a time of personal sadness. He had had his first tiff with Naomi, she had turned down the invitation he had given her to the wedding, afraid that her father would object.

"If you are still ashamed of me, I suppose I had better leave you alone!" He had snapped. He was mortified by his outburst almost immediately, as he noticed her eyes fill with tears.

"Don't you, you of all people, talk about me being ashamed! You know what my father is like. I love him dearly but, he will send me away, and forbid me to see you, if he suspected I was seeing you. Neither of us is 'of age', just be patient for another two years. She was pleading, almost begging. It was an appeal that made him hate himself for causing her such distress. "I'm sorry." He replied taking her in his arms and kissing her lightly on each weeping eye, tasting the saltiness of her tears, it's just that my sister is getting married, you would love one another. I want you to meet all my family, they are nice people, even though they are coal mining stock!"

"Don't start again!" She warned, "It's my father you have to convince, not me. If your family are half as pleasant as you are I'm sure I will love them all!" She looked up into his coal black eyes and continued, "I promise, the first chance we get, I will visit your family in Cwmcarn. But my father must never find out, not before I am twenty-one anyway! He hugged her, realising that all that she had said was true. Her father would never allow them to marry! He was only tolerated at the office because he had the backing of the Earl. It made no difference to Hay Jones that he was the most able worker in the company's office. They had kept their secret from the merchant through 1912 and 1913, although they were certain he must have suspected they were more than working acquaintances. Anyone who spent more than five minutes in their company, became aware of the electricity, the attraction that sparked between them whenever they were near one another, like a semi hidden longing, almost a sadness that yearned to be released. He hugged her close as she buried her head into his shoulder, giving herself up to the huge sobs of hopelessness that consumed her.

"Hush dearest!" He said softly, "We only have to put up with this deplorables situation for another 12 months, and then you will be free! We will then have the rest of our lives together!" He gently lifted her head until he was staring into her tear-stained eyes. "Will you still want me if your father turns me out of the company?" He spoke earnestly, almost afraid to hear her answer. "Think carefully because the only other job I know is coal mining! It isn't a way of life that you are suited too."

She returned his deep stare, as she wiped away a tear that was running slowly down her shining cheek. "It's you I love, not your job! I will go wherever you take me. But you are underestimating yourself, you are intelligent, and very, very, talented."

He felt utterly distraught, having been responsible for her abject wretchedness, "It's just that I fear for the future, I don't know what is to become of us if your father decides to send you away, and get rid of me from the company."

It had been the first time he had ever brought tears to her eyes, and he swore it would be the last.

Mam had arranged a wedding feast at home in George Street. She had borrowed a trestle table from the Chapel and had laid it in the front room. It contained A mouthwatering assortment of food covering the entire alphabet of things edible. The house gleamed and the aroma of Mansion Polish assaulted every olfactory nerve that was exposed to it! The bride and groom had led the wedding procession that walked from the Chapel to the house. The best man, Eric's brother Sam, had scattered the expected handful of farthings and ha' pennies to the raggedy gang of children, waiting expectantly for a chance to scramble after each thrown coin.

Elsie Cousins, Doris Morgan, Pam Smith and several other resident's of Feeder Row had gathered outside the Chapel gates to see the happy couple emerge.

"Lovely girl," said Doris, "looks as pretty as a picture. All the sisters helped Kate make the dress, young Victor bought the material from a swanky shop in Newport!"

"Yes!" Added Elsie, "It's the poshest wedding seen in Cwmcarn for ages!"

How do you make that out?" Asked Pam.

"It's a big wedding! Smirked Elsie, "And the bride isn't pregnant!" The ladies all rolled with laughter.

"If she is," joked Pam. "The poor little bastard will be choked under a bodice that tight!"

"She's a good girl is Christine! Elsie continued, kept her hand on her ha'penny until her wedding' night!"

The house had almost burst at it seems, it appeared to Victor that the entire village had been invited. The men were eternally grateful that it was a sunny day, the barrel of beer was propped on a wooden trestle in the backyard! Kate had refused to allow alcohol into her house but had agreed, after a great deal of persuasion to let Tom put the beer in the garden. You must let the lads toast the bride an' groom, it's tradition! Had been his final remark. She had relented on the understanding that not a thimble full of alcohol was to be brought into the house, not while the minister was present anyway! It developed into a dual, reception, the minister, the Chapel deacons, the women and the bride and groom chatted happily inside, whilst the men and the barrel of beer, laughed and sang outside. And all the while, the luckless groom wished he had something to drink instead of a constant stream of tea! Tom watched the way in which Victor dispatched several glasses of the honey brown liquid in a most practised manner. It was obvious that his nephew had certainly broadened his education in the two years he had been in Newport. Stuart and Evan made a beeline for Victor and began pulling his leg and unmercifully.

"I thought you would 'have 'had a woman in tow by now." Laughed Evan as he thumped Victor playfully on the back, "Somebody earning' as much as you should have to fight them off!

Stuart joined in the conversation, "Come on Victor, be honest you are too old to be still starching' the bed clothes! You'll end up blind if you don't find yourself a good little woman." Both men doubled over with mirth as they noticed the first tinge of embarrassment creep slowly up on past his collar and run gleefully through his scalp. Despite the importance and responsibility of his work he was still vulnerable to the Wiles and humour of his friends and neighbours.

"Leave the lad alone you pair of sarcastic bastards!" Shouted Huw Stevens, coming to Victor's aid. "How do you know he hasn't got a nice little girl that he doesn't want you nosey buggers to find out about!" Victor looked gratefully at the mining deputy and wondered if he knew anything of his romantic anguish and problems. Victor made a momentous decision, if he didn't confide in someone, he would go insane. He decided to tell Hugh about Naomi and himself. He grabbed his old friend and minster and pulled him out into the back garden until they were alone, he poured out his heart to the wise old deputy. Who listened in silence, making no interruptions until Victor had finished. He looked at the shadow of despair that seemed to haunt the youth's eyes then replied. "You seem to be in the middle of quite a problem. You know her class look down on us, we are lower than dogs. Do you think they'll let you marry one of their own? I can tell you it won't be easy. He spends the next ten minutes trying to persuade the youngster into seeking a more attainable wife but failed miserably!"

"I agree with every word you say!" Victor replied, "But I love her, and she loves me! If I don't marry her, I'll never marry!"

"I know one thing," he replied, "It's time you told your family about this young lady. You know as well as I do, no matter who she is or where she comes from, she won't be good enough for your mother!"

The two men talked together for several minutes, oblivious to the screams and laughter that came from the house. Victor decided that he would have to go in and enjoy the celebrations, he couldn't spoil Christine's wedding day, this had to be a perfect day. He would break the news soon, but not today.

CHAPTER 25

ALL THROUGH 1913 VICTOR AND NAOMI KEPT THEIR SECRET FROM her father, Victor was certain the old gentleman knew but he seemed to be content with the situation as long as nothing appeared to be official or permanent.

The company had improved its trading position steadily, and its dealings with South America were showing a handsome return, coal to the River Plate, with grain on the return voyage. Victor had coped with the procurement of the stores necessary for such a long and novel voyage, with consummate ease. A fact which caused several of the company's senior clerks' considerable displeasure, particularly Earnest Owen and Michael Porter. Two gentlemen, who were waiting, far from patiently, for Victor to make an error of judgement, or better still, a serious mistake. They made long and horrendous threats behind his back, yet no one, whilst he enjoyed the backing and favour of the Earl, did move against him. Brian and Trevor, for their part, enjoyed his success and were scornful of the doubters and antagonists. They wished him well, hoping that he would advance himself to an impressive impregnable position before the earl succumbed to the ultimate and certain fate that awaits us all.

April had been an especially wet month, with both the River Usk and Ebbw riding high in their courses. Anxious glances had been cast at the stability and security of their banks, but fears proved groundless. Victor gazing out through the tall window was watching the rivulets of water as they streamed down the slick panes before gurgling into the cast iron drainpipes returning the endless streams of water on their never-ending journeys to the sea. The docks had enjoyed more than a year's comparative peace, only a few minor disputes, usually concerning the Bouldon Brothers and their companies had disturbed this smooth co-existence of the port and its employees. He sat back in his chair a deep feeling of contentment and well-being flooded through his veins, when suddenly he heard a scream! His blood ran cold as the scream was repeated and he barely recognised the anguished sob of Naomi's grief-stricken exclamation as she called his name! "Victor! for God's sake come quickly!" He jumped to his feet and was through the door in less than half a dozen enormous strides.

"Hurry! Oh God! I don't know what to do!"

The screams led him to the merchant's office, for the first time he went into a room without knocking, he was followed by Trevor and the office manager William Hyde. Naomi was slumped at her father's desk, staring wide eyed and terrified at the ashen apparition, that Victor realised was her father! Hay Jones was jerking convulsively on the floor; his unblinking eyes were rolling drunkenly around their sunken sockets. The old man's face was covered in blood, which was splashed over the table and chair legs, because, in his frenzy, he had almost bitten through and severed his tongue.

"Get Naomi out of here now!" Victor bellowed, as he ran quickly to the fallen merchant. Kneeling beside the injured man, he held his head firmly between his strong hands. Holding him in a vice like grip, Victor ensured that the merchant did no further damage to himself, he was amazed at the strength of the spasms that ripped through the old man's frame. He held on until the last ripple subsided and the merchant slumped unconscious in his arms. Lifting the inert body with ease, he carried it to a large leather sofa, where he made the merchant as comfortable as possible.

"Get on the telephone and call the doctor!" He ordered Trevor, who was standing shocked in the doorway, tell him to hurry! Looking out into the other office he caught sight of Naomi, she was crying bitterly at her desk, her head cradled in her arms.

"Come here Naomi". He called her into the office. For her own sake, he decided, she must sit by the still form of her father and comfort him. The merchant was oblivious to everything that was happening. Help me look after your dad he needs you! Consoled Victor.

She lifted her head and with tears streaming from her tormented eyes she wasn't bravely into the room with Victor. He closed the door behind them.

"Your father has suffered a massive stroke my child." Said Doctor Cormack, the family's physician. His broad Irish brogue almost singing the words. I've been telling him for months now, it's time to slow down! He wouldn't listen. Naomi, Victor and the doctor stood quietly at the merchant's bedside in the Newport and Monmouthshire hospital. Lewis Hay Jones had been rushed there, straight from his office a little more than three days previously. He had remained in the bed since his admittance, he had neither opened his eyes nor moved! The only sign of life was the slight rise and fall of his chest that witnessed his shallow breathing. The erratic beat of his heart was causing concern to all who listened to it, a great deal of anxiety. "You must prepare yourself for the worst. I don't know if he's going to regain consciousness, but if he does, he will probably be an imbecile or a cripple for the rest of his days!"

You callus bastard thought victor, what a wonderful way to tell someone, already grieving, there is no hope for her father. He put his arms protectively around her shoulder and she buried her head into his chest as she gave herself up, once again, to the sobs that engulfed her whole body. She had remained at her father's bedside the whole time, and Victor had been no more than three feet away from her.

"Go home and get some rest, you need your sleep. You can't do anything here. They'll send for you if there is any change." She looked into Victor's eyes, pleading with him, but he replied, "Let me take you home, you are exhausted. If you don't have some sleep soon, you are going to need a bed here yourself! I promise to bring you back if it becomes necessary."

She slept for more than 15 hours, thanks to a sleeping draught provided by the doctor, Victor had given it to the housekeeper and told her to put it into a warm cup of cocoa for Naomi. "Make sure she drinks it!" Had been his parting remark, before he made his weary way back to Stow Hill. They returned to the hospital every day to sit at the bedside, clutching hands, and saying nothing. Afraid to speak least they disturbed the comatose figure lying motionless in the bed beside them.

Lewis Hay Jones died six days later, without regaining consciousness. Victor had remained resolutely at Naomi's side throughout the ordeal. He was buried at the Holy Trinity Church.

Relatives, Naomi hadn't seen for more than fifteen years and others she didn't even know, turned up for the funeral and waited like vultures for the reading of her father's will. Victor remained staunchly beside her, impervious to the snide remarks and hostility he received. On more than one occasion the Earl had prevented him from splitting a scornful skull. The covetous fraternity gathered in the drawing room, waiting insatiably for the family's solicitor, Ivor Pugh, to read the will. They sat expectantly like gormandising locusts waiting to pick the bones clean. The attorney placed his tattered briefcase on the table before him and took out a large manilla envelope. He broke the wax seal and spread several foolscap documents onto the table. The rapturous gathering sat still, as the lawyer coughed.

"This is the last will and testament of Lewis Hay Jones; he began to read through the lengthy document and his expectant audience waited hungrily for him to reach the monetary sections. It was a lengthy document and would take the aged lawyer several minutes to read. He paused however, and took a small envelope from his open case, opening the flimsy paper, He smiled up to Naomi and declared, "Your father provided this codicil to his will a little more than six months ago, his instructions were that it be read before the will.

'To whom it may concern, it has come to my attention that my daughter Naomi has been involved with one of my employees, a common pit boy of whom I thoroughly disapprove. He is an able and intelligent worker, whom, under his present patronage will probably advance far in the company's hierarchy. Despite his obvious talents, I cannot sanction the alliance. Naomi has always been a headstrong and self-willed young woman and will probably do as she chooses, but I will not allow any of my estate to go to any fortune, hunting schemer. If she decides to waste her life with that young man, my house and fortune are to go to my second Cousin Sidney Martinson.' The solicitor paused as an excited buzz ran through the listeners. He coughed loudly, and scowled harshly at the persistent offenders, before continuing with the letter.

If she decides to marry Victor Leslie, my daughter Naomi, is to be given five hundred pounds and told to leave my house forthwith! She is to be allowed seventy-two hours from the reading of this, my codicil, to reach a decision. If she renounces the miner, my will is to be read. If she decides otherwise, I revoke my will and the instructions given in the letter are to be followed implicitly.'

Mr. Pugh looked up and said, "I tried to advise your father against such action, but he was determined. There was no way I could persuade him otherwise." Naomi looked neither left nor right but stared into the kindly old lawyers yellowing eyes, she squeezed Victor's hand tightly and replied in a faltering voice, "Thank you Uncle Ivor, but I know how much of a bigot my father could be!" This remark caused several angry murmurs which were silenced by some long and threatening stares from Victor, as he pointedly balled his right hand into a granite hard fist!

"I must ask everyone to leave so that I can think clearly for myself. I will let you know of my decision in a day or two." The startled witnesses began to vacate the house, leaving only the Earl, Mr Pugh, Victor and Naomi in the room. The Earl gave Naomi's arm a gentle squeeze as he followed the departing relatives.

"I'm very sorry Naomi, but one way or another, I must have your answer within three days." He sadly collected his belongings before thrusting them angrily into his briefcase and leaving.

"I've never wanted your father's money Naomi. I've not considered it, come away from this house and let me look after you, we don't need his money!" Naomi looked unhappily at Victor, "How dare daddy!" How dare he, inflict this on me at a time like this. He was my father and I loved him deeply. Didn't he realise that I would want some time to grieve over him, not count his inheritance!" She took Victor's hand in hers and caressed it gently. His once coal calloused palm was now soft as the down on an eider chick's breasts. "I want you to be patient and also leave me alone." Victor began to protest but she pushed her flawless index finger quickly to his lips, "Hush my darling, I must think this through all by myself. Come back tomorrow when I will give you, my answer. You will have it, before anyone!" Victor began to argue, then plead, but she merely pushed him to the door and begged him to leave. When she heard the front door close, she turned towards the fireplace with its picture of her parent's arm in arm, hanging above it. Smiling unhappily at their contented faces she threw herself onto the table and surrendered to tears that had been threatening to engulf her for the last two hours.

Victor walked back to The Woodlands home with his hands thrust deeply into his pockets. He stamped his feet angrily onto the dry pavement and kicked out mercilessly at a poor tomcat that happened to cross his path, a reflex that he regretted bitterly the moment he had done it, fortunately the old Tom had the sense to disappear into a private hedge before further retribution could be exacted upon it. He began to wonder how much he was asking Naomi to give up for him. Could he expect her to settle for an ex-miner, even one that loved her, when she had the chance of receiving a fortune and the hundreds of suitors it would bring. Did he love her enough to give her up, so that she could inherit what was hers by right? He reached the front door turned the handle and went in.

Victor had squirmed uneasily at his desk for no more than twenty lifelong minutes, when a loud knock at the door, catapulted him back to reality. He stood as the earl entered. He waved Victor back to his chair and sought out a comfortable seat for himself. He smiled reassuringly at his young protégé.

"You look as happy as my head gardener when he's lost a Bob and found a penny!" The old man remarked. "Don't be so gloomy, after all, if she wants you more than the old goat's money, you only have to ask the permission of her guardian." Victor looked up, his eyes frozen with terror at the thought of more obstacles being placed in their way, if she should choose him!

"You don't know who it will be, do you?" He asked.

"'Afraid I do old chap. Mischievous old devil! Don't know if he'll like you anymore than Hay Jones!" Victor buried his face dejectedly in his hands and missed the twinkle that appeared in the old man's eyes.

'Lord what have I done to deserve this treatment', He thought to himself. He began to worry about how he would handle this new situation and approached this new, formidable representative. Before any more could be said, the door burst open, and Naomi hurtled into the office with the energy of the Cardiff to London express! Victor swept her into his arms and eagerly sought her Ruby lips, she unashamedly returned both his kiss and embrace. The earl's polite cough caused them to part.

"Am I to assume from what I have just witnessed, that you have reached a decision?" The Earl inquired.

"There was no decision to be made Uncle Horace," Naomi said. There's only one way I'll ever be separated from Victor, and I hope that doesn't happen for another 50 years! I needed some time alone to grieve for my father, perhaps daddy will be happier now that he's with mother!" Her eyes were ablaze with desire and commitment, as she stared deeply into Victor's burning orbs, catching sight of the sadness lurking at the rear.

"We are no nearer to marrying now, than we were before! We still have to obtain the consent of your new guardian, and from what his lordship has just told me about him, that won't be easy!"

Naomi turned and glanced at the earl, "Just what have you been telling Victor about yourself Uncle Horace?" Victor turned to face the smiling face of his old Patrician.

"You mean you are...?" Victor began but the old man interrupted him before he could finish.

"Forgive an old man who has a foolish sense of humour!" He bowed low to the young couple before him.

"Sir? said Victor, never the one to miss an opportunity, I love your ward deeply, although I won't be able to keep her in the style to which she has known for all her life, I will do my best to look after her and take care of her. Will you allow me to marry her?" Naomi turned towards him and, as she had done so frequently in the past, she allowed him to kiss her deeply, with all the passion that his youthful inexperience could manage. The kindly old man looked fondly at the youthful couple and smiled.

"I don't think my permission will be a problem, but what about Victor? He's still underage, will his mother allow him to marry?" Asked the earl. Victor looked at Naomi, then turned to the earl before answering. Once Mam, Uncle Tom and the girls meet you," he said to Naomi, "They will love you as much as I do! I go home tomorrow evening to play for choir practise, will you come home and meet my family?"

"I've been waiting for this invitation for several months, but now it's come I feel petrified!" Naomi said. They decided to travel to Cwmcarn on the 6:20 train the following evening. It would be a surprise for the family, Victor hoped it would be a happy one. He was sure they would accept Naomi, especially once they knew how much she was prepared to give up to be with him.

The earl walked over to the beaming couple, he pecked his ward lightly on her flushed cheek and shook Victor's hand vigorously." My wedding gift will be to promote you to office manager when I make William Hyde the companies new merchant." He announced, "I will leave instructions that you are to receive a salary of eight pounds five shillings a week!" Naomi, allowed herself a secret sigh, with the five hundred pounds from her father, one hundred pounds she already had in trust from her mother, together with Victor's new wages, they would have a very comfortable life together.

CHAPTER 26

THE TRAIN PULLED INTO THE DESERTED STATION WHERE ONLY Victor and Naomi descended onto the Platform. Naomi looked nervously around, half expecting to see a vetting committee waiting for them!

"Relax" Victor ordered "No one knows you're coming; you are going to surprise a few people tonight!". The casual remark filled her with dread and apprehension, she couldn't descend unannounced on his family, like an unwelcome washing day shower, what would they think of her? She made up her mind, and once it was made up, she was as obstinate as a mule.!

I'm staying here in the waiting room, until you tell your family about me." He began to argue, but she shut him up. "I know how I would feel! I've been worrying about it all the way here. Tell them about me and I'll meet them when it's more convenient. I'll wait here until you return". Victor was unable to crack her resolve and despite all the arguments and pleadings she stayed behind.

Victor ran all the way to George Street, by the time he reached number 26 he was panting for breath. He rushed into the kitchen in such a state of exhaustion that Kate almost fainted. Ivy jumped to her feet and dragged Victor to one of the fireside chairs.

"Sit still Victor" Ivy commanded, catch your breath then you can tell us what's the matter." It took several deep breaths before his head stopped swimming and he felt confident enough to talk. He looked around the entire family everyone except for Christine, had come into the kitchen to find out what had caused the commotion.

"I'm glad everyone's here, I've a story to tell you...." He began telling them of his meeting with Naomi, the way their feelings had grown and developed. He told of the secrecy that they had been forced to adopt because of the hostility and bitterness of her father. He continued with the tale of his death and the condition laid down in his will. By the time he had finished the story, the girls were all in tears.

"Victor!" sobbed Ivy. "That was probably the saddest story I have ever herd. I think my heart is going to break in two! I didn't know you could be such a romantic. It sounds as if she must have really suffered, just because she loves you!".

"I never met her father," snapped Glenys angrily, "But I will hate him forever, he sounds a horrible beast!"

Kate had remained silisn't, listening thoughtfully to her son's story, and the comments of her daughters. She stood and went over to him, she put her hand gently on his shoulder before running her fingers affectionately through his lush black hair.

"If you love her, and she seems to love you I will give my blessing, but I would like to meet her first," said Kate.

"She's at the station," Victor announced, "She was afraid to turn up out of the blue! She said I had to tell you about us first just in case you disapproved!".

Kate's eyebrows reared up onto her forehead, in the way that the family recognised as a premonition of impending explosion. "Victor!" she snapped "Do you mean you left that poor girl all alone in a strange station?" She pulled her hand roughly out of his hair making him yelp painfully. "She's in a strange village and is probably still grieving over her father, because despite it all he was still her dad!". Kate marched purposefully to the door, snatched up her shawl, which she wrapped around her shoulders and went out through the door. "I'll fetch her you all wait here." She ordered over her shoulder as she disappeared with a voice that no one dared dispute.

Naomi huddled herself into a corner of the austere room. Looking around she was faced on three sides with brown varnished panelling, a single window next to the door overlooked the platform. A lacquered wooden wall clock was the only decoration. She closed her eyes and hoped Victor would soon return, not since her mother had died had she felt so completely alone" She closed her eyes as the tears began to fall. "Hurry Victor, I need you!" she whispered to herself. She watched the clock run endlessly through forty minutes, when the "prison" door opened. A kindly old lady walked confidently into the room but whispered nervously "Naomi?"

Naomi looked up through her red tear-stained eyes and answered, "Yes I'm Naomi!".

The old lady went to her and gently took her hand. "Wipe away those tears you are coming home with me! I'm Kate, Victor's Mam. Only I might not have a son by the time I've finished with him, fancy him leaving you here on your own. I'll skin him alive the little toe rag!"

Naomi, gathering her composure she began to defend her Victor, "It wasn't his fault, I told him I was going to wait!"

"He should have made you. If you are to be part of this family the first rule, is we are a family. We don't leave anyone on their own, especially in times of trouble. Come on there are a house full of people who want to know all about you, not the garbled version we had off our Victor". Kate led the smiling young woman out of the station and began the long walk to George Street. Kate took a secretive appraisive look at the young women walking beside her. In the beauty stakes, she decided Victor had chosen well!

She found it easy to talk to this young woman as they strolled slowly homeward. Kate discovered, much to her pleasure, the depth of feeling that Naomi held for Victor and with every passing step she found herself warming towards her. By the time they reached home they were strolling arm in arm and laughing merrily together, a fact which amused the girls greatly as they entered the kitchen.

"Mam" Exclaimed Ivy with an enormous grin that broke out from one side of her mouth to the other. "What are you doing with that young lady, we all thought you had gone to scratch her eyes out! After all she wants to take little Victor away from his Mammy" She jumped to her feet rushed to Naomi and hugged her so tightly that everyone heard her ribs cry out in anguish. Welcome to the Leslie household, I'm Ivy, soon to be your big sister. Naomi was almost trampled underfoot as the family rushed forward to greet her. The fervour of the welcome opened the flood gates once more, and her tears began falling like rain.

"Give the poor girl some air" Kate ordered "You're all going to frighten her away if you're not careful." Naomi took out a small silk handkerchief and gently brushed the tears from her cheeks.

"Please don't mind me" she apologised, smiling at the concerned faces that surrounded her, "I didn't know what to expect that's all, I didn't know if I would be welcome or not" Tom who had been standing at the rear of the throng of excited sisters pushed his way gently to the front. He took Naomi's dainty fingers in his gnarled shovel like hands, looked deeply into her eyes and said, "I am pleased to meet you, I hope you don't mind me saying, but you are far too pretty for our Victor, you have definitely got the worst end of the deal!".

Naomi looked harshly at the man who was doing his best to crush her fingers into a pulp when Kate interrupted. "Take no notice of the sarcastic so and so, he's just trying to wind you up" Tom leaned forward pecked Naomi lightly on her cheek and did his best to squeeze every last drop of air out of her petite frame.

"I was merely complimenting the young lady on her beauty" he said. "Victor you've got yourself a dazzling vision of loveliness!" He pecked her once again on the cheek and added, "We think our Victor is special, so it will take someone as perfectly unique as you to deserve him." He stepped back and took a long carful look at her." And I think he has made a wonderful choice."

"You must have made the right sort of impression" laughed Glenys, "You've been in the house for almost five minutes and mam hasn't wanted to put the kettle on!". The family sat cosily around the blazing coal fire, kept high in the grate despite the warmth of the late June evening. Everyone wanted to know every detail from their first meeting to the trip to Cwmcarn on the train. Naomi sat contentedly in the comfortable chair as the warmth of the affection crept slowly through her aching heart and began to fill her with a sense of belonging.

It was Tom who broke the spell when he announced that if both, he and Victor did not leave for choir practice straight away the members would skin them both alive.

"Let them go so that we girls can have a real get to know you chat. Suggested Kate.

Tom and Victor were soon walking briskly toward the Chapel schoolroom. "You sly old bugger!" exclaimed Tom looking proudly at his young nephew. "You kept her secret didn't you, she's a cracker and will certainly raise a few eyebrows around the village I can tell you" The two men hurried into the Choir's practice room to find an impatient gang of men awaiting their late arrival.

"Slower than a fart own a spinster's privy" quipped Stuart Thomas, as Tom mounted the conducting dais at the front of the choir.

"The only hot air in this buildin' comes out of your mouth Stuart" retorted Tom." It just so happens that we 'have a visitor at 'home and' it was touch an' go whether we was coming' or not tonight! But seeing as how we are here let's get on with the practice. We'll start with "Glory and love to the men of old.' Victor searched through the tall pile of music at his feet. "Ready to die for Father Land! Echoed through the hall as the resounding climax of "Gounod's Soldiers' chorus reverberated. Tom took the choir through the entire piece once again, before commenting "Not bad! In a year or two we should be singing it quite well" The usual moans and groans regarding Tom's parentage and reluctance to praise were stilled, as the school room door opened to admit Kate, Ivy and Naomi. It was Naomi, as the stranger who was attracting all the attention and interest. Tom put down his white baton and announced, "Gentlemen may I introduce Miss Naomi Hay Jones our Victor's intended." He glared at the choir to silence any comment before whispering "Double barrel name see dead posh, so anybody swears or farts out loud will have my baton where the sun don't shine!"

The women unaware of the interest they had aroused, sat in chairs that were arranged in a neat row near the door. Victor turned and smiled at Naomi, a knowing affectionate smile, if she had been brought to the choir practice, she was accepted!

"If you can take that 'lapdog' smile off your face for five minutes Victor" added Tom "Perhaps we can try, 'The song of The Jolly Roger!" Victor Played as if he was possessed and the choir returned the compliment by singing superbly. There followed an hour's uninterrupted singing of almost the choir's entire repertoire. It was impossible to say whether the choir, or their small audience, enjoyed it more! Tom put his baton on the piano top for the last time, before announcing, "I let you off lightly tonight, there was lots of mistakes, but I wanted to let Victor swank a bit! You won't get away with it next week." Most of the choir made their way slowly out of the room, after a short word of greeting or a nod of welcome to Kate and her 'guest'. A small group formed itself round the piano and Victor.

"You sly old sod!" shouted Evan Wilkinson, "Congratulations, it isn't so bad being' married! It 'has got its compensations, 'specially at meal times!" "Bedtimes you mean!" laughed Stuart. "She looks a bit of alright from here Vic. What's she like close up?"

"Not much if she falls for a toss pot like 'him!" added Bryn Smith. "I'm going to give you only one piece of advice," said Huw Stevens seriously holding out his hand to shake Victor's "And it's "Never fart under the bedclothes!" warned Stuart Thomas "cos it's a real passion killer!" The entire group laughed heartily at his crude interruption.

By the time the laughter had ceased, Huw said, "I can't remember what I was going to say so, it couldn't have been that important! Are you going to introduce us to your young lady?"

Victor took the men and introduced them to Naomi, they all shook her hand warmly and agreed that she was, 'A cut above' the sort of girl they had expected Victor to end up with. By the time they left the silisn't school room, the summer night was beginning to cast its shadows and the sparse gas lamps were appearing as solitary sentinels against the advancing darkness.

It was time to return to Newport. For the first time since he had left Cwmcarn, the family accompanied Victor to the railway station, more truthfully, they escorted Naomi and Victor went too! They reached the station just as the locomotive was pulling noisily to a halt, Victor ran to purchase the tickets as the family said their goodbyes to their soon to be accepted member.

"Come and see us properly" invited Kate, as she kissed Naomi warmly on her unblemished cheek, "Stay for the weekend so that we can get to know you even better" The sentiment was endorsed by each member of the family in turn, especially Tom, who whispered, "You're just what he needs, a good women to bring the best out of him!"

Naomi nestled contentedly against his warm, strong shoulder as they enjoyed the short dark journey back to Newport.

CHAPTER 27

Naomi, saw the earl and her solicitor Ivor Pugh, in her living room. There was a great deal of sadness etched into the faces of both men, we've studied the will in great detail but have been unable to find a way of overturning its conditions.

The lawyer apologised, "The plain fact of the matter is, if you marry the young man you stand to lose the house and slightly more than fifteen thousand pounds!"

Naomi, smiled cheerfully at the two disconsolate figures before her, then replied.

"Thank you, but you needn't worry. I loved my father and mourn his passing, however, I deplore his decision and will never forgive him for his bigoted opinion of Victor. We intend to marry. I met his family last night and I have never felt so much warmth and affection, it's worth the price! For the first time in more years than I can remember, I have felt at peace with myself. I can look forward to friendship, courtesy and freely given love. Can you say the same gentleman?"

The Earl sat back, have a long sigh of resignation, which was followed by a smile of acceptance. "I think you are like your mother, wilful and obstinate, too headstrong for two old codgers such as we, to change your mind. I will wish you well, and give you my blessing to marry your 'rough black diamond'. Good luck my dear, I fear you are going to need it!"

The elderly solicitor shook his head and reached behind him for a sheaf of documents, "I'm afraid you will have to sign these disclaimers, renouncing all rights to your father's estate!" He placed the documents before her and Naomi, without a moment's hesitation signed each one with a carefree flourish, before passing them to the earl for him to witness! "Your cousin." The solicitor continued, has agreed to your remaining in the house for as long as you require.

"I'll make him wish he had never been born. If he doesn't!" promised the earl.

The thoughtful luminary gathered the papers together and left. For several minutes the aged guardian and his ward sat quietly talking with hushed voices. "The next couple of months are going to be quite difficult ones my dear," The earl said with more than one hint of regret in his voice.

"Unfortunately, I'm not going to be here to help or advise you. Lady Charlotte and I are going on the S.S Monmouth to South America. We've never seen that neck of the world so we are taking a bit of a holiday, then onto the United States, we will be away for at least a year. I've left instructions about Victor's position at the company and Pugh's my written consent for your wedding. I'm sorry we can't stay but the arrangement's for the trip were made some time ago, and we can't alter them now."

"Don't worry! Victor and I will be fine. I was hoping you were going to give me away, but that doesn't matter. I've more than enough money to buy and furnish a house and keep a large nest egg for emergencies, and we will be able to live handsomely on Victor's new wage."

The couple continued their conversation for more than three hours with the old man giving as much advise as he thought relevant. Eventually he stood and said "Well my dear, I'm afraid I have to catch a train to London in an hours' time. The next time I come to Newport will be to board the 'Monmouth'.

The earl left a resolute Naomi, determined to make a successful future for herself with Victor. She closed the door, as if she were ending her past life, ready to begin her bright future with the man she loved and who loved her.

The train screeched to a halt at Cwmcarn and the young couple jumped gleefully onto the platform. Naomi was the first one through the wrought iron barrier, urging Victor on, as he handed their crumpled tickets to Evan. Who, true to form complained about their condition. They strolled over the narrow bridge that spanned the dark brown sludge that had once been the crystal-clear River Ebbw. Victor had never known it to look like water, it had always reminded him of a severed vein, slowly bleeding itself to death! Perhaps one day, his children or grandchildren might see its pure glassy waters once again. Arm in arm they strolled through the village, climbing gradually through Park Street until they came to George Street and were standing before number 26.

Kate had watched them strolling up the hill and silently opened the door for them to enter. She kissed each of them affectionately and ushered them inside, where a freshly brewed cup of tea stood steaming on the table for them. This was their third weekend visit, and Kate looked forward to each one with relish.

"Hello Mam" said Naomi with genuine affection "I thought the weekend would never come. It's been a busy week in the office with ships in from Spain and Italy, poor old Victor hasn't known whether he's coming or going!"

They sat at the table, but Naomi was too excited to either eat or drink, "If I don't tell you soon I will burst," she announced "We've seen a lovely house and we have paid a deposit, Mr Pugh is arranging it's purchase for us and thinks the sale will be completed in about a month We were hoping that you would see Mr Morgan and ask if we could get married in the chapel in four weeks' time, on a Saturday." She noticed Kate's surprise as she mentioned the local chapel and quickly added, "I know it ought to be in my own, but I have no family left in Newport, you have become the only family I know." Kate smiled at the compliment and was pleased at the way this young woman had settled in so easily into her extended family.

"Of course, I'll arrange it! If Berwyn says anything, he'll have me to reckon with!" Kate replied.

Victor smiled to himself secretly enjoying the way that Naomi had Mam, almost eating out of her hand!

"As you know my father has died and the earl is away, do you think Uncle Tom will give me away?"

"Of course he will!" Kate answered. "If he knows what's good for him!"

"You can't answer for Uncle Tom mam!" Victor insisted. "Naomi must ask him, and it must be his decision!"

The young couple decided to take a short stroll over the mountainside and enjoy the clear, warmth of the summer's evening. The bluebells had almost faded, only a few solitary dying stalks were visible, but the foxgloves were standing tall, happily enduring the strong sunlight, as it encouraged them to unfurl their mighty bells. They walked over the lush green turf of Peggy's field, no one knew why it was so named, it had always been so. Victor gleefully pulled Naomi up its steep slopes as the melodious song of the hiding black birds echoed from the tall clumps of spiteful bramble, that guarded the approach to the tall stands of birch and beech. Naomi looked up, high, high above them almost to the sparse cloud, a single buzzard circled majestically, attentively looking for any sign of a careless rabbit that would provide it with the meal eagerly awaited by its ravenous young. They strolled higher, here the mountain was unblemished; no sign of coal mining or stone quarrying; that might offend nature or the discerning eye of the walker.

They sat beneath the shade of a magnificent silver birch, its gnarled bark bearing witness to the ravages of decades of protection against harsh winters and sweltering summers. She nestled in his arms, as they looked down at the sleepy village. His lips found hers and they hung together in a passionate embrace, his tongue hungrily engulfing her willing mouth. His hand sought out a firm hard breast and was pleased to feel its nipple hardening to his touch. Naomi lay back enjoying the sensations that were coursing through her body, tingling electric shocks that were setting her aflame. she felt the stiffness developing deep within his trousers carnally craving for the release that only she could bring! She jumped to her feet "Victor! Don't force me into something we will both regret. Please, you only have to wait a few more weeks. I want to come to you a virgin!" She pleaded.

His passion subsided, they ambled down the worn track, back to the home where his family were waiting. Tom, when told of Naomi's wish, coupled with the fact that she had no living relative that she wanted to ask, agreed to give the bride away. Victor reached into his pocket and took out a crisp, white five-pound note, which he handed to his mother. "I want you to arrange our wedding supper, you must ask whoever you think should come. We have already asked eight people from Newport."

Kate looked at the note and replied, "With this much money I could feed the whole village!"

"We don't want that mam." Victor replied, "Just family and friends for a nice spread."

"If I know your mam," Tom added, "She'll do you proud, it'll be a day to remember!"

Victor smiled at his uncle before handing him two 10-shilling notes. "This is for the yard!" He said giving his uncle a blatant wink, "There must be something for the boys outside! It's thirsty work attending a wedding."

Leaving the men to attend choir practice, Kate took Naomi to see the Minister so that the wedding arrangements could be made. As they were walking to, 'Nazareth' they met Pam Smith, Elsie Cousins and Doris Morgan, making their way to the Cwmcarn Hotel. The three ladies were joining their husbands for the usual night's session at the pub.

"Good evening, Mrs. Leslie." Greeted Elsie.

"Have you met Naomi?" Kate introduced Naomi to the ladies from Feeder Row. They shook her hand so violently that Naomi was almost pulled off her feet. "She is going to marry my Victor."

"So this be the girl 'who is going' to' marry your Victor?" Asked Elsie, as she winked at her two friends, "It isn't what it's cracked up to be dear!" she concluded.

They only want you for one thing!" Laughed Pam.

"Yeh, cooking' dinner an' darning socks!" Interrupted Elsie.

"A bit of 'how's your father is a waste of bloody time! They will 'usually be too drunk and it's all over an' done with in two seconds!" Bellowed Doris.

"They all boast about how big it is, but at night you can hardly find it!" Added Pam.

Kate raised her eyes skyward and took a firm grip of Naomi's arm ready to haul her away to a less embarrassing climate.

"Come with us and 'have a glass a stout, at least if you are drunk you will fall on your back of your own accord!" Laughed Elsie. The three women crossed the road and were making for the large black door of the Hotel, when Naomi called out to them. Her ears were a flame with scarlet embarrassment," It was wonderful to meet you I hope we meet again soon. Doris, who was almost through the door turned back and shouted If you need any advice on your wedding' night don't be afraid to ask! Kate knows where to find us."

"Only Piece of advice is don't do it!" shouted Pam as she entered the public house, "But, if you do, strap your ankles together, and tie your nightie to your toes!" She disappeared inside, leaving Kate and Naomi standing outside the hotel, mouths gaping, like a pair of floundering goldfish.

Kate began to quickly search her mind for a suitable answer to the idiosyncrasies of the women, when Naomi began to laugh. It began as a high-pitched giggle but developed into a raucous, contagious bellow that soon infected Kate. Both women stood in the middle of the street with the tears running down their faces.

"I didn't realise there was so much I had to learn!" Naomi exclaimed. "I would have sworn they were drunk already!" Kate shook her head and without answering, led the way to the manse to discuss the wedding arrangement's with the minister.

There was, she decided, nothing she could add to the wisdom of the three old sages.

Tom, took a sideways look at his nephew as they walked to choir practice. The boy was a good two inches taller than he and there was a spread to his shoulders that showed the lad possessed considerable strength. Victor was earning more money in a week than he did in a month! Good luck to the lad, he was proud of him. Naomi showed every sign of being the perfect woman for the youngster. I know I've never been married but I've been about quite a bit so if there's anything you need advice on I'll try to advise you!!!"

"Don't worry uncle." Victor replied. "I know you've 'seen to' the, needs of several widows in the village, and have lots of first-hand experience, but I know where everything is and how it's supposed to work, though I'll admit to not having any practice! Only to you mind!" He added quickly.

"I hope your skin is pretty thick tonight. "Warned Tom. "Only you can expect quite a bit of leg pulling from the choir."

Much to his surprise, choir practice passed without any sarcastic comments. Victor could hardly believe his luck. As he was preparing to leave the hall, he found Stuart and Evan waiting for him.

"I hope you intend taking the boys out for a little drink before you join the married club?" Asked Evan.

"I hadn't thought about it." Victor answered truthfully, "But I will, it'll be a good idea to say goodbye to my single days!" Tom who had overheard the conversation made a mental note to warn his nephew, when they were alone, against such foolishness. The last person who had gone on such an outing wasn't found until two days after the wedding! He was tied up inside a coal wagon at Swansea Docks! It was a tradition to have a skinful of beer before getting married, but he would make sure that Victor was there for the wedding, he had never given a bride away before and he intended to make sure that these dopey buggers didn't spoil the wedding. With friends like Evan and Stuart to look after you. You didn't need enemies!

CHAPTER 28

KATE HAD FUSSED HER WAY THROUGH THE PREVIOUS THREE WEEKS. The wedding arrangement's had been finalised and everything had run smoother than a well-oiled wheelbarrow! She looked around the chapel, it was spotless, and the floral decorations were superb, old Mr Smith's Garden had produced some magnificent blooms. Everything looked wonderful. Tom had ensured that Victor hadn't drunk too much beer and was in a fit state to participate in his wedding ceremony. She had witnessed far too many weddings with a sozzled bridegroom, supported rubber legged at the alter by an equally incapable friend! It was often the only way some of the men could face up to the future of literally spending a lifetime with some of the old hags, they had been unlucky enough to put in the family way. The chapel began to fill as the guests arrived, everyone in their Sunday best, starched collars and bowler hats! The smell of camphor began to pervade every nook and cranny of the building bearing silent malodorous witness to the demise of a thousand ravenous moths, as everyone used their one and only suit and best frock for its annual airing; usually it was a funeral, but today according to most, a happier occasion! Victor arrived with his best man, Trevor Bailey. He pecked Kate affectionately on her cheek and marched confidently to the front pew of the chapel. He was stopped three rows from his seat by Morag Thomas, Stuart's wife.

"If you have any doubts or feel trapped!" she whispered as he leaned over her "Nip out the back way you can hide in our attic, nobody will know you're there" Victor smiled and pecked her appreciatively on her lips before replying.

"I want to get married don't worry I'll be fine, you'll see." Kate glanced at the congregation before taking her place at the front with her other children. Only Owen and Evan showed any sign of the previous night's ritual, drink till you fall over performance. She smiled proudly at everyone she passed but saved an excruciating scowl for the two unfortunate miners, one that would have seared a robin off a starch box, before taking her seat. It was unusual to see Megan, Berwyn, Morgan's wife, sat at the organ, in place of Victor, her skeletal fingers poised nervously over the gleaming white ivory keys, as she awaited the signal to begin.

Tom marched stiffly down the aisle with the slim figure of Naomi clinging shyly to his powerful arm. The ceremony passed in a blur, with Kate returning to reality when the coins jingled and jangled outside the chapel, as Trevor threw them to the scrambling mass of unwashed children, waiting expectantly outside the gates. The procession began its short stroll back to George Street, and the veritable banquet that awaited them.

"Doesn't she look a beautiful bride?! Announced Doris Morgan, as they stood watching the wedding procession walk along the road. Naomi noticed the group of women and smiled happily at them and waved in greeting. "If she really is a virgin!" Elsie replied "She won't have that smile on her face for too long. 'He's got something to wipe it off with!" The group began to giggle and wave at the wedding couple.

"Don't be daft!" Quipped Doris in reply. "That's Victor Leslie's mam, she won't have told 'him what it's for!" Pam Smith, joined in the joke and added, "Trouble is they find out about it soon enough. Me, I quite like it, as long as 'he don't bang me head on the bed's 'headboard!"

"Well I'll bet anybody with a mam as religious as Kate Leslie won't have the first idea where it goes!" Asserted Doris.

"You are forgetting' one very important thing." Stated Elsie, to her two friends and neighbours, "Tom Owen's is 'his uncle, an' Tom don't get you on your 'hands and knees to pray!" All three women squealed with mirth and howled with delight.

"M mm!" Answered Doris wistfully, "He is a randy old bugger alright!"

"You never hear of 'him with a married woman though!" continued Doris." 'He just takes care of the widows."

"Yes, and from what I've heard, there's more than enough to go round!" whispered Pam.

The procession continued along its merry way, ignorant of the speculation it caused as it marched forward. Several doors were opened and shouts of 'good luck' were yelled as they walked by.

The wedding party had been buzzing merrily for some time before Tom was able to corner Victor "I hope you remember your wedding performance tonight or the bedroom will be a pretty bloody hopeless affair."

"Don't worry Uncle Tom" Answered Victor, "I'm a quick learner!"

"That's what I'm afraid of!" Snapped the older man. "Take your time or it will all be over before you get started! Take your time, think of Naomi, you mustn't be a little excited boy let loose in a sweet shop for the first time". 'And, remember you can always go back for a second' helping!" He left behind a blushing bridegroom as he went into the yard in search of a glass of the beer, from the barrel that had been banished from the house to the outside.

Herbert Humphries pushed his way through a crowd of well-wishers until he stood next to Victor.

"I met Albert Kinsey of the National Amalgamated Labours Union a few weeks ago and he spoke very highly of you. Said that it was thanks to you that the management were made to see sense and settle for a reasonable agreement at the docks." Said Herbert.

"I was glad I could help." Victor replied. "They are fighting the same kind of battles that the FED is! The faces are different, but the disputes are the same!"

"Glad to hear you haven't forgotten where you came from or who your real friends are." Herbert replied. He slapped Victor heartily on the back and continued. "I realise this isn't the time to be talking of such things, but I had to let you know how they feel about you. And, as far as we are concerned, it won't be forgotten!"

Naomi had enjoyed meeting Victor's family and neighbours. She would never again think of them as common miners! Coarse they may be but each and every one of them had a heart that was bigger than a lion's, added to a wisdom that was as deep as the mine where they worked, it was only education and the refinement it brings, that were missing, they cared about people, 'things' didn't matter!

She slipped away unnoticed to Kate's room, where she changed out of her wedding dress. She put it preciously on the bed and changed into her travelling clothes, it was almost time for her and Victor to leave. She met Kate and Ivy as she left the room.

"We were coming to see if you needed any help to change." Said Ivy, looking enviously at Naomi's new dress, "But obviously we are too late!"

"Thanks." She beamed, "But it's almost time for us to be on our way to the station." She took Kate's hand, looked her softly in the eyes and continued, "I don't know how to thank you. I've never known such kindness and caring," Said Naomi." I want you to know that I will make Victor a good wife, and more importantly, make him happy! The three women began to cry and hugged each other, extracting as much comfort as they could from one another's strength.

Naomi continued, through tear brimmed eyes, "Don't think that I am taking him away, I don't think anyone could do that. We will visit as often as we are allowed. I will expect to see you all regularly in Newport, coming to visit us. I know that Victor sends money, I'll kill him if he ever tries to stop, I've seen how hard it is for you to cope. Please use some of it on train fare to come and stay with us."

It seemed to take an eternity for the train to reach Newport, but eventually they were stood outside their new home. Number 47, Bridge Street.

"Welcome home dear," said Naomi, as Victor pulled her close and lifted her into his arms. "Put me down at once!" she pleaded, "You never know who's watching us out here in the street." He released her and began to open the door. He was stopped as the door was wrenched open in front of him. Eva Woodland and Melanie stepped out beside them. "We just popped in to light the fire and leave you a spot of supper. Just in case you were hungry." She nudged Victor in the ribs and whispered, "You got to keep your strength up!" Turning to her maid she said, "Come along Melanie, Let's leave these two lovebirds alone." And with a wink she concluded, "I expect they've got a lot to talk about" Taking hold of Naomis hand, Victor pushed her quickly inside, smiled at Eva and shut the door.

"Victor!" Naomi scolded, "What a thing to do! What will they think of us, with you shutting the door in her face like that?" Victor gave her no chance to protest further as he swept her into his arms and gently brought his lips onto hers. He began to excite the tip of her tongue with his own. They clung together like two limpets until breathless they broke apart.

"Eva won't be offended; she knows we want to be alone as he breathed the words passionately against Naomi's neck. "We'll apologise tomorrow, if we go out but food is the last thing I want right now, I want you!" He kissed her again deeply this time unable to disguise his longing. She returned his embrace forcing herself against his growing manliness and the strange sensation that caused her nipples to swell against his chest, making her moan deep within her throat, Victor Kissed her again, almost brutally this time, as animal passion began to take control of his every action. He began to tear at the fasteners on her dress.

Naomi stirred and looked at the still form of Victor sleeping peacefully beside her. She became aware that, for the first time in her life, she was naked in bed, what surprised her even more was, she didn't feel any embarrassment! She placed her hand on her husband's muscular shoulder, he too, was as naked as a newborn baby! Her gentle caress brought him out of his trance like sleep in an instant, he turned to face her. "Good morning, Mrs. Leslie I hope you had a wonderful night's sleep?" He said cuddling her securely in his arms.

"Eventually! Thank you!" she smiled, recalling his earlier passion and repeated ardour. "I was wanting to tie my nighty to my toes, but I didn't even have chance to put it on! I brought such a pretty one!"

Victor rolled so that Naomi was pinned beneath him and said. "I think you look much better this way," Both felt his masculinity rise at her nearness and touch. He kissed her passionately and she slipped her legs apart to allow him entry.

"Oh God" she moaned. "I didn't think I would enjoy it as much as this!" She surrendered herself to both his, and her own passion and delight. It was several minutes before either of them was capable of coherent talk.

"We have to get out of bed Victor." Naomi announced as she pushed Victor playfully towards the edge of their feather mattress, "We are booked on the 'Britania' to sail to Weston for the day."

Victor pulled Naomi to him and answered, "I can think of a dozen things I want, to do again, rather than catch a paddle steamer to Weston!" Naomi sighed and slipped back under the eiderdown, a knowing smile on her flushed face. The tide was probably out in Weston, it could wait!

Both Victor and Naomi enjoyed their honeymoon weekend, but Monday morning, which arrived far too quickly, saw an almost exhausted Victor entering the company's office. He was met by a very unsympathetic Brian who remarked, "You young fellows are all the same, can't leave it alone!" Victor managed a smile before pushing past and seeking out the sanctuary of his office. He collapsed into his chair and blissfully closed his eyes. His cat nap was disturbed as Trevor pushed his head around the door and warned, "If you don't take it easy, they'll never get that grin off your face, and If you should die, they're going to struggle to get the coffin lid down !" Victor managed a feeble grin. Both were interrupted as Muriel Evans, Naomi's replacement came bursting into the office.

"You are to see Mr. Hyde at once" she announced her pretty face etched with concern "There's been a message from the docks it seems a Bouldon brother collier docked about an hour ago and has sent word that it's heard the Chepstow's' sunk after colliding with another ship in fog two days ago, not far off Land's End! The merchant wants to see you at once, then you are to go to the docks to see that ship's Master." All thought of tiredness and exhaustion evaporated from Victor's mind, like a dockside puddle out in the noonday sun. He jumped to his feet and ran Pell mell to his employer's office.

To say William Hyde despised Victor, was as near to the truth as any God-fearing man could put it, loathing, detestation, resentment were all words that sprang to mind. The unfortunate problem was the Earl! Hyde hoped that the day would come, in the not-too-distant future. When his opportunity would arise to discredit the loutish upstart completely! Until that time came, he had to use him.

"Get yourself into the south Deck Mr. Leslie," Ordered the Merchant coolly. "See the master of the Bouldon Brothers collier and try to find out if we've lost a ship full of iron ore?"

Callous bastard thought Victor! You've fitted perfectly into the merchant's seat, only concerned about a ship load or ore, it had a crew of nineteen men! "I'll find out all that I can, before I report back." Victor dashed from the offices, and without any thought of his own safety ran across the road after a departing tram. He managed to leap onto the rear platform where he was confronted by an irate conductor. The man's temper cooled as he learned of Victors errand. He hurled himself from the tram at the dock gates and began running like the wind along the quay side. He slowed to a walk as reason began to return to his muddled skull. He didn't know the name of the ship or where she was berthed. He set off in search of George Jackson, the seamen's representative in Newport. He rapped loudly on the union leader's door before entering. Jackson sat upright in a hard wooden chair. Victor peered into the haze filled office, catching sight of a bearded figure mulling over a batch of papers on the table in front of him, Eye watering billows of blue smoke poured from the wooden pipe that was clamped between his broken, black, stumps of teeth. Jackson looked up and smiled, a leer that would have done the devil himself proud, as the black teeth parted to give the impression of the very gates of hell! "I thought you'd be here. I just heard the news myself. Don't know if it's true!"

"Which ship brought the news?" Asked Victor, choking in the appalling atmosphere of the office, which was ten times worse than any dust filled coal mine! "I've been sent to see the ship's Master."

"As near as I can tell," Replied the representative, exhaling further clouds of smoke into the already clogged room. "It's the S S 'Durkin' she's sat at the Bouldon wharf."

"Thanks!" Gasped Victor as he dashed out into the fresh air. He have his tortured lungs a minute to recover before rushing off into the ship's direction.

"I spoke to Harold Wise, master of the S.S.'Durkin', "Reported Victor. He stood before the merchant's desk and recounted the information he had been able to illicit from the ship's master. "It seems that there was a fog bank. The 'Durkin' didn't see the collision but heard it. They believe that a collier out of Hamburg ran into the 'Chepstow' and cut her in two. It seems as if the' Chepstow', went down in less than two minutes. It was so, foggy that searching was almost impossible, and they found no survivors. But they are certain it was the Chepstow; they found the wreckage of an empty lifeboat!"

William Hyde sat stoney faced throughout Victor's report, his tension obvious as he curled and uncurled his fingers around a slim pencil. He sat back in his chair, closed his eyes, and balanced on its back legs before muttering.

"My God! That's the first ship we've lost, 11500 pounds worth of ship and cargo at the bottom of the sea!"

"It is a grievous loss sir." Victor replied. "Master and crew all lost. And many of them family men too."

"Crew? Oh yes!" William Hyde answered, his mind working overtime, trying to devise a plan that would ensure no possible blame could be levied in his direction. "We mustn't forget the crew. Ask Brian Cuthbertson to bring me a copy of the articles for the voyage and include a copy of the crew. I'll inform the directors at Lloyds insurance.

Victor decided his safest course of action was to collect the ship's manifest from Brian, if he remained with the merchant, he would probably throttle the mercenary bastard, until his last breath. He left and went in search of Brian Cuthbertson, who quickly found the ship's documents. "I expect the little weasel has phoned his masters and laid all possible blame at someone else's door by now." Stated Brian as he watched Victor leaving, carrying a large manilla envelope. "The bloody shit will be worried about the cash flow until the insurance money is paid up. Those poor bastards at the bottom of the sea!"

The ship's articles and manifest were strewn around Hyde's desk like confetti as he pondered over them together with sheets of figures and calculations.

"She delivered a full cargo of coal to the naval station a Gibraltar and was en route from Huelva on the Spanish coast with a full load of iron ore." Announced Victor, as the merchant scribbled calculations onto a foolscap piece of paper.

"You are to oversee the processing of all the details regarding the value of the ship. Telegraph Spain regarding its iron ore cargo, check all the listings to see if we have any other claims of value to make and ask the crewing section to make a list of widows and orphans." Hyde ordered. "I'll have to contact the necessary authorities and prepare a report. No doubt the newspapers will be here fairly soon, although, you can handle that. I am not to be disturbed!"

Victor closed the merchant's door silently behind him. Trust the swine to put the widows and orphans last! He visited each office issuing orders to each department. Rumours were flying through the dusty corridors of the building faster than a tropical dose of diarrhoea! Everyone was eager for news of the company's first disaster. Victor told the clerks all that he knew.

"Keep me informed of all developments Hyde." Sir Michael Fairfax. Bellowed down the phone. He had listened to the Newport merchant's report for more than five minutes. "The earl is in the Americas' and isn't expected to be back for at least another 10 months so keep me up to date with all developments. I'll call a special board meeting when we know a little more. I will reinforce your approach to Lloyds, there are several 'names', at my club." Fairfax replaced the receiver. This 'Chepstow' had proved a sound investment and had repaid herself ten times over in the twelve years or so that she had been owned by the company. Her loss would affect their trading position, but once the insurance money appeared, a replacement could be sought. He decided to inform the other members of the board and picked up the telephone.

"Those poor men!" Sobbed Naomi, as she sat listening to the news of the ship's sinking. "What's to become of their families!"

Victor took her small hand within his shovel like mitt and squeezed it gently and said, "Something must be done. I can't sit idly by and do nothing. The directors line their pockets and widows and orphans suffer."

, "Be careful my darling!" she warned. "You know Hyde is waiting for you to make a mistake."

Victor nodded his agreement but made a mental note that he could not just stand back and do nothing.

"I don't intend giving them a chance like that." He assured his worried wife, "I was thinking that we could start a hardship fund for the dependant's."

"I tell you what," Naomi answered, "I'll do it, I've plenty of time it will mean you won't get into trouble with the company, we can always say I knew the crew and wanted to help."

The following day, a determined Naomi descended on the unexpecting offices of the Newport 'Merlin', the local newspaper. She told the story of the loss of the Chepstow and its crew. The editor's eyes opened wide as she placed two five pound notes on his desk and announced she wished, with the papers help, to start a fund for the widows and orphans.

Leaving the newspaper offices, she crossed to the Maindee area of Newport and called at the house of the Member of Parliament Lloyd Haslop the liberal member. She knew that Victor wouldn't be pleased that she had gone to him, but she didn't know any socialist MP's and anyway, there weren't any in Newport. She had met the gentleman in the past and felt certain that he would want to help such a worthy and self-advantageous cause. He pledged five pounds himself and promised to contact both the local and national press, 'to raise the public awareness and appeal to their generosity'.

"I had no idea such a thing had happened to a Newport ship!" He answered, rubbing his hand through a substantial growth of mutton chop side burn. "I'll see a few friends and try to get something organised, isn't it one of Beaumont Harris' ships?"

"Yes," Naomi replied, "But the earl is away on an extended vacation in America. No one knows how to contact him. In fact, we don't know where he is!"

"Dammed awkward that! Still never mind, we'll do what we can, thank you Naomi."

Naomi stayed with the Gentleman for only a short while before she made the excuse that she had to return home to meet her husband and was able to leave. It was an extremely smug and self-satisfied young woman that rode on the upper deck of the tram as it returned to Westgate Square.

"Have you seen the newspaper this morning?" Demanded an angry Willaim Hyde of a completely flummoxed Victor. "The Chepstow loss is splashed all over it, together with news of a fund in aid of the crew's dependants, it says the fund was begun by the local MP and your wife!" Victor did his best to look shocked, as the old merchant continued, "She's put ten pounds, ten pounds!" He repeated, to start the fund aid!" Victor stood in front of the merchant's desk, he stood as tall as he could without actually standing on his tiptoes, in this way he could ensure he was looking down at his employer.

"You know Naomi almost as well as I do Mr. Hyde." Victor answered. "I believe she knew some of the missing Crew members personally. She is a very caring person. There is no way I would have been able to stop her carrying out such a generous gesture, but what is more, I support her completely in this wonderful act!"

"I don't know if the board of directors will see all this unnecessary publicity in much the same light!" Retorted the merchant. He Clasped his head in his hands and began muttering to himself. "This would have to happen, just as soon as I'm in charge!"

"Mr. Hyde!" Victor said quietly, "It was an accident, a terrible accident. This company won't suffer, the insurance company will take care of its financial losses. We need to give some thought to the families who have lost their loved ones. They need all our compassion now!" A terrible thought crossed Victor's mind as they were talking he said, "You have informed the families of the crew members, haven't you Mr. Hyde? I hope they haven't found out about this by reading about it in the papers!" Victor was able to answer his question with the look that crossed the merchants face. "Good God!" Was all he said, as he strode from the room.

Ten days later, Victor met George Jackson at the Wharfside, he didn't think he could survive another indoor session with George's pipe! He watched the gulls screaming and swirling in the breeze as they howled their displeasure at the wind that had picked up to disturb their slumber, as it whipped up the placid sea into a myriad of choppy wavelets.

"That waster, Haslop's been to see me!" Snapped George "Said he was pleased with the way the fund was going'. 'Bastard's trying' to take all the credit for it." He pulled the steaming pipe from his lips, before spitting venomously into the briny foam.

"The important thing is" interrupted Victor, Is its raised almost fifteen hundred pounds for the fund. It has to be shared out I know but at least it's more than the families. would have had without it."

"Seaman's union would have given some hardship money. But it would 'have been a bloody pittance! Thank you for all your help young man and give that wife of yours a big thank you from me and' the seamen's union."

"How the hell did you let the newspapers get hold of the story, Mr. Hyde? Michael Fairfax snapped down the telephone. "The board felt obliged the throw in two hundred smackers each. And I don't like wasting money on dozy bastards who can't find their way at sea. It is going to take a few months to replace the Chepstow, we are going to see what's available. Keep the rest of the fleet at sea as much as you possibly can. We will need them working to full capacity if we are not to lose any income."

"I didn't let the press know sir!" Hyde stammered down the telephone, "It was the wife of that damn pit boy who spilled the beans!"

"Ah yes, Hay Jones' little tart, the one who married that prodigy, Leslie! Keep your eye on him, we don't want him costing the company any more money!" He slammed the phone down and muttered. "More to the point I don't want that bastard costing me any more cash!"

CHAPTER 29

Naomi and Victor stepped onto the Cwmcarn station as they had done a hundred times previously, since their wedding. There was a decided chill in the air. November had almost become a memory, the trees were brown ruins, their summer splendour vanished, replaced by the stark austere boughs, that supported the few dead remnants that had once been a magnificent royal coat. It was time for nature's annual dying. Naomi pulled her coat warmly around her neck, as she experienced the full weight of the valley's icy blast, without the canopy of protective leaves she could see all the way to the Prince of Wales Collery. She shuddered as she recalled the miners still entombed there for more than thirty years since that horrible explosion at Abercarn. Wherever she cast her eye, the flora seemed to be perishing. The colours were magnificent, but Nature was being slaughtered. Victor put a comforting, protective arm around her. She glanced at the riverbank where a single holly tree was standing tall in all its majestic splendour, its barbs immune to the freezing squalls that had accounted for all its neighbours. Naomi smiled, despite all the apparent death and decay that surrounded her, she felt full of life and vitality.

"We are telling the family before anyone else finds out." Naomi announced to everyone as they sat cosily around a blazing coal fire. The honey flames cast haunting shadows that danced around the ceiling. "I am expecting a baby. The doctor thinks it should be born in June, she concluded proudly.

Kate was on her feet and hugging her daughter in law, Tom was next to jump to his feet pumping Victor's hand as if he were turning the chapel's pipe organ handle.

"Well done, Victor!" He whispered. "You've rung the bell already. 'I knew that advice would come in handy, but I suppose 'handies', have got nothing' to do with it!"

"What are you mumbling about Tom Owens?" Demanded Kate as she gave him one of her sulphurous looks. "It's Naomi you ought to be congratulating, she's the one that's expecting!" Tom went to the woman and have his niece a bear hug that threatened to shorten her life by at least six months.

"Careful with what you are doing you clumsy ox!" Kate snapped, "Not so rough she's carrying the latest member of the family". She turned back to Naomi and continued, "I thought I was going to have to wait forever to be a nana. Christine's been married nearly two years and still no sign!"

"Just goes to show dunnit!" Beamed Tom, his face lit up with a grin, wider than one that was seen on the cats face when it found an old salmon tin! "There's plenty of vim in Cwmcarn mining stock. By God, that was quick work you two!"

The talk turned to knitting and baby clothes. Tom growing more irritable by the second grabbed Victor and pushed him through the door, shouting over his shoulder "You sort out all that between you, I'll take Victor out to wet the baby's head!"

"You can't wet it's head yet!" Called Ivy, as the two men disappeared through the door, "It hasn't been born yet!"

"You randy little bugger!" Tom congratulated his nephew as he passed him a glass of dark foaming beer. "Well done."

They were joined by Owen, Evan and Stuart who were more than willing to toast the expectant father.

"By God!" Agreed Stuart, "You didn't hang around!" Evan joined the fun by slapping Victor manfully on the back, "Soon found out how it all works, didn't you?"

"That's the easiest bit over." Stuart continued "From now on it'll be shitty arses, and tits just for the babies. It'll stop your gallop my boy. No more 'how's about it, she'll be too tired after feeding' the nipper!"

"Leave 'him alone!" Owen said, "It's wonderful having kids! I wouldn't be without mine for the world."

"If you lot don't shut up we'll drink somewhere else!" Interrupted Tom. "We've come here to drink the good 'health of the baby what's going' t' be born in May."

"May!" Exclaimed Stuart, "You didn't waste any time. Bloody hell" She hardly had time to take her wedding' veil off, never mind anything' else!" The laughter which greeted this last remark stopped all conversation, glasses were raised in a toast and quickly drained. Victor threw a handful of coins on to the varnished bar top and ordered a refill.

"Don't forget!" Slurred a well-oiled Tom, as he and Victor staggered homeward, "If you see the' minister tell 'him you wanted to start a family straight away. Don't tell him you enjoyed it!"

Winter had come and gone in a frenzy of snow and ice. The company continued to prosper and a replacement for the stricken 'Chepstow' had been purchased. She was renamed, 'Caerphilly', to conform with the company's policy of ships named after Welsh towns. She was of the raised quarterdeck type and was of 1100 tons gross. She joined her sister ships in their never-ending voyages between the Mediterranean and Newport carrying coal and iron ore.

Victor had observed Naomi swell with every passing day, and with each day that passed his love and longing for her became more intense. He watched with concern every twitch and flinch as she endured the discomfort of carrying their first child without complaining or showing a sign of displeasure or anger. He had been working longer hours as the business improved. Despite strikes and stoppages, coal exports were booming. He would often sit in his warm luxurious office thinking of old friends and neighbours who would be toiling away on their hands and knees more than quarter of a mile underground, winning the very coal he was shipping around the world. He had begged Tom on more than one occasion to leave the pit and work as an office messenger boy, but had been refused, far from politely by his extremely irate uncle. "I'm a miner! It's all I bloody well know so Don't offer me charity!"

Kate had spent more and more time with Naomi as her time came nearer. At the beginning of May, Kate and Ivy descended on Bridge Street like a pair of Regimental Sergeant Majors and took over the running of the house. Naomi was warned not to touch even a feather duster for fear of being confined to bed for the remainder of her pregnancy.

"You just take care of that grandchild -. Victor will do as he's-told. Kate's answer to every problem seemed to be, put the kettle on "Everything gets better after a nice cup of tea!" It seemed to ring in her ears night and day! She sat back in her chair and closed her eyes enjoying five minutes of peace and quiet. She looked down at the swelling below her stomach that had for the last nine months, completely dominated her every thought; Soon it would be a living breathing individual with its own needs and aspirations. Patting it gently she said, "Come on you, whatever you are, it's time you stood on your own two feet, all this carrying you around is killing my back".

Everyone had been kindness itself, and that had been a major part of the problem. She hadn't been allowed to do anything for herself, even a bed had been brought downstairs for her as the midwife thought it unwise for her to climb the stairs.

"I'll close my eyes for five minutes'. She thought.

Kate and Ivy tiptoed into the room and found Naomi sound asleep, a state she occupied for more than three hours, they left the exhausted young mother to her much-needed rest. Kate was busy sifting a large bowl of flour, preparing to bake bread, whilst Ivy was outside pegging out a line of washing.

Naomi woke with a start. She felt a sudden cramp in her tummy followed quickly by another.

"Ivy, Mam!" She bellowed afraid to move, "Come quick! I think it's time!" Kate and Ivy arrived almost simultaneously, although Ivy had more than three times as far to run as her mother. They found a grimacing Naomi perched on the edge of her chair, holding her tummy and pleading. "We might be willing to wait but I don't think this baby is going to wait much longer!"

"Into bed with you." Kate ordered, as Ivy helped the young mother. "You'll feel much better if you are lying down."

Once the two women had Naomi safely tucked up in bed, Kate turned to Ivy and said, "Fetch the midwife, Ivy." She looked at Naomi before continuing, "Run! And you had better tell Nurse Thomas to run back with you!"

"What about Victor?" Naomi panted.

"The last thing we need at a time like this is a man cluttering up the place!" Kate replied. "We'll worry about Victor when all the work is done!"

Ivy ran through the front door and out into the street as if the devil himself were after her.

Victor came home anticipating a wholesome meal, after a hard day at work. "Hello I'm home!" He called out pleasantly, his voice resounded thought the four corners of the house. He sniffed deeply expecting to be rewarded with the aromatic sensation of a meal being freshly prepared in the kitchen. There was nothing. The only smell he could detect was one of polish, feeling puzzled, he called again. "Where are you I'm home and ready to demolish a sheep between two bread doorsteps.

Ivy appeared grinning from ear to ear, put her fingers to her lips and announced "Hush Daddy! Typical of all men, never here until everything's finished. Come and see the latest member of the Leslie Clan!"

"Wha? Wha? What do you mean?" Victor asked, "Who's here?"

"The baby silly!" she repeated urging Victor to follow her and repeating that warning for silence. Victor was met with a scene that was never to be bettered. It was one of total tranquillity. Naomi was sleeping peacefully in the bed; he had never seen her look more radiant. Beside her, was a lace covered cot that contained the small, most perfect being that Victor had ever seen.

"W W W What is it?" He stammered, as he bent low over the cradle to gaze down at the slumbering form beneath him.

Ivy came up and planted a congratulatory kiss on her brother's cheek squeezed his arm affectionately and answered, "It? He's a boy! A perfectly wonderful little boy. He's beautiful, black hair just like his dad and what a pair of lungs! You should have herd him scream when the nurse smacked his backside as he was born!"

Victor carefully removed the unblemished, pure white sheet that hid his son's face and gazed proudly down. Leaving the slumbering infant, he wasn't over to his wife's bedside, he kissed her lightly on the forehead and whispered, "Well done my darling, he's perfect in every way!" Kate appeared in the doorway and purred faintly but sternly. "Come out of there Victor! Naomi needs to rest. I know you feel like the cat that's just found the cream, but she must sleep. She's done a wonderful job now let her recover in peace!"

Naomi announced that the baby was to be named Peter, after her maternal grandfather. It was a name of which Kate approved. "Peter is a wonderful Biblical name!" She often remarked, "A name of strength and one that's full of character."

Victor was pleased that he had a son! One that appeared to be fit and healthy. He hoped to tell him much, especially about his roots and the toil and heartache that had been part of his family's history, for at least two generations. He had some treasured possessions that he wished to pass on to his son, in the not-too-distant future.

Victor entered the company's offices feeling more than ten feet tall. Most of the congratulations he'd received were warm and genuine although some were grudging and insincere. As he sat at his desk, he found a message from the merchant ordering him to report at his earliest convenience. Victor wasn't straight to Mr. Hyde's office. He knocked and waited for permission to enter.

"Come in Leslie." The merchant commanded. Victor could see from the expression on Hyde's face that something was troubling him. "I have here a message from the board of directors, commending you on your action when the Chepstow sank six months ago. I disagree with their recommendation, but I am only the company's merchant! I see first-hand the way you are currying favour with the dock workers, their union and representatives. I am most displeased with this involvement, and regard it as a position, that is slowly undermining my own, and gradually eroding the control and discipline of the company! I will expect your total commitment and sole loyalty to the management of the Gwent Coal and Steamship company. I have nothing further to say on the subject, expect that I will be monitoring your performance and actions most carefully in the future! You may now return to your office, where no doubt, you have much important work requiring your urgent attention!"

Hyde picked up a document off his desk and with a cursory wave of his hand dismissed Victor. "Oh, by the way." He concluded. "My best wishes to your wife following the safe delivery of the baby boy!"

Victor left the office; he expected no favours from the merchant and was damn certain he would not receive any. He was determined to enjoy the sensation of being a new father with a baby son. No suspicious, envious old man was going to mar the day for him. It was a wonderful spring day. May had chosen one of her best days for him and he was intent upon remaining composed and cheerful despite all the problems and difficulties that would be placed before him. His only sorrow was that music had, had to take a back seat in all his plans. The doctor had been correct his fingers weren't flexible enough for further progression, but he had a family to care for and support, and now music was only a hobby! It startled him to think he now regarded it in a frivolous way. A few short years ago it had seemed to be his way to improve his life, his means of escape he shuddered, then smiled and began to examine the ship's manifest that lay on the desk in front of him.

They had taken to travelling back to Cwmcarn most weekend's.

Peter was now more than two months old and Naomi had asked that her son be entered onto the chapel's cradle roll, and as he was blooming in the July sunshine, now seemed the perfect time. The request had delighted both Kate and the family and the dedication service was completed, with Kate preening herself like a mother hen. Peter remained sound asleep throughout the entire event, despite the continual oohing and ahhing that was usually guaranteed to wake even the soundest of sleepers.

"Have you heard the news?" Berwyn Morgan enquired as he munched his way through a doorstep sized slice of fruit cake. "Some Archduke in Sarajevo, wherever that is, was murdered to death about a week ago." Victor looked at the old minister as he innocently enjoyed his cake. "We have discussed nothing else at the office, some of the staff feel it could start a war between the Austrians and the Serbs. If that happens, who knows who might get dragged in. It could even affect the company's trade if they start hostilities on the open sea!"

The old man looked up kindly at the young man, sublime in his elevation to parenthood. "I hope you are wrong, after all it's so far away. The wicked murder was done by a young hot head called Garvilo Princip. Killing is evil, but I hope the young fool isn't going to be responsible for even more deaths."

"The merchant is concerned about the possibility of danger to our ships but thought that we could benefit from a foreign war because their warship's would need coal, and ours is the best steam coal in the world!"

Kate noticing the two men talking intently, interrupted them and ordered, "This seems to be too serious a discussion for a day like this, come on you two! Let's join the rest of our guests and enjoy ourselves. Whatever it is it can't be important enough to spoil a day such as this!"

William Hyde called all the senior staff members into his office, he looked drawn and pale as Victor took his seat at the board table next to Brian. "You've all been reading the grave reports of the situation that exists on the continent. I have received a correspondence from Sir

Michael Fairfax. He is convinced that war is inevitable. The French are bound to be dragged into the conflict and then it will only be a matter of time, before we get involved. Myself I have never experienced such a situation before." He looked toward Brian and stated I have been told it will all be over in a few weeks. I know there are some members of staff with plenty of experience of military service who are concerned that we may become involved. I repeat I have been assured that it will be over within a few weeks!"

Brian laughed scornfully at this suggestion, before stating forcefully, "If there is a war, and I hope to God there isn't, it won't be over in a few weeks, that's politicians talk, they never have to fight or spill their blood, it will last a bloody sight longer than a couple of weeks! Silly Buggers! It'll take months to mobilise the country!" The group look devastated as Brian Cuthbertson predicted a long and bloody campaign. The younger men fearful of the carnage that would probably become a living nightmare that everyone would have to face. The older men, although thankful that they would not be expected to take up arms, realised that they had sons and friends who would not escape the appalling predicament of total war.

"I hope Mr. Cuthbertson's ghastly prediction doesn't come true!" Answered William Hyde, "But let's try to carry on as usual and hope that sanity and reason will prevail. It's Sunday tomorrow and Monday is a holiday, when some of the staff will be having a well-earned day off. I will be working, but under the circumstances, I think everyone else should spend the day with their families!"

CHAPTER 30

THE SUN SHONE BRIGHTLY AS THE LESLIE FAMILY STROLLED WITH the crowds happily along Commercial Street, Kate, as proud as a peacock, strutted along the busy road, pushing the apple of her eye in his carriage. Peter, for his part remained oblivious to the milling throng, and refused to wake. Victor and Naomi walked arm in arm slightly behind the adoring grandmother. Glenys and Ivy brought up the rear as they gazed and marvelled at the wondrous displays and curios that filled almost every shop window. Wherever you looked, people were laughing and smiling. A Jollity that was almost a falsehood, born of desperation as they tried to deny the inevitability of the sorrow and heartache that most surely would come! Naomi rested her head on Victor's shoulder as they stopped to admire the latest fashions displayed in Reynold's store window. Victor took her hand and squeezed it reassuringly, his love for her completely dominating his entire existence, looking at the still form that slept peacefully in his carriage, he had every reason to remain alive and unaffected by the madness that was overtaking the world!

Victor left them for a short while, promising to return home soon. "I won't be long I have to fetch something I've forgotten. I'll see you all back at the house. I won't be more than half an hour."

If he hurried, he would have time to complete his task and return home in two shakes of a puppy dog's tail!!

Newport awoke on Tuesday 4th August to find itself at war! Victor read the report in the newspaper in stoney faced silence. He kissed his worried family members before leaving the house for work.

"Don't you do anything silly!" Snapped Naomi, as she waved goodbye from the doorstep. "You've a family with responsibilities for a son don't get worked up about joining any army!"

He turned, smiled and blew a long lingering kiss, he had no intention of getting killed because of some Austrian Archduke. He had never heard of Sarajevo, and he had isn't ships to most areas of the globe.

The silence that enshrouded the office was complete. Victor was overcome by its completeness. He was used to the long faces that seemed to follow him around the company's building, but even the faces of his friends seemed to have grown an extra bottom lip and chin! Several employees seemed to be sneering openly at him.

"You are to go to the merchant's office immediately!" Muriel Evans ordered as soon as he walked through the front door without her usual smile or greeting. Victor, somewhat taken aback by the brusque order wasn't straight to the designated room. He tapped on the door and entered. The merchant was sat smugly behind his desk, there were three other men in the room, Earnest Owen, the storage clerk, and two police officers. A Sergeant and a police constable.

"This is Victor Leslie, sergeant. Do your duty!" The merchant ordered as soon as Victor appeared at the door.

The police sergeant swaggered toward Victor and announced.

"Yesterday five hundred pounds disappeared from these offices. You are one of the only three men in possession of keys to this establishment." He indicated the other two company executives, "Both these men saw you leaving here yesterday evening! A time when you were supposed to be enjoying the holiday." He coughed before continuing. "They both observed you leaving the premises with a brown paper parcel under your arm!" He paused to allow the seriousness of his words to sink into Victor before concluding "I therefore arrest you under suspicion of stealing your company's money!" Victor stood completely still, unable to comprehend the magnitude of the situation. The police constable took him forcefully by the shoulder whilst the sergeant snapped a pair of skin cutting handcuffs around his wrist.

"I don't like thieves at the best of times!" Scoffed the policeman, "But to rob your company at a time like this!" He pulled hard on the cuffs, enjoying the pained expression that crossed Victor's face as the metal circles chaffed his skin.

"Just goes to show a leopard can't change his spots!" Barked William Hyde, "Breeding shows in the end! The earl trusted you and this is how you repay him. Were you intending to use the money to run away to a foreign shore, where you would be safe from the fighting?"

Earnest Owen, three years of hatred frothing and bubbling to the surface, snarled, "Mr. Hyde is right we saw him leaving the empty offices with a parcel last night. We wondered what he was doing here. Now we know!" The police officers dragged a shocked Victor through the hushed offices, Victor his glazed eyes fixed on the floor wasn't quietly, his mind in a turmoil of doubt and apprehension. A Particularly sharp, stinging tug on the manacles, drew blood and momentarily forced him from his stupefied trance and he searched the gloating onlookers for any sign of a friendly face. Noticing Brian Cuthbertson, he called out quickly." Tell Naomi what's happened! I'm innocent!" The police constable hauled him through the door out into the street.

"I want to see my husband!" Demanded Naomi, as she stood beside a long mahogany counter at the Commercial Road Police Station. "His name is Victor Leslie, and he was brought here this morning!" She was pleading and the tears were streaming from her worried eyes. "Please let me see him. It must all be a mistake; Victor wouldn't do anything wrong!" The constable stood immobile behind the desk, tears rarely moved him, he had seen too many of them in his fifteen years with the force. He hadn't met a villain who hadn't always been innocent. He looked at the lady weeping unashamedly before him, she didn't look like the usual 'customer', he had to placate.

"I'm sorry ma'am," He replied, "No one is allowed to see any of the prisoners. He's been well treated and fed you'll be able to see him at the magistrates' court on Thursday. I can't let you in I'm sorry." Naomi stood staring at the policeman, not fully comprehending his refusal, she was certain it wasn't her Victor, he wasn't capable of anything so despicable as stealing from the company. "It can't be Victor!" she begged, "We don't need money we have everything we need!"

Naomi realising that she was getting nowhere with the policeman, have a loud sniff and, with a loud stamp of her heal turned and left the police station.

Victor sat cross legged on the straw mattress that covered almost a third of his cell. He looked at the brick walls that surrounded him. He had been shut here for....? He tried to remember! How long he had been here? They had taken his pocket watch; he had no way of measuring the passage of time. He closed his eyes and tried to 'see', Naomi and Peter. He couldn't even picture their faces in his mind! He stood up and hammered on the thick door, "Let me out! I'm innocent, I haven't done anything wrong. Why don't you go and look for the real thief?"

He continued to bellow and yell until a panel opened in his door and he saw a pair of cold blue eyes.

"I'll give you one minute to shut your gob!" Said the grey eyes viciously, "Then me and a couple of mates will come in an' shut you up! Make your mind up, what's it going' to be." Victor sat down!

"Thought so, you gutless bastard!" Snarled the eyes and the panel was slammed shut, leaving him to his isolation.

Naomi wasn't straight to her solicitor; he had promised to represent Victor at the magistrate's court.

The hearing began at 10 o'clock. Victor was stood before the magistrates' bench, he felt dirty, unclean, in fact he hadn't been able to either wash or shave for the last forty-eight hours he had been detained in the police cells. The solicitor hadn't raised much hope of an acquittal, because of the weight of evidence and the quality of the witnesses against him!

Victor looked up at the bench of magistrates', hoping to see some vestige of compassion or benevolence. Three sets of severe, puritanical eyes glared down at him. These magistrates typified the intolerance of the authoritarian middle classes dominating the country. The charge was read out and the witnesses called. The most damning evidence was gleefully provided by William Hyde and substantiated by an equally exuberant Earnest Owen. Throughout the hearing Victor strenuously pleaded his innocence, but his employer's together with his colleague's evidence couldn't be refuted.

Naomi had tried to contact the earl, but no one knew where he was. The company had no forwarding address. The only detail that was known was, that he had last been herd of somewhere in Texas and was intending to travel on to California via Arizona. The problem was that even if she could discover his where abouts, there was no way that he would be able to influence the proceedings. She sat impassively in the court together with the entire Leslie clan, listening as the witnesses blackened Victor's character. Tom had protested loudly and leaped to his feet but had been forced to sit down under threat of legal proceedings from the chief magistrate, and the truncheon of a policeman!

The magistrates huddled together at the conclusion of all the presentations, nodding grimly and glaring pitilessly at Victor. They sat upright and the chief magistrate cleared his throat.

"Huu Hurhmm" Victor Leslie we have listened to the evidence presented to this court and have no hesitation in finding you guilty." He paused as anguished gasps travelled around the court room. Naomi slumped back into her seat whilst Kate began to moan and wring her hands as the tears began to deluge down her worried face.

"You have been of previous good character. If you wish this court to look favourably upon you, we demand that you return the stolen money."

"I cannot return it sir." Victor replied earnestly. "I cannot return it because I have not stolen it!" He looked the magistrate squarely in the eye and repeated. "I am innocent of this trumped-up charge!"

"You leave us little choice. A man that has been given every chance to better himself at such a benevolent firm and then acts in such a despicable way, deserves harsh treatment. You have turned against those who have tried to help you."

He looked around the courtroom as he prepared to pronounce sentence "This crime is made doubly worse by the fact that we are now at war with Germany and all her allies!"

His speech was interrupted by one of the fellow magistrates who leaned forward to whisper into his ear. He paused to listen and nodded in agreement. He turned for the third member of the bench and conferred briefly with him before turning back to Victor. My good friend has reminded me that perhaps we are in a position to serve our country. We will be as lenient as we can be!" Naomi and Kate grabbed hands hoping for some sign of hope. We are mindful to send you to prison for five years, but because of our country's need we will allow you to volunteer for active service in his majesty's army if you wish too!"

Naomi drew blood as she sank her nails into Kate's hand.

Victor leered at the three magistrates and then answered, "My only choice is no choice! I'll take the king's shilling, but I'll not end up as cannon fodder you'll see, I'll prove my innocence even if I have to kill the Kaiser's entire army to do it!" He turned to face his family and shouted. "Don't worry, I'll be fine, take care of Naomi and don't let her waste money on lawyers, she'll need all we have to live on!" The magistrates banged his gavel loudly and replied. "Take the prisoner away constable! He is to be released into the custody of the recruiting officer once, he has signed his enlistment papers. He is then to be taken straight to his training depot!" Victor was marched away with Naomi's screams and his mother's sobs echoing in his ears!

Three days after his court appearance Victor found himself bouncing fitfully along in the rear of a Pontypool Urban District Council water cart, being pulled by two of the poorest excuses for horses that he has ever seen! The wagon had been commandeered as part of the Second Monmouthsire Battalion's transport and Pontypool's donation to the mechanical warfare that was to come! The driver a pock faced private, with a tthemper and disposition to match his complexion, swore and cursed at the two unfortunate nags every ponderous inch of the way. Victor's other companions proved to be two sullen 'volunteers' in similar situations to that of Victor. One of these, was Steven Burns, who gazed moodily at the others throughout the entire journey, as they tried to engage him in conversation during the transfer to the battalion at Oswestry. Burns was at least three inches taller than Victor and a good two stone heavier, he rebuffed every attempt by Victor and the others to include him in their conversations and share confidences and home memories. He glared evilly at everyone for the entire journey. The journey took three days! Three days of sleeping under the wagon with meals of dry biscuits and dried meat washed down with large draughts of scalding tea! Victor's clothes were beginning to look much the worse for wear, his shirt hadn't been washed for ten days along with his under clothes. His socks were so stiff they rubbed his feet in his shoes. He was certain they had been stinking for the entire journey, yet his travelling companions hadn't complained, their noses were either immune or their body odours at least matched his own! They reached the Battalion's headquarters at five o'clock that evening. To Victor's untrained eye, it looked as if the field were growing a sea of tents. White and green canvas covered the landscape, but order reigned!

The sergeant took Victor and his two companions before the adjutant Captain Royce. The sergeant and his party stood stiffly to attention before the officer.

"You three men have the extraordinary privilege of coming to the second Battalion the Mons regiment." The officer announced proudly, "We know of your past problems, but if you obey orders and work hard you will find us fair. We are at war! That means no preconceived ideas, do as you are told and be good soldiers. We will allow you only one mistake, after that you go back to jail. The choice is yours!" He paused waiting for a comment, then continued, "Take them to the quarter master, and get them kitted out and for god's sake, burn those bloody foul-smelling clothes they are wearing! Dismissed!" The sergeant marched them out as the captain bellowed, "Get them fed and billeted as well!"

Victor was beginning to feel human again; a clean uniform, a wash and shave and his first warm meal for a week; all he now had to adapt to was sharing a tent with twenty-two men! His billet was filled with a mix of single young men and older married ones. They all seemed apprehensive about what the future had in store for them. With only one exception every recruit was from a similar working background, miners and steel workers with the occasional farm labourer. The exception was Steven Burns, he was arrogance itself. Burns' physique dwarfed everyone's in the tent, and from his arrival, his truculent behaviour and malevolent temper set him apart as a scurrilous bully. His fists bludgeoned a fair headed youth, who had the misfortune to trip over his outstretched feet.

Five or six blows from Burn's mighty fists reduced the youngster's face into a blood-soaked mask. The tent's occupants began wondering who the next person would be to fall foul of the belligerent Steven Burns. The tent flap was raised, and a voice yelled, "Lights out! Turn in you lot, real training begins tomorrow. Reveille will be five thirty!" The order was met with loud moans and groans. The voice, oblivious to the dissenters continued. "I don't give a bugger about your beauty sleep; this battalion's got a proud record, and we will be joining up with the Welsh Division very soon so get some sleep!" The more he listened, Victor became certain that he ought to recognise the voice. The orders continued, "When we meet the Germans, you'll thank the good lord you were so well trained! Get to sleep, that's an order! Private Leslie, step outside the tent for inspection." Twenty-one sets of eyes looked quizzically at Victor who merely shrugged his shoulders and stepped out of the tent flap into the gathering gloom. He could hardly believe his eyes as he looked at his sergeant. Dressed as impeccably as only a Company sergeant Major could, stood CSM. Trevor Bailey!

"What the bloody hell are you doing here Trevor?" Victor gasped, as he recognised his old friend best man and workmate.

"That's enough of the language, private Leslie!" Laughed Trevor as he held out his hand in greeting. I have been in the reserve Force for almost 10 years, Brian and I were at your trial and when we herd the court's decision, we moved heaven and earth to get you escorted here. Brian has lots of army friends, so he was able to call in a few favours and get the right strings pulled."

"I didn't do it Trevor. It wasn't me!" Victor stated.

"That doesn't matter here. This is the last time you are to call me Trevor. I want us to remain friends, but I am a sergeant major, and I must maintain discipline at all times. And believe me the only thing that is going to keep you alive through all this is discipline!" He pointed to the tent. "In you go, follow orders and do your best, we both know how good your best is. I'll be looking out for you and will put in a good word for you whenever I can."

"Can we get word to Naomi and the family to let them know I'm alright?" Trevor have him a small sheet of paper and a stub of pencil, "Write a little note on this and give it back to me some time tomorrow, I'll try to get it delivered, but I can't promise." Victor took the piece of paper and went back into the tent.

"I like me kip!" snarled Burns "so no noise to disturb me and if anybody thinks about farting in this tent, they'll have my boot up their arse."

One by one the soldiers drifted off to sleep. Victor lay back trying to bring Naomi's face to mind but somehow it always seemed to elude him. He sighed and closed his eyes.

He began his training at six the following morning, by midday he began to realise that office work left much to be desired when compared with the physical effort he had taken for granted when he had worked down the pit. His legs ached, his arms felt as though they were constructed of lead and his chest was heaving as he fought for breath to replenish his lungs, which felt as though they were on the point of bursting.

Throughout it all he was under the protective and watchful eye of C.S.M.Bailey. It was an extremely weary Victor that sought the luxury of his bunk that night, following a sumptuous banquet of yet more dry biscuits and bully beef. He stretched and wriggled his toes within the suffocating and restrictive highly polished army boots that were slowly strangling his toes to death. He did not remove them, wanting to break them in to his feet, before they broke him. He reached under the blanket covering his 'bunk' and took out the pencil and paper. He put the date ... 16thAugust at the top and added 2nd Battalion Monmouthshire Regiment.

Dear Naomi.

'I am in a billet somewhere in Wales and am alright. Trevor Bailey is my sergeant; he has promised to take care of me and said he will teach me all I will need to know to stay safe until I can come home to your loving arms and warm bed. I miss you terribly and hope and pray that I will be spared to return home to you and Peter. If you have any Problems my darling, go home to mam. Use the money we have shaved but stay with the family, they will look after you until I can do it myself. I love and ....

"What are you doing Leslie?" Demanded Steven Burn, as he noticed Victor writing the letter. "Writing a letter to some Floozie, I'll bet! Give us a look." He made a grab for the letter but Victor pushed the bully's hand away a move which really incensed the lout. Jumping to his feet Burns snarled, "Stand up Lesile!" As he spat out the word's saliva dribbled along his chin and sprayed into the room. "I'm going to smash your face so that even your own mother won't recognise it, never mind the tart you are writing the letter to."

The Lamp

While he was not afraid, this still left Victor in somewhat of a quandary. Would he be taken back to rot in some jail to serve out his sentence or should he fight the bully and to hell with the consequences'? The thought of prison didn't appeal to him at all. But neither did the idea of running away from a loud-mouthed braggart like Burns. He thought of the advice his uncle had given him not long after he had started work in the pit! If you get into any serious bother don't think about fighting' fair. That's a daft bloody load of ballocks. They lose all interest in fighting' if you cream their taters!" Victor carefully put down the paper and pencil and rose slowly to his feet. The other occupants, having witnessed the power in Steven Burn's fists, all jumped aside leaving plenty of room for Burns to fulfil his threats. The bully stood on the balls of his feet, his legs slightly apart, with his fists cocked in the classic fist fighter's pose.

"Come on you pompous turd!" He spat as Victor approached clenching and unclenching his fists, "I've wanted to smash in your poxy face from the moment I clapped eyes on you! Come and get what's coming' to you!" Victor went up to the bully, but instead of bunching his fists brought up the toe of his right boot between Burns' legs. A look of pure undiluted, excruciating agony crossed the stricken man's face as the torment burst up from his tortured genitals and burst from his mouth in a breathless grunt of suffering and anguish. Clasping his stricken equipment, Steven Burns sank to his knees. Taking deliberate aim. Victor smashed the lace holed instep of his boot flush into his antagonist's face, splitting both nose and eyebrow with a blood splattering gash. Burns fell to the floor an insensible hulk.

"That'll teach the mouthy bastard!" said Tony Brown, an ex-miner from Crumlin, who was using the next bunk to Victor. He added "I hope 'he don't want to use his family jewels for a while!"

The tent rocked with laughter.

"Yeh!" Added Eddie Griffiths another miner, "I don't think I ever want to eat mashed taters again!" He thought for a while then concluded. "Let's all get to bed before the sergeant comes in. We'll all, say 'he fell down, and hit is head on the tent pole. I 'hope his skull is busted so they can't bring 'him back here to cause more trouble. Come on lads let's get to bed an' remember it wasn't Victor or any of us. The miserable bastard fell over 'his own feet!"

Steven Burns, still unconscious was carried to the battalion surgeon's tent where he was diagnosed as suffering from severe concussion, lacerations and a broken nose. He was transferred to the cottage hospital. He was never seen by the second Mons again!

Victor finished the letter to Naomi and gave it to Trevor. "I'll ask the chaplain if he can send it for you." Trevor promised.

Training continued for the next three days with the emphasis placed upon physical fitness. Victor found himself in a detachment that was ordered to dig trenches. It was the first time in almost four years that Victor had touched a pick and shovel. His hands blistered, but within two hours of starting to dig he was moving earth with the best of them. Once a miner, always a miner! The battalion, together with the rest of the Welsh Brigade moved to Northampton and the training was stepped up. Victor was given his first sight of a Short Magazine Lee Enfield rifle and introduced to its idiosyncrasies. He enjoyed its feel and the confident way it kicked back into his shoulder as he squeezed off several clips of ammunition. The older, more experienced soldiers proved heir worth in training the new recruits and preparing them for the conflict that was to come. August turned into September with the relentless drills and practice being repeated day after day, until the battalion began to gel into a formidable fighting force as the trust and camaraderie between soldiers developed. Throughout all the drills and training, Victor earned the admiration and confidence of his newfound friends and won the respect of his officer. Finally, after a further six weeks of unstinting training, on the 5h November, the battalion as part of the Welsh Brigade embarked for France.

CHAPTER 31

The battalion arrived at Harve on the 7th November. A day later, they were taken by train to St. Omer, a journey that was to take two weary, uncomfortable days, with the men packed into evil smelling trucks. "You was educated Victor." Stated George Lewis a corporal from Blaina. "What does them Froggie words on the side of these trucks mean?" Victor smiled as he thought of the inscriptions that had been stencilled on all the trucks, in heavy black paint… 'Hommes 40—Chevaux 8'! "It means that a horse gets more room than you do corporal. Perhaps we are fighting this war to make sure that all the French horses are comfortable and well fed!"

"You mean we are in horse trucks?" Asked Howard Roberts a miner from Crosskeys, "I wondered what the smell was."

"And we all thought it was you" Interrupted Trevor Bailey "It might bloody stink but as my old mam always used to say. A second-class ride is better than a first class walk! Don't complain too loud, because before any of you get home you will have walked your bloody feet flat!" The talk mumbled on about the transport and the fact the officers were travelling in 'proper' railway carriages.

"I expect they are having to rough it as well." Added private Tony Brown. "I didn't see one 'First Class carriage on the train!"

At St.Omer, Sergeant Bailey's words were proved correct. The battalion left the train and marched and marched. They were fortunate to stop for a week at Wizarne. Once again, billeted in the comparative luxury of twenty-two to a tent! The week was spends in exhaustive fitness training.

"If I see a German!" Panted a bewildered Howard Roberts, "I won't shoot him I'll challenge 'him to a bloody race an' whoever wins can win the sodding war!"

"Stop moaning Private Roberts." Ordered Trevor Bailey. "If you aren't fit, how do you intend to catch the enemy when he runs away?"

"What the bloody hell do I want to catch 'him for? If 'he's got the sense to run away he can piss off all the way to sodding Germany! I Don't want to catch 'him!"

"Quite right Howard." Added Tony Brown, "I don't want to catch a German either, I wouldn't know what to do with 'him once I'd caught him!" "Perhaps 'he's got a sister!" Chimed in Jack Evans, huddled at the back of the column, he was another ex-miner from Crumlin.

"You wouldn't be able to catch even her!" Scoffed Tony.

"Silence in the ranks!" Warned Sergeant Bailey, "If you've got enough breath to argue we haven't done enough physical jerks! Perhaps I'd better ask the officer for another hour!" The suggestion was met with an absolute silence. Victor smiled and winked at Trevor.

"We can laugh and joke now." Victor thought quietly to himself, "But how will we react when the shells and bullets start flying?"

The false peace ended with the Battalion undertaking a two-day forced march to a small village called Le Bizet, it was a name that seemed ironic to Victor, an identical name to the French composer. But there was nothing musical about their reception. They were instructed into the art of fighting from, and defending their trenches, by the 2nd Lancashire Fusiliers. Two companies, 'C' and Victor's 'D' went straight into the front line while 'A' and 'B' remained in reserve.

The trench was no more than five feet deep and the bottom a morass of churned mud. Bundles of brushwood had been thrown into the bottom of it. Taking up his station Victor's feet were sodden and his toes chilled through to the bone.

"Keep your heads down below the parapet when you move around Lieutenant Edwards ordered as his platoon began milling around trying to find the safest part of their allotted sector. The Bosche have some pretty good snipers in this area and if you don't keep your heads down its going to find itself a target for a bullet! Sergeant Major see that the men are distributed as evenly as possible and that a vigilant watch is made of the enemy's lines." He pointed over the top of the mud-spattered trench, "They are about a hundred and fifty yards that way." Victor was placed with Jack Evans and corporal George Lewis. Their section of trench was no more than eight yards long, three feet wide and at its deepest, no more than five feet deep. The edge of the trench was protected by a small parapet of loose earth that had been thrown out of the trench. A few strong points had been provided where the trench wall was reinforced with sandbags and wooden props, but the nearest one to Victor was almost fifty yards away.

"I'll keep watch for the first hour." Said Corporal Lewis as he leaned near the top of the parapet, with only his eyes exposed. "You two use your shovels and try and hollow out the rear of this trench into a dugout so that we can have a bit more room." Victor and Jack attacked the trench wall with a vengeance and had soon hollowed out a drier area that was large enough to seat two soldiers in reasonable comfort.

"Keep your head down Jack!" yelled the corporal, without turning around," But come over here and take the next watch." Jack Evans was soon looking over the trench's edge lying beside his corporal. "If you see anything shout out as if the devil was after your sister!" George slithered down to join Victor in the dugout. Looking along the battalion frontage of trench, Victor could see that soldiers were busy with picks and shovels widening and improving the trench. The battalion was recruited in a mining area, and more than ninety percent of its soldiers were colliers and it's officers mining engineers!

It was comparatively quiet. In the distance they could hear the deep grunts and bellows of artillery and the crash of exploding shells, but it was as silent as the grave to their front,

"Can't see anything' happening' in front of us!" Said Jack Evans, as he craned his neck up to get a better view to the front.

"Keep your bloody 'head down!" snapped George quickly, all in vain as the top of Jack Evans' head exploded into a bloody pulp and his lifeless corpse slid down slowly to the floor of the now blood-soaked trench!

"Oh God!" Yelled Victor, being the first person to react to the, soon to be all too familiar, sight of friends and enemies, bloodied, mutilated and dead! He looked down at the motionless figure that had just ceased to be private Jack Evans of Crumlin. Victor had never seen so much blood! It was seeping through the brushwood that had been thrown down in an attempt to provide a dry footing in the trench, now it was blotting up Jack's life blood!

He stooped over the still body, hoping to see some sign or faint spark of life, there was none.

"Keep your heads down!" Bellowed Lieutenant Edwards, in response to the outcry that greeted the shooting. "Observers! Did anyone spot where that shot came from?" Silence greeted his question. "You have been warned about being vigilant at all times, if you make one mistake here, it will be your last!"

Trevor Bailey was the first soldier of authority to appear. George Lewis just sat trembling in the recently constructed dug out. "Victor!" The sergeant ordered, "Keep watch, but for God's sake keep down!" He turned to the corporal and put his hand on his comrade's shoulder and shook him gently. "Come on George, there are men depending on you. This is War! Time to forget the romantic nonsense they put in the papers. Jack's dead his war is over, take care of the living!" George looked up through red rimmed eyes and choked back the tears as he replied. "I know that, but I put him there on watch. I told him to stand there!" The older Sergeant looked down in sympathy and responded, "You accepted that responsibility when you took the stripes and pay. Now you must stand up and be counted. There are going to be times when you will have to make certain decisions and give orders, and these soldiers." He waved his arms to indicate the men crowded into the trench, "Would rather take them from you, than some toffee-nosed officer with little regard for their worth or safety! Trevor saw two men smoking a dozen yards along the trench, "You two get a spare blanket to cover the body and carry it to the command post." He leaned cautiously against the parapet and whispered to Victor, "Did you see where the shot came from?" Victor could only respond in the negative. Trevor continued. "Keep your eyes on George he's taking Private Evans' death particularly badly, He slipped down into the trench and made his way back to Lieutenant Edwards.

Victor kept his head as low as he possibly could, and was careful to remain immobile, so that no movement would give away his position to an enemy, sniper. His eyes however, raked back and fore straining to catch any sign that would indicate where the deadly bullet had come from. He could see a similar parapet to his own, no more than two hundred yards ahead. Everything looked silent and empty, but he was certain that it contained, just as many worried souls, frantically looking in his direction, searching for him and his position!

The endless monotony of head down look to your front continued for two grubby days as the battalion was instructed by the Lancashire's. He wondered how they would survive the usual practice of eight days in the front line, followed by a similar time in reserve! The trenches were little more than cess pits, an ocean of mud, blood, vomit and flesh! The battalion was lucky in as much as more than three quarters of its number were miners, men used to working with the pick and shovel in filthy conditions, but they were allowed home to wash and sleep at the end of each shift. The battalion raised many an eyebrow at the way in which it improved the trenches, by means of sheer muscle power and ingenuity.

Another man died and three more were wounded before 'D; company moved back into reserve for a 'rest', Victor was glad he didn't know the soldier, it was hard to lose friends! The company's 'rest, involved working every night on trench construction or repair. The repairs proved the more hazardous occupation, as it generally involved improvement's to trenches, little more than a hundred yards away from the enemy. The only protection was darkness, although bullets followed the sound of picks thudding into earth and the crystal-clear ringing of spades against stone!

The battalion was soon deemed to be sufficiently 'blooded' and was declared competent enough to take over their own stretch of trench. In early December, they relieved the 2nd Essex Regiment. December brought the cold weather and rain. The rain made movement almost impossible, and the drainage of the trenches became extremely difficult. Nothing kept the rain out successfully. Mercifully no engagements with the enemy took place, although frequent exchanges of fire had resulted in thirty six soldiers being killed, with another one hundred and thirty wounded.

Victor looked at the slime mud filled hole that had been his home for more than four months. He had forgotten when he had last had dry feet! If she could have smelled the things he called socks Naomi would have been appalled. His thoughts drifted to Naomi and Peter, he had to fight back the tears as he imagined her sitting at home worrying if he was alive or dead!

"It's a good job we all smell bloody awful!" Joked Eddie Griffiths, Victor smiled, his nose had been blocked up for more than a fortnight, mercifully he had lost his sense of smell. "I'd love to be able to smell freshly baked bread or a pair of clean sheets, after a day's drying on the clothesline!" He added.

He looked around him. Soldiers were sheltering under sacks, planks of wood, behind sandbags, anywhere to get out of the continual downpour. Nothing worked! The rain and mud seeped through greatcoats, boots, tunics, leggings and socks, nothing was impervious. The continual drenching was having a serious effect on the battalion's health and moral. More and more men became sick or suffered from frostbite. On the occasional day that the rains stopped the intense cold took over. Worst of all, was 'Trench foot', an agonising swelling of the feet caused by the appalling wet conditions and the continual damp.

"At least the Boche aren't any better off than us!" laughed Eddie. "I wouldn't want to shoot one of them so he could get away from this bloody awful weather."

Sergeant Bailey came slopping through the mud, he stopped by Victor and said, "Lieutenant George is taking a detachment of men on a mining operation, I thought you would welcome the chance to get away from these trenches for a while!"

"Anything's better than this water-soaked mud hole!" He replied. "I thought you might appreciate a break away." Trevor laughed, "Sorry it's not two weeks by the seaside. Get yourself down to the command post and report to second lieutenant George."

Nightfall, found Victor, accompanying the officer and fourteen other soldiers as they crawled out of the trench and made their way towards the rear. For once, Victor was pleased to feel the rain beating a tattoo on his helmet. The trees had been obliterated months earlier, the cannon fire had taken its toll on them, as well as on the humans who had tried to shelter beneath them. This dreadful weather would hide them from even the sharpest of lookouts! They slithered and slopped through the mud for several hours, when they were met by another group of soldiers. Lieutenant George, who had been peering frantically into the gloom ahead appeared to be mightily relived at their appearance. Victor could not hear what was said between his own lieutenant and the officer accompanying the other detachment. He merely fell in at the rear of the column and followed when they were marched away with the rain drops beating time as they disintegrated loudly against his tin hat.

A few hours before dawn, they marched past a derelict farmhouse and reached their destination. It was a trench little different from his own! Its sides were reinforced with wooden planking, into a parapet that was strengthened with sandbags.

"Keep down men!" Lieutenant George warned, "There are some ruined houses by the enemy's trenches, and they have some crack shot snipers posted there. I've been informed that they can shoot the eye out of a rabbit at a thousand yards!" The men needed little urging to flop exhausted into the bottom of the trench, too tired to care about the mud and filth that lined it.

"Headquarters want a mine tunnelled from here right under the houses those Bosche snipers are using." Lieutenant George announced to the weary dishevelled rag bag troops crouched around him. "If we can get under their position, we'll fill the mine with explosive and send them straight back to the Kaiser! The Wiltshire regiment have tried, but this damned rain keeps causing their attempts to flood and collapse. You are all ex-miners, so we want you to try."

Victor looked at the tools and timbers that had been provided. He looked at the officer and said, "Excuse me sir." The detachment turned to look at him. "There's no way even we, are going to tunnel through this mud!"

"Privates, don't say anything is impossible, in this army soldier!" The lieutenant reprimanded, "We all try until we succeed, or die in the attempt!"

Victor turned his attention to the officer who had accompanied them the previous night, he was a captain, and he was listening intently. Victor faced his lieutenant and continued, "I didn't say we couldn't do it sir." He hesitated before continuing, he could see the young officer was becoming more annoyed, with each word. "The ground here is too waterlogged sir, but we could…"

"When we want a private's advice, we ask for it, snarled the lieutenant." If we weren't at war, I would have you placed on a charge for insubordination. Now get a shovel and start digging. The sergeant will tell you where!" The men began reaching for the tools that were strewn about the trench floor, when they were stopped by the captain. "Just a moment Lieutenant. This army of ours is made up of soldiers from all walks of life." He indicated the Mons detachment, "Your men are all miners, we need mining savvy, not just brawn!" He looked at Victor, "You were I think about to offer a solution to our problem, because problem is what it is! The snipers in those houses have killed or wounded almost three hundred of my solders. At the moment I'd listen to the devil himself if he knew how to blow up those ruins! Out with your idea soldier that's an order!" He glared at lieutenant George daring him to interrupt.

Victor took a deep breath and continued," We need dry ground to start with!" "Exactly Private Leslie!" Barked the lieutenant. Victor continued, "This ground is so wet and muddy that no matter where we dig it will collapse "I'm sorry we can't oblige with dry ground," snarled the lieutenant it has been raining if you haven't noticed!" The other solders began to snigger at the officer's sarcasm.

Undeterred, Victor continued, "Yes sir, I know sir, but we walked past a farmhouse a few yards behind our lines, if we can get in there, and if it has a cellar, we can start tunnelling from it, the ground will be dry!" "Bloody hell!" Shouted the Captain, "Of Course! It was so simple; the solution was right under our noses. We'll cross to the farm tonight and start digging. Well done private! All of you get some sleep if you can!"

One hour after the sun disappeared over the horizon Captain Watkins took the detachment over to the derelict building. The upper floors were completely destroyed, and huge holes were visible in the roof, but the kitchen was almost intact, it was at the rear of the house and consequently had missed the worst of the shelling and rifle exchanges. The detachment reached the ruin unscathed and more importantly, undetected. Captain Edwards detailed the Lieutenant to take four men and to start preparing trenches to the rear of the cottage. "If the Bosche discovers we are in here they'll start pinging over a few shells and we'll need those trenches in a hurry." He informed his subordinate. Victor found himself in the farm's cellar, where candles were lit, and work began on the tunnel in the shortest direction towards the enemy houses. It was dirty, dusty and bloody hard work. But it was dry! For the first time in more than six months Victor was not up to his backside in mud!

"Well done private!" enthused Captain Watkins, pleased that the work was showing every sign of being successfully concluded, "How long do you think it will take?" "I don't know Sir." Victor replied, "It all depends on the ground ahead. I would guess we are going to have to tunnel about seven or eight hundred feet!" that's going to take several weeks, sir." "Well let's get on with it and see how far we can go today. That might give us a better idea of a probable time." Captain Watkins ordered. "Please sir." Asked Victor, "May I make another suggestion?"

"Certainly private." The captain replied. "Your suggestions have proved top notch this far."

"Once we start tunnelling proper, can you bring a few more men over to help shift the earth, we will do the digging, but you'll need a few fresh troops to do the carrying."

"Good idea private I'll see to that at once. The officer replied. "One last thing sir. And it's probably the most important of all. You had better ask for an engineering officer, or perhaps you can borrow one of the officers from our battalion who was a mining engineer in Blighty. We need to know if we are going in the right direction and how far to dig!" The captain left the cellar to ponder on the questions raised by Victor leaving the second Mons detachment to the tunnelling and digging.

CHAPTER 32

KATE WAS IN THE KITCHEN PREPARING TOM'S MEAL, HE WOULD BE home from the pit in a few hours. Looking out of the window she could see Naomi, with Peter gurgling happily on her lap. Tears welled up in her eyes as she thought of his father. They hadn't seen or heard from him since he had been dragged away from them, more than six months previously. The catastrophe of war was running through the village like a plague. News was being received daily of deaths and mutilations, there wasn't a street that hadn't lost fathers, sons, neighbours or friends. The death toll was evident everywhere, and the pall of gloom and despondency shrouded the community like a hungry vulture. She looked at Naomi and managed to force a smile through her tears. Her daughter in law was heavily pregnant. Victor had been a busy boy before they had dragged him off to God knew where! From her size and appearance, Naomi wasn't going to be carrying for much longer. Peter was already a perfect replica of his father and with every passing day the likeness intensified.

Looking down the valley she caught sight of Berwyn Morgan, his red cheeks bulging as he panted his way beside the remains of the dam that had burst may years ago. She watched as he clambered up the footpath, rushing upward. He was waving a small piece of grubby white paper in his hand. More bad news for some family she sighed, who's turn is it today? She lost sight of the old minister as he reached the bottom of the street and began climbing up the hill. She took one last look at the mother and child sitting in the garden before returning to her cooking.

Her heart missed several beats when she heard a pounding on the door she rushed to open it and was appalled to see Berwyn standing there with that, piece of paper! The aged minister, realising the significance of his unexpected arrival, blurted out, "It's alright, it's good news! It's a letter from Victor." The minister thrust the soiled paper into her hand and concluded, "It's for Naomi, it's from Victor!"

Kate took the precious document out to Naomi. Without saying a word, she picked up Peter and gave the radiant mother the letter and took Peter inside the house. Naomi stared at the letter for several minutes before she had the courage to open it. With trembling hands, unable to restrain herself a moment longer she tore it open. Kate was watching from the window, clutching Peter tightly to her aching bosom in a silent prayer as she saw the delight and ecstasy that transformed the young woman's face.

"Mam! Mam" Naomi screeched, as she dashed into the house, "It's a letter from Victor! It's several months old, but he was fine when he wrote it." The two women hugged each other, and a totally relieved family passed Peter from one to the other and subjected him to the sloppiest kissing he had ever encountered in his short life. Kate decided there was only one thing to do before reading the letter, put the kettle on!

"Brian Cuthbertson has written to me that Sir Michael Fairfax will be in the shipping office at Newport tomorrow." Naomi announced to the family as they sat around the table, following their daily meal. "The letter has filled me with new hope, I intend catching tomorrow's train to town to see him. I am going to try to clear Victor's name I'll offer to replace the missing money."

"Don't be daft girl!" Tom replied, "You know as well as I do. Victor didn't steal that money!" He looked around the table and everyone was nodding with agreement.

"I know!" She replied "But the money is missing, and Victor has been blamed. I will feel better if I can replace that money, then we can try to redeem Victor's name!"

"It's five hundred pounds!" Kate added, "I don't know anyone who has that much money, let alone anyone willing to give it away! Have you got that much?" She asked incredulously. "If you have and you give it away, what will you live on?"

Naomi stared down at her hands before looking up and saying. "If I sell the house in Newport. I can pay the money back and still have a few hundred pounds left. If I do that, can I live here with you?"

"Of course, you can!" Kate replied. "You're my son's wife, his son is asleep upstairs, and you are carrying his other child! You are family." "I still say you will be daft to pay the money back! You don't owe a penny. Someone else has stolen it and Victor has been blamed!" Tom insisted.

"It will make me feel as if I am helping Victor survive this terrible war." Naomi stated, "If God spares him and he can come home to us all, we will be halfway to restoring his good name!" She fled from the room with tears pouring down her cheeks in torrents.

The steamship office appeared unchanged from the day she had left it. To Naomi's practiced eye, as she glanced around, even the cobwebs seemed to be in the same positions! It was like walking back into history. Sir Michael Fairfax, jumped from the chesterfield sofa on which he had been slouching, as she entered the room. His face dropped when he noticed her condition.

"Welcome back Naomi. I was delighted to hear from you. It's been far too long, come in. Take a seat, I had no idea you were pregnant!"

She smiled sweetly at his attempt at politeness and replied. "Thank you, Sir Michael, it has been a tiring journey." She sat on the sofa, a more accurate description would probably have been, she perched uncomfortably on its edge.

"What can I do for you my dear?" He asked oilily!

It took her less than two minutes to explain her wish to repay the money and attempt to clear her husband's name.

"I would love to be able to help such an attractive young beauty as yourself." He replied, reaching over to rub his hand along her knee and thigh. "A man in my position, has many friends and much influence and I'm sure you could be extremely grateful and reward a generous benefactor!"

Naomi said nothing but sat rigidly upright and steeled herself against his unwelcome touch, it was making her flesh creep. I'll tell you what!" He continued his eyes aflame. "You pay the money back and..." He looked at her swollen stomach. "When your condition alters, come and see me again and I'm sure that together we can find a solution that is mutually acceptable!"

Naomi, withholding the urge to lash her hand into the lecherous old codger's face, got to her feet and replied. "I'll arrange for the money to be paid into the company's account!" She made for the door as quickly as her condition would allow. Fairfax intercepted her a few strides from the exit, turned her around and placed one hand around her buttocks and the other cupped a swollen breast.

"I think we understand one another, Naomi. If you are suitably grateful." His hand toyed with her nipple through the material of her dress. "I'm sure there will be something I can do to help!" His other hand was fondling her buttocks cheek forcing them apart, his fingers striving to reach between. "What a pity you're pregnant, but do you know? I've never had a pregnant woman!"

She tore herself away and rushed through the door. Once outside the office, she turned and said loudly, "I'll see the money is forwarded to the company as soon as possible." She left with all the speed she could muster. Standing on the pavement in Commercial Road she shuddered and shuddered again, she felt unclean. His touch burned to her very soul. She returned home, determined to try to wash away every memory of his offensive touch, wondering if there was enough soap in the entire world, for such a monumental task. 'I'll never feel clean again!' Was her last thought.

"We're almost under the house sir." Victor reported to Captain Watkins. He was stripped to the waist and the sweat glistened on his grime-streaked chest. "If the engineering officer is right, we have only about twenty feet more to go.".

Captain Watkins nodded and investigated the four feet shaft that led from the cellar. He had not placed his head inside the tunnel, but had remained in the cellar, urging the men on. "Well done private, keep the men at it. I for one won't forget your part in this little escapade. I'm off upstairs, we are mounting a pair of Lewis guns in the ruins of the living room, they'll command a wonderful field of fire if the Bosche try to over run our trench." He turned and marched up the stairs.' Little escapade, be buggered!' thought Victor, 'We've been slogging our guts out in this little hell hole for nearly four weeks, and you haven't even got your hands dirty! Tell that to the families of the men who have been killed by the snipers in the houses!' He turned and began crawling back into the tunnel.

The mine had been completed. They started transferring the bags of ammatol and boxes of gun cotton into the tunnel. They charged the mine with ninety-six bags of explosive ammatol and sixty boxes of gun cotton. The explosives were ready! The miners crawled back wearily to the spacious cellar and its fresh air. Where they could enjoy a few hours well-earned rest. It was the first chance that Victor, had, had to sit down and look around the roomy cellar. The flickering candles cast eerie shadows that crawled around the room, like spiders searching for an unwary fly. He caught sight of a small box, half hidden by the dust in the far corner of the room, when a draught caught the candle flame and it flickered, the metal box glittered brightly. Curious, he got to his feet and was soon holding the tiny box in his hand. It was only eight inches long, and no more than two inches wide or deep. Victor took it to the nearest candle. The lid of the box was hinged. He blew the dust away from the tarnished lid and lifted it. His eyes could hardly believe his good fortune. The box held a harmonica. Victor had seen one like it years earlier in Crane's Musical store window. He took it out and put it gently to his lips. It worked! Within two minutes, the cellar was reverberating to the haunting strains of 'Tipperary', as Victor played the instrument. His playing soon attracted an audience. As the miners gathered round him to add their voices to his playing. He continued with a rendition of 'Hello, hello who's your lady friend for all those present, Victor played most of the soldiers' favourites and requests, as the impromptu concert was enjoyed by all those present. Eventually exhaustion forced him to replace the harmonica in its box, which he then tucked securely into his tunic breast pocket. He was asleep within five minutes.

Victor was deep in the middle of a home cooked meal with Naomi, and Peter, when he was suddenly tugged back into reality. The noise was ear shattering, ten times louder than any underground explosion that he had experienced at the colliery. The walls of the cellar were vibrating and creaking, as explosion after explosion shattered the early morning silence. He covered his ears with his hands and cowered down as near to the floor as he could, attempting to escape the thunderous bombardment. The walls creaked, complained and cracked, but they withstood the barrage that was being concentrated on the trench system. Victor, grateful that he was inside the cellar, was ashamed to admit afterwards, that he gave little regard for the safety of the soldiers sheltering in the trenches. The piercing detonations intermingled one with another, until Victor was certain his ears and mind could stand no more. His mouth was open wide, and he was screaming soundlessly, the only sounds audible, were the interminable blasts as the high explosive and shrapnel shells burst all around!

The barrage ended as suddenly as it had begun, but a shrill ringing sound continued to fill his head and clog his ears. Victor stumbled to his feet and made his way, shakily, up the stairs. The farmhouse was little more than a disorganised pile of masonry and rubble. Mindful of further explosions, and the ever-present snipers, he made his way to the front of the farm. Four of the soldiers were seriously wounded, two dead and Captain Watkins was sitting against a pile of sandbags with a large cut running from his forehead to his left ear. Victor swathed the officer's head in bandages in an attempt to staunch the blood that was running down his face.

"I'll be alright!" Groaned the officer. "G g got to g g get the L L Lewis guns mounted and the sandbags rebuilt!" They began rebuilding the sandbag barricade that the barrage had knocked flat. Victor, with the help of another three soldiers from the cellar piled the bags high.

"That b bb barrage means the B b boche are going t t to attack!" He stammered, dragging himself behind the barricade, "T t these Lewis guns are g g gg going to be needed, hhhelp me!"

Victor, helped the Captain position himself behind the automatic weapon and then slid over to the other machine gun. Picking up the 47 round circular magazine he attached it to the top of the gun. Looking around he found two boxes, each containing a dozen magazines. The soldiers who had been sheltering in the cellar with victor, were slowly appearing and began constructing barricades and loading their rifles. Looking ahead at the trenches, Victor, could see that they were a hive of activity, despite the devastating bombardment, as the survivors prepared to repulse the anticipated attack.

"Get the dead and wounded into the cellar!" He shouted to some of the others. He looked for support from the captain, who turned painfully and barked, "Dd do as you are d d d damn well told!"

Victor glancing ahead noticed that the barrage had produced many gaps in the barbed wire in front of the trenches' parapet. No man's land was now swarming with thousands or grey uniformed enemy infantry. The Allied artillery was slow to react as only a few rounds were seen to explode around the advancing soldiers. A pair of Vickers machine guns opened up with their deep throated chatter as they began to decimate everything in front of them, the infantry began responding to the order to open fire.

Despite horrendous losses the grey uniformed horde, rolled on!

"Stupid b b b bloody general s s staff!" cursed Captain Watkins as he watched the battle unfold, "They only allow t t t two machine guns to a battalion. How are we expected to stop that lot with just two?"

Victor looked and was appalled at the carnage being wreaked, by just two machine guns. It was gruesome!

"No one fire until I do!" Croaked the injured Captain. "Once I start p p p pour it into them. We'll be a surprise they won't be expecting. Remember it's them or us!"

Victor watched as the grey lines advanced, closer and closer. Many fell but empty spaces were filled from the rear. Mills bomb grenades were filling the air like confetti at a wedding, except they were not sent with good wishes, those were the last thing on any of the soldiers lips as they waited for the advancing enemy. The carnage was about to begin as man murdered man. The enemy front ranks were within fifty yards of the trench parapet when Captain Watkins screamed the order to fire, and cut loose with the machine gun, hosing death and destruction through the enemy ranks. Victor found himself squeezing the trigger and began scything down every German within sight. The Lewis gun was kicking into his shoulder with an intensity ten times worse than any mining drill. Six seconds! That's all it took, six short seconds and he had poured forty-seven murderous rounds of ammunition into the advancing lines. All around him soldiers were firing as quickly as they could work the bolt actions on their rifles! He detached the empty drum magazine and replaced it with a full one. He was a slave to the blood lust that seemed to have accompanied another magazine of death! He had emptied nine magazines, before the grey coated soldiers began to waver, less than fifteen yards from the parapet. They had hesitated under the murderous hail of grenades, rifle and machine gun bullets. Many threw their rifles down and ran, most began to retreat in an orderly fashion, still facing forward.

"Pour it on!" screamed the injured Watkins, "Don't let the bastards get back!"

To his dying shame, Victor emptied another magazine, into the retreating and terror stricken, enemy? Watkins continued firing till all signs of life in front of him had ceased.

The general order to hold fire went up and down the trench. The whole area was awash with blood and destruction.

"Well done men!" Captain Watkins congratulated his small but deadly detachment. He turned to Victor and added, "I'll see you are remembered in full for your part in this Private Leslie!" Noticing the look of abject horror that was on Victor's face, he said, "You'll get over it, war is the nearest thing to hell on earth. Now you've faced this you will never fear or be revolted by anything again. Just remember if you hadn't used that gun, that trench would have been filled with British dead, how many mothers back home will be thanking you tonight and tomorrow." "But', he thought to himself, 'how many German mothers will be cursing me?

Boxes of 303 ammunition were produced and trembling fingers started recharging the discarded magazines.

"Play us a tune private, we need a song!" Captain Watkins shouted to Victor. He opened the precious box and began playing. 'Pack up your troubles'! The men around him started singing and soon the song was being taken up by the hundreds of men in the trenches in front of him. The enemy regrouped and assaulted the trench system again and again. They were repulsed each time. Captain Watkins hosed the attackers relentlessly." God forgive me!" Victor whispered to himself, as darkness descended on the battlefield, 'because I don't think I can ever forgive myself'.

CHAPTER 33

The battle raged for a week with every attack being repulsed with horrendous casualties on both sides, The scale of the losses could not be sustained indefinitely. The routine of attack and counterattack gradually subsided. The antagonists totally exhausted remained behind their blood-soaked barricades observing each other malevolently. Not one single yard of ground had been gained or lost by either side. The battle ground was covered with hundreds of decaying corpses. The only gainers were the callous pachydermatous general staff of both sides who would dine out on their militaristic propaganda and memoirs for decades, without having entered any active battlegrounds. The thousands of injured and wounded were taken from the Aid Posts, by the overworked field ambulances to the advanced Dressing Stations, where the overwhelmed doctors did their best to cope with the depravity and trauma of man's inhumanity to man. The wounded still lucky enough to be alive were shipped to Hospitals in the rear. Those left uninjured contemplated the next aggressive moves, more bombs, more shells and more bullets, interspersed with a few feet of cold hard, liberally used bayonet steel!

Victor had been lucky! His only injury was a slender gash more bloody than dangerous, where a 7.92mm Mauser bullet had run a furrow that had grazed his seventh and eight ribs. His shoulder was bruised black and blue, from the continual recoil of the Lewis gun!

They were told of a terrible new weapon that had been used a few days previously. The rumours had flown up and down the trench of a poisonous gas, a hideous green yellow pall that crept slowly along the ground, choking and suffocating everything it encountered, be it man or beast. The descriptions of men choking and coughing their lungs out had been frightening. Victor said a silent prayer for those poor unfortunate souls who had suffered such an agonising death, and selfishly thanked the Lord that it was them and not him!

Captain Watkins called the mining party survivors to him and ordered, "It's time for you to rejoin your battalion." Of the original twelve men, led by Lieutenant Edwards, four men were left. The corporal had been one of the first casualties. The last had been the young lieutenant, shot through the lung by a sniper, as he moved between the ruin and the front-line trench. He was still clinging onto life, a situation that showed every sign of being temporary. "I hope you can remember the way back?" Questioned the Captain, "Because we can't spare a single man to help you. You're on your own." Victor answered for the others, "I think I can find my way back to the second Mons, Sir." He replied.

"Good show" He looked at the other three, "I'm promoting private Leslie to acting corporal, he's in charge until you get back. Find a stretcher and take Lieutenant Edwards with you, he'll have more chance with your surgeons. If he stays here, he's just going to bleed to death. If you keep your ears open, you should hear the explosion of the mine. Hope you are able to enjoy the fireworks, but you've seen enough action for now." The moon and stars were blanketed in the smoke from thousands of smouldering shell holes. They set off taking turns of half an hour carrying the heavy stretcher, and half an hour's rest per pair. The delirious officer groaned each time someone stumbled or slipped.

Victor hoped he would be able to remember the way back to their own communication trench in the rear. It would have been hard enough in the daylight, now, it was almost impossible! Every landmark and feature had been obliterated by the intensity of the Huns rolling barrage. Victor led the small group in the direction he hoped was the right one. The sky was beginning to adopt a grey mantle, as it prepared to accept the metamorphosis of night into day, when Victor caught sight of a hastily erected parapet. It had to be the battalion's reserve trenches! "Ow are we going' to get up to the trench without the boys taking a couple of pot shots at us?" asked Iwan Morgan, from the rear of the stretcher.'

'Now there's a point!' Thought Victor, then he had an idea he said "Stand tall lads. We'll march in singing a song." Taking his precious harmonica out of his pocket he began blowing as loud as he could. 'It's a long way to Tipperary', He paused for a moment then shouted. "Sing you dozy buggers! Sing."

The three soldiers croaked their way through as many words as they could remember.

"'Alt! Who goes by there then?" Came the command from the darkened trench ahead. At least they had called before firing!

"With voices like that you buggers 'have got to be English! You aren't Welsh!" The voice called.

"Private Leslie and the survivors of the mining detail. Returning to second Battalion We've got Lieutenant Edwards with us, he's badly wounded!" Victor replied.

"Wait there!" The voice ordered, "But keep down, and stop that bloody awful racket!"

The detail was allowed into the trench, where the injured lieutenant was lowered carefully down, where willing hands rushed him to the Regimental Aid Post.

Victor, after reporting to a Lieutenant George, asked if he could rejoin his own company. The lieutenant pointed an arm to the right and answered, "Company D, what's left of them, are about three hundred and fifty yards over there! Off you go. "Victor set off, the light was improving, with every step he took. He passed men, who showed every sign of having been involved in a hard prolonged fight. Everyone looked weary, and totally drained of vitality. They were all unshaven, with trench grime on their heads, arms faces and uniforms. Many showed the dark stains of old, dried blood. Victor walked through this debris of human exhaustion, trying not to disturb those who were sleeping or those who were too afraid to close their eyes! Eventually he came to a few faces that he recognised as belonging to some of the platoons from 'D' Company. Dawn broke, bathing the area in a sea of shimmering light. Just as he came to the company command post, where Captain Hughes the company commander was deep in discussion with Trevor Bailey. Victor stood to attention, near the two men. Until Trevor caught sight of him. "My God Victor! You look like a ghost from the past I didn't think I'd see you again! Come and report to the Captain."

Victor gave his report in a matter-of-fact way, telling of the casualties, the fighting and the rumours of the new weapon. The officer listened intently before saying.

We've taken quite a pounding here private. Grab something to eat the sergeant will assign you to a position. We know about that weapon, its gas. It annihilated 'B' company! I've never seen anything like it!" He shuddered, lost for words.

"We've taken a hammering Victor," Trevor announced. "The company's lost more than a hundred and thirty men! And of the seventy left, no more than fifty are fit to fight. The captain is expecting orders for us to pull back and regroup. How's everything with you?"

Victor told of the mining and his horror at the savagery of the fighting "It's the shelling that's worse." He concluded. "You never know where to try and hide. The noise eats right inside your skull." Looking round he could see only three of his original tent mates. "Three out of twenty-two," Said Trevor. "It got so bad when we were in the front line that we just had to throw the dead out of the trench and pick them up for burial at night! At least we couldn't see their faces in the dark!"

Their conversation was disturbed by a low rumbling explosion that occurred some way off to their front right. "There goes that bloody mine!" Victor announced more carnage and death than I've seen, I pity the poor Germans on top of that lot."

Trevor was correct in his assumption, shortly after midday Captain Hughes being the ranking surviving officer announced the battalion was to be pulled back and be relieved by the Essex regiment. It was a weary, depleted group of soldiers that made their way silently to the rear. The battalion needed a rest and a chance to rebuild. They marched all day, until they were just outside a town called Armentieres. They were told to halt in a field that formed part of a flax washing factory. The field was dotted with tents and the NCOs were busy detailing men into various canvas billets.

"We won't need squashing twenty-two in a tent this time!" said Victor.

Lying on his mattress, Victor closed his eyes. He tried to think of Naomi together with Peter, safe at home in Newport, and the rest of the family in Cwmcarn. Whenever he recalled them to memory, the guns would blaze in horror and a curtain was drawn across his mind. He closed his eyes again and thought of the captain's last announcement. "Fresh change of clothing and a bah tomorrow men." It was a chance to be really clean! There was even a bar of soap for every ten men!

Trevor had borrowed paper and pencils from a quartermaster sergeant and had loaned them to Victor. For the first time in more than nine months, he had the chance to write home. He didn't worry about the fact that the letter might never be delivered, he was able to write his love and longings, and how much he missed everyone. He closed his eyes, then began 'My Darling Naomi.'

You may never receive this letter my Dearest, but you will certainly know how much I miss and love you ... .

In a few short minutes he had filled two sides of paper, and his eyes were moist with despair and yearning. He put the pencil and precious letter carefully away, closed his eyes and surrendered to blissful oblivion for eight hours.

The tubs were arranged in Pairs, in an outbuilding that had once housed the water supply for the factory. The men were marched to the shed and once inside were ordered to strip. The one piece of clothing they were to keep was their boots. Victor's eyes were transfixed on the tub full of bright clean water. He was handed a cake of soap and told, 'You have five minutes!' No one needed a second urging and soon each tub held a soldier scrubbing away at his skin as if it was dispensable. The war seemed a million miles away as some started singing to the tune of the old 'The Ash Grove':-

'One black one, one white one.'

'And one with a bit of shite on.'

'And the hair on her Dickie Dido' hung down to her knees.'

The song was cut short as a scream of "Attention blasted through the building, "Stand up you dozy load of buggers! Get ready for inspection!" Twenty soldiers stood to attention each one as naked as the day they were born, in walked his Majesty the King, the Prince of Wales and Field Marshall Sir John French. The inspection was over in no more than three embarrassing seconds, as the royal party wandered through the building with the instruction, 'carry on men!'

"Bloody hell!" exclaimed Eddie Griffiths, a private from Pontypool. "The King 'himself inspecting the privates' privates!"

"We seen you, standing' to attention!" Laughed Howard Robert in the next tub." Every bit of you was standing' to attention! What were you doing' under the water?"

"It's mine and I'll wash it any way I like" Replied Eddie happily. "Well, I reckon that's the first time the King has inspected the troops todgers!" continued Howard, "And 'he could inspect every bit of yours, you haven't been taking the medicine they're supposed to give us!"

"I was listening to some of the officers talking this morning" Victor interrupted, his hair a mess of soap suds. "It seems we have just made a withdrawal from the battle of Ypres."

"What the hell is a withdrawal." questioned Eddie." The only withdrawal I know about, is when you have to pull out quick, spray it all over the ceiling or else you pay for it nine months later!"

This one was a tactical withdrawal!" Laughed Victor, after submerging his head to rinse away the soap suds. "It means they have brought us here to rest, so that we can be ready to fight again. "Sod that!" Quipped Howard as he too rinsed his hair, I fought plenty of Germans with my bayonet last going off. I was so scared I pissed my pants! I don't think I can do it again.

"You can piss your pants any old time!" Replied Eddie.!!

"I meant fight with a bloody bayonet, you silly bugger!" Laughed Howard. The survivors had, had a refreshing bath less than twenty four hours rest from the constant shelling, and they were laughing and joking with one another. Victor looked around, the haggard look that had infested everyone's' face a few hours earlier, had lessened "Rinse off!" came the order, "I 'hope none of you dirty buggers has pissed in the bath water cos there's another five men supposed to use that water!"

A clean, happy group of men marched out into the fresh air, where they were handed a clean towel and told to dry. A pair of army surgeons examined each man with a spatula and stethoscope, before they were marched off to the delousing tent, where each man was powdered from head to foot in an evil smelling flea powder. "Work it well into your crutch!" Snapped an orderly, fed up with powdering naked bodies. "it'll kill the crabs."

The next stop was the quarter master's, where, joy of joy! Every man was given clean uniform and cleaning utensils with which to polish his boots.

Trevor Bailey marched into Victor's tent and ordered, "It's Sunday tomorrow. Church parade at nine. The padre's a Londoner. He's expecting some special singing seeing as this is a Monmouthshire Regiment. I hope he isn't going to be disappointed, cos then, I'll be disappointed, and you wouldn't want that, would you lads?" He was answered with a chorus of 'No sergeant Major!" Someone added, "If the king wants to inspect our dicks, some bloody Chaplin may as well inspect our throats!" Trevor turned and snapped. "Something wrong with your privates, Griffiths? What's different about it! You ashamed of it or something?"

"I don't think so sergeant major." Answered Howard, with not a trace of emotion on his face. "Private Griffiths knows how to stand to attention as does every last bit of him." Trevor turned on his head and marched swiftly out of the tent, it wouldn't do for the men to see him laugh!

The one hundred and eighty-six survivors of the second Mons Battalion stood bare headed in the cold morning sunshine, ready to mourn the loss of their comrades. The battalion's visiting chaplain, the reverend Captain Edward Jordan, stood at their front his head bowed in prayer.

"We are here to worship God, who's purposes are good and who's power sustains the world he has made, who by his holy spirit leads in this war. We give thanks that he has spared us and remember those who have died in his service, fighting the forces of our enemies. With God on our side the victory will be ours." He looked up and said," Let us all sing a hymn of praise to Almighty God. I'm afraid the piano was smashed when the transport was shelled, but we shall do our best without music. I have heard that Welsh men are the best singers of hymns in the Christian world. Let us try to sing "All people that on earth do dwell. Captain Hughes interrupted the Chaplin, "Excuse me padre but we have an answer to the problem. Private Leslie front and centre."

The order struck Victor like a bolt of lightning. He took a few paces forward to the front and then stood to attention, in front of the captain.

"Sir!" He replied flourishing his salute.

"Private, I have been told that you are something of a musician, and you have obtained an instrument, that you er, um liberated. Do you think you could play to accompany the padre's hymns?"

"It is only a harmonica, sir." Victor replied, a wide smile on his face, "But, if the minister thinks it suitable, I can play most hymns. I used to play the organ at the chapel every Sunday."

Captain Hughes turned to the minister and said. "Do you think it would be too sacrilegious for the hymn singing to be accompanied by a mouth organ?"

"My dear Captain!" The minister enthused, "The lord knows we are at war. I do not believe that He will take offence and I will welcome this young man's accompaniment. I will not take offence and I will welcome this young man's accompaniment. We will have to imagine we are at home, and he is playing in his local chapel." He turned to Victor placed his hand on his shoulder and said, "Thank you my boy. Are you able to play, 'All people that on earth do dwell?'"

Victor smiled and said, "A wonderful choice sir! Would one line's introduction be sufficient?" The bemused minister nodded, and Victor turned to face his comrades and began to play. The haunting melody drifted over the field, like a calming blanket of bitter, stupefying laudanum. The harmonica's eerie notes made the entire group swallow hard, as tears started to well up in the eyes of even the most hard-bitten warrior. The soldiers joined in with one accord. No one ever forgot the service or the singing that took place on that Belgian field as approximately two hundred Welshmen sang, as only an exiled Welshman could sing, each one dreaming of his own valley, his own Beulah land! They sang Hymn after hymn that morning, 'O God our help in ages past', Praise my soul the king of Heaven', 'Now thank we all our God'. And many others. The service ended in a four-part harmonising of the National Anthem.

The sergeant major dismissed the battalion, and the soldiers marched off to their tents. The elderly minister called Victor, before he joined his comrades.

"Thank you, young man." He said his voice trembling with emotion. "I don't know how many of us will be spared the supreme sacrifice from this war, but today, I saw the gates of heaven, and if the Good Lord calls me right now, I am content!" He paused to collect his thoughts and settle his thumping heartbeat, before continuing, "I have been told the Welsh could sing, but that was wonderful. Only to be interrupted by Victor, "We don't sing well on our own but put us together and singing is in our blood. It is at the very base of every Welshman's soul." They talked for several minutes, Victor found himself warming to the old man's honesty and sincerity.

"I enjoyed playing for the battalion sir, I wish it could have been on a proper church organ, but I wondered if you could do me a Favour?"
"I've written a letter to my Wife and family, could you see that it's delivered?"

"I will do my very best my boy!"

Victor took the letter from his tunic breast pocket. He carefully wrote the address on the back and have it to the minister.

"I will have to show it to your commanding officer for censorship of course." The old man stated.

"I don't care who reads it first, just as long as my Naomi reads it eventually!"

CHAPTER 34

THE BABY HAD BEEN BORN THREE LONG MONTHS PREVIOUSLY following a full-term pregnancy and Naomi had carried the child without a moment's complaint. It was probably the fear of not knowing where Victor was, and afraid to raise a single murmur of discontent in case she should say or do something that might result in his certain doom. He was the father of a little girl, someone of whom he knew nothing, "Please God bring him home!" was the prayer that crossed the entire household's lips at night.

Kate and Ivy had been wonderful, accepting her and the children, without a moment's hesitation. Tom was, just Tom! He never complained, moaned or used a cross word with anyone. It was he, who had the patience to play with the fast-growing Peter, throwing him in the air taking him for walks, with the baby perched high on his shoulders. No one ever mentioned Victor, but he was at the forefront of everyone's thoughts. Laura had been born in the September, she was a baby who smiled at everyone, never cried and always appeared contented.

"A Pigeon pair!" Announced Elsie Cousins, one day, when Naomi was taking the baby down to the main road. "What a beautiful little bugger she is!" "Hush Mrs Cousins!" Naomi scolded mildly, "You shouldn't swear in front of children!!"

"Don't be daft" the old woman retorted. "it's better to hear that, than be deaf."

"She's right dear." Added Doris Morgan, "and anyway that's not swearing you should hear her Joseph when he's 'had a skinful, that's swearing. Not feeling in the mood to argue, with the two old crones Naomi replied can't stop, I've got to go into the village, we need some sugar and a bag of flour from Jones and Porter's. If I don't hurry, they'll be closed for lunch!"

"We don't have lunch in places like Cwmcarn dearie!" Elsie answered, we have dinner, they only 'have lunch in places like Newport!"

"Glad to see you 'know how to carry the baby wrapped in a shawl, 'Welsh' fashion. After carrying' the squirming' little bleeder for nine months your back feels rougher than a badger's arse, so every bit of help you get is welcome!" Concluded Doris.

Naomi hurried on, hoping to leave the cackling old women far behind, thankfully they made no attempt to follow her. She looked down at the small baby snuggling cosily in the shawl that was wrapped around her head and shoulders. "It's the easiest way to carry the baby." Kate announced as she wrapped the shawl around her. "Safe for you and safer for Laura and a lot easier on your aching back!"

Now, whenever she had to fetch or carry anything she wrapped Laura securely to her chest with a silky soft, woollen shawl. At last, she reached Jones and Porter's doorway when she herd her name being called.

"Mrs Leslie! Mrs Leslie!"

She looked up to see the postmaster coming towards her. She faltered and her complexion paled as Mr. Hearne came towards her holding an envelope!

"It's a letter, from Newport. "He emphasised the Newport knowing the devastating effect that letters and communications had on families in the village. "I was just about to send it up to George Street but I caught sight of you, "He gave Naomi a small brown paper envelope. She recognised the small, neat, cursive script at once. It was a letter from Brian Cuthbertson. Thanking the postmaster, she wasn't into the village grocers.

"My heart skipped a beat when I saw him coming with it!" Said Naomi, before she dropped the letter and packages on to the table.

"I recognised the writing at once, it's from Brian. I wonder what he wants?" "There's only one way to find out!" Kate replied, as she took the sleeping baby from her mother and placed her snugly in her cot. Naomi picked up the letter and tore it open.

"It is from Brian!" She confirmed. "He says they are all well in Newport and hopes we are too. "It says the Earl and Lady Charlotte are expected back in Newport soon. He'll let me know. when he knows more. He thinks it will be around April ". They are sailing into The Queen Alexandra Dock from America on the S.S Monmouth!" She looked up and continued. "I must go and meet them, if anyone can find out what's happened to Victor the earl can!" She finished reading the letter in silence, it being little more than polite small talk.

"I'll write back to Brian and ask for more details." She said to Kate. "The Earl will help; I know he will."

We are expecting a train load of replacements tonight." Trevor told Victor as they stood at the edge of the tunnel, watching the sun, a vivid crimson orb, slipping below the turquoise horizon. "I've recommended you as 'acting corporal', to the captain. First task, you are to pick out half a dozen men and accompany Lieutenant Bennett to the railhead in Armentieres and help escort the replacements' here."

"More bloody cannon fodder!" Swore Victor, his thoughts a thousand miles away. "Twenty-two to a tent again I expect!" He concluded.

"We just obey orders and try to stay alive, that's all Victor, say nowt just try to stay alive."

At three thirty that morning, following a two-mile moonlit march. Victor and his party, led by the young lieutenant, were waiting at the trackside when a locomotive hauling twenty-five cattle trucks screamed to a halt, "Brought to the slaughter like bloody cattle!" Victor whispered to Eddie Griffiths, who was stood beside him, "At least they pretended a little better when we arrived." The cattle trucks disgorged almost a thousand men and their equipment in less than half an hour!

"Bloody hell!" Swore Eddie, "It's a new battalion!"

Lieutenant Benett went in search of the commanding officer. Victor, and his small section were soon marching back to their tented billets at the head of a large body of men.

They reached the bustling camp shortly after the sun had raised its tired head suspiciously above the shell-shocked horizon. The NCOs were left the task of billeting the men into tents. The officers were messing in what was left of, the factory owners mansion and soon disappeared. Victor stood close to a far from amused Trevor, as they watched the replacements mill around until they were allocated to a tent.

"Green as the grass!" Trevor swore, his face etched with both anger and pity, "Well they won't have much time to learn!" "The trouble is," Victor added as he watched the newcomers laughing and joking as they entered their canvas 'homes'. "They are only allowed one mistake! Do you think the folks back home know how bad things are here?"

"That's a daft bloody question" Trevor replied as he pointed to the several hundred soldiers, still waiting in the early morning mist. "Do you think they would be here if they did!" A furrow appeared across his brow before he continued, "Alright, I suppose they would come for country and all that! But I don't think they would appear to be so happy about it."

"We've got to have a laugh and joke! It's the only thing that makes tomorrow bearable." Victor answered, "if we didn't, I know I couldn't go back into those bloody trenches!" He stopped and stared and shouted, "Bloody Hell!" His outburst was so sudden and unexpected that it startled Trevor, a man used to the continual cacophony of bombardment and the agonised screams of mutilated soldiers.

"What the hell Victor?" Trevor snapped.

Victor pointed to the next group of men about to enter a tent. "I've just seen a friend from Cwmcarn and he's with another six or seven men, from home as well! Shit! I thought they would be at home working down the pit! Even that is better than being here!" Evan Wilkinson, the mountainous rugby player from Abercarn was entering his allotted tent, unaware of the interest that his presence had caused. "You daft fool!" Trevor admonished his companion. "He probably has some news of your family! Get over there and ask him. Do it now while the officers are away, playing at being gentlemen! If anyone questions you, say you have been sent by me to inspect their tent!" Victor began to argue, but Trevor dismissed all protests and concluded. "Acting corporal Leslie, inspect that tent!"

Victor lifted the tent flap and bellowed, "Attention!" He herd the startled shouts as twenty men sprang sharply to their feet. "What's an idle load of toss pots from Cwmcarn, hoping to do in this man's war?" He called, before stepping into the tent. The anger that flamed on Evan's face, melted like a snowflake on a vicar's backside as he toasted himself before hell's fire, when he saw Victor!

"Bloody hell Victor! We all need fresh knickers now, you dozy bugger." He shouted, as he stepped forward to hug his friend. "I just pwped myself!" He picked Victor up as though he were no more than a wiff of hot air. "Put me down you great ox!" Victor laughed, "Is this any way to treat one of your corporals?" The gentle giant put the protesting Victor reverently down.

"Sorry corporal!" He answered, his mouth alight with a beaming smile that split his face better than a gash from Sweeny Todd's razor. He stood stiffly to attention. His head almost out in the fresh morning air as it rubbed against the tent's protesting ridge pole.

"Relax all of you." Victor ordered, as he thrust out his hand towards Evan, and returned his grin. "What the hell are you doing here? I thought you had more sense."

"We didn't want to miss all the fun." Evan answered, as he mangled Victor's hand in his gigantic paw, "We wanted to come out before it was all over. What's it like Victor?" Victor noticed everyman was watching him intently, waiting for his reply.

"You can't begin to imagine!" He answered, "Think of your worst nightmare, and then imagine that you can't wake up! When I arrived,

I was in a tent just like this one, the only difference now, is there are only four of us alive out of the original twenty two!"

"We'll show those huns a fing or two!" Answered a soldier.

"Say that as you watch your best friend die!" Victor exclaimed, "I'm not exaggerating or telling fairy stories, I'll leave that for the papers and the propaganda artists back home. Listen to your sergeants and corporals and anyone who has survived so far. Do as you're told or die. He grabbed hold of Evan and pulled him outside.

"I won't say it's good to see you, Evan!" He said, "I wish you were safe at home down the pit!"

"Is it really that bad, or were you winding us up?" Evan asked. "It's worse! There's filthy mud, disease, and death. Not dignified death but the sordid kind where soldiers are herded just like sheep and made to charge into machine guns. Compared to this, the pit explosion was like heaven and at least we had hope that we would be rescued. Not here, I hope you survive. I'll try to help you, but, when the shells start falling the only one who can help you is yourself! Find the deepest hole you can, stick to the bottom of it and pray!" What I really came over to ask about is the news from Cwmcarn."

"Don't know a lot." Evan stated, "You know I'm not a nosey person. I seen your Mam and sisters a bit, they were worried about you but they was alright."

"What about my wife! Do you know anything about Naomi" I haven't seen her at all, I have been training and haven't see your family for quite a while. It's great to see you though you big bugger. I wasn't joking about what this war is like. When we go back to the front it's worse than hell. He spent several minutes talking with his old friend before walking deliberately back to his own tent. He threw himself onto his mattress and reached for his paper and pencil. Perhaps they would have another church parade and he might see the padre!

It was a resolute Naomi, who found herself knocking at the harbour master's door at six thirty on a cold morning. The weather had looked grey, as cold as a bank manager's heart. She walked along the quayside; Docks held no fear for her. She had been around them for most of her life. She entered the office. It contained a large desk surrounded by shelf after shelf of documents and ledgers. The master sat slightly to the side of the single desk, warming himself at a large coal fire that blasted invitingly. He smiled as she entered, he recognised her immediately, he beckoned her over to share the warmth.

"You're Lewis Hay Jones' daughter, aren't you?" The old man enquired politely. "I recognise you immediately. I was sorry to hear of his passing. He was a gentleman in all our dealings."

Naomi returned his smile and replied, "I am."

His remembrance made the visit somewhat simpler. "I'm here to meet the Earl of Gwent and Lady Charlotte, they are docking today on the S.S. Monmouth." She moved gratefully to the fire and held her hands in its welcoming warmth loathing the sensation of agony as the feeling returned to her frozen fingers, as if an army of mice were nibbling their way through her scalp. "Do you know what time they are expected, and which berth she'll use?"

"She's arrived my dear." He replied, "Thank the Lord! The war has claimed plenty of good ships this year. There are too many that will never arrive! She's berthed in the Queen Alexandra Dock, right outside the Clory Warehouse. She's not staying long, just long enough to coal, then she's off again!" He paused to pick up his gnarled pipe, which he lit with a long taper from the fire. "Not the best place to be at the moment. That warehouse is full from floor to bloody ceiling with bombs and things. The navy's moving them out in a couple of day.....!"

Without waiting for the aged master to finish, she rushed out into the icy chill of the damp morning air. Clory's was one of the biggest firms on the dockside, her father had taken her there many times and she, knew the way as well as she knew the shoes on her own feet. She ran as if the rent man were after her. "How long before she would see the Earl her lungs were bursting in her breast as she ran to the Quayside.

She saw the dock, and there, tied securely fore and aft was the 'Monmouth'. She slowed to a saunter, enjoying the ship's graceful lines. She stopped to savour the moment and observed the fevered activity that was happening on board. Coal was being showered into her holds and the dust was hanging on the early morning mist like a dark funeral overcoat. Every exposed inch of metal had become coated in black grime, in the race to complete the coaling. Pulling her coat tightly around her shivering shoulders she quickened her steps until she stood at the foot of the steeply angled gang plank. She shouted to the seamen stationed sleepily at it. "May I speak to the Earl and Lady Charlotte please!"

The startled seamen jumped as if stuck with a hat pin! He looked at Naomi and replied.

"Strewth lady! You didn't arf make me jump!" He stood to attention as the second mate appeared and asked Naomi, "Who wants the Earl?"

"I do!" Naomi replied. "The Earl is my godfather, Please tell him Naomi Les..... Er." She paused, perhaps the earl wouldn't recognise her married name and refuse to see her. "Naomi Hay Jones wishes to see him on a matter of the utmost urgency!"

"Stay there miss," the officer replied, "There's an awful mess up here, I'll tell his lordship you're down there." He disappeared into the bowels of the ship, leaving Naomi shivering on the quay.

"Naomi, my darling child what are you doing here?" The earl asked.

"I must speak to you; it is most important." She shouted, her eyes misting with happiness as she saw her friend and benefactor for the first time in more than three years.

"Wait there. "He called, "I'll come down to you!" He began climbing down the gangway. He had almost reached the bottom step when the air was shattered with a piercing shriek of at least half a dozen police whistles. Soon they were being joined by the sirens of all the ships moored in the harbour. The caterwauling was deafening, ear shattering! Hands pointed skyward; Naomi looked up. Drifting lazily towards them, was the strangest sight Naomi had ever seen it looked like an enormous cigar, floating through the air, high over the docks.

"Good God!" The Earl exclaimed. "It's an airship, a Zeppelin' It's going to drop bombs on the docks!"

Naomi and the Earl stood and watched, like fascinated statues as the airship approached, they could hear the deep throated roar as its three engines were throttled hard. Small black cylinders started to cascade from the rear of the gondola and began their screaming descent to the ground. Water, metal and flame began to erupt all around. One bomb pitched through the roof of the Clory's warehouse which disintegrated with a blast that rocked Penarth Pier, to its foundation piles, ten miles away. One high explosive bomb landed in the water, close to Naomi and the earl and they were both blown cartwheeling off their feet into the water and knew no more, as flames, masonry and shrapnel bloodily devoured, everything in its voracious path!

This must be your lucky day." Said Trevor, "We have been selected to form a 'Pioneer battalion'. No more trench fighting, just bloody hard work digging trenches!"

The second Monmouthshire's had been selected to help provide the trenches and roads that were needed. They were nearly all ex-miners, well used to the spade work and digging that would be required. They were to join the 29th Division at the Somme. Their tools were soon issued, they were mainly shovels and picks and thousands of empty sandbags, that needed filling together with stand after stand of riveting timber, that would be used to provide firing and jumping off steps. The battalion's transport requirements doubled, because there were so many tools to be moved, the men walked! As pioneers they would not be required to garrison the front-line trenches, but would be billeted in the rear, moving forward at night, to undertake whatever pioneering duties they were allotted. Casualties, however, were still heavy! They were shelled as they moved forward and when they returned to their camp. Snipers and shelling also took their toll as they worked at night. The battalion was busiest whenever the division was ordered to attack. The pioneers had to improve the assembly positions and the roads so the artillery could move forward. They, had to dig out the trenches so the infantry could advance.

CHAPTER 35

Kate paced nervously around the house, without looking or touching the mantel piece before dusting it twice. Tom looked up from the table where he was trying to arrange a manuscript of popular songs for the male voice choir.

He recognised the haunted look that had occupied Kate's face for the last three hours.

"It's no good you walking' round with a face like a snacked arse, our Kate!" He announced, "I'm sure Naomi will do her best to try and persuade that earl to help Victor. You know as well as I do how determined she can be."

"Don't you use language like that in this house Thomas Owens, thank you very much!" She retorted, pausing to pick up a photograph off the mantelpiece before absent mindedly dusting under it. It's the not knowing that is the problem. We don't know where Victor is, and it's that, that is slowly killing us all!" She replaced the picture frame and ran her finger along the dresser's edge. She glanced down at her spotless digit expecting to find a slight trace of dust.

"If you don't stop wandering around like a lunatic, I'll help them put the straight jacket on you." He answered. "Sit down and try to relax. Better still make us both a cup of tea."

The moon had been shining brightly, for several tension filled hours, and was halfway through its journey across the sable dark sky. Anxiety and disquiet filled the house with a flaying apprehension. Tom's pocket watch showed it to be well past ten thirty!

"I expected her home hours ago!" Kate stated, beginning to become worried about her.

"You know how wilful she can be." Tom answered, his quiet tone betraying his bravado, "Perhaps she's staying in Newport with the Earl and Lady Charlotte. You know she'll do almost anything to find out where Victor is. She's even more desperate than you are! But I can't stay up and wait any longer, I've got to be up at five in the morning. I'm going' to bed." "I don't think she would leave the children with anyone, no matter how important it is, not even us!" Kate stated, as she began to clear away the cups and saucers. "I'm beginning to worry and don't think I could sleep even if I went to bed. I'll wait up for her, she shouldn't be long. "She watched her brother climb the narrow staircase before stoking the fire with half a dozen large lumps of glistening black coal. Kate slumped into her well-worn fireside chair, kicked off her slippers and extended her toes luxuriously towards the welcoming warmth of the glowing coals.

"Kate! Kate!" Tom shook his sister gently, "Don't sleep down here get up to bed, you'll give yourself a stiff neck sleeping' in the chair." "Wha.... Wha.... What time is it? She asked sleepily, opening her eyes to see her brother bending over her. "I must have dozed off for a minute." "Minute!" Laughed Tom. "It's five in the morning what time did Naomi come in?"

"Naomi" Queried Kate, still half asleep, she sat up and stretched her already stiffening arms, "I don't remember I must have fallen asleep. Just after you went up the stairs. As she pushed herself up from the chair, every one of her creaking joints protested at the unwelcome disturbance. "I'll make you a cup of tea and I'll look in on her and the children before I have a lie down myself." She picked up the heavy poker and stirred the embers into glowing life before adding fresh black nuggets to the rekindled fire. Soon the kettle was singing merrily, and Tom was presented with a cup of steaming golden brown tea.

"I've made your box so you can get to work once you have drunk your tea." Kate said, "I'm going up to bed now, I'll try to get a couple of hours sleep." She left her brother sipping contently at his brew as she tiptoed up the creaking stairs, passing the room she shared with her daughters, she peeped into Naomi's. The children were sleeping soundly but Naomi's bed was unused! It had not been slept in!

"I've just received a first-rate report about you, Leslie." Captain Hughes announced, to the soldiers of the newly formed 'D' company. "It's from captain Watkins of the Wiltshire's. He said you were instrumental in the success of the mining operation and then helped him man a pair of Lewis guns and beat back a regiment of Germans. Under the circumstances. I am going to confirm your promotion to corporal. Well done soldier!" He paused whilst he finished reading the report he was holding, "Incidentally," he concluded. "He says he has recommended you for a medal." Victor felt just like the cat that had run off with the cream and enjoyed the sensation of being the centre of attraction as his captain praised his exploits. Trevor looked on proudly and could hardly contain his own exuberance as the young soldier was honoured by his contemporaries.

"Bloody hell, Victor!" Evan swore, as they sat in their tent after the morning's muster, "If the captain had said any more, they would have had to get You a bigger cap!"

"Evan!" Victor replied, "I was absolutely petrified the whole time I was there!"

"I think I would have crapped my trousers if it had been me." Evan replied.

Victor took out his harmonica and began playing, Gilbert and Sullivan's 'With Cat like Tread'. It was a piece he had herd with Naomi, on one of their frequent trips to the Lyceum. The tent was eerily quiet as he played, but a voice piped up, "Stop fartin' about with all that fancy stuff, play something the boys can sing."

Soon the tent was reverberating to the strain of, 'Hello, Hello, whos' your lady friend', and like a disease ten times more infectious than measles, the singing spread from tent to tent, until the whole Battalion joined in.

"That's better!" The voice shouted. "Has anybody got a spare woman, my hand isn't what it used to be!"

"Wait until you get the shakes from a really good bombardment!" Eddie Griffiths replied, "Then try your 'hand again, it's ten times better than any French tart!"

"Bugger off" Snapped Evan, "Nothing's better than a tart, French or otherwise."

"Wait until the stuff they put in your tea starts to take effect!" Victor added, "You'll forget about any kind of tart then!"

'D' company, along with the rest of the battalion, were given the task of constructing a new front-line trench less than sixty yards away from the enemy.

"We are going to be digging less than a hundred yards away from the enemy." Ordered Captain Hughes, to the assembled company. "We will be working at night. We will probably have a peaceful first night's work, after that ….!" He looked pointedly around at his assembled men. "Get stuck into it and get down as deeply as you can. You will need all the shelter you can get. I know I don't need to talk like this to the veterans, but you replacements, you just obey orders and we should get the job done fairly quickly."

At six thirty the company began the short march to the front lines and from there it was out into no man's land! They found three officers waiting, sheltering in a deep shell hole. The officers had already been marking the position of the new trench with tape. Victor wasted no time in allotting thee members of his squad a length of ground. He did this with the remainder of his troops.

"Don't waste time." Victor warned. "Just dig like buggery. The ground is frozen as solid as a polar bear's dick so put your backs into it!" He watched the men start to dig, before he moved to an area, he had set aside for himself. He carefully placed his rifle and pack down on the ground before he started. He lost count of the number of times he raised the pick above his head and brought it down hard, into the frosty concrete hard soil.

. He set to his own task with a vengeance, and within a few hours had made a three feet deep hole. Peering into the darkness he was able to discern the vague silhouettes of soldiers, as busy as behavers tunnelling their way down into the ground. Climbing his way out of his recently excavated half completed burrow, he cautiously moved from soldier to soldier, offering each of them a few words of advice and encouragement. Most had excavated to a depth similar to his own. Evan, being by far the strongest man in the battalion, had mined down to a depth of almost five feet, and was already enlarging his hole to meet his neighbour's.

"Well done Evan." Victor complimented his friend. "We'll all be back in camp before we know it."

"Don't talk to me while I'm working.'" Evan replied, his face a mask of sweat, despite the sub-zero temperatures, "But would you mind passing' on a message to the general for me corporal? I joined the army you fight the enemy, not too bloody well dig 'oles!"

Victor returned to his own little niche and resumed work, with the blistering shovel and exhausting pick. As he began to dig deeper, he became aware of a worrying phenomenon, the ground was excessively chalky and the edges of the trench were becoming marked with long lines of thrown out, white chalk, which were visible even in the midnight's half-light!

"Oh shit!" Victor thought to himself, "This is going to mean trouble tomorrow. The Bosche are bound to see all this in the morning and use it to range in their guns ready for us tomorrow night!" Once his fox hole was dug to approximately six feet, the task of joining his hole with the neighbouring one began. Once one section of trench was joined the freed soldiers began helping friends and butties complete theirs. Riveting timber and sandbags were soon produced, and the trench sides reinforced. It was a simple task for the miners to provide the trench with firing steps. Well before dawn the company was heading back to its own trenches. Not a single man had been lost or injured.

"We were lucky today!" Victor warned his section of weary, dirt encrusted soldiers. "Try to find somewhere to have a kip. We will be out there digging again tomorrow." He decided against telling them about his fears concerning the tell-tale chalk. Let them have one day's worry-free sleep!' He thought. 'If the Huns don't send over too may shells!'

At four that afternoon, Victor found himself summoned, along with all the other NCO's by the captain. They, together with the junior officers, squatted as he have his orders.

"I expect you all noticed the chalky nature of the soil, we can be sure that the Huns did. We are expecting a dangerous night and want your chaps to dig as deeply as they can. The chalk is going to reveal us. So, the Colonel has promised artillery if we come under machine gun fire, that should make the blighters keep their heads down!"

Victor could see the worry lines that had appeared around the officer's face as he spoke. "I am expecting the Germans to send over several patrols to find out what's going on. Each platoon will provide its own covering party of four men and an NCO. They are to draw a dozen mills bombs each, I hope to God, they bring them all back!" He concluded. "Believe it or not Victor," Trevor declared as they were marching back to their own platoons, "You are the senior corporal in the platoon. All the others are replacements. You know what that means don't you?" "Yes, I am now acting sergeant." He replied, realising the full implication of Trevor's words, "I'm expected to volunteer to take charge of the covering party! At least I'll be excused from digging." Make sure you choose experienced soldiers, men who have done some fighting in these trenches. The diggers will be depending on you."

Victor had never before felt this exposed, or vulnerable as he waited in the darkness of 'No man's land', for the mayhem to begin. He placed his covering party about twenty-five yards ahead of the workers and almost thirty yards apart, before throwing himself into a particularly deep shell hole. He peeped nervously over the top. Searching the gloom for any signs of an enemy squirming towards the company. His ears were straining to hear the slightest sound that might give away an approaching sniper or patrol. The company began digging, the sound echoed through the still evening like a ha'penny rattling in an empty oxo tin! The Germans must have herd the digging. Sure enough, several flares shot skyward bathing the area in bright light. A hundred soldiers dropped onto their faces as a pair of maxim machine guns began raking the area, with their deadly messages of annihilation and extinction. The air above his head sang as the calamitous projectiles sought a ruinous home in unsuspecting flesh, whining like the persistent drones of a swarm of hornets, only a thousand times more deadly. Victor tried to close his ears to the screams of both terror and agony, as the weapons wreaked havoc among the poorly hidden soldiers.

"For God's sake start the barrage!" Victor herd himself scream, over and over again at the top of his voice. As if by answer, artillery bursts began to engulf the enemy trenches and silence the murderous Maxims. The uninjured were urged to their feet to resume digging. They dug as if their very lives depended upon it, which they did! The dead and wounded, their life blood seeping rapidly away, remained on the ground, awaiting the over worked stretcher bearers. So, it continued all night, flares, murder and mayhem, silenced by covering artillery! It is surprising how quickly and how far a frightened rabbit, or petrified man can dig, when his very life is on the line. Victor, who was used to watching colliers undercut a seam when they needed the bonus money, had never seen miners worked so hard or rapidly. Despite all that the enemy threw at them and the mounting list of casualties, the trench progressed. The same procedure took place night after bloodthirsty night. It was on the sixth night's digging that the Germans tried to rush the workings. Victor was a little over fifty yards from the first explosion, as mills bombs exploded, with a detonation of orange doom, accompanied by several ear shattering scream. Forgetting his own safety, he rushed towards the sound of the slaughter. Seeing dozens of indistinct human shapes looming out of the gloom he pulled the pins out of a pair of his grenades and hurled them among the shadowy figures. They exploded with a gruesome suddenness. Others, following his example were lobbing grenades amongst the furtive attackers. Rifle fire began to crackle as the company took up their rifles and began pouring a hail of bullets into the enemy, adding their destruction to that of the bombs. Fierce hand to hand fighting was occurring in several trench holes as the surprised miners defended themselves with shovels or bare hands. One hole had been overrun by three enemy soldiers who were bayonetting the occupant. Victor raised his rifle and working the bolt, as quickly as his numbed fingers would allow, poured shot after shot into the attackers until his rifle was empty, and they were pulpy corpses lying in front of him. He fumbled to fill the rifle's magazine with, a full charging clip from his belt, he eventually reloaded the weapon. The Company's concentrated fire was driving the German's back towards their own trenches. Victor hurled another two Mills grenades after the fleeing enemy, to help them on their way. He turned and wasn't back to inspect the victim, still lying at the foot of his trench hole. His heart was in his mouth as he saw the mortally wounded soldier. It was Evan Wilkinson, he had been bayonetted five or six times and was trying to hold his shattered intestines together with his blood-soaked arms, "Evan!" screamed Victor "Oh Evan! Don't move I'll fetch the stretcher bearers!"

"Don't leave me!" Begged Evan breathlessly," "I d d don't think any doctor can fix this! D d don't go, I couldn't bear to die alone!" He moved his hand slightly and Victor felt the bile rise in his throat at the sight of the bloodied, intestinal coils that slipped from his grasp. "I wanted to kill a German before the war was over, not dig bloody holes! W w w well it's a bloody hole alright, and I didn't even dig that properly."

"Hush!" Soothed Victor, as he cradled his butty's head in his arms," Don't talk, shave your breath. You'll be alright."

"Oh Victor! It hurts, hurts worse than anything you can imagine. When you get 'ome tell my mam I didn't kill anybody. They've killed me instead!" He shuddered, his back arched and he died in Victor's arms.

Victor looked at the shell that had once been his lifelong friend. The tears ran down his face in torrents and sobs racked his harrowed body, to the very depths of his suffering soul! 'If I could catch the bastard who said war was glorious.' He thought to himself, as he hugged Evan's broken body, 'I'd make him eat every last lying word. Dying like this, is a sordid, meaningless waste of life. There was no one here to really grieve over him, or to be with him. He had me as a friend to care for him and I'm no more than a poor second best!'

The family were at their wits end. It had been six days since Naomi had gone to Newport, and since that time, not a single word or message had been received. During that time Kate had managed only a few hours restless sleep.

"Something has happened, it must have done!" She repeated over and over again to Tom and all the others gathered around the kitchen table, "She wouldn't leave the children, not knowingly anyway!"

"Theres only one thing for it," Tom announced to his sister and nieces, "I will have to take a day off work tomorrow and go to Newport, I'll go to the docks and ask if anyone knows anything of her where abouts."

The argument raced from one member of the family to another, it was a strange debate, rather like two blind men trying to find their way out of a maze at midnight. No one knew where to go and if they were in the right place anyway! Their talk was silenced by a tapping on the front door.

"Who can that be at this time of night?" Ivy asked. All eyes turned toward Tom, who stood up and wasn't towards the door.

"That's the silliest question I've ever heard." He replied. "We'll never know who it is until I open the door. I'm coming!" He shouted, pausing to light an oil lamp that stood on the parlour mantlepiece. Carrying it carefully by its polished brass base he used its dim glow to light the way to the front door. Slipping back the well-greased bolt he looked out, "Mr Owens?" asked a voice he struggled to recognise. "We have met, I'm Brian Cuthbertson. It's about Naomi!"

"Come in Mr. Cuthbertson, it's far too cold to stand out there, we were just talking about her. You can tell us the news." He closed the door against the cold dark evening and led the way to the cosy and warm kitchen.

"Come in and sit by the fire and warm yourself." Kate invited, taking Brian's thick overcoat and hanging it on the hanger behind the back door. "Catch your breath. It's a long old walk from the station." "I don't think what I've got to say can wait!" He replied, his face showing the wretchedness and suffering that he was obviously feeling. "What's wrong?" Tom asked. "If there's anything wrong, the best way is to come straight out with it."

Brian sat up and looked at the sea of concerned faces that surrounded him. "I don't know where to begin!" He started, "You all know that Naomi went to Newport to meet the earl and Lady Charlotte on the Monmouth." He Paused for the nods of assist. "Well, there was an attack on the docks by a German Zeppelin. It dropped more than twenty bombs!"

"Dear God!" Kate exclaimed, as she clasped her hands together as if in prayer.

"Stop interrupting our Kate!" Tom ordered, "Let Mr. Cuthbertson finish." "Call me Brian, please." He replied before continuing, "There was a large munitions warehouse at the dockside, right beside the Monmouth's berth. It took a direct hit from at least two bombs and exploded!"

"Is Naomi badly hurt?" Kate began ……

"Let the man finish, Katey!" Warned Tom, noticing how uncomfortable Brian was becoming.

"It was high tide so all the ships that could were ordered to sail. Apparently, there was pandemonium at the docks, the warehouse was full of Naval shells, and they were exploding all over the place. The Monmouth was one of the ships to sail. Naomi was last seen talking the Earl on the dockside as the warehouse went up." He looked uncomfortably at his fingers and began picking at his nails, his voice began to tremble as he continued. "They found what they think is the earl's body floating in the water three days ago, but aren't sure! It's a charred wreck, almost unrecognisable." There was no sign of Naomi". There are dozens of dead and at least twenty people unaccounted for!"

Following Evan's death, Victor decided that he would stay aloof from the members of his platoon and company. It simply hurt too much when you had a friend die in your arms. There was no way he could ignore Trevor, he would have to hope that nothing happened to him, but there would be no new friendships. Some of the companies were involved in carrying ammunition and supplies to the attacking troops, but most of the work involved the blistered palms of dig, dig, dig. Casualties occurred, but Victor closed his eyes to the maiming's, mutilations and deaths. He simply carried on and thanked the Lord it was someone else!

The battalion was relieved and moved out of the Somme. They wasn't by the time-honoured manner of all infantry battalions, they walked. They marched straight to a railway station, where thankfully the second-class ride, albeit, in a stinking cattle track, beat the first-class route march that no one enjoyed. They found themselves, once again in the Ypres area. 'D' Company were billeted in the cellars of Ypres. The sector was quiet, compared with the fighting on the Somme, Ypres was tranquillity itself. It was hazardous to move around in daylight, the enemy had the entire sector under constant observation. Anyone providing an observer with an open target brought down swift and often deadly retribution. Victor's platoon was allocated a pair of cellars under what had once been a baker's and butcher's shops.

"Let's get this pig stye cleaned up!" Victor ordered his depleted section. "We don't know how long we are going to be here so we may as well make the place clean and comfortable.

"Bloody spit an' polish again sergeantl!" said an unknown voice.

"Stop your moaning Private Griffiths." Victor retorted, "Just listen to that!"

Eddie listened intently then answered, "What the hell you on about sergeant? I can't hear nuffink!"

"Exactly!" Victor replied, "wonderful isn't it. Perhaps we'll get a few hours' sleep tonight without being shelled!" The soldiers began making their cellar as comfortable as they could.

"Let's get some sandbags filled to block up those holes." Victor ordered. "And Private Roberts and Watt's scrounge around to find some way of sealing the entrance. We haven't been gassed yet, but there's always a first time. If we can seal this up, we'll be as snug as bugs in a rug down here."

As the soldiers carried out their given tasks, Trevor Bailey entered the cellar.

"Well done Victor I see you've started improving your billet, from what the captain was saying we could be here for a few months."

"I don't know about the men, sergeant major." Victor replied, "But I can certainly use the rest. We have been here for at least an hour, and we haven't attracted more than half a dozen rounds of artillery!"

"Peacefull isn't it!" Laughed Trevor. "We are going to be trenching tonight, and every night, until we've dug a communication trench from here to the front line. Don't work the men too hard during the day, let them get some rest ready for the nights."

The men began to find corners and niches where they began to settle. Victor looked round, there wasn't one soldier who didn't show the haggardly, sunken eyed expression of fatigue and strain. More and more of his squad were becoming irritable and jumped nervously at anything unexpected or strange. Unheralded, noises had many of them shaking fitfully. It was during sleep that Victor most noticed their distress, none of the platoon slept peacefully, everyone showed signs of agitation and ment al turmoil. Several cried out in horror or for wives and mothers.

"Damn all Archdukes, Kaisers and Kings who expect young men to fight and die, just to sate their greed for wealth and power. The greedy bastards !" Muttered Victor under his breath. "Perhaps one day they'll get their comeuppance! I wonder if I look as ghastly as the others.!" He slumped to the floor with his back against a distempered wall and within seconds, exhaustion took control, and he joined his comrades in shuddering slumber.

The night was eerily quiet as the men began constructing the communication trench.

"If they put all the bleedin' trenches we've dug together." Joked Eddie Griffiths, as he swung his pick high, it's razor sharp point gleaming in the bright moon light, "We'd 'have dug all the way to Piccadilly and back!"

"Where the hell is Piccadilly?" Asked Bill Watkins one of the original survivors, as he shovelled.

"It's a place in London haven't you been to school?'" Eddie Replied.

"I went to Sunday school and they teached me to read, and write my name." Bill replied.

"Well Piccadilly is in London see," Eddie repeated, "And' they have some wonderful women there. They'll do it for a thruppenny bit!"

Bill started digging twice as fast as he had been previously and called out to Victor, "Oy Corporal we 're digging' this trench to Piccadilly, to find some of them tarts Eddie's on about."

"Get out of here you dozy bastard!" Eddie laughed. "You wouldn't know what to do with one, even if you had the thruppence!"

That's the problem." He replied sadly, "I'll probably be dead before I learn!"

From that day on the trench was given the name Piccadilly. The men dug and dug, with the hope that a pair of well filled tarts knickers would be found at the ended of it.

"It's worse than looking for the end of the rainbow!" thought Victor.

CHAPTER 36

Kate and Tom were sat before their blazing fire, both too numb to speak. It was Tom who broke the dreadful silence.

"That poor girl!" He whispered, "She left here so full of hope, and look what's happened."

Kate looked at her brother. She had cried herself, dry, she felt empty inside, totally drained. How much more could happen to her family? There was only one more thing, Victor! And she refused to even contemplate that appalling prospect.

"What are we going to tell Victor when he comes home?" She replied. "His last words, were, "Take care of Naomi and Peter."

"We will look after Peter and Laura, until their father comes home." He answered. "God knows there's enough love in this house for a hundred children. I just wish things were different." He shook his head sadly and gazed into the orange flames as they flickered and twisted concluding in smoky trails that made their lazy way up the chimney. He thought, 'Please Lord, bring Victor home safely from all this madness. I don't think this family can take much more heartache.'

He wasn't quietly over to his sister, wrapped his powerful arms about her delicate shoulders and whispered, "well old girl, it looks like it's up to us again. Two young ones to look after and I am willing to bet that Victor, if we could ask him, wouldn't trust anyone else to take care of his children, other than us!" He squeezed her gently and pecked her affectionately on the cheek. He knew the hidden energy, the vitality that was deep within this woman. She had raised her own children after burying her husband, her grandchildren would present little problem. "Oh Tom" She replied, her voice little more than a subdued whisper, "The children are no problem I can't help thinking about Naomi. What about Victor! I don't think I could bear it if something happened to him!" Let's get a night's sleep, God knows we need it. No argument," insisted Tom," let's get up them apples and pears".

It seemed as if their heads had hardly touched the pillows before they were woken by a hammering on their front door. "What the hell," Yelled Tom," You all stay in bed I'll go and see who's hammering the living daylights out of our door. Pulling his trousers on he rushed downstairs pausing only to light a candle. He rushed to the door which was still being hammered. "This ad better be important or I'm going to rip your head off your bloody shoulders". He pulled open the door to see an agitated Brian Cuthbertson waiting outside on the pavement!

"I came straight away they've found her!" It's Naomi they've got her she's alive!" He shouted breathlessly. Hearing this an eavesdropping Kate rushed to the front door and dragged a dumbstruck Brian into the house. Kate sank to her knees in a silisn't prayer. Tom followed the pair into the kitchen. "Quickly Brian tell us what's happened. All I know is she has been unconscious for six days in the Newport and Gwent hospital. At first no one recognised her then a neighbour saw her and told the police who she was. They came straight to me, and I got the night train to Cwmcarn to tell you. She's quite poorly and badly burned but alive!" Ivy burst into tears on hearing this and said I'll look after Uncle Tom and the children mam, you need to get to the hospital."

The moon had long begun its languid journey through the glittering stars, when Captain Hughes led the company into the Piccadilly trench for the fourth night. Work began, picks and shovels were blurs of motion in the pale moonlight, and despite the cold, sweat began to pour in torrents. The digging continued unchecked for several hours in the bright moonlight. Suddenly the company stopped and listened, the ear piercing shriek of a rapidly approaching artillery shell was heard.

"Take cover!" Shouted Captain Hughes, as the projectile exploded thirty yards short of the trench. "Heads down, the buggers never come on their own!" He concluded.

The first ranging shot was followed by another thirty rounds, in quick succession.

"What the ...?" Shouted Victor peeping over the top of the trench as the barrage concluded.

"Gas!" Yelled the captain, "Gas attack! Gas helmets on everyone, quickly! Make sure you are sheltering in a sound part of the trench." The soldiers dropped their picks and shovels and swiftly pulled their gas helmets over their heads. "Every man is to stand perfectly still; the helmet will protect you if you stand still. Let the gas blow away."

Victor stood rigid, his body too petrified to move. He was too terrified to even blink his eyes. He became aware of an unpleasant damp feeling between the cheeks of his backside. The ghostly white phosgene gas swirled around the soldiers, every one of them as fearful as Victor. The ghoulish mist swept over them. The gas was so dense that Victor lost sight of the opposite edge of the trench, just four short feet away. Squinting out of the helmet's frog eyed goggle, it appeared to Victor as though he was standing in the centre of the mass of a quivering blancmange. The temptation to disobey orders and run away was almost unbearable. He thought if its green colour that was the gas, he had heard about, but this white one was twice as deadly. It was the feeling of total isolation that he found the hardest to bear. The phosgene, cut you off from friend, foe and even the entire world. They had been trained to stand still, Victor did so and said a silent prayer, that everyone else followed orders. The three minutes that it took for the gas cloud to pass was, like an eternity of forevers. Gradually the mist thinned, he was able to see soldiers standing rigidly around him, each one as taut as a nuns knicker elastic!

"Helmets off and prepare for attack!" Screamed Captain Hughes at the top of his voice. The gas masks were ripped off and rifles picked up and loaded. There was still an acrid taste to the air, it burned the back of the throat. Many soldiers coughed and spluttered, before spitting forcefully onto the parapet in front of them, in an effort to rid their mouths of the incredibly sour sensation.

Victor scanned the moonlit horizon, but could detect no sign of attacking infantry, had it just been an isolated gas attack. The first one the company had experienced, he hoped it would be their last.

'Those poor bastards who were suffocated when we didn't have any protectors' He swore to himself. 'I wonder if it's any different than being killed by a bullet or bayonet? The result's the same anyway, you're dead!'

Seven men perished in the phosgene attack, three died almost immediately, four more were found writhing on the trench floor, their faces contorted as they gasped for breath, their mouths' a mass of foam, they died as they were being stretchered to the aid post. "Not bad, these respirators." Announced Captain Hughes, as the casualties were hauled away, "Only seven failures out of two hundred!" Once it became apparent that no attack was to follow, the company returned to it's trenching. The Piccadilly trench had to be completed.

The remainder of the night passed quietly, and they returned to their warm, dry cellars, it took Victor several hours of sitting quietly, in the relative security of the cellar, before he stopped shaking. The gas was a constant reminder of the pits back home. God, how he would love to be back home in the safety and security of a firedamp pit!!

Naomi opened her eyes and struggled to see in the glare that came from several tall windows, her eyes began to water in the bright light. She realised she was face down in a bed, when she became aware of excruciating pain coming from the skin of her back, her legs and backside. She attempted to turn around but was prevented by a nurse who rushed like an express train to prevent her from moving. "Stay still miss, you are face down to help you heal!" said the nurse. "We have been praying that you would wake up, you've been unconscious for almost ten days! Doctor Flannagan is coming to check on you right now." "What about my family, my children!" She pleaded!

"Don't worry!" said Doctor Flannagan, "Your family is fine. At first, we didn't know who you were, and being unconscious we couldn't ask you any questions. You were recognised by a Mr Brian Cuthbertson who contacted your in laws and they raced here in the middle of the night. Your mother-in-Law, Mrs Kate Leslie has been here for days hoping and praying, especially praying for some improvement. She's been threatening to break the door down now she's heard you are awake, but she will have to wait for a couple of hours until visiting time. Nurse will also need to change your dressings, which I'm sorry will be painful.

"Corporal Leslie?" The call came from lieutenant Bennett, the platoon commander. He stood at the top of the cellar steps. "Corporal Leslie?" "Yes sir!" Victor replied, jumping to his feet and standing to attention.

"Captain Hughes wants to see you, toot sweet, old boy" He ordered.

"Ah Corporal." The captain stated as Victor entered the command post. "Good news for you and the battalion you have been awarded the Military Medal. Major General Do Isle has agreed it, you are to be decorated with it when we are relieved."

'Bloody hell' Victor swore to himself,' A bloody gong for butchering dozens of Bosche soldiers. They are just like us, a load of bloody sheep who go wherever their silly old farts of commanders tell them too!

Word of Victor's decoration, spread through the company like wildfire. He could do no more than grin weakly as he was congratulated and patted on the back! His hand ached with the number of times it was wrung by well-wishers.

A recently decorated Victor accompanied the battalion when it returned to the Somme on October 6th. He looked at the members of his platoon, they still showed the signs of complete exhaustion, many were sick with high temperatures and racing pulses. The officers were able to arrange plenty of rest for themselves, due to there being a sufficient number of them, but the mounting casualty and sick list meant that the men had to work without relief, if the allotted work was to be completed on time. "The lads can't take much more." Victor complained to Trevor, as they marched to their new camp in Montauban.

"I've watched lots of them crying themselves to sleep!" He replied, "Yet every night they are ready with their shovels to go out and face whatever the Hun throws at them. They are bloody marvels!"

"I'm afraid to look at myself in the mirror!" Victor added.

"You are still an ugly looking bugger." Trevor joked, then added more seriously, "We all look like death warmed up, but the captain was telling me that he's been told by the colonel that we are going into reserve, for real rest shortly before Christmas."

"That'll be a blessing." Victor replied, "I wonder how many of us will be left to enjoy it, God I miss home! Peter must be walking and talking by now. I bet he's a real handful for Naomi. That's another thing Naomi! That stuff they are supposed to be giving us to help manage without women, it isn't working! I wake up every morning ready to go pole vaulting over to the Germans' trenches!"

"I'll tell the medical officer to double your dose of dicky powder!" Trevor laughed.

They reached their new camp site. It proved to be a muddy field; pock marked with shell holes. It took several hours of hard shovelling before the battalion was able to pitch tents in comparative luxury, no more than twelve men to a tent! They had hardly settled in when the weather broke. The rain came down as if every cloud in the sky had been lacerated from end to end and positioned over the Somme. The rain, added to the shell ravaged soil, produced an agglomeration of the most viscid mud that Victor had ever encountered. It got everywhere! It glued his toes together, penetrated through every layer of clothing that he could dress in, and turned every meal into Oliver Twist type gruel!

"How the hell are we supposed to dig trenches in this shitty stuff!" Snarled Eddie Griffiths, as he slurped his glutinous coated shovel from the trench.

"Stop asking questions Private Griffiths!" Victor ordered, "Just dig." "But Corporal. Howard Roberts added, I've dug headings in Risca, Crumlin and Rose Hayworth, and some of them have been damp pits. But this, it's impossible! As fast as you dig down, the walls fall in!"

"Stop complaining and get stuck into it!" Ordered Victor again.

"Very funny corporal!" laughed Eddie Griffiths. "Stuck is the only thing were going to get!"

The work was both punishing and thankless. The battalion would work all night digging out a trench. it would be reverted with side timbers and left. Returning the following night, the trench would be found half filled with water, the timbers floating soggily in the bottom and the sidewalls washed away.

"Here we go again!" Quipped Eddie Griffiths as he peered into the morass that confronted them. "It's too bloody cold for swimming!" "If you don't pipe down and get on with it. I'll make you permanently cold and save some Germans the job!" Victor snapped. "Clear this mess up quickly so we can get on with the new section.!"

It was back breaking work digging drainage ditches, ditches that could hardly cope with the amount of water that was pouring incessantly into the trenches. The battalion stuck to their task!

Dawn was breaking and the order was given to leave the trench and form up ready to depart to their camp.

"Help!" Yelled Eddie Griffiths, from the bottom of the trench in which he had been working, "I'm stuck solid! Help me please." Victor peered into the trench and there at the bottom was Eddie Griffiths Glued into the quagmire. "Stop wriggling you daft bugger" Yelled Victor. "Stay still and well pull you out. Victor detailed two soldiers to pull Eddie out. They caught hold of his outstretched arms and heaved. They did no more than almost dislocate his arms from his sockets. "Hold it, you two, what are you trying to do to me!" He screamed. He was well and truly stuck.

"If you don't stop yelling, we're going to leave you here for the Germans to find!" Warned Victor. Eddie ceased his struggling and complaining immediately.

"Well do something corporal. You are supposed to be the brains. Get me out!" He repeated urgently.

Victor thought for a while, then a smile crossed his lips before he joined the two men trying to pull the deeply entrenched soldier free. He pushed his hands into the mud covering Eddie's waist, feeling gingerly around the oozing swill.

"Careful what you are doing down there!" Eddie whispered. "There are a few bits and pieces I am quite attached too. I hope to have plenty of use for them when this bloody war is over. In fact, if it comes down to it, I don't want to leave this 'ole without any of them!" "Found them!" stated Victor. Eddie screwed his eyes uptight fearing the worst. "That's those two now for the other two." "Other two?" asked an incredulous soldier. "I knew Eddie was special, but not that special!"

"If you 'isn't careful with them 'ands." Said Eddie, as he opened his eyes." We'll 'have to get divorced and then I'll insist on marriage!" "It's a pity it's your arsehole that's full of mud and not your cakehole!" Snapped Victor. "I've told you already, stop moving." "What's wrong down there corporal?" Asked Captain Hughes.

"Private Griffiths is stuck in mud right up to his waist, sir." Victor replied.

"Hurry up with it corporal, Dawn is only about thirty minutes away. When the sun comes up all hell will break loose if you are still out here." The office stated.

"I'm undoing his braces sir, then we should be able to pull him out of his trousers and boots." Victor added as he fumbled blindly in the mud and darkness, searching for Eddie's braces and rear trouser buttons. "I'll leave you another two men, just in case you need any extra muscle. I can't endanger the Company for the sake of one silly arse who gets himself stuck! I'm taking the men out, join us as soon as you can." The captain stated. Victor heard the men begin slipping and sliding their way back to the comparative safety of the camp.

"You won't leave me here, will you?" Asked a frightened Eddie. "If you don't stop wiggling I bloody well will." Victor replied. "There that's all your buttons undone. Bet you didn't feel a thing as the actress said to the bishop !" Victor eased himself onto solid ground and -turned to the two soldiers and said. "On the count of three. pull." Victor ordered they were going to pull this dull bugger out of this mess." Eddie, I know you have been frightened by this little escapade, but, there had better be nothing but mud in your long john's, when we get you out! One, two, three!!" They all heaved. "Put your backs into it. He's moving!" Victor shouted as every vein on his neck could be seen pumping with the strain and effort of extracting the soldier from the slough. Gradually, Eddie began to be withdrawn from his slimy pit. "Keep it up. Like a cork from a pop bottle, Eddie was propelled up and out of the quagmire, to land in a heap in No Man's land. "Let's get out of here before the Bosche decide to investigate all the racket that's been going on." Ordered Victor and he led the small contingent of men back towards the safety of their own camp, with Eddie hobbling along at the rear, minus his trousers and boots!

"Well done, Leslie." Said Captain Hughes, speaking with Victor in his tent during the late afternoon. "Cool thinking and positive action. First rate!" He picked up a sheet of paper off the small table in front of him. "I've just received this order from Division approving your promotion to sergeant. You are to replace Sergeant Ruck who was wounded three days ago. Congratulations sergeant."

A humourless smile played it's way across Victor's face, as he thought of his inauspicious entry to the Battalion. "Thank you, sir, I'll do my best not to let you or the men down." Victor replied. He left the tent thinking, 'Why me? It's hard enough looking after myself without worrying about others.'

It appeared as though the battalion was to spend another Christmas in the front line, when orders confirming Trevor's prediction of a relief away from the front line arrived. The 29th Division, including the 2nd

Mons were to move back to rest, away from the fighting, for several weeks.

On the 19th December, a weary but thankful battalion, left their tents and marched to the railway track, where they entrained, in their usual cattle trucks and headed for the rear. The weather was intensely cold, and the entire battalion had great difficulty in keeping warm, but No one complained. The sound of shellfire was growing less and less, as the train took them further and further away from the fighting! They stopped at a small camp, set in the grounds of a small chateau in Foundry. The officers established their headquarters in the sumptuous mansion the sergeants and other ranks erected tents in the lawned grounds. Victor found himself billeted in the sergeants' quarters and to his utter amazement and joy, discovered that the sergeants mess was situated in the cellar of the chateau, a huge frost-free basement that was used to store unwanted furniture and household goods and ornament's. "Let's have a look around the place." Suggested Trevor handing Victor a lighted candle. "There's nothing like looking through people's cellars and unwanted items. You can learn a lot about people by looking at the things they used to utilise or don't use anymore."

The two men set off to explore, the cavernous vault, their candles flickering lazily as they moved around the dust covered boxes and cupboards.

"If you had suggested this to me a couple of years ago." Victor stated bravely, "I would have been too scared to enter a place like this, I've read too many Edgar Allan Poe stories, and they often left me too afraid to go to sleep. But now! after the things we've seen, since coming overseas, I don't think anything will frighten me again!" Macabre forms danced from wall to wall as the pale flames sent spectral shadows bouncing from the dismal darkness.

"Dear God!" Breathed Victor coming to a sudden stop. "It can't be!"

"What the hell!" Snapped Trevor, himself coming to a rapid halt, "Are you trying to scare me or what?"

"Look!" Victor continued, pointing towards a large, covered object just ahead. "Unless I'm mistaken, that's a piano. I wonder if it still works. Come on."

He rushed over to it and began pulling away the sheet that had been carefully draped over it. Sure, enough gleaming beneath the dust laden cover was the polished mahogany of a Knaus Coblenz' upright piano. His trembling hand gingerly lifted the cover to expose the gleaming keys. Placing the candle carefully on the piano top he ran his fingers lightly over the keys.

"Not perfectly in tune, but good enough. "He remarked. "The sergeant's mess will be having a Christmas concert. He began playing 'Pack up your troubles in your old kit bag.' When the slightly off-key notes began to reverberate around the ghostly space. Soon voices were heard along with footsteps. The area became bathed in the warming glow of dozens of candles, as the inquisitive sergeants reached Victor and the Regimental Sergeant Major. Eager arms dragged the piano back to the section of the spacious cellar that was acting as the sergeant's mess.

Victor was amazed once again, that hot meals, uninterrupted sleep, and the cessation of shelling transformed the battalion. Soldiers walked around in better spirits. The haggard sunken eyed appearance that had haunted everyone was slowly disappearing. The battalion was being brought up to full strength with the influx of replacements and recruits. The only problem, as far as Victor was aware, was that he began to brood more and more about Naomi and the family back home.

"The trouble is!" He confided to a sympathetic Trevor. "When I'm at the front I'm too worried to think about how Naomi and the family are coping at home. All I think about when I'm up there is will the next bullet be mine, or will I be pulped by the next explosion but here there is too much time to sit around brooding, and dreaming of home!"

Fresh troops meant raw troops which meant plenty of drill and training. The company practised and practised. Practised attacking deployments, drilled how to execute defensive positions, and generally honed its fighting skills. Victor enjoyed the training; guns now held a fatal fascination for him. He enjoyed the rifle's sleek lines as it nestled against his cheek. He revelled in the way it, thumped back against his shoulder when he gently squeezed the trigger. He had never been fitter or stronger, his muscles were hard and his body lean. He led the drills; he was not a passive observer. As a 'seasoned' sergeant Victor took an active role in preparing the troops for the pleasures that lay ahead. It was a job to be loathed. "Look at it this way." Trevor advised, "A lot of us are going to be killed or wounded. We know what it's like in those trenches, these poor kids don't. It's people like us who must prepare them for it, so it isn't a total shock. And if our training saves just one life it is worth it. "I suppose you're right!" Agreed Victor "It just seems such an awful waste, Lord above, have you looked at them? They are only fresh-faced babies!"

"They are the same age as you Victor!" Continued Trevor looking back at his 'young' friend. "You used to look like them, a youth at the front!" Victor was too disturbed to reply.

CHAPTER 37

Christmas had always been a happy time at 26 George Street love flowed in abundance from every room, through every corner of the household and out of every pore of every person." Unfortunately, there is a tremendous void in all our lives at present," said Tom. "Victor would want us to enjoy Christmas" continued Tom taking Kate's trembling hand into his calloused mitt.

"At midnight on Christmas Eve his thoughts are going to be on us. So, our whole family's thoughts will be on him, and we make sure his children enjoy Christmas. I've' spoken to Naomi in hospital and at midnight she will turn her thoughts to Victor, her children and us."

"Oh Tom!" Kate replied, her eyes awash with salty tears that gave her eyes a crystal-clear reflection. "How much longer is it going to go on! Every day I expect the worst, dreading each day expecting it to be the time when his name appears among the casualties. Poor Evan Wilkinson is gone Big Evan too gentle to even hurt a fly!"

In the Village and on the mountainside, winter was making its presence felt, the cold was bitingly hard and although it hadn't snowed, frost gleamed on every roof, like a freshly polished mirror, and ashes had been scattered liberally along every pavement, in an effort to make them walkable in the icy conditions. They crunched loudly underfoot. Everywhere, people were trying to celebrate Christmas, but the daily additions to the casualty figures that were displayed in the Post Office window, filled the village with an air of dread!

"All we can do is keep thinking happy thoughts." Added Ivy as she nursed Laura on her lap. The infant slept soundly, unaware of the heartache and turmoil that was surrounding her. "I know that thought won't keep Victor safe but it's all we can do."

"We are going to celebrate Christmas and that is an end to it!" Ordered Tom.

"I've been saving a couple of pounds of sugar." Kate announced, "I've kept it in a tin at the back of the pantry, I thought I might make some toffee we might even have toffee apples."

"That would be wonderful mam!" Ivy replied, "It will be a wonderful treat for Peter. I bet he will like toffee almost as much as his father used to! "Does you mean!" Kate corrected her daughter sharply.

A Little after seven that evening, the family were sitting contentedly around the fire. The girls were reading, and Kate was busy knitting a warm pullover for her grandson. Tom was snoring contentedly in his high-backed chair with his feet stretched luxuriously out, toasting in front of the fireplace. There was a firm rap at the front door. "Who can that be at this time of night?" Said Kate as she went towards the door. "Wake up your uncle, tell him someone's at the door. Kate lit the lamp in the passage, and called, "Just a minute!" She slid back the bolt and saw Brian Cuthbertson illuminated in the lamplight. "Come in Mr. Cuthbertson. Don't stand out there in the cold." He limped on his wooden leg it caused him problems during the winter months.

"I wanted to come and see you all just before Christmas." He said happily, gazing around at the close-knit family gathered before him. "I hope I'm not intruding. I so wanted to come and see how young Peter and little Laura are doing." He sat by the fireside, next to Tom in the offered chair.

"You are welcome here anytime Mr. Cuthbertson, you know that." Tom answered. Kate began to prepare her mandatory pot of tea, whilst Ivy set out the Sunday best China. Glenys, rushed to the larder to fetch the milk and cake.

"I hope you don't mind but I've brought a little something for the children for Christmas?" Brian announced, "We have had a few ships in from across the Atlantic and I was able to get hold of this!" He placed an enormous two-pound box of chocolates on the table behind him." Don't ask where they came from, just let the children enjoy "them". "Mr. Cuthbertson!" Kate spluttered, "You shouldn't have."

"If this family doesn't start using my given Christian name of Brian. I'm going to explode!" He interrupted, then continued. "Christmas is a time for chocolates, especially when they are given to young children, by silly old men who have nothing better to do!" "Thank you Mr. Cuth .. er.. I mean Brian!" Answered Glenys. "I'll see that the children get some on Christmas Morning."

He reached inside the large frail he had brought with him. "I brought a few other presents, if you don't mind?" He took out some oranges. "I adore these they are my favourite." he continued;" I want to share some with you. I also have this;" he took out a goose and said, "Roast it and think of me".

Tom protested this must have cost a lot of money. "Hush!" Brian snapped, waving aside all arguments. It didn't cost hardly anything, most of it came off a ship no questions, asked if you know what I mean!"

He reached into his bag for a third time saying." This if for you Tom." He handed over half a bottle of whisky, "To keep the cold out when you have to start on a freezing Monday morning."

The tea arrived and Kate handed round the steaming cups. She revelled in the murmurs of delight as Brian devoured three large slices of cake.

The talk drifted onto news of the war and the effect it was having on the Shipping company. Before anyone realised, it was nine thirty and Brian announced. "I'm afraid I must leave now, there's a train at ten fifteen and it will take me quite a while to hobble to the train station!" "I'll walk with you." Tom replied, not wishing to turn the old man onto the cold dark street alone at night. "It's quite slippery and we can't have you falling, can we?"

They walked in silence for several hundred yards before Brian said, "I'm glad you came with me Tom, I wanted to speak to you alone." "I thought there was something on your mind." Tom replied. "I could tell there was something worrying you. I waited for you to buck up enough courage to tell me. You haven't heard any bad news about Victor, have you?"

"No nothing!" He answered, noticing Tom's sharp intake of breath. "No, all I want to say is, there's still no sign of the earl's body although there are still more than eight people unaccounted for.

I hoped that he had escaped on the Monmouth, when it sailed. We know it reached Miami in America, but it was sunk on the return journey. We haven't heard of any survivors!"

As they walked slowly back to the station Tom said, "Death has visited so many houses in Cwmcarn these last few years, that we accept such things as common happenings. Mind you, we've all had more than our fair share of death and misery from that damn pit! Naomi rushed to Newport the moment she heard the earl had returned. That's when she was badly burned" The maddening thing is, I doubt if the Earl could have done anything to help Victor!"

Tom helped the old man sit in a well-lit compartment before the train pulled away, "Don't worry about the children we'll look after them until their mother is able to come home from hospital and we'll keep you informed."

Willing hands had pushed the piano into the middle of the cellar where it stood proudly in the section set aside for the sergeants' mess. "Here you are Victor!" Trevor announced, to the incredulous gathering who were standing around staring quizzically. "I asked Father Christmas to drop it down the chimney for you, but he left it in the cellar instead!"

"Christmas present my arse!" Yelled company Sergeant Major Fred Jennings. "Can he play the bloody thing?"

"Give him a chair and listen." Trevor replied. A wooden box was pushed towards the piano and Victor sat at the keys.

"It isn't a bleeding piano stool!" Shouted Fred, "But it'll have to do."

Victor began to play, 'Hold your hand out you naughty boy!' his fingers ached, he hadn't played a piano for more than three years, but the notes soon began to flow. An impromptu concert followed with the sergeants adding their voices to the notes of the instrument.

"Bloody marvellous, Victor!" Shouted Fred. Now we can have a proper Christmas concert with carols and all! We'll sort out a few songs and invite the officers for a Christmas evening 'get together'".

Victor played until his fingers were on fire, and still played on. He forgot the War, forgot the trenches and forgot the enemy. His eyes misted over, and he could see the Woodlands' large room in Stow Hill, with Naomi standing at his side, on that first evening. Singing happily.

The regular meals added to the soundless, hushed nights, performed miracles on the mood and condition of the battalion. Victor closed his eyes and furrowed his brow in concentration, but no matter how hard he tried, he couldn't hear the sound of a single gun or cannon!

"Excuse me sergeant." Announced the battalion chaplain, The reverend Captain John Williams, "I'm sorry to interrupt your minutes reflection, but I hear you are playing for a concert on Christmas night?"

"Yes sir, that's correct." Victor replied coming swiftly to attention.

"Stand easy, my son." The officer replied, "I was wondering if you could perhaps play a few Christmas carols there for everyone to sing. It is Christmas after all!"

"I was intending to do that sir. The lads will enjoy it." Victor replied.

The weather became colder and colder, as the frost steeled the ground. None of the second Mons Battalion, complained, not too loudly anyway, even though several cases of frostbite were reported. The war was more than twenty miles away and they were about to enjoy a peaceful Christmas.

At three minutes to midnight Victor silently left his bunk and wandered out into the star-studded night. He faced west, closed hie eyes and said quietly to himself 'Merry Christmas my darling, kiss my baby for me, tell him his daddy is thinking of him, and is praying to the Lord that he will be able to come home to you both! The tears were unashamedly washing down his face stinging both his eyes and cheeks as their wetness became a frozen victim to the icy chill, 'God bless mam and all the family, remember to pray for me! Dear God, I've had enough of this madness and killing, please send me home safely, he stood immobile in the field for several minutes, lost in his own thoughts. Opening his eyes and turning to go, he became aware for the first time, that he was not alone. Dozens of similar figures were out in the midnight iciness facing home!

In far off Cwmcarn a candle lit Vigil was being held on the kitchen table, glasses were raised and fervent wishes of, 'God bless, Victor, and Naomi!' repeated by everyone before the fiery whisky was drunk. Tom had insisted that even Kate drink to her son's health. Eyes were closed and silent prayers were offered for Victor's well-being and safe return together with Naomi's complete recovery.

They dined in the sergeants' mess on corned beef, onions and potatoes. The meal was completed with several football size Christmas puddings, and the whole lot was washed down with pints of foaming beer.

The concert began with Trevor Bailey reciting Kipling's, Green Eyed Yellow Idol', followed by, 'When the red red robin' and 'Hold your hand out you naughty boy.'

Fred Jennings and the quarter master sergeant brought the house down with their comic version of the General Staff's, they were only playing leapfrog!

A young second lieutenant Alfred King, who hadn't started shaving the bum fluff off his chin, ended the concert with a tenor solo of, Keep the home fires burning'. His effort was met with silence. Most of the audience were in tears and too upset to respond to his wonderful performance. The concert ended with several well-known carols, that were sung and enjoyed by all present. The Chaplin ended the evening by leading them in prayer and blessing all present.

"Well done, Leslie!" Congratulated Colonel Brewer, First rate job. Perfect morale booster, just what the doctor ordered." Victor jumped to attention. "Thank you, sir, I was glad to help out." The concert was Sergeant Jennings' idea sir, he had the idea."

"I'll credit him with the idea don't worry sergeant." He looked at the decoration ribbons on Victor's tunic and added, "Military medal as well I see. I don't mind admitting I had my doubts about you in the beginning, but the sergeant Major was very persuasive. I must concur with his judgement; you have proved to be an asset to the battalion."

"Thank you, sir!" Victor replied, I have always done my best, it's a family trait, it is my most fervent wish to get home and clear my name."

"Sergeant, you have redeemed yourself a hundred times over! Just go and enjoy the rest of your Christmas and forget about this damn war for tonight at least."

By the tenth of January the Battalion was back to full strength, replacement's, like lambs to the slaughter, had been drafted in. Most of them had no experience of trench warfare and many of them had hardly completed their basic training.

"Do as you are told, watch the experienced soldiers around you and do as they do!" Victor warned the new additions to his platoon. On the 12th January, the battalion entrained and marched! Victor found himself back in the middle of a trench at Montane here they took up their pioneering duties of trench digging and improving roadways once again. The work, although carried out at night attracted the usual accompaniment of machine gun and shell fire with its inevitable numerous casualties!

'D' company were ordered, along with the other companies to dig a new length of trench at Le Transloy. It was to be used to launch an all-out attack on the enemy.

"This trench must be dug tonight." Victor ordered his section. The ground is quite hard, but we can do it."

They followed the taping ribbons to their allotted portion and began. "This ground is worse than undercutting a seam of top-grade anthracite!" Moaned Eddie Griffiths.

"Don't talk bloody daft!" Answered Howard Roberts. "You have never done anthracite, it's steam coal back home!" Bugger off, Robbie!" Snapped Eddie. "After them couple of weeks away at Christmas my 'ands have gone soft. I've got more blisters on them than there are on a parson's prick after confession!"

"Ands 'aren't the only thing that'll be soft from now on." Quipped Robbie. "You all complained about the funny taste to the meal."

"Shut up and dig!" Victor ordered his hard-working men. "We can't leave until the job is done. If we are still here at daylight, the Huns will send us all a present."

In spite of all the complaints and warnings the battalion were safely in their reserve trenches well before dawn. With more than six hundred yards of trench completed, the attack went in a week later, the enemy were driven back several hundred yards before the attack gradually ground to a halt with the troops consolidating their gains. The Battalion were ordered to provide two Communication trenches from the old front line to the new. Victor found himself in reserve as the work was performed by 'B' and 'C' companies 'B' company's work began well, despite the hardened ground, until the communications trench was ready to break into the new front line so recently won from the Germans. The area was found to be still in enemy hands, who poured Volley after Volley of rifle fire into the pioneers, inflicting several casualties. Colonel Brewer taped out on a new direction for the trench that hopefully led to an area held by friendly forces. Covering fire was provided by the South Wales Borders.

'C' company began their task and had been digging for only a short while when a barrage of shells began falling all around them. The experienced soldiers had dug more than eighteen inches into the ground and were able to throw themselves flat into their frozen refuges, replacements however were not so fortunate, and were tossed like chaff in the wind, as the shells began to wreak havoc among them. Arms, legs and dismembered, torsos were blown skyward to descend as a bloody rain upon those fortunate enough to be sheltering. By the time the counter bombardment began dozens of mutilated, dead and dying filled the area. 'A' and 'D' Companies were called up to help with the trench construction. Victor found himself leading the platoon. As soon as they started digging in the iron hard ground the baby-faced lieutenant Alfred King was killed as a bullet took him in the throat and almost decapitated him, he died in Victor's arms a frightened bewildered little boy!

"Come on lads!" Victor shouted, as he reverently lowered the lifeless body of the young officer onto the red stained snow. "Let's get this trench dug, then we can get the hell out of here!"

The platoon set to their task with a will. The top two feet of the ground was as hard as tempered steel and required muscle power a plenty. Once through the frosted layer the digging became easier.

"Don't stop to rest until you get through to soft soil. Eddie advised the party of replacement's who were digging alongside him. "I know it's hard going, but a bit of sweat is better than a German shell blowing your balls off!"

"He's right boys!" Howard Roberts added his voice to the advice being freely offered. "Dig as if the devil was after you cos the only thing between you and the devil is a deep hole to hide your arses in." Victor smiled at the survival tips being given by his lifelong butties. "They are right men!" He warned, "The only safe place to be when the shelling starts is ...."

"Safe between some tarts legs in Cardiff!" Eddie interrupted. Even Victor laughed at Eddie's quip. Remembering where he was, he snapped. "That's enough private Griffiths!" He reprimanded the soldier but secretly couldn't fault his logic! "What I was going to say was the only safe place is deep underground!"

"An' the sergeant doesn't mean buried in a wooden box!" Howard added.

Looking a little more than fifty yards ahead, Victor could see Trevor and a large party of soldiers, illuminated in the bright moonlight, beavering busily to complete their excavation, which was progressing well. They had tunnelled to a depth of at least five feet and were hollowing out the cavity, ready to marry into the adjoining sections, suddenly the entire excavation was levelled by a gigantic explosion as a 150mm howitzer shell landed alongside its trench section and totally obliterated it!

"Trevor!" Exclaimed Victor, "Oh my God, No!" Victor's heart missed a dozen beats as he saw the trench sides collapse in on the men sheltering inside it. He made a rapid decision and barked an order. "Corporal Evans." He spoke to the platoon corporal," Keep the men at it until the work is finished." He turned and picked half a dozen soldiers, "You men follow me, let's see if we can help those poor devils ahead bring your tools and rifles. They set off toward the ruined trench going from one shell hole to the next until they reached their objective, the remains of the excavation. A scene of utter carnage met them. The blast had killed several soldiers outright, eerily they appeared unmarked the shell blast had just snuffed out their young lives totally and completely. Other soldiers lay around moaning many had grievous wounds or broken limbs. What struck Victor immediately was the almost total lack of blood! The explosive force and resultant shock wave was the cause of nearly all the injuries. He instructed one of his men to return to the company command post and request stretcher bearers for the large number of casualties, which he estimated to be as many as eighteen. The remaining soldiers began to search for other survivors. Moving to the front of the trench to examine what remained of the excavation, Victor could see a pair of boots sticking out from a large mass of soil and debris, they struggled for a few moments, then went still it was obvious that this was the section that had taken the full force of the impact. He began tearing at the pile of earth and debris with his bare hands before shouting. "Private Griffiths and Robert, get over here with your shovels quickly. There may be some more men buried here they may still be alive." He continued scraping at the loose earth until he had exposed legs that belonged to the boots. Eddie and Howard continued with the task with a vengeance. Both were ex miners and knew the horror of being buried alive. Exercising extreme caution without reducing speed, which was of the essence, the two privates moved huge quantities of frozen soil. In less than a minute the trapped soldier was pulled from the trench by some miracle he was still alive, but unconscious. Happy with this success the three soldiers continued with their grisly task. Victor by now using the tarnished butt of a Lee Enfield rifle to push back the alluvium. They soon came upon another pair of legs and began to delicate task of freeing up this victim without causing more hurt. As more of the torso appeared. Victor began to recognise the uniform and brassard of Trevor Bailey. Eddie Griffiths cleared more and more fallen earth from around the sergeant major's waist and shoulders whilst Victor grabbed Trevor's legs and began to heave his friend from his unwanted tomb. A muted cry of agony was music to his ears as he slid the soldier out of the rubble. A large shard of rock was implanted in his left forearm, which was almost severed at the elbow. He ordered the two soldiers to continue digging for other survivors. Victor wound his belt tightly around Trevor's wound to stop the blood that was dripping profusely onto the hard ground. The tourniquet stemmed the gory flow so he began to wipe dirt and soil from around his butty's face and eyes. He was pleased to hear the rasping breathing as his unconscious friend clung tenaciously to life.

"Do yourself a Favor old friend." He whispered. "Don't wake up until we can get you to an aid post, or better still the dressing station because that wound is going to hurt worse than the hobs of hell," He ducked instinctively, throwing himself across the sergeant Majors injured body as another great explosion sprouted into the air about thirty yards to the rear of the trench. Loose stones and frozen earth cascaded onto the trench occupants, clattering viciously on their helmets like a thousand enraged hornets. When it was safe to do so he glanced over his shoulder to see the stretcher bearers entering the excavation and beginning to remove the wounded and injured. He called a pair of them to him and ordered.

"Take good care of Sergeant Major Bailey. I've put a tourniquet around his left arm about three minutes ago, its badly injured." He pointed to the collapsed side wall. "He was buried under there for a few minutes." He watched as they placed his comrade onto their stretcher and hauled him away, before he turned back to help the search for further survivors. They found one other man alive, totally uninjured except for his ordeal, but four other soldiers were dug out dead. "Who's in charge here?" Called Major Royce who was leading a platoon from the reserves.

"What's happened? I want a report off someone quickly." Victor, crouching low, returned to the other end of the almost completed trench, he saluted and reported. "At the moment sir, I am." He quickly explained the situation to the officer and concluded. "We've dug three survivors out of the slip at the forward edge. Other casualties are being ferried back to the aid post. We haven't found Lieutenant Thomas the platoon commander!"

"Now you're here to take charge sir, may I return to my platoon, Lieutenant King's been killed and I am needed there."

"My God sergeant, we are all going to remember Le Transloy for a long time, we've taken a right pasting. You have my permission to return to your men. You are to be commended for your work here this evening, well done.

CHAPTER 38

Victor felt totally isolated. He was a platoon sergeant in a battalion, that was almost eight hundred men strong, yet he was alone. For the first time in his army career, Trevor Bailey wasn't at his side as either his guide or mentor.

Trevor's army days were over. He had returned home without his left arm! The tourniquet had shaved his life, but there was nothing the surgeons could do to shave his arm, it had to be amputated at the elbow. At least he was home, although not in one piece, he was away from the insanity and wanton slaughter.

Victor soldiered on. Days drifted into weeks and weeks into endless months. The cold was pitiless, entering every shell hole and trench, with its painful beastly teeth that gnawed agonisingly at every piece of exposed human flesh, nothing would keep it at bay. With a thaw, came the cloying ooze that sucked at feet, boots and the very will to live. Movement became impossible, rest inconceivable and sleep an elusive dream, yet he did all of these, his desperation and determination to return home to Naomi and the family drove him with a blinding resolve. Spring saw the battalion involved at the battles of Scarpe, where they fulfilled their pioneering duties with distinction. Numerous casualties were suffered because of the wholesale shelling of the entire area.

They moved next to Pilkthem, Langermarck, and then Poelcapelle. The names meant nothing to Victor, but the consolidation work continued at each one. As each position was earned in blood, so the battalion added their gore to the price for each yard of ground gained or lost. November, found the battalion busy at the battle of Cambrai. The battalion were carrying few weapons except for gas helmets, and greater quantities of construction materials.

"This is bloody daft!" Eddie Griffiths stated. "Agreed!" Victor replied, "But as we are going to be building, the generals don't think you will need your rifle."

"I don't know what we want a rifle for any how." He added," we are 'hopeless shots. I don't know about you but none of us could hit a cow in the backside with a shovel. They dropped off supplies behind the guards' trenches and watched the new wonder weapons roll into no man's land.

The new wonder weapons called tanks rolled forward to take down the enemy machine guns. Victor soon realised why they called them wonder weapons as they seemed to be impervious to the machine gun fire. Previous attacks had failed, and the enemy counter attacks needed to be repulsed, which the tanks accomplished. From a hilltop position what was left of 'D; company, watched the guard's division counterattack. They were accompanied by a battalion of recruits, recently arrived in the war zone. Victor was amazed to see that the vast majority of the new soldiers went into battle wearing only their khaki felt hats. They were ordered to strip steel helmets from fallen comrades, who would have no further need of them! When the battalion returned, every survivor wore a helmet.

Victor supervised the issue of rifles and ammunition to D Company. The Mons held the line for two weeks of continual fighting until the division was relieved. Their 'rest'. proved to be road and track repairing! The intense fighting, together with the diminishing numbers, of recruits meant that, the battalion was reduced to just three companies. Victor's 'D' company was absorbed into the other three. They had to begin the task of constructing a road from gravel and stone. The ground was pock marked and scarred with shell holes and craters, a testament to the intensity and ferocity of the shelling that had occurred.

Join up the shell holes alongside the road!" Victor ordered his platoon, as they began their filthy task. "Dig a channel from hole to hole so that all the water drains into the holes and ditches." Thus began the task of reconstructing the road. The next task was to drain the water from the shell holes on the road itself, into the side ditches. It was a filthy task, every hole was filled to its oozing brim with gallons and gallons of muddy swill.

"What the bloody hell!" Exclaimed an incredulous Eddie, as he watched the murky liquid drain from a particularly large hole. His startled shout brought Victor to his side. He gazed down into the hole as the bloated body of a horse, gradually appeared. The unfortunate animal was still hitched to a field gun!

"Just shut up about it Private!" Warned Victor, "When the wagon brings the road materials up, just bury the lot or would you rather pull it out?"

"I 'haven't seen nuffink sergeant!" Eddie replied.

The Germans launched their final attempt to gain Victory at the battle of Lys, in the Somme area. The 20th Division including the 2nd Mons were rushed to reinforce the battalion which marched quickly to Baillieu where every mule was used for transport.

-Bloody hell", Whooped Howard Roberts, as he looked at the line of buses waiting at the roadside. "We aren't going' to walk we're going to have a bus ride!" said Eddie.

The battalion began to climb into the buses. Eddie strolled up and down the bus holding out his half open hand," that'll be a half a penny each please," he joked. "Sit down in a seat Private Griffiths damn it!" Ordered Victor a smile playing on his face or you can run behind!"

"Not bleedin' likely sarge!" The soldier replied. "This is the first time I've 'ad a ride that hasn't been in a cattle truck. My feet are going' to enjoy this trip more than me. Every last bleedin' inch of it!"

The buses progressed but were soon impeded by streams of French refugees escaping from the front of the German lines. Late in the afternoon the leading bus was fired upon. The column halted and the battalion began to dig in at the roadside.

"Oh balls! Me and my big mouth!" Moaned Eddie Griffiths, swinging his pack into a shell hole before burying it deep into the rich soil. "Just when I was getting used to being here the War starts again."

Trevor entered the shipping office unannounced and surprised his old friend. Tears rolled abundantly and without shame from Brian's aged eyes, he leaned forward over his desk and his body jerked spasmodically as sobs consumed his heart, mind and soul. It was several minutes before he was able to stand and greet his long-lost colleague. Clasping Trevor warmly around the shoulders, he welcomed him, as only one ex-soldier, could to another. He felt the wrath welling up inside him, as he observed the empty sleeve and the lines of pain and agony, etched upon Trevor's face for all to see. Anger not aimed at the enemy that had caused his suffering and pain, but spleen bursting enmity at war itself, and any situation that allowed it to proliferate and prosper. He sat Trevor in his old chair.

"Welcome home old friend." He said, wiping away a last stray tear that appeared on his cheek. "I am glad to see you home safely. This room can become our office again, now that you're back. It feels comfortable once again. Together we are like a well-worn suit, comfy and at ease with one another."

"I don't think I will ever be at ease again." Trevor replied. "I have seen and done things that will shame me until the day I die. Then perhaps the Lord will forgive me."

"We all do things, in times of total war." Brian replied noticing the way his friend nursed the painful ruin that had once been his left arm. The urge to survive is a strong one and we all go to extraordinary lengths and resort to any means to ensure we do. The best thing is to leave such memories on the battlefield, but if it will ease your pain to talk, I am an expert listener." He tapped his wooden leg, smiled and continued. "I am not without experience in these matters." They sat and talked for several hours. Brian listened attentively as he was told of the horrors of the trenches, their squalor and carnage his ears picked up at the mention of Victor and his exploits, promotion decoration and timely rescue of his old friend. He allowed Trevor to talk without interruption, letting his fears and tensions slowly evaporate in the telling.

"You have answered many questions without them being asked" Brian remarked, as Trevor concluded his tale. "I am sure Naomi, and the family will be relieved to hear it as well."

"Tell it second hand please!" Trevor said again I don't think I could face Naomi, knowing that Victor is still out there, possibly never returning." Brian shook his head sadly, looked his old companion in the eye and said "A lot has happened since you left for France. I must go to Cwmcarn, there are people who will want to hear your story."

The battalion found themselves occupying a defensive position near Pen D' Achelveri They dug the trenches all through the night, exhausted they slumped where they were. Confusion reigned. What became obvious was that the defensive position was a shambles.

"I've just received orders that we are to move in a few hours." Victor passed the word along to his platoon. "We are to dig a defensive trench. The forward troops will retire to it tonight, so it's got to be ready."

The battalion moved to their assigned position and waited for the wagons to deliver their tools. The situation had changed for the worse and they marched with their weapons and ammunition, the tools followed. "What a bloody mess!" Snapped Howard Roberts as he entered a less than half completed trench.

Tools were distributed to the platoon who began working to improve the trench. Victor issued orders though his thoughts were on Trevor and the problems his absence was causing, mayhem was bound to be the result.

There's movement to the front!" Someone yelled. Picks and shovels were dropped, and rifles distributed.

"Wait for the order before you fire." Victor warned his troops. "no one touches a trigger until the lieutenant says so!"

"Shit a brick!" Eddie Griffiths announced quietly. "They are our troops!"

The battalion watched as the forward troops passed through heading for the rear.

"Carry on with your orders!" Shouted Captain Hughes, "Get this trench finished!"

The trenching work continued with renewed enthusiasm although extra lookouts were posted. At night there were no troops to move into the trench, so the battalion took up positions ready to repulse any enemy attacks.

"What a pig's guts of a position!" Victor swore! "Eddie was at his side leaning against the freshly dug soil. Victor looked towards their left flank. If the Germans attack now, we could end up surrounded!"

"I expect some silly old fart of a staff officer chose to put us in this position because it looks good on his map!" Bill said from a little way along the trench.

"Let's concentrate on what happens in front of us," said Victor his voice raised so that it carried along the trench. "We can't worry about what is happening elsewhere." He fixed his eyes forward," if they get behind us, we are done for!"

The battalion was trying to hold a thousand yards of trench a task that was usually given to a full-strength regiment, not an under-strength company. The second Mons were trying to hold their line. The attack came early the next morning it was proceeded by a fearful barrage of artillery and trench mortars. Within five minutes of the attack starting a direct hit on 'A' Company's command post killed all officers except for a replacement one. The bombardment lifted and Victor could see and hear a large number of grey uniformed enemy soldiers streaming towards his position. "Look to your front!" He yelled, "Here they come, stay down and shoot when ordered. When the order comes pour it on!" He looked toward the young officer, who was gratefully returning his stare.

"Open fire!" screamed the Lieutenant.

The company began shooting into the massed ranks, that were rapidly approaching. Lewis guns were adding their constant chattering as they spewed out their deadly projectiles into the enemy waves who were killed by the furious fusillade. Many enemy were killed more were injured.

"I will shoot anyone who I see, firing at any wounded enemy!" Warned Victor. "We concentrate on the living and uninjured. The main attack has broken for the moment. Be on your guard for small numbers of the enemy wasters who will try to find weak spots!"

He crawled through the trench over many dead and wounded soldiers before he reached the lieutenant.

"We held them that time sir, but our flanks are very weak. If we don't receive any support, we are going to be cut off."

"What will they do now?! Asked the younger officer.

"They will probe our defensive line until they find our weak spots."

"What do you suggest?" Lieutenant Hopkins added.

"We've no reserves, so we can only hope the men can hold." Victor answered. "At the moment we've plenty of ammunition, if they try to engage you here at this section at close quarters use grenades, we've plenty of them."

Victor returned to his own platoon, encouraging all the bleary red eyed soldiers he passed on the way. The Mons held their line all day and into the next, but casualties and lack on ammunition were beginning to make their position impossible. The enemy began making inroads from both the battalion's flanks. Colonel Brewer sent runners to each company with orders to withdraw. Victor's platoon along with the survivors of 'A' and 'C' companies began to fall back to an embankment held by 'A' company of the Royal Newfoundland Regiment, about three hundred yards backwards to be reached rearwards step by step. Victor bringing up the rear saw, Eddie, Howard and Bill stopped dead in their tracks by an entanglement of barb wire. "Shit what a bloody mess!"

Advancing cautiously around the wire using a small hillock as cover, they found the colonel's bat man up to his waist in a bog. The soldier had evidently found the colonels bottle of rum, he was trying to put it where the Germans couldn't capture it, down his throat!

"'He's as pissed as a fart sergeant!" Laughed Eddie, He's floundering around in that mud as happy as a pig in shit!"

"Keep your voice down!" Snapped Victor, aware that pursuit was fast approaching. "let's try and get the drunken sod out of that mess." Despite their best efforts they were unable to free the unlucky soldier. "We'll have to leave him." Victor ordered, "The Germans will have more time to pull him out than we will."

"If he breathes on any of them, they're in real trouble." Quipped an amused Howard," 'His breath will kill at a hundred yards."

"At least he prevented the colonel's booze from being' captured!" Laughed Eddie as they left the drunken soldier, singing happily to himself, as the group continued their retreat behind the rest of the battalion. Thus, one batman, complete with rucksack containing all his commanding officer's kit was captured.

To their horror, once they had rejoined the battalion, they discovered that 'B' company had been completely surrounded and captured. The battalion's strength was now approximately one hundred and fifty officers and men! They held the embankment until ordered to support their Brigade at La Creche. By this time, the Mons were near collapse. The strain and tension resulted in almost total exhaustion.

"How much more are we expected to take sergeant." Asked Eddie Griffiths wearily. His bloodshot eyes, unshaven chin and filthy dirty appearance giving him a vampirish appearance.

"Not much more I hope!" Victor replied. "We hold until we are told otherwise. Anyway, if the Huns get too close, we are going to put you up on a pole in front of them. One look at you will send them all running. God you are an ugly bugger at the best of times, but now?" This raised a slight laugh among some of the surviving troops and lieutenant Hopkins added. "I've had a good look at all the men sergeant, and they all look like death warmed up and shattered."

"They have all been involved in hard fighting something that they have not been trained for. They have held the line for three years with little training or experience for the tasks they have performed.

Nine buses took the survivors to the rear. This time there was plenty of room on every vehicle. For a few days the battalion was rested and replacements were drafted in. their duties returned with orders to construct new replacement trenches. They were also charged with improving the roads and reinforcing the railway tracks.

CHAPTER 39

"Well done," Sergeant! "Colonel Brewer congratulated Victor after he'd been decorated with the Distinguished Conduct Medal by Lieutenant General Hunter who simply stated," Richly deserved, without thought of your personal safety or the danger you faced you rescued Sergeant Major Bailey and his party. It was an inspiration to us all." He shook Victor's hand.

"I didn't act alone Sir." Victor replied." I had soldiers with me, and they did all that was asked of them." "Quite right Sergeant but without you they wouldn't have done anything at all!" The Colonel smiled pleasantly before continuing, "You took all the decisions and led from the front. Consequently, you have been confirmed as company sergeant major for the reforming of 'D' company. We hope to be back to full strength in three days' time." "Thank you, Sir," Victor replied whilst inwardly he was seething and thinking why me? I don't want to be responsible for getting another batch of young soldiers killed!

"It's difficult, isn't it?" Said the Colonel when he noticed Victor's concern at the mention of his new promotion. "Being responsible for making life or death decisions! Someone's got to do it, I am confident that most of the new and experienced soldiers feel more at ease with someone like you, giving them their orders. Someone who knows what he is doing and has done it before and not let them down. Victor saluted and let the Colonel rejoin the general.

Victor lay on his bunk listening to the distant rumble of artillery fire. Thankfully they were several miles from the front, he could hear only the heavy guns.

He turned over and closed his eyes. What a turn up for the books, old prison lag, to Decorated Company Sergeant Major, not bad for a common pit boy. Losing Trevor had left him feeling isolated in his new promotion, it had turned him into a semi recluse. He worried incessantly about all the young soldiers under his command. He maintained a barrier, a distance around himself he became afraid to show friendship or involvement. The battlefield made a mockery of all relationships. Friendships were fleeting suffering from the mortality of flesh versus steel. God, he was fed up with this senseless futile slaughter!

The battalion returned to the front. Luckily, they were employed in strengthening the rearward trenches and defences. Although they were well beyond machine gun and rifle range, they were continually bombarded by artillery. The gas shells were particularly virulent. The battalion suffered many casualties to the new mustard gas that the Germans had developed. The trouble with it was it looked like ordinary smoke with barely any smell! If it touched your skin, it burned to huge blisters and if you breathed it in!!! "Warn your men this new gas is awful Sergeant Major!" warned an officer, "They must cover themselves up, it's hot digging I know but I've never seen such blisters!" "Tell your men, train them, they must not leave any exposed flesh during or immediately following any bombardment. If you suspect mustard gas light fires get the stuff to evaporate.

Victor lost count of the number of trenches his Pioneers Dug or roadways that they improved. But at least it was better than being in the frontline!

The battalion returned to the practise of several days frontline work and then back to reserve and more consolidation work. More and more of the battalion's tasks of late seemed to involve consolidation of ground recaptured or taken from the enemy. The Pioneers were ordered to prepare the forward roads for the heavy transport that follows an army on the offensive. They were now living under canvas, always ready to be on the move. Each company was in a separate field, because of the probability of bombardment, as they were following hard on the heels of the offensive. The tents moved forward as The Pioneers advanced with their constructions.

On the 21st of September, the Mons moved back to the Ypres area and began preparing the roads to support the movement of artillery and waggons. No sooner had the first shovel been buried in the ground than the rain began to fall.

"I'm glad about that my little beauties." Eddie Griffiths shouted at his digging detail, "Now you'll have a chance to find out what it was like for us in the old days!"

"And I'm glad you didn't say the good old days." Added Victor as he came along to inspect the progress being made. "This rain is going to turn the road into a quagmire. Keep them at it, it's going to become very busy in a few days."

"Don't worry!" Laughed Eddie, looking at victor, "I was trained by a right old bastard!" He turned back to his men and yelled, "Put your backs into it, this isn't rain it's only a little bit of gnat's piss!"

The enemy was losing ground continually and by October the battalion had recovered more ground than had been taken in the previous twelve months. The Mons followed closely behind the next major attacked at Courtrai, on October 14th. They helped the Royal Engineers rebuild bridges and repair railway lines, which had been blown up by the retreating Germans. Platoons were selected to follow closely behind the attacking troops to enable them to cross streams and marshy ground. Victor hardly ever ventured near the front line being more concerned with the organisation of working parties and their supply. By the 20th of October the battalion was assisting the engineers as they built bridges across the river Lys. The Germans were in full retreat, and it was extremely difficult to keep up with them. Victor was given orders by the Colonel telling him to prepare for the battalion to take part in an attack to cross the river Scheldt, but the objective was obtained without opposition. The Mons we're continually on the March, following closely behind the Division's fighting troops. They had just reached a place called Celles, when he was called to the command post.

"Ah, Sergeant Major Leslie." Announced Colonel Brewer, as victor stood to attention in front of a map covered trestle. "I've just received a communication. I intend assembling the battalion and reading it to them immediately, but I am letting all the officers and the non-coms know first." He picked up a message off the table and read.

"Hostilities will end at 11.00 on the 11th of November. The battalion will hold its present position. Full defensive precautions must be taken. You will not fraternise with the enemy. Concentrate on communication work."

He dropped the dog-eared piece of paper down in front of him before continuing.

"In other words, Sergeant Major, the war is over! Thank the Lord no more killing!" He looked at victor and asked, "Am I right in assuming you have been here from the beginning?"

"Yes Sir!" Victor replied "if you remember, I joined the battalion straight from prison, and landed in Flanders on the 7th of November 1914 of the original 'D' company that came there are now four of us left. I haven't heard from my family, for more than four years!"

"Don't worry about that now, I'll see you are discharged with the honours you have earned and will get!" Colonel Brewer concluded.

"I'm glad it's a proper bloody train this time!" Laughed Eddie Griffith as he settled back luxuriously in his seat, "I have travelled in enough cattle trucks with bullshit up to my eyeballs, to last me the rest of my life!"

"What's the first thing you are going to do when you get home" asked Howard Roberts.

"I'm a married man!" Bill Watts answered, "What do you think?"

"Stupid question I suppose, but what if the Dickie powder hasn't worn off?2 Laughed Howard.

"See that!" Said Bill, pointing to his steel helmet. "That's for the wife! It's the only thing that will stop her brains being battered out against the bed headboard when I get home Dickie powder be buggered".

Victor said nothing, he closed his eyes and slept, dreaming of his dark haired beauty and of strolling barefoot through the lappy and the soft warm feel of her breasts as they caressed one another and strolled through the warm grass.

They boarded ship at Antwerp and sailed for Tilbury. Three days later the train reached Pontypool, the battalion's headquarters. A reception was waiting for them complete with a blaring brass band. The civic dignities dressed in their starched collars and camphorated suits met them at the station.

The company had been marched out of Pontypool, in 1914 and marched back in 1918. The battalion formed up on the platform before marching through the town towards the drill hall for the civic reception.

Victor looked this way and that, hoping to catch sight of Naomi or some other members of his family.

The following day, a grey half lit one, so common to the valleys of Monmouthshire, saw Victor standing before the company's commanding officer, Major Hubert Ellis.

"Well Sergeant Major, I suppose you are anxious to be away."

"Yes Sir!" He replied, "I haven't seen my wife and child for more than four years, they don't even know I'm home, it's going to be quite a shock for them when they see me."

"Here are your discharge papers, you've served your country well!" The officer held out his hand and shook Victor's warmly "good luck!"

"Thank you, Sir. You know how I came to the battalion?" Stated Victor, the officer nodded. "I intend to clear my name; I did nothing wrong!"

"Take a tip from me." Advised Major Elis, "The slate has been wiped clean. You have more than repaid your debt to society go home and just try to get on with your life."

Victor was given a travel warrant and two shillings. He went straight to the station where he caught the first train he could to Newport. It made its way slowly down the valley. He waited as the small stations drifted past as the wheels clattered towards his destination at Bridge Street. Eventually the train arrived, and he jumped off. He resisted the urge to run as he didn't want to arrive home out of breath. Hoisting his knapsack, he arrived at number 47.

The house was boarded up and grime lined all the windows "What the hell!" He shouted, his voice startling a passerby.

"en't no one livin there soldier, en't been nobody for a while or more." The person advised.

Victor tried the front door, it was locked! Dropping his sack, he jumped over the wall and ran to the back. He peered in at a window, but could see nothing, the inside was dark, and the window caked with dust and dirt. He ran back to the front door and grabbed his rucksack and raced frantically to the station, she must be in Cwmcarn!

The smoke from the Abercarn tinplate works hung like a pall over the valley floor as the train wound lazily along the mountain side at Pontywaun, before slowly grinding to a halt at Cwmcarn. Victor jumped from the carriage before the train had stopped and set off full pelt running for the exit. All eyes turned towards him as his army boots banged their way up the metal steps and over the bridge. He had clutched his ticket all the way from Newport and when he threw it at Evan, who was manning the exit, it was badly battered.

"Oi" What do you call this soldier?" Demanded Evan when he examined the tattered ticket.

"Sorry Evan!" Shouted Victor, without pausing, but running to the river bridge. He turned and shouted over his shoulder. "It's all there, I'm in a bit of a hurry!" 'That's the understatement of the century!' He thought to himself. Chapel Farm and Jamesville passed in a blur, as he raced towards George Street. He reached number 26, where he halted. His thoughts we're in turmoil, he wanted to rush in, but he had been away for four years. What differences would he find? Then it dawned on him, it was the family home, differences and changes didn't happen in family homes! He reached out and pressed the latch, the door swung open in front of him. The spotlessly clean passage was empty. He walked quietly to the living room door and opened it.

Kate was out in the garden, pegging clothes on the line Glenys, was just pushing the prop under the heavy line. Young Peter was running around dodging in and out of the bare gooseberry bushes while Laura was toddling in and out of Kate's legs. Suddenly they were both stopped dead in their tracks by a full-throated scream from Ivy, who was inside the house.

"Mam! Mam! Oh mam come quick!" Ivy yelled. "Dear God mam hurry! Please mam!"

Grabbing up Laura, Kate made a beeline for the door, at a speed that made a mockery of her sixty-two years.

"What's wrong Ivy?" She bellowed as she reached the kitchen door, "What's the matter, we're here!"

"Nothing's wrong mam, that's just it!" Ivy replied, "Everything is perfectly wonderful come and see!"

Kate went into the Kitchen where she found Ivy, her eyes crying unashamedly, clinging like a limpet to Victor!

Victor looked up, let his sister loose and said, "Hello mam long time no see!"

"Oh Victor, my son!" Were the only words she could utter, before Glenys hurtled past her, like a star shell hurtling from a howitzer canon and dived head long into her brother's arms. Victor lifted her as though she was a feather duster and whirled her around in the middle of the kitchen floor.

"Thank you, Lord!" Kate whispered, stooping to her knees as the tears began to flow. "I knew you would take care of my boy and bring him home safely to us."

Ivy took a frightened Laura from her grandmother's trembling hands just before Victor swept his mother into his brawny arms. He buried his nose in the clean smell of her hair, feeling its silky texture against his smooth face. "If only you knew how much I've been looking forward to this moment was all he could say."

Kate freed her arms from his vice like grip, and kept his face in her hands, she looked deeply into his eyes, examining them for any imperfections or injury. She loved his every pore and whisker. "Others were worried! But I knew you would come home safely!" She replied. She placed a kiss on each of his eyelids, before burying her head in his shoulder once again.

The three women crowded around the prodigal son hugging him, reassuring themselves that he wasn't a figment of their imaginations.

"I'll make a nice cup of tea for us all, and you can tell us all about it. I once made a bet when we were sheltering in a trench that they would be your first words when I got home, and I walked in the door. Kate beamed and walked to the kettle.

"Who's this little girl?" Victor asked, looking at the tiny bundle clinging nervously to Ivy. "Aren't you a little darling!" "Oh Victor!" Ivy replied, "This is your daughter, Laura, she was born not long after you had gone away." She tried to hand Laura to her father, but the child began to scream and cry at the prospect.

"Wha wha when did it happen, I didn't even know!" Victor stammered. He smiled at the precious bundle hiding securely behind her aunt's head."

"I went to Newport, but the house was boarded up." Victor stated, looking from one face to another, "Where are Namoi and Peter, he must be out of nappies by now?"

Kate dropped the kettle, the water hissed and boiled as it met the flames. The question she had been dreading, was out! She left the kettle and turned tearfully to her son.

"Peter's playing out in the garden, he's wonderful, so full of energy and full of mischief."

"Has Naomi popped out for a while then?" He continued beginning to worry as he recognised the melancholic expressions that his question evoked. Kate wrapped herself in her son's arms and said, "Victor, Naomi was badly hurt" in a Zeppelin attack She told a numbed Victor of the story of-the ill-fated errand that had taken her to Newport. He buried his head, as he had done so many times in his childhood in his mother's breast and wept. He wept until his lungs hurt. His throat was aching from the dryness that was the result of crying 10,000 tears. "She's much improved" and we are counting the days until they discharge her from hospital and she comes home!" Stated Kate. Victor looked deeply into his mother's eyes, "Where is she I must go straight to her. "This bloody war! Damn all bloody archdukes, all their greedy spawn that expect us to fight and die to preserve their positions and power!" He uttered through tightly clenched teeth.

"Let it all out my darling." Kate soothed. "We've all cried until we're empty. It's no good looking for anyone to blame. Blame isn't going to change anything! But if it helps you carry on, we understand. Let it out, don't bottle it up inside yourself" she grimaced as his hands clenched hers in anguish, crushing her fingers tightly, but she said nothing, they remained locked together for several uncounted minutes until Victor stood back. "I'm sorry mam, I shouldn't be crying like this not in front of you and the girls." He apologised, wiping away the salty tears that dripped along his cheeks.

Kate reprimanded her son." Don't talk daft if you can't shed a tear and let your feelings out here with me where can you?" "Naomi is in the Newport and Gwent Hospital. She was badly burned on her back and legs. It's been a long painful recovery but she's much better now." Kate said. I'm certain that once she sees you, she will want to come home straight away!" Victor grabbed his jacket and added," I must get to the hospital; I'll be back when I can."

The train seemed to take an eternity. "Glad to see you back safe and sound, "Shouted Evan from the opposite platform. "Pleased to be back among my own!" Shared Victor. "I'm off to visit Naomi in the hospital, in Newport." "The next train will be along in fifteen minutes!" Evan replied.

The walk from the station to the hospital passed in a blur, his eyes becoming more and more tear filled with every pace. The imposing building beckoning him on. "Where do you think you are going soldier boy?" Croaked an elderly orderly. "It isn't visiting time for another hour and a half." Victor stepped back and looked at the orderly standing in his way. "Come on butty, I've been away fighting Germans for more than four years, is it too much to ask that I be allowed to visit my injured wife". "Tent up to me. If matron finds out, she'll have my guts for garters and my nadgers will be floating in formalin in a specimen jar!"

"Fair play Butty, we haven't seen each other for more than four years and I've been in the front line for all of it. Naomi doesn't even know I'm alive, come on cut us some slack."

"Did you say Naomi?" said the orderly, "I'm Geoff. You must be Victor." She's been shouting the place down asking for you ever since they said the war was over!" He stared at Victor's chest, "Judging by them ribbons you really have been in the thick of it. Naomi is on the first floor up them steps. The ward is the big door on the left. Go up the stairs, if anyone spots you, I haven't seen you."

Resisting the urge to dash noisily up the stairs he tried to tip toe up the steps in his hob nailed army boots! He reached the door and peered through its glass window. A nurse was standing at her desk in front of three people. Victor joyously recognised all three. He saw Brian Cuthbertson and Trevor Bailey arguing with the nurse. But his eyes were drawn to the most beautiful sight he had not seen for many, many years. It was Naomi, standing on her own two feet, conversing with the nurse. Victor quietly opened the door and marched in.

"Here's a sight for sore eyes!" He announced walking swiftly towards Naomi and gently enveloping her in his arms before crushing his lips hungrily to hers! "My darling, darling how I have missed you". They clung together for several minutes despite the audience they were attracting. "Naomi's been driving us mad with her orders to find you" said Brian," But I see you've beaten us all!"

"I went straight to Bridge Street once I was demobbed. It was shut up and I started to panic."

My next stop was Cwmcarn that was a surprise I can tell you. No one was expecting me. They told me about you being bombed. I gave everyone a kiss and cuddle before rushing here."

We have been asking the nurse to discharge Naomi, "said Trevor." I've told you all before I am not allowed to do that. It must be Dr Flannagan, he won't make a decision before tomorrow. Your wife was grievously wounded, and he wants to ensure she is well enough to go home." Stated the nurse. Brian interrupted, "It's obvious that we are not going to succeed now. Let's leave the two love birds alone as they have four years to catch up on. Victor can stay for visiting this evening and return tomorrow to persuade the Doctor to let him take Naomi home to Cwmcarn where she can be with her children, and Victor's family where I am certain his mother will ensure she doesn't even pick up a feather duster!" This was agreed by everyone. As they were leaving, Trevor looked over his shoulder at the happy pair before uttering," Make sure you wear your uniform, with its rank and all your bravery medals tomorrow!"

With his lips clinging hungrily to hers they sought a quiet section of the stairway. My darling, darling, he murmured as he cuddled into her neck playfully running his tongue from side to side. You are all I have thought of for four lonely years. They remained entwined together until they heard a bell ring and a voice say, "all visitors must leave immediately patient's need their rest."

Victor tiptoed away to the train station as soon as he had planted a long lingering kiss on her lips.

The reunion with Tom was both joyous and sorrowful. The two men met quietly together in the back garden. Tom, his pride in his nephew obvious for all to see. At first, they faced each other in silence clasping hands, both enjoying the pleasure of their first meeting since the outbreak of war. It was Victor who spoke first, the anger still strong within his heart.

"If I ever lay my hands on the bastard who stole that money, I'll swing for him! None of this would have happened if I hadn't been sent away. Four years of squalor and suffering! Not just for me but us all." Tom put his arm around his nephew's shoulder and replied "What good will that do? Revenge isn't going to give you back those four years or erase the memories of what took place! Do you think we would want you to waste your life seeking revenge? I bet Naomi doesn't want you to waste your life doing it. You 'have two young children and a hurt wife to look after, you have to bring your children up properly. I know it's 'hard but you must look forward to the future you mustn't look back. There are two reasons in our house and one in Newport why you have got to get on with your life. You took care of your soldiers now you do it for your family you have to be as good a father as you were a sergeant. Children need love and despite that terrible war, love is something I know you are full of." Let's go inside." Looking at his cold soiled clothes, he added." I need my bath you can tell me about the war and how you won your medals when I wash."

"I'll tell you when mam and the girls are not listening. It was worse than hell itself! I don' want to talk about it when they can hear. I don't think I'm ever going to feel clean again!"

It may have been his wish to forget, but it wasn't t what was granted. Word of his return had spread through the locality like wildfire. Visitors filled the house from dawn till dusk, many were old friends, glad to hear of his safe return. Others came to visit the 'celebrity' out of ghoulish curiosity. The family were polite to them all.

What are you going to do now?" Tom enquired, as they sat before a blazing fire later that evening. "You can stay here with us, but have you got a job in mind?

It had been a thought that had been at the forefront of Victor's mind for the few hours he had been back.

"I don't know uncle. I suppose I could ask for a job back at the pit. Mam will go spare, but I don't know what else to do. They still think me a thief at the shipping line, so I won't be welcomed back there so it looks like the pit!"

"I'll have a word with the manager on Monday, see if we can get you a start." Tom replied.

"There's one or two things I must do before I do." Victor replied. He closed his eyes and shuddered at the thought, then continued "I haven't even said this to a soul, but Evan Wilkinson died in my arms. I'll never forget the look in his eyes, it will haunt me forever. I promised him I'd visit his mam; I can't put it off much longer even though I'm dreading it!"

My number one priority will be to go to the hospital and discuss Naomi's discharge. I need to go to the house in Bridge Street I've left a few special things there that I must have. I'll need to talk with Naomi about Bridge Street I can't work in Cwmcarn and live in Newport.

"I have played piano a few times for the Mons, and I still love it! Even though the instruments were way out of tune the audience loved it too. Do you have an opening for a choir accompanist?"

I intend catching the five thirty train to Newport in the morning. I want to go to Bridge Street before the hospital there are a few important things I left there. Victor went quietly to bed.

Victor awoke at 5:00 AM. It was a time he was used to, what with surviving in the trenches and getting up for work. He tiptoed out of the bedroom and went downstairs being as quiet as he could not to wake his mother sisters or the children. Thomas was already up and dressed ready for his shift at the pit.

"I'm catching the train to Newport." Said Victor, "I hope to be back before mealtime." He left the house and headed towards the station. The sun was just beginning to peep through the grey layered blanket of cloud when he boarded the train. He alighted at Newport.

"Hey Victor, Victor Leslie!" A voice boomed across the Newport platform through the cold twilight, "it's good to see you" This is a fortunate encounter! "It's saved me a journey to Cwmcarn to find you."

"I'm sorry" said Victor "I don't believe I know you. "Have we met!" The old gentlemen smiled, looked at his companion and said,

"We have never met, but I know all about you, a mutual acquaintance, Trevor Bailey spoke of you and said you were just the sort of man we were looking for!" He turned to his companion and confirmed, "My friend's name is David Jones, and I am Evan Harris." David, this is Sergeant Major Victor Leslie, ex pit boy and war hero. The pit boy who helped to resolve the seamen's strike!" He held out his hand to Victor and they shook hands. I know a lot about you, and I know your uncle Tom very well and since talking to him you are just the kind of man we're looking to employ!" Said Evan "I don't understand," Victor remarked! "How can I be this person?

"It is six o'clock in the morning and we are standing on Newport station which isn't the best time or place to be discussing business!" Continued Victor.

"I agree" replied Evan. "Can we meet tomorrow in Nazareth Chapel School Hall at eleven am?" Before then may I say something for you to think on!" finished Evan.

"I represent the Miners Federation, The Fed. You are just what we need to persuade more miners to join the Fed and help us try to improve the working conditions of all miners, by taking on the bosses and coal owners."

"I will see you tomorrow morning and we can talk. I must say I'm intrigued." said Victor. as he walked towards Bridge Street. "I will try and persuade you to work for the Fed," said Evan as they parted, "it pays 6 pounds ten shillings a week."

Victor dashed off as quickly as he could, puffing and panting, across the road dashing to Bridge Street. He hailed a tram that came rattling around the corner.

"What an unexpected proposition!" Victor thought to himself.

He put the key into the door and went into the cold damp house. He went upstairs to the smallest bedroom and pulled up two small sections of floorboard beneath a rug in the corner. Bending down he took out a brown paper parcel. He Replaced the boards and locked the door before heading for the hospital.

Naomi was pacing up and down the ward eagerly awaiting the appearance of her Victor. Once she caught sight of him, she flew into his arms like a rushing typhoon. Burying her head into his shoulder as the tears fell in torrent's once again.

Victor sought out the nurse and said," Has the doctor seen her and said I can take her home to look after her?

"The doctor would like a word with you Sergeant Major. Doctor Flannegan is in his office waiting for you, Mrs Leslie will have to wait here while you talk."

"Wait here my darling, I won't be long. He picked up his parcel that stood at his feet and followed the nurse to the doctor's office.

"Please sit down," said the doctor. It's good to welcome back our brave soldiers doubly so in your case as I look at your gallantry medals!" He waited for Victor to sit down before beginning." Your wife has been with us for a considerable time. At first, we didn't think she would survive and recover from her injuries because they were so severe. Despite agonising pain, she has shown steady improvement. Your wife is a fighter with a determination to survive and see you. I have never witnessed it's like before."

"Naomi has always been a determined individual and has successfully fought adversity all her life. "Said, Victor. "Her fervent wish is to leave hospital and be reunited with her family and children. Please tell me I can take her home. We will take great care of her and treat her like a queen. I implore you, don't keep us separated any longer." War has kept us apart for four long years!"

If you guarantee that she will spend the next three months resting and avoid all hard work. I can see no reason why she can't leave with you now. Her burns have left scars but are completely healed. She can go!"

The words resounded joyously through Victor's ears, and he jumped up and grabbed the doctor's hand which he pumped gratefully. He picked up his parcel and dashed through the door.

"It's all clear my darling, you can come home if you promise to avoid all housework and strenuous activity. You must become a lady of leisure for the next three months at least. Warned Victor"! "I can do that without even trying." Naomi replied.

"I just need my outdoor clothes to keep me warm as we travel". The nurse pulled around the bed screens, it took Naomi moments for her to dress as Victor clung onto his parcel as if his life depended on it.

A perplexed Naomi glanced at the brown paper package and asked, "Whatever have you got there?"

He looked at his wife as he explained, "This is what sent me to war for four years. It's the so-called evidence that William Hyde and his lackeys used to condemn me in court." He placed the package on the bed and carefully undid the string around it and opened it. "Here's the five hundred pounds, which according to them, I stole." He took out a rusty headed mandrill mining pick and a gleaming miner's lamp from the parcel and placed them on the bed. "They were both my father's the only things of his I have. They are more precious than money to me!" He pointed to the lamp. "This is the supposed five hundred pounds they say I stole and hid in this parcel!!!"

Printed in Great Britain
by Amazon